A Cursed
Inheritance

A Cursed Inheritance

Kate Ellis

PIATKUS

Copyright © 2005 by Kate Ellis

First published in Great Britain in 2005 by
Piatkus Books Ltd
5 Windmill Street, London W1T 2JA
email: info@piatkus.co.uk

The moral right of the author has been asserted

A catalogue record for this book is available from the British Library

ISBN 0 7499 0725 8

Set in Times by
Action Publishing Technology Ltd, Gloucester

Printed and bound in Great Britain by
Bath Press

March 1985

The child stood, frozen with terror, staring down at the place where the man's face should have been, hardly aware that the slick of blood seeping from his head was soaking into the hem of her flowered cotton nightdress.

The others lay by the drawing-room door, gazing up at her with accusing eyes as the drying blood from their wounds, vivid as freshly butchered meat, crusted on their ivory flesh. Scarlet blood had splattered up the walls and the metallic scent of the slaughterhouse hung in the air like a mist.

The child moved her naked toes in the warm, sticky fluid, unable to cry, unable to run. And when the sound of a distant scream and a muffled shot echoed down the staircase, she stood, petrified like the victim of some fairytale witch's curse.

Then came a heavy, brooding silence and the child suddenly became aware of the urgent need to move. To return to her hiding place and keep perfectly still, quiet as a mouse in the wainscoting.

Mr Death was visiting the house. And Mr Death was hungry.

Twenty years later

In life, the corpse floating face down in the River Trad had been youngish and fairly fit; a patron of his local gym until boredom had set in. But now his dead limbs moved only with the rise and fall of the murky tidal waters. The river had embraced him. And there was no escape from its cold grasp.

The man on the wooded river bank, mistaking the corpse at first for a pile of old clothes, prodded at the torso with a dead branch; the final indignity. But then, realising his mistake, he took a mobile phone from his pocket with trembling fingers and summoned the outside world.

Chapter One

*On the fifth day of April in the year of Our Lord 1605
we set sail for the New World from the port of
Tradmouth aboard the* Nicholas. *I took this for a good
omen for in the old faith Saint Nicholas was the patron
of sailors. And in Devon, unlike in London, we still
favour the old ways.*

*We are numbered sixty-five – mostly men but some
women and children – and in our company we have
persons of all ranks: gentlemen, artisans and labour-
ers. Captain Barton hath authority over all until the
sealed orders in his care are opened. Then we will
know the names of the Council that is to rule over us
when we reach our journey's end.*

*There were many sick in the first days of our voyage,
yet I myself did not succumb. By unprosperous winds we
were kept five days in the sight of England. Then we
suffered great storms, but by the skilfulness of the
Captain we suffered no great loss or danger. By the
Lord's grace we have now reached land. It is a place
called Virginia in honour of the old Queen.*

*We entered into the bay of Chesupioc directly
without let or hindrance and when we landed we found
fair meadows and goodly tall trees with such fresh
waters running through the woods I was almost
ravished at the first sight thereof.*

I went ahead with one Joshua Morton, a large, red-faced gentleman from Dorset who travels with his brother, Isaac. This Joshua's wife – a most comely woman, small and dainty and a full score years younger than her husband – feared what we would find once ashore. Her brother-in-law, a foolish man, had been telling her tales of savages and fierce wild creatures, taking pleasure in seeing her fear and placing his fat arm around her waist. I did my best to reassure her that I am at her service.

Set down by Master Edmund Selbiwood, Gentleman, on the Nicholas *this first day of June 1605.*

Emma Oldchester knelt on the hard wooden floor and took the tiny figure between her thumb and index finger. When she had placed it carefully in the drawing room she brushed back her long fair hair with her left hand and stared at the scene she had created.

She had painted the house carefully, just as she painted all her doll's houses. But this one was different. Special. She had tried to get every detail right, making alterations as the memories crept back. The wallpaper, the fabric of the curtains, the exact position of each item of furniture. The blood spattered on the walls.

She recalled some details about the house – the huge oak door and the dark green walls in the kitchen – quite clearly. But the important things were vague like a half-remembered dream. There were times when she wished she remembered more. And yet perhaps it was better that she didn't.

She looked down at one of the dolls lying on the table, the one dressed in a tiny cloak of black felt, the one with no face or gender. She stared at it with unblinking eyes for a few seconds before throwing it down.

When she stood up she placed her heel on the small figure and ground it into the floor, twisting until the thing broke with a satisfying snap.

*

'So where are we off to, Wes?'

'Report of a body in the river?'

DCI Gerry Heffernan sighed. 'Life got too much for some poor bugger, I suppose.'

'The call said it looks suspicious.'

With Heffernan slumped in the passenger seat beside him, DI Wesley Peterson drove the unmarked police car out of Tradmouth and turned on to a narrow lane fringed with high, budding hedgerows. He had taken down the directions carefully as usual – half a mile before Knot Creek on the Tradmouth side of the river. Unlike his boss, he liked to be ordered and organised.

When they reached their destination – a small car park next to a footpath leading down to the river – he saw that Dr Colin Bowman's new Range Rover and the police photographer's battered Fiat were there already, parked next to a brace of patrol cars. The show had begun.

The path skirted round the edge of a field and they trudged towards the water's edge, watched by staring ewes and their small woolly lambs. Eventually, they arrived at the river where overalled figures were working industriously beneath the overhanging trees. The area had been taped off – a crime scene.

Following the bright flash of the police photographer's camera, they located Colin Bowman, the pathologist. He was squatting by a human body which lay, waterlogged and still, on the ribbon of sparse grass next to the water. When Colin spotted them he straightened himself up and peeled off his latex gloves.

'Good to see you both. They fished him out of the river an hour ago. Come over and have a look,' he said, greeting them with a genial smile. Always the perfect host. The man would be a pleasure to work with if it weren't for the fact that every time they met him, they had to share his company with some rotting corpse or other.

'So what have we got?' Heffernan asked, staring down at the corpse with distaste.

3

The dead man was tallish, not old, not young. Sodden jeans and sweatshirt clung to his dead flesh and his longish dark hair was matted with river weed. The wide, sightless eyes and the open mouth gave him an expression of astonishment.

'Healthy male. Mid thirties or thereabouts.' Colin squatted down again. 'He's not been dead long enough to float to the surface under his own steam, as it were. His clothes had been caught by the branches of an overhanging tree. See that tear in the sweatshirt? There's a matching wound in the flesh underneath. I think our friend here was stabbed. Probably with a fairly narrow blade but I'll be able to tell you more ...'

'When you've done the postmortem. Thanks, Colin. Don't suppose there's a chance that it could have been an accident? He might have fallen on a spike or ...'

Colin smiled. 'You know the score, Gerry. I won't know for certain until I've had a closer look. You'll just have to be patient.'

Heffernan pulled a face. Patience had never been his strong point.

Wesley turned to a young uniformed constable, the sort people have in mind when they complain that policemen are getting younger – this one looked all of fifteen. 'Who found him?'

'An artist, sir.' The constable's winter-pale cheeks turned red. 'He was painting when he spotted the body in the river and he dialled 999 on his mobile, sir. He's over there.' He pointed to a man who was deep in conversation with a uniformed officer.

Heffernan grunted something incomprehensible and turned away. But Wesley gave the young man what he judged to be a sympathetic smile. The lad seemed keen. No harm in a bit of encouragement.

'Thank you, Constable ...'

'Dearden, sir.' He blushed again. He had heard of Inspector Peterson, the only black CID officer in the local

4

force, but this was the first time their paths had ever crossed.

Gerry Heffernan was making a beeline for the man Dearden had pointed out; a stocky man in his early sixties with long grey hair tied back in a ponytail. He wore a paint-stained, Breton smock which marked him out as an artist as much as a uniform labels a police officer. Wesley followed his boss. The old police adage that the person who finds a body usually becomes the prime suspect hardly seemed to apply in this case. But more surprising things had happened.

Heffernan stayed silent while Wesley asked the necessary questions but, as expected, the answers weren't much help. The artist had been setting up his easel when he noticed what he thought was a bundle of old clothes caught up in overhanging branches. On closer inspection he realised it was a dead body so he rang the police on his mobile phone like a good citizen. The artist's hands were shaking. He looked as though he needed a drink.

Wesley concluded that he had probably been in the wrong place at the wrong time so, after thanking him for his cooperation and noting his home address, he told him he could go. Heffernan, however, was frowning at the unfortunate man as though he suspected him of all manner of heinous crimes from the Great Train Robbery to the Jack the Ripper murders. But he said nothing so it seemed that he agreed with Wesley's verdict.

When the artist had gathered up his possessions with clumsy haste and scurried back to his car, Wesley and Heffernan were left on the river bank, staring at the grey, flowing water as the undertakers zipped the body into a bag and placed it on a stretcher. It had probably been a point-less exercise to tape off this section of the bank: the crime had most likely been committed elsewhere and the body carried there by the river's treacherous currents.

'Have they found any ID?' Wesley asked hopefully.

The chief inspector shook his head. 'In an ideal world,

Wes, he'd have his name and address tattooed on his back-side. But ...'

Wesley smiled and turned away. In his world things were never that easy.

Mrs Geraldine Jeffries sat in her room on the first floor of Potwoolstan Hall, staring at the large patent leather handbag that lay open on the bedspread. She'd checked its contents three times and she'd searched her drawers and wardrobe. She wasn't as young as she used to be and some-times she forgot where she'd put things – but two hundred and fifty pounds in twenty-pound notes and the diamond ring her late husband had given her for their silver wedding anniversary ... Geraldine Jeffries had always kept her hand firmly on her valuables.

They had been there first thing that morning – she had checked – so they'd been taken while she was down at breakfast. There were no locks on the doors at Potwoolstan Hall, something Mrs Jeffries had complained to Mr Elsham about on her arrival. He had assured her that, rather than being an oversight, it was a symbol of openness and trust. And this was the result.

She stood up, her thin scarlet-painted lips pressed together in a determined line. She didn't care what Elsham said or what excuses he gave – she was going to insist that the police were called.

And if he refused, she'd call them herself. All the Beings had been obliged to give in their mobile phones on arrival at the Hall, but Mrs Jeffries would walk to the nearest vil-lage to make the call if necessary, in spite of her arthritis.

She had been robbed.

Pam Peterson slammed the phone down. Wesley was working late again because some inconsiderate corpse had found its way into the River Trad. She lifted the howling baby out of her cot, seething with resentment. She needed Wesley there, just to take over for a couple of hours, to

6

relieve the pressure. He was fond of telling her that she was lucky to have her mother near by, but she was always quick to point out that Della was usually more of a hindrance than a help.

The doorbell rang just as she was making her way downstairs, carrying baby Amelia over her shoulder, and when she reached the hall she held on to Amelia's small, soft body with one hand while she opened the front door with the other.

'Wes not about?' Neil Watson stood on the doorstep with a bashful grin on his face.

'He's at work.' She hesitated. 'He's just called to say he'll be late home ... again. Come in.'

As Neil brushed past her, she felt there was something different about him, but she wasn't sure what it was. Then it came to her. Ever since they'd met at university, Neil had invariably worn ancient jeans, usually stained with the mud of some archaeological dig or other. But today the jeans were spotless and so were the white trainers and black T-shirt. Neil had cleaned up his act. Pam wondered fleetingly if it was for her benefit but then pushed the thought out of her mind.

'Shame. I was hoping to see him before I went.' Neil and Wesley had studied archaeology together at Exeter University. They had shared a flat and in those half-forgotten, distant days Pam had abandoned Neil, the dreamer, for Wesley, the practical, quiet spoken one.

Pam led the way into a living room littered with toys and baby equipment; the detritus of early childhood. As she put Amelia into her baby chair, she held her stomach in, conscious that she hadn't yet lost the weight she had gained during her pregnancy. Wesley assured her that he didn't mind. But sometimes she suspected that he was too busy to notice. Or maybe he just didn't care.

'So where are you going?'

Neil sat down, his eyes aglow with excitement. 'I'm off to the States,' he announced. 'There's an excavation at a place called Annetown in Virginia. Some of the first settlers landed there.'

'The Pilgrim Fathers?'

'No ... before their time ... around 1605.'

Pam smiled. Neil might be vague about most things but history was an exception. 'How long will you be out there?'

'Only three weeks initially. Depends on the powers that be. It's a sort of exchange: one of their archaeologists is coming over here to see how we do things. I volunteered to take part because there's a Devon connection. It was too good an opportunity to miss really and ...' He hesitated. 'How's, er ...' He pointed in the baby's direction. It was typical of Neil to have forgotten her name.

'Amelia. She's fine. You were going to say something? And ...?'

Neil studied his hands. The nails still bore traces of soil, an occupational hazard. After a few moments he looked up. 'I went up to Somerset to see my grandmother last weekend.' There was a pause and Pam wondered what was coming next. 'She's really ill. Cancer.'

'Oh I'm sorry,' Pam said automatically. 'Should you be going to the States when ...?'

'She wants me to go. She's asked me to do something for her while I'm over there.'

'What?'

Neil hesitated. 'She's asked me to contact someone.'

Pam sensed that Neil wasn't altogether comfortable about his mysterious mission and this made her curious. But before she could question him further, Amelia decided they'd talked long enough and began to howl. Neil looked awkward; babies were uncharted territory for him. He mumbled something about having to go and took his leave, bending to kiss Pam on the cheek.

She stood up and flung her arms around him. 'Take care,' she whispered in his ear, ignoring Amelia's urgent cries.

He broke away gently. 'I'll email you. Tell you how I

get on. Gives Wes my regards,' he said before walking out to his car.

Pam stood at the front door with Amelia grizzling in her arms and watched him drive off, staring at his old yellow Mini until it disappeared out of sight round the corner. And experiencing an unexpected feeling of loss.

There was a hushed air of expectancy in the CID office when Wesley and Heffernan returned. Word had got around on the ever-efficient office grapevine that the body in the river was a murder victim. But until Colin Bowman had given his definitive verdict there wasn't much they could do. Apart from discovering the dead man's identity and tracking down his next of kin.

Wesley was wandering back to his desk when a voice behind him made him jump.

'Sir.' Wesley swung round and saw DC Steve Carstairs leaning on a desk with a sheet of paper in his hand. He was wearing his black leather jacket as usual: Wesley had concluded long ago that he probably slept in it. 'There's been a report of a theft at a place near Derenham; calls itself a healing centre. Money and jewellery taken from a woman's room. It sounds similar to those others. You know, the Dukesbridge health spa and that arts place outside Neston. And that cookery place in Morbay. I reckon there's a pattern.'

Wesley looked at him, surprised. It wasn't often Steve used his imagination.

'Well, if you're free you'd better get round there. Let me have a report when you get back. And get a list of residents and staff, will you? See if there's anyone staying there who was at the other places.'

'It's Potwoolstan Hall,' Steve said significantly with what Wesley thought might have been a wink.

Wesley looked blank. The name meant nothing to him.

But Detective Sergeant Rachel Tracey, who had over-heard the conversation, took pity on him. Wesley was from

London after all. He could hardly be expected to be familiar with every major crime that had been committed in his adopted county over the past twenty years – even one that had passed into local folklore so that the very name of the Hall was synonymous with evil and death.

She ran her fingers through her hair before she spoke, a subconscious action. 'It's a big old house near the river halfway between here and Neston. About twenty years ago the housekeeper there shot the family she worked for then she shot herself.'

Wesley frowned. 'That rings a bell.'

Rachel leaned forward. 'Every so often there's a newspaper article or a TV programme about it. The usual rubbish. Was it part of some satanic ritual because the woman who killed them had nailed dead crows to the doors? Was she a member of a local coven? That sort of thing.'

'So it passed into local mythology?' Wesley knew the public appetite for horror stories as well as the next man.

Rachel smiled. 'You could say that.'

'So what's this about a healing centre?'

'The Hall was turned into a healing and therapy centre a few years ago. Very New Age,' she added with a slight sneer: Rachel Tracey, a farmer's daughter, was a down-to-earth young woman who had no time for anything she considered to be silly or pretentious. 'It stood empty for years after the murders, which is understandable, I suppose. Who'd want to live in a place where six people were killed like that?'

'Who indeed?' said Wesley, starting to edge away. Interesting though this gruesome slice of local history was, he had present-day misdemeanours to deal with. The corpse in the river had to be his priority before the trail, if any existed, went cold on them.

'You could still see the bloodstains years after it happened,' Steve said with relish. 'I had some mates who broke in when it was empty and they . . .'

10

Wesley turned away. The last thing he needed was to hear tales of Steve's misspent youth. Steve caused him enough trouble as it was. 'Well, you'd better go round there and see what's been stolen. They might show you the bloodstains while you're at it.' He grinned. 'But if they charge you for the privilege, don't claim it on expenses, will you?'

Rachel took a deep breath. 'I'll go with him. I could do with getting out of the office.'

Steve scowled, suspecting a conspiracy; that Rachel was really being sent to keep an eye on him. He made for the door, trying not to let his disappointment show. The theft would be a boring routine matter and if he was stuck with Rachel that ruled out a visit to the pub on the way back. But at least he'd get a good look at Potwoolstan Hall.

When Steve and Rachel had gone, Wesley made for Heffernan's office. The DCI would want to be told about this new distraction, so that he could complain about it if nothing else. Wesley poked his head round the door.

'Just thought you'd like to know, Steve's on his way to investigate a report of a theft.'

Heffernan shuffled his paperwork. 'Can't someone from Uniform deal with it?'

'It sounds as if it might fit the pattern of those others. Same MO – money and jewellery stolen from a guest's room. This latest one's at a place called Potwoolstan Hall. Steve mentioned the famous murders.'

Heffernan raised his eyebrows. 'Did he now?' He sat back and there was a long silence as he stared into space. Finally he spoke. 'I was sent over there as a raw young constable to patrol the grounds not long after I joined the force. Not something you forget in a hurry.'

'Rachel said the housekeeper shot the family she worked for then shot herself.'

'That's the sanitised version. It was a bloodbath. She blasted the elder daughter's fiancé with a shotgun in the hall – almost blew his head clean off: blood and brains everywhere. Then she shot the son, the daughter and the parents before killing herself in the kitchen.'

'What made her do it?'

Heffernan shook his head. 'There'd been some sort of row but I can't remember the details.'

'Rachel said the Hall's a healing centre now.'

'So I heard. It was empty for years so they probably bought it at a knockdown price.' He sighed. 'So what exactly has been stolen?'

'Money and jewellery. That's all I know. No doubt Steve'll find out the details.'

'I wouldn't bet on it,' Heffernan mumbled under his breath.

The sound of the doorbell made Emma Oldchester jump. She wasn't expecting visitors. She put the final touch of brown paint on the tiny staircase before wiping her stained hands on her apron and making her way downstairs.

She often wished they had a glass front door instead of the solid wood one Barry had chosen so she could see who was calling. She had asked Barry to fit a spy hole but he had never got round to it. She hesitated, her hand on the latch. Surely it wouldn't be him. He wouldn't visit without warning. Cautiously, she slipped the security chain on and opened the door a few inches.

'Hello, Emmy, my pet. Aren't you going to let me in?'

Relieved, she took the chain off and flung the door wide open. 'Sorry, dad, I thought . . . I thought you might have been him.' She stood on tiptoe to kiss the newcomer, a big, weather-beaten, man with a shock of grey hair and a beard that tickled her face.

'Has he been in touch again?'

'Not for a couple of days. I expected . . .'

'I told him I didn't know anything. Perhaps he's given up.'

Emma began to chew at her nails.

'Look, Em, you don't have to speak to him if you don't

want to. Tell him to get lost. Let sleeping dogs lie, that's what I say.'

Emma made her way into the small, neat lounge and the big man followed.

'Maybe I won't. Barry says I shouldn't. Maybe I'll just tell him I don't want to see him if he phones again.'

There was an awkward silence. Joe Harper stared at his daughter. She looked so fragile, so vulnerable. Just as she'd always looked.

'How are your houses going?'

Emma forced a smile. 'It was a good idea of Barry's, the website. I've got four new orders through it: one from Wales, two from London and one came in yesterday from a lady in Tradmouth. She wants a traditional Devon cottage for her daughter's birthday.'

Joe smiled. 'You're doing well, maid. I'm proud of you.' He reached out a large hand and brushed a strand of fair hair off her thin, pale face. 'Doll's houses have always been your thing, haven't they?' Joe's face clouded, as if some sudden unhappy memory had sprung into his mind.

Emma took his hand in hers and squeezed it. She wouldn't mention what she was planning. The last thing she wanted to do was to worry him.

Colin Bowman was due to conduct the postmortem on the unidentified body from the river the following morning, but until then they had to be content with idle speculation. According to Gerry Heffernan, who was an experienced sailor and knew about these things, the body probably went in further up the river towards Neston. Now all they had to do was to find out exactly where.

Heffernan had checked with the harbour master and the coastguard just in case anything untoward had been reported by any of the river's many sailors. But there was no word of anything out of the ordinary. The victim might have been murdered on a boat and the body thrown overboard. Or else he might have been thrown into the river after an attack on dry land. Either way, Wesley's workload was due to expand at an alarming rate. He hoped Pam would understand. But somehow he feared that she wouldn't.

The perfunctory search of the dead man's pockets on the river bank had yielded no clue to his identity and Wesley suspected that the killer had stripped the corpse of belongings to make identification – and his life – more difficult. The next step was a trawl through the missing persons reports. DC Trish Walton made a start.

Gerry Heffernan emerged from his office and announced that it was lunchtime. Wesley's morning walk by the river had given him an appetite and somehow, by unspoken agreement, he and Heffernan found themselves in the Fisherman's Arms on the receiving end of two pints of best bitter and two large hotpots which steamed temptingly in oversized bowls. Wesley tucked into his enthusiastically. Since Amelia's arrival in the world, hearty meals were in short supply at home and he and Pam existed on ready meals and takeaways. But then, as Pam normally worked full time as a primary school teacher, things hadn't been much better before Amelia's birth. Only in the school holidays had the Petersons ever experienced anything resembling domestic harmony.

Wesley gazed at the roaring open fire as he finished his pint. The low-beamed cosiness of the Fisherman's Arms with its worn red leather seats, its well-polished horse brasses and its motherly landlady, the widow of a police sergeant, who always provided a warm welcome for members of the local constabulary, was a perfect antidote to a morning spent stuying a cold corpse on a chilly river bank. But, like a pleasant dream, it couldn't last for ever. They had promised Colin that they'd call in at the mortuary that afternoon. It wasn't something they were looking forward to but, on the other hand, Colin did serve a very decent cup of tea.

Tradmouth Hospital was a short walk away so when they had finished their meal they walked quickly down the narrow streets to keep their rendezvous with death.

'Wonder how Steve and Rachel are getting on at Potwoolstan Hall,' said Wesley, raising his voice to make himself heard over the screaming sea gulls.

'Rachel's been quiet recently. It is something to do with that Australian boyfriend of hers?'

Wesley hesitated for a moment. 'That was over ages ago.'

Heffernan looked at him, curious. 'You seem to know all about it.'

Wesley felt his face burning.

'Is it true she's moving out of the farm?'

'So she says.' He knew all about Rachel's intention to find a flat of her own in the town, away from the farm where she had lived all her life with her parents and three brothers. She had told him about her proposed bid for freedom in great detail. But somehow he didn't feel like discussing it.

When they reached the hospital they followed the signs to the mortuary. Once they had passed through the plastic swing doors a faint odour of decay masked by a heavy dose of air freshener hit their nostrils. Wesley felt slightly nauseous. It was the same every time.

Heffernan, however, charged ahead along the polished corridors towards Colin's office where they were greeted like long-lost friends and provided with Earl Grey tea and biscuits made on the Prince of Wales's own estates from organic ingredients. Nothing but the best would do for Colin Bowman.

Colin always liked to chat – probably, Wesley thought, because his own patients were hardly in a position to be talkative – and he asked about Pam and the children before moving on to the subject of the forthcoming wedding of Wesley's sister, Maritia, and her move to Devon where she had applied to work as a locum GP. It was only when the subject of Maritia's plans had been exhausted and Colin had made extensive enquiries about the progress of Gerry's two children at universities up north, that he led the way to the stark white room where the body of the man from the river lay in a refrigerated drawer, awaiting Colin's undivided attention the following morning. They viewed the body briefly before Colin pointed out a set of plastic bags containing the man's clothes.

'Nothing very exciting, I'm afraid, gentlemen. Nothing you can't buy in any high street in the land. Ralph Lauren sweatshirt, Levi jeans, Nike trainers, Marks and Spencer's underwear. No bespoke suit made by a little tailor in Savile Row with a detailed list of all his customers, I'm sorry to say.'

'Pity,' said Wesley. A spot of individuality would have been too much to hope for in these days of globalisation.

'But I did find this in the back pocket of his jeans.' Colin produced a small bag containing what looked like a scrap of paper. He passed it to Wesley, who stared at the thing and handed it to Heffernan.

There was a small, satisfied smile on Colin's lips, as though he had a secret he was longing to tell. 'I know what it is, of course,' he said.

'Well, don't keep us in suspense.' Heffernan passed the bag back to Wesley.

'It's a book of matches. I recognised it at once because I was there on Saturday for the local pathologists' annual dinner: very jolly affair. I picked one up myself.' He delved into his pocket and produced a glossy book of matches with a familiar name printed on the front.

'The Tradmouth Castle Hotel,' said Wesley, handing the bag to Heffernan. 'He might have called in there for a drink.'

'Don't be such a pessimist, Wes. At least it gives us somewhere to start until we hear from missing persons.'

As they took their leave of Colin Bowman, Wesley glanced at the drawer containing the mystery man and shivered. He would be there when the man's body was cut open the next day. And there was no way he could avoid it.

*

16

DC Steve Carstairs drove too fast along the narrow, high-hedged country lanes. Rachel Tracey sat beside him, gripping her seat. Steve suspected that she was there to make sure he didn't miss anything vital or cause offence to the natives – and he seethed with resentment. He was quite capable of dealing with a simple theft on his own.

Rachel hadn't said a word since they set off and it was Steve who broke the silence.

'Still going out with that Dave? The Aussie?'

'No.'

'But I thought that's why you were looking for a flat.'

'Well, you thought wrong. Dave's gone back to Australia. You can transmit it on the office grapevine if you like. In fact, I wish you would. I'm sick of all the questions and innuendoes.' She folded her arms. That was all she had to say.

But Steve wouldn't let the subject drop. 'We were all hoping for wedding bells.'

'You've just missed the entrance.'

Steve slammed on the brakes and they were both flung forward. Rachel put her head in her hands as he backed the car rapidly back to a large gateway and a prominent sign bearing the words 'Potwoolstan Hall Therapy and Healing Centre' beneath a logo; a stylised version of a naked female figure reaching for what looked like a beach ball. Or perhaps it was the moon. It was a difficult entrance to miss, Rachel thought. But somehow Steve had managed it.

He sped up the winding drive, ignoring Rachel's suggestion that he slow down. If he was showing off, he'd picked the wrong woman, she thought as she tightened her grip on her seat.

'Well, this is it,' said Steve as the car came to a halt with a satisfying crunch of gravel beneath the tyres. 'Scene of the massacre. You'd think they'd have changed the name, wouldn't you?'

Rachel said nothing as she climbed out of the passenger seat. She wanted to get this over with. The front door stood wide open so she walked in. The Hall looked old from the

17

outside; mellow Beer stone with mullioned windows and boastful decorative gables. The height of chic in the sixteenth century.

From what she'd heard over the years, Rachel half imagined the interior to look like the set of a horror film; all black and blood-red with fraying tapestries and cobwebs. But the reality came as a disappointment. The large, square hall had a newly decorated, slightly institutional look. The floor was pale wood and the smooth walls were painted a calming light green. Instead of dark ancestral portraits, a selection of modern watercolours hung on the walls, the kind usually found in local amateur art exhibitions.

Rachel stood for a few moments looking around, wondering what it had looked like when the Harford family had lived – and died – there. Probably nothing like this.

Ahead of them was a magnificent oak staircase, deeply carved and black with age; the one feature of the entrance hall that hadn't fallen victim to modernisation. A tall man was walking slowly down to greet them. His hair was frosted at the temples and he wore a short, spotless white jacket of the kind favoured by dentists. He had a wide mouth and his eyes, focused on Rachel, were a pale, piercing blue. Rachel instinctively smoothed her hair and straightened her back as the man approached with an outstretched hand.

'Welcome,' the man said, taking Rachel's hand in both of his and holding it for a few seconds. He turned to Steve but the handshake he received was considerably briefer.

'Mr and Mrs Jackson, I presume. Welcome to Potwoolstan Hall,' the man continued, his voice silky smooth.

Steve made a noise which sounded like a snort and Rachel shot him a hostile look.

Rachel produced her warrant card. 'I'm Detective Sergeant Tracey and this is Detective Constable Carstairs, Tradmouth CID. I believed someone here reported a theft, Mr ... er ...'

The man took a step back and Rachel noticed a flash of alarm in the bright blue eyes. 'I'm so sorry. I was expecting new guests. Elsham. Jeremy Elsham. I'm the facilitator.'

Steve thrust his hands into the pocket of his leather jacket. 'Does that mean you're in charge?'

Elsham gave a patronising half-smile. 'I suppose I am. But here we prefer the concept of my being a facilitator rather than a dictator. The Beings take responsibility for their own healing and ...'

'Beings?' Rachel sounded puzzled.

'I suppose some less enlightened establishments might call them patients. Those who come to us for healing. We like to refer to them as Beings – each one unique and individual.'

Rachel pressed her lips together disapprovingly. She was a woman who preferred to call a guest a guest and an owner an owner. 'So what exactly has been stolen?'

Jeremy Elsham looked uneasy. 'Mrs Jeffries, one of our Beings, claims that somebody has taken two hundred and fifty pounds and a valuable diamond ring from her handbag. She left it in her room during breakfast.'

'We'll need to speak to Mrs Jeffries. And if we could have a list of all your guests. And your staff too, of course.'

'Oh, I'm sure nobody here ... Perhaps the thief came in from outside. We don't lock doors here and ...'

He fell silent when a woman appeared, fashionably thin and wearing a crisp white uniform. She was a platinum blonde with the manufactured beauty of one familiar with the cosmetic surgeon's knife. Steve stared at her chest admiringly, and Rachel gave him a sharp nudge with her elbow.

'This is my wife, Pandora. Darling, these people are police officers. They want to see Mrs Jeffries.'

Rachel tried not to show her surprise. Pandora appeared to be much younger than her husband. She wondered if there was a first wife somewhere discarded in favour of this newer and racier model. But when she looked more closely at Pandora's neck, she realised that first impressions might have deceived her: the neck belonged to a woman who wouldn't see forty again.

Pandora consulted the clipboard she was carrying. 'Mrs Jeffries is in meditation at the moment. But the session finishes in five minutes. Then she's booked in for another regression.' Pandora's collagen-enhanced lips turned upwards in a cross between a smile and a snarl.

Steve edged closer to Pandora. 'What's this regression?'

It was Jeremy Elsham who answered. 'We regress our Beings to their childhood, and sometimes beyond that to their former lives. It helps them to resolve issues of their inner being and ...'

'Perhaps we could have a word with you in your office until she's free,' Rachel interrupted. She wasn't going to be sidetracked by what she considered to be hocus-pocus.

Elsham glanced at his wife and led them into a spacious room off the main hall. The words 'Strictly Private' were printed in gothic letters on the door. Perhaps a small hint that behind every facilitator lurks a dictator, Rachel thought as she recalled a phrase from a book about a farm she'd been forced to read at school: 'All animals are equal but some are more equal than others.' Being a farmer's daughter she'd found this concept quite interesting.

Elsham's huge office was furnished with an expensive simplicity which would have done a top executive proud. There was a thick beige carpet on the floor and the soft leather seats were modern in design. At one end of the room, a black leather sofa and two armchairs were grouped around a sleek beech-wood coffee table. Elsham hadn't stinted himself: but then, having sneaked a surreptitious glance at the price list on the desk, Rachel concluded that he probably didn't need to. Potwoolstan Hall was no charitable institution.

The only thing that looked out of place in the room was

a gloomy painting hanging on the wall behind the desk. Two young men in Jacobean costume – doublets and wide ruffs – stiffly posed against a dark background with faint lettering and a coat of arms barely visible between them. It was obviously as ancient as the Hall itself but it didn't seem to fit in with the image Elsham wanted to project.

Elsham sat behind the desk, leaning back, relaxed, as if to demonstrate that a visit from the police didn't bother him in the least. He answered their questions clearly and succinctly, the perfect witness. But Rachel somehow couldn't rid herself of the suspicion that it was all an elaborate act, a performance.

The first Elsham had heard of the theft was when an agitated Mrs Geraldine Jeffries burst into his office just after breakfast to report that her money and a valuable ring were missing from her room. The staff had undertaken a discreet search but nothing had been found. The other Beings hadn't been questioned of course: he was hoping it wouldn't be necessary. People came to Potwoolstan Hall to find spiritual peace and healing and the last thing they needed was to be interrogated by the police. When Rachel said they might have no choice in the matter, Elsham didn't look happy.

Geraldine Jeffries's arrival was announced by the clanking of heavy gold jewellery. Mrs Jeffries, a lady of a certain age, had dyed her hair jet black and her tanned flesh – the product of too many holidays on the Côte d'Azur with follow-up sessions in her local sunbed parlour – was the texture of leather. With her large, even teeth and her long nose, she reminded Rachel of a crocodile.

And like a crocodile she snapped, first at Elsham for allowing such a thing to happen in his establishment in the first place and then at the two police officers for not having arrived as soon as she called to haul the thief off to the cells. Rachel made soothing noises and suggested that they examine the scene of the crime, mentioning that the police had been investigating a spate of similar thefts in the area.

21

Mrs Jeffries, satisfied that someone was willing to do something constructive at last, led the way.

As they walked up the stairs, Rachel found herself wondering where exactly the massacre of the Harford family had taken place. Then she put the thought out of her mind. It was ghoulish. On a par with people who visit the scenes of major accidents. She felt mildly ashamed of herself.

Mrs Jeffries's room – a large and well-furnished chamber worthy of any five-star hotel – yielded no clues. The thief, if there was one, hadn't conducted a disorganised search – he or she had merely dipped into an unattended handbag and extracted the valuables, as though he or she had known exactly where to find them.

The money and ring – containing a hefty diamond, valued at six thousand pounds for insurance purposes – had apparently disappeared during breakfast when the Beings had been in the dining room munching their morning muesli. Only three had been absent: a Mrs Carmody, who was confined to a wheelchair as a result of a road accident; a Mr Dodgson, the Being in the next room to Mrs Jeffries who had missed breakfast because of a stomachache; and a Ms Jones, a young woman who claimed to have overslept.

As Mrs Carmody's room was on the ground floor and her spinal injuries made it impossible for her to walk even a few feet, and certainly not up two flights of stairs, Rachel considered that she could probably be ruled out, although she might have witnessed something. She would speak to her along with Mr Dodgson and Ms Jones. And she would see any staff who had been on the premises as well, in spite of Elsham's assurances that they were all entirely trustworthy and their whereabouts accounted for.

Pandora brought Dodgson to the office first. He sat down on the edge of his seat, twisting the gold ring on his left little finger round and round. He was in his forties with thick brown hair that showed no sign of grey and a deep, well-modulated voice that any Shakespearean actor would be proud to own. Somehow Rachel suspected he would have been more comfortable in a suit than in the snowy white T-shirt and expensively faded jeans he wore. And she was certain she'd seen him before but couldn't think where it was.

Dodgson's account of events fitted exactly with Elsham's but, although the hand that signed the statement was steady and the voice clear and confident, his failure to make eye contact made Rachel suspect that he was hiding something.

But if Dodgson was nervous he hid it very well. Almost like a professional. Perhaps he was an actor, Rachel thought. Perhaps that's why his face seemed familiar.

She caught Steve's eye. 'I'm sure I've seen him before somewhere.'

Before Steve could reply, there was a knock on the office door. Pandora opened it and stepped aside to let in the next lucky contestant.

'Ms Jones?' Rachel asked as the girl strode confidently into the office. Her scraped-back ponytail accentuated the sharpness of her features and Rachel's first thought was that she had been too heavy on the make-up.

But the girl's wide eyes were focused on Steve Carstairs, whose mouth had fallen open.

'What are you doing here?' he asked.

'I could ask you the same thing,' she replied boldly.

Rachel, watching Steve's face, reckoned that he looked terrified.

When Emma Oldchester heard her husband's key in the front door, she rushed out of the spare bedroom where she worked on her doll's houses and hurtled down the stairs to meet him.

She waited for the door to open, holding her breath. She could feel her hands shaking and she clenched them by her sides.

Barry Oldchester stepped into the hall and when he saw his wife waiting at the bottom of the stairs he smiled.

23

'Hello, love,' he said as he put his bag of tools down on the floor where it landed with a metallic clatter. 'I finished early. The woman in Stokeworthy only needed a tap washer replacing. I'm out later though; central heating on the blink just outside Whitely; woman won't be in till after four.' He leaned forward and gave Emma a kiss on the cheek. 'Any chance of a cup of tea?'

Without a word Emma turned and made for the kitchen.

'You OK, love?' Barry followed her, concerned. He sensed something wasn't right. A stocky five feet eight inches tall with a shock of sandy hair, Barry was a well-meaning, if unimaginative man. He had met Emma when he had serviced her parents' central heating boiler and had been entranced by her long blond hair, her pale blue eyes, her pretty heart-shaped face and her quiet vulnerability. She had an air of untouched innocence which at first had excited and aroused him. But later, when he had discovered the deep damage beneath her placid mask, he had begun to treat her almost as an invalid. More a sickly child than a wife.

'Of course I'm OK,' she said unconvincingly. She filled the kettle and felt her hands trembling.

Barry put a protective arm around her shoulder. 'How did you get on at that craft fair in Neston?'

Emma shook her head. 'I had a headache this morning. It went after a while so I just worked on one of the houses. I had another Internet order from someone in Birmingham. And there's another fair on Thursday.'

'Good.' Barry was only too aware that Emma's houses made them a good profit. And they needed every penny they could get. He was keen to start a family, sooner rather than later. He was fifteen years Emma's senior and his mum said they should get a move on.

But he was reluctant to put pressure on Emma. He had never forgotten the words her father, Joe Harper, had said to him on their wedding day. They were etched on his mind, always there. Like a barrier between them. 'Look after her. She's seen things in her life that nobody should

have to see so just be patient with her.' Barry hadn't understood then and Joe had made no effort to explain. But later,
Emma's late mother, Linda, thought he should know the
truth. Sometimes he wished she'd never told him.

The kettle had boiled and Barry took over, putting the
teabags in the pot and pouring the boiling water over them.

'My dad came round today. Just for a cup of tea.'

Barry glanced at her nervously. 'Oh yes?'

Emma took a deep breath. It was best to get it over with.
'I want to go on one of those healing courses they run at
Potwoolstan Hall.'

Barry looked alarmed. 'Why? Why there?'

'You know why.' She looked at her husband and saw the
fear in his eyes.

'It might make things worse, raking it all up again. It's
a load of nonsense what they do at that place. And have you
seen how much it costs?'

Emma said nothing.

'I don't want you to go. And I don't want you to see that
man.' He grabbed her wrist and held it tight, looking into
her frightened eyes. Then he released his grip and began to
stroke her cheek. 'He'd only upset you. Has he rung
today?'

'No.'

A smile played on Barry's lips. 'I didn't think he would.'

Emma looked at him. There was something in the way
he'd spoken that worried her. 'Why?'

But Barry Oldchester poured the tea in silence as Emma
stared out of the window.

Chapter Two

As we were anchored, Captain Barton broke the seal upon the box and the orders were read. They named a Council of eight men – Lord Coslake, Master Richard Smith, Captain John Radford, Master Isaac Morton, Master Fulke Oldfield, Master Henry Barras, Master Christopher Heath and Master Henry Jennings – and we must choose a President who shall govern with the Council.

We landed all our men and some were set to work upon the fortification, and others to watch and guard. The first night of our landing there came some Savages, sailing close to us. Yet it is not the Savages we fear so much as the Spanish who would conquer this land for their King and their faith.

Master Joshua Morton, the younger brother of Master Isaac, is much occupied by the building and in the evening he favours the playing of card games with other gentlemen so that his wife is often alone. There are many strawberries and other fruits unknown to us and the woods are full of cedar and cypress trees. Mistress Morton fell and hurt her ankle while gathering strawberries and I carried her back to the safety of the settlement. She was as light as a bird in my arms. Her husband seemed not pleased at my presumption.

It was almost two thirty when Wesley and Heffernan returned to the station. Wesley was looking forward to a cup of tea and half an hour spent gathering his thoughts about the man in the river, but he spotted Steve Carstairs swaggering across the office towards his desk. Steve's touch was the opposite of delicate, his chief talent being the building of fruitful relationships with an unappealing variety of informants. He seemed to have a rapport with the criminal classes, which didn't altogether surprise Wesley.

'How did you get on at Potwoolstan Hall?' Wesley asked.

Steve thrust his hands in his pockets. 'Some old bag had cash and a ring nicked from her handbag. She'd left it in her bedroom. Stupid old cow. There's some funny people in that place.'

'What's the setup?'

Steve was about to open his mouth when Rachel appeared in the office doorway. 'Has Steve told you about the theft?'

Steve shot her a resentful glance. If that's how she wanted to play it, he'd let her take over. It would save him the effort of explaining. He slunk back to his desk and pretended to study a witness statement.

Wesley turned to Rachel. 'He started to. Well?'

'When we arrived we were met by a man called Elsham who called himself the "facilitator" – probably a twenty-two carat charlatan but good at the old charm. Anyway, it seems this healing centre,' the words were said with heavy irony, 'specialises in something called regression therapy. The guests – or Beings as they're known – are hypnotised and taken back to their childhood, and even back to former lives. If you left that Elsham in a field of sheep he'd have them fleeced in two minutes flat.' Rachel was at her judgemental best, her mouth set in a hard line.

'Not a man you'd trust with your life savings then?' He

27

smiled and she smiled back, the ice melting. 'Was the victim's room locked?'

'The guests aren't allowed to lock their doors. House rule. According to the victim, the stuff was pinched while they were all having breakfast. We've interviewed everyone who wasn't at breakfast.' She suddenly grinned wickedly, as though she had a juicy secret she was longing to impart.

'What is it?'

Rachel looked over her shoulder at Steve. He appeared to be engrossed in paperwork but she was taking no chances. She walked out of the office into the corridor, motioning Wesley to follow her. He obeyed, full of curiosity.

'There was a girl there called Serena Jones,' she began when they were out of earshot. 'Steve met her at a club in Morbay and they've been out together a few times. He got the shock of his life when he saw her there. Somehow she didn't seem the type you'd usually find in a place like that so I asked Steve what he knew about her, which turned out to be very little.'

'You think she might have something to do with these thefts?'

'Not sure. But she looked as if she was hiding something.'

'Have you checked whether anyone at Potwoolstan Hall was staying at the other places? The health spa or the ...?'

'Yes, I've been through the lists but there's nothing obvious. Mind you, there's nothing to stop the thief using a different identity in each place, is there?'

'So, apart from Serena Jones, are there any other likely suspects?'

'The man staying in the room adjoining Mrs Jeffries's wasn't at breakfast: claimed he had a stomachache. It checked out: he asked Mrs Elsham for some indigestion tablets. There was a Mrs Carmody who's in a wheelchair. Her room's on the ground floor and the place has no lift.

She usually has breakfast in her room.'

'So we should probably concentrate on Ms Jones and your man with stomachache. What was his name?'

'Charles Dodgson.'

Wesley smiled.

'What's the matter?'

'Charles Dodgson was the real name of Lewis Carroll, the man who wrote *Alice in Wonderland*. Perhaps someone's trying to lead us down a rabbit hole. You'd better run a check on him. Did you ask if you could search the rooms of the three who weren't at breakfast?'

'Yes. Dodgson and Carmody were keen to cooperate but Serena Jones got a bit uppity about it. We didn't find anything suspicious, of course.'

'Pity. I would have liked to get this one cleared up.' He looked at his watch. 'I'm going to the Tradmouth Castle Hotel to see if they have a name for our corpse in the river. The boss wanted to come with me but the chief super's called him to a budget meeting.'

'Bet he's pleased about that,' Rachel said with a laugh.

He called across the room. 'Are you busy, Trish?'

Rachel gave her a sharp look. 'Can you run a check on a man called Charles Dodgson on the PNC?'

'I'll do it now, Sarge,' Trish said sadly. She turned and wandered back down the corridor. Wesley knew that Rachel had just taken advantage of her rank. And he wasn't sure how he felt about it. There had been times when the prospect of an afternoon alone with Rachel Tracey, even in the course of work, would have excited him. But he had put all that behind him now. He thought of Pam and felt a pang of guilt.

'Fancy coming to the Tradmouth Castle?'

Rachel didn't need asking twice. She went into the office to fetch her coat.

The Tradmouth Castle wasn't generally regarded as the smartest hotel in town. It was the comfortable, slightly old-fashioned home of chesterfields and hunting prints, the natural habitat of the mayor and the Rotary Club. Professional men held their annual dinners there and middle-aged, middle-class men took their wives to eat there on their wedding anniversaries. They took their mistresses elsewhere. Wesley had never frequented the place and he strongly suspected that Gerry Heffernan hadn't either. Rachel, however, announced that she had once been to a Young Farmers' dinner dance there. Wesley was glad that somebody knew their way around.

The young woman behind the reception desk stared at them like a rabbit caught in car headlights when they produced their warrant cards and Wesley guessed that, as she obviously wasn't a master criminal, she probably hadn't encountered many real police officers at close quarters before. She was a thin, nervous-looking girl in her late teens and her brown hair was scraped back from her face, making her brown eyes enormous against her pale skin. Wesley made a special effort to put the girl at her ease before she chewed her ragged fingernails down too far and did herself a serious injury.

'It's just routine,' he said. 'Nothing to worry about.' He knew he sounded like a doctor reassuring a terrified patient that a potentially unpleasant medical procedure wouldn't hurt a bit: as his parents were both doctors he concluded that he'd probably picked up the bedside manner by osmosis. The tactic seemed to work. The girl stopped chewing at her nails and visibly relaxed.

'You'll have to see the manager. It was him who rang the police.'

Wesley glanced at Rachel, who looked as puzzled as he felt.

'The manager called the police?'

'Only a few minutes ago. We didn't expect you to be so quick. I mean you hear about the police not turning up for hours and ...' The girl's voice trailed off. 'I'll tell him you're here,' she added feebly before picking up the phone.

She looked at the instrument, consulted a sheet of paper then pressed three buttons carefully. She was definitely new to the job, Wesley thought.

The manager hurried straight out of his office behind the desk. It would probably have been easier for the girl to knock at his door to announce their arrival but she had decided to do things by the book. He was a slim young man with slightly receding hair and the keen, intelligent look of a police sniffer dog. Like policemen, hotel managers seemed to be getting younger by the minute.

He held out a confident hand to Wesley. His handshake was firm and he looked Wesley in the eye and introduced himself in a strong, clear voice, as Matthew Fellowes. Wesley didn't know whether his apparent self-confidence was natural or if he'd learned it on a management course of some kind but he reserved judgement. He and Rachel were led into Fellowes's office, which was smaller than he'd expected and fitted out with uninspiring chipboard furniture.

Fellowes sat down behind his desk and began to thank them profusely for turning up so promptly. Wesley, unused to effusive praise from members of the public, basked in the admiration for a few moments before asking the man to explain exactly what was wrong. He hardly liked to admit that they hadn't rushed there in answer to his summons: he'd make the most of the situation while the going was good.

'It was the chambermaid who found it like that ...'

'Like what exactly?' Wesley asked, hoping a full explanation would follow.

Fellowes looked uncomfortable for the first time. 'As I said on the phone, one of the first floor rooms has been ransacked. Things thrown all over the place. Terrible mess. Of course we won't know what's missing until Mr Evans gets back.'

'Mr Evans?' Rachel asked.

'The guest who's been staying in room fourteen. I've

questioned the staff and nobody's seen him for a couple of days. And now the chambermaid tells me that she doesn't think his bed's been slept in for the last two nights.'

The two officers exchanged glances. 'Can you describe this Mr Evans?'

Fellowes proceeded to give a remarkably good description of the corpse in the river. Wesley tried to keep the excitement he felt under control and asked to have a look at the room.

As Fellowes led the way upstairs, the girl at reception looked terrified as they passed. 'She's new,' he whispered to Wesley when they were out of earshot. 'Owner's niece. Not the brightest pixie in the forest, if you get my meaning, but we have to work with what we're given, don't we?'

Wesley smiled. He could say the same about several of the police officers under his command.

They reached the door and Fellowes let himself in with his pass key. 'I told the chambermaid to leave everything as she found it. I thought you'd want to take fingerprints and all that.'

Wesley stepped over the threshold, followed by Rachel. The chambermaid had been right. The room had been ransacked. Clothes had been pulled from the wardrobe and from the chest of drawers that stood beneath the window. The bedclothes had been ripped from the bed, probably in an effort to search beneath the pillows and mattress. A suitcase lay open and empty on the floor. Someone had been anxious to find something.

'Nobody heard anything,' Fellowes said with what sounded like disbelief.

Wesley wasn't surprised. This kind of search wouldn't necessarily be noisy.

'Will you ... er ... be all right here on your own?'

'I think we can manage.' Wesley felt relieved when the manager hurried off. He never liked to be watched when he was working: not many people do.

'Not a professional job,' Rachel observed, pointing at the

chest of drawers. Wesley saw what she meant. The drawers had obviously been opened from the top downwards – the professional thief always finds it quicker the other way around. And something about the way the clothes were strewn about suggested a haphazard rather than a methodical search.

Wesley knelt amongst the clothes on the floor and began to feel in the pockets. He pulled out a half-finished packet of low-tar cigarettes from the inside pocket of a linen jacket and four pounds thirty-three pence in change from the back pocket of a pair of jeans. But there was nothing much else. If the man had credit cards or a driving licence he would probably have been carrying them with him in a wallet. And if the occupant of the room was indeed their mystery corpse, that wallet was either in the possession of whoever killed him or at the bottom of the river.

Wesley pulled on a pair of latex gloves and began to examine the room in more detail. But there was nothing much to find. A toothbrush and a tube of toothpaste still stood in a glass in the en suite bathroom beside an electric razor. Mr Evans, whoever he was, hadn't decided to stay with friends or a woman he'd just met if he had left these essentials behind. It was looking more and more likely that Evans was their man. He could feel it in his water, as Gerry Heffernan would say.

They left the room, closing the door carefully behind them, and made their way down the thickly carpeted stairs to Fellowes's office. He invited them to sit down but no tea was offered, much to Wesley's disappointment. Gerry Heffernan would have demanded some but Wesley lacked his audacity.

Wesley drew a photograph from his pocket and handed it to Fellowes; a picture of the corpse, tastefully arranged so as not to alarm the sensitive. 'Is this Mr Evans?'

Fellowes went pale and nodded. 'Is he . . .?'

'I'm afraid so. I suppose you have an address for him?'

'Of course.' Fellowes wrote the address on a piece of

paper and handed it to Wesley. 'He arrived the Sunday before last and booked in for a fortnight, saying he might want to stay longer. He gave us his credit card details. Usual practice.'

'In case the guest disappears without paying?' said Rachel.

'A precaution.'

'Can you tell us anything else about him?' Wesley asked. 'Did he say why he was here? What his line of work was?'

Fellowes shook his head. 'I presumed he was down here on business but I've told you all I know, I'm afraid.' Fellowes assumed an apologetic look.

'I'll arrange for some officers to come over and talk to the staff and the other guests. He might have talked to someone.'

Fellowes looked alarmed. 'I hope they'll be discreet. Our guests . . .'

'You won't even know they're here,' he said with a reassuring smile.

Wesley studied the piece of paper in his hand. Evans's initial was P and the address was in south-east London. The only thing he knew about the district was that it had once been a no go area but now it was facing an invasion of young professionals courted by developers of smart warehouse-style apartments. It wasn't an area he knew well: London was a big place. One of the reasons he had been glad to get away from it.

As they left the Tradmouth Castle Hotel they saw two uniformed constables making for the entrance. 'Will you tell them or shall I?' he said to Rachel.

Rachel did the honours: Fellowes would still be convinced that the two CID officers had rushed there in answer to his call. Why disillusion the man?

They returned to the office, to report their findings but Gerry Heffernan was still in his budget meeting. He'd be in a foul mood when he got back, Wesley thought. Budget meetings always affected him that way.

After sending a couple of DCs back to the Tradmouth Castle to interview the staff and guests, Wesley made for his desk and tapped the name P. Evans and the address into the computer. If Evans had been convicted of any crime under that name, the details would come up in a matter of seconds.

But he drew a blank. P. Evans, whoever he was, had either been a law-abiding citizen or he'd never been caught. But at least Wesley had an address. And he had friends in not so high places.

His heart began to beat fast as he picked up the telephone. It was a long time since he'd spoken to his old friend in the Met, Pete Jarrod – now, like Wesley, promoted to DI and posted at P. Evans's local police station. Pete and Wesley had been graduate recruits together training at Hendon and they had always got on well. But such is the way of the world that their only contact now was a card each Christmas with a scribbled note.

He asked the switchboard for DI Jarrod's extension and waited, fearing that Pete would be out fighting the capital's crime. But his luck was in. Pete answered, surprised to hear Wesley's voice. The two men spent five minutes catching up on news – half-envious questions about life in Devon and enquiries about Pete's wife, Becky, who worked for an investment bank – before Wesley was able to steer the conversation round to P. Evans.

Pete promised to run a check on Evans at the address he'd given and get back to him. Wesley harboured a vague hope that Pete might be able to pass on some unofficial local knowledge about his man; that Evans might be some Mr Big, as yet untouched by the law but under surveillance by the local CID. But no such luck. P. Evans was a mere member of the public. A victim rather than a perpetrator. Pete and his colleagues had nothing on him. In spite of this, Wesley thanked him profusely and said he'd be welcome down in Devon any time. It was an invitation that he didn't expect Pete and Becky would take up – and he wasn't sure how Pam would react if they did. She had her hands full at the moment without a couple of extra mouths to feed. And once she returned to work when her maternity leave ended after the Easter holidays, things would hardly improve.

As Wesley predicted, Gerry Heffernan wasn't in the best of moods when he returned from his budget meeting. He lumbered through the office muttering ominously and disappeared into his lair. After a few moments, Wesley followed him and found him slumped at his cluttered desk.

'If I'd wanted to be a ruddy accountant, I would have bought myself a calculator.'

'That bad?' Wesley sat down and assumed what he considered to be a sympathetic look.

'Give me an honest armed robber any day. Anything new?'

Wesley told him about his fruitful visit to the hotel.

'So we've got a name for our corpse.'

'Looks like it. The photo's not good but the manager recognised him all right. I've rung a friend of mine at the Met. He's going to send someone round to Evans's address.'

'Good. The question is, what was whoever searched his room looking for? And did they find it? We've got to find out more about Mr P. Evans. I suppose it would be too much to hope that the Tradmouth Castle has CCTV cameras dotted all over the place?'

Wesley gave him a regretful smile. 'Afraid not.'

Wesley looked at his watch. It was five o'clock already. Another night when he'd arrive home late.

He returned to his desk to catch up on his paperwork. There was a note from Trish: Charles Dodgson didn't appear on the PNC. He had no convictions – under that particular name at least. But that could wait for another day. Murder trumped a series of thefts.

He was surprised when Pete Jarrod returned his call an hour later. Being familiar with the workload of the Met, he hadn't expected such efficient service.

'Hi, Wes. I've asked around but I'm afraid nothing is known about Evans and I sent someone round to the address but there was nobody in. According to the electoral register his first name's Patrick and there's a Kirsty Evans at the same address. Probably the wife. I'll arrange for her to be informed as soon as she gets back from work.'

Somehow, Wesley had hoped for more; that perhaps one person at Evans's local police station would be aware of his existence. But it was hardly surprising. It was only villains who ended up 'known to the police'.

'Thanks, Pete. The wife will have to come down here to make a formal identification.' He hesitated, making a decision. 'If all's well I'll come down tomorrow to see her and I'll bring her back to Devon. I'd like to see where he lived for myself.' He looked at the heap of files on his desk. 'I've got a mountain of paperwork here but ...'

'I understand – have the same problem myself. If we don't manage to track down the wife I'll let you know, save you a wasted journey.'

'Thanks. Ring me at home if you can't get hold of me here.' Wesley put the phone down, suddenly impatient to find out more about the dead man's life. In the meantime, he'd bring Gerry Heffernan up to date on his plans.

He looked at his watch again, thinking of Pam alone in the house with Michael and Amelia and experiencing a sharp pang of guilt. He had never wanted to be an absent father. But circumstances conspired against him.

Pam rushed into the hall when she heard Wesley's key in the door. She was carrying Amelia over her shoulder, hoping she would drop off to sleep. But the baby's eyes were wide open and alert, as though she knew Daddy was home.

Wesley greeted his wife with a weary smile and planted a kiss on her forehead. He took Amelia's tiny, golden-brown hand in his and she gripped his fingers tightly.

'Neil's been round,' were Pam's first words. The look in her eyes told Wesley that Neil's visit hadn't been a routine one. Something had happened. 'He's off to the States tonight.'

Wesley frowned. 'What for?' Neil didn't usually take holidays: he enjoyed his work too much.

'He's going on a dig in Virginia. Something to do with the early settlers. He said he'd keep in touch by email while he's out there.'

Wesley made his way into the living room, where Michael was sitting on the floor constructing a tower of brightly coloured plastic bricks. As soon as he saw Wesley he jumped up and charged at his legs, demolishing his tower in the process. Wesley caught him in his arms and lifted him up.

'So we won't be seeing Uncle Neil for a while,' he said, addressing Michael, who nodded earnestly. At almost three he was becoming a serious child. The uncomfortable thought that his long absences at work were responsible for this flashed through Wesley's mind. But then, according to his parents, he too had been a solemn, studious child. Perhaps it was hereditary.

'I have to go to London tomorrow,' he said, trying to sound casual.

Pam looked at him as though he'd disappointed her in some way.

'A man's body was found in the river and we have an address for him in London. I have to see his wife and bring her back to identify the body. I'll stay the night in Dulwich – with my parents.'

She hesitated. 'Can't someone else go?'

Wesley shook his head. If he told her that he wanted to see where Patrick Evans lived for himself and find out as much as he could about his life, he feared she wouldn't understand.

He was about to open his mouth to ask what they were having for supper but the look on Pam's face made him think twice. If he had had a hard day, so had she. He whispered something in Michael's ear and the child slipped out of his arms. They would make the supper together; a spot of father–son bonding.

Emma Oldchester had never liked telephones. She had always felt nervous about making calls, although she never really knew why this was. But she had finally done it. She had booked into Potwoolstan Hall for a week, starting on Easter Monday.

She glanced at her watch. Barry was late and she didn't like being alone, especially in the dark. From the window she could see the trees in the fields opposite the house reaching for her like gnarled fingers against the deep grey sky and she suddenly felt afraid. The outside world had always been a threatening place but this house was her refuge. Somewhere he could never touch her.

Emma switched on the television news. There was a strike at an airport up north; a civil war in some African state with an unfamiliar name; share prices had fallen. But she wasn't really listening – she just liked to hear the sound of human voices. It made her feel less alone in that empty house.

She sat quite still for a while, staring at the screen. A casserole was bubbling away in the oven for when Barry returned. Everything was under control.

Until the telephone rang.

She ignored it at first but as it carried on ringing she slumped down in the corner and stared at the instrument, her body trembling as she willed it to stop. It would be him. Even when she'd refused to see him, he had kept on calling – pestering, Barry had called it – and although he hadn't called for a few days, she knew he was out there somewhere, biding his time.

Eventually the ringing stopped. But she knew he wouldn't give up. Patrick Evans would call again.

Chapter Three

Two days since we were set upon by a party of Savages. It seems they are led by a cruel and powerful Chief who has conquered many tribes and has many warriors under his command. By all accounts he is a clever and conscientious leader and a man to fear.

Captain Radford, the President of our Council, observed that these native warriors greatly outnumber the settlers and this Chief could have slaughtered us if it had been his will. It may be that he is willing to establish a truce between our people and his and to trade with us.

We passed through excellent ground full of flowers of divers kinds and colours and strawberries four times bigger and better than our own in England. We met with a Savage who brought us to a Garden of Tobacco and other fruits and herbs. He gathered tobacco and distributed to every one of us then we departed as we mistrusted some villainy.

Our fortifications are as yet unfinished and even the gentlemen amongst us have laboured beside the artisans to erect the walls as we fear for our lives and the safety of our womenfolk.

On the twentieth day the Chief sent forty of his men with a deer to our quarters but they came more in villainy than in love. They would have lain in our fort all night but we did not allow them for fear of their treachery.

I try to allay the fears of Mistress Morton as her husband gives her no such words of comfort and reassurance. Her name is Penelope ... the name of a faithful wife.

Set down by Edmund Selbiwood, Gentleman, at Annetown this twenty-first day of July 1605.

When Wesley left home at seven the next morning, Pam kissed him on the cheek and instructed him to drive carefully. He sensed that she wasn't happy about his journey to London. But there were some things a policeman's wife had to put up with, he thought, trying to banish his nebulous feelings of guilt.

As he knew he had a long journey ahead of him, he tucked into a hearty full English breakfast in the police station canteen. Sitting alone at a table by the window, he gazed out at the view of the river as he ate. The weak spring sun was shining and the clement weather had lured a number of sailors on to the water. And he had noticed some early tourists in the town over the past few days, strolling at a leisurely pace along the waterfront, getting in the way.

The canteen was empty apart from a noisy quartet of uniformed constables in the corner, just come off their shift and tucking into bacon, sausage and eggs. They ignored him and he ignored them, which suited him fine. As he stared out of the window, he thought of the day ahead. Colin Bowman had booked the postmortem on Patrick Evans for eight fifteen. Over the years, Wesley had taught himself to watch some of the gruesome procedures without being physically sick but he still looked away when the first incision was made in the corpse's chest and when the brain was removed from the open skull. Wesley looked down at his now empty plate, wondering whether he'd done the right thing. Perhaps it would have been wiser to witness the postmortem on an empty stomach.

As soon as he had finished at the mortuary, he intended to set off for London to see Evans's wife – or rather widow. Pete Jarrod had rung him at home the previous night to say that when a DC had called round to break the news, the widow had seemed to take it calmly. This came as a relief: Wesley didn't know whether he was up to coping with hysterical grief. He had come to rely on Rachel to deal with that sort of thing because she was good with the bereaved, possessing just the right mixture of sympathy and common sense. But this time he'd be alone. With the investigation into Evans's suspicious death gathering pace, Rachel was needed in Tradmouth.

Of course there was always a chance – a slim one admittedly – that they had made a mistake about Patrick Evans; that someone who resembled Evans had stolen his identity and the genuine article was alive and well somewhere. But Wesley dismissed the idea. The hotel manager had recognised the photograph of the tidied up corpse and once his wife had identified the body the question would be settled beyond doubt.

Wesley looked at his watch and at his empty, greasy plate. It was time to meet Gerry Heffernan. With a sigh he stood up, his chair legs scraping loudly on the hard floor. The group of uniforms in the corner looked round then averted their eyes.

As Wesley arrived in the CID office, Heffernan hurried in, breathless. He had the dishevelled look of a man who'd overslept. But then he'd lived alone since his children had left home for university. And his wife had died some years ago so there was nobody to make sure he got out of bed on time in the mornings. His tie was askew and there was a grease stain on the front of his shirt. Pam concluded long ago that Gerry Heffernan was the type of man who needs a good woman. Trouble was, good women seemed to be in short supply these days.

'Ready for our rendezvous with Colin, Wes?' The chief

inspector sounded inappropriately cheerful, his accent betraying his Liverpool origins.

'Ready as I'll ever be,' Wesley mumbled. Heffernan charged ahead, setting the office door swinging and Wesley followed, regretting his choice of breakfast. His stomach was already starting to complain at the earlier excesses of that morning.

Colin Bowman was waiting for them at the mortuary. As usual, the two policemen observed the proceedings from the far side of the white-tiled postmortem room, Wesley hardly saying a word and looking away at the most gruesome moments while Heffernan chatted cheerfully, as though Colin was doing something quite mundane, like preparing a meal or working on a car engine.

Colin announced that the victim had been a healthy man in his thirties. He had good muscle tone, probably as a result of working out regularly in a gym, and Gerry Heffernan couldn't resist observing that all that healthy living hadn't done the man much good.

The cause of death was undoubtedly a stab wound to the heart. The blade that had ended Patrick Evans's life had been narrow, sharp and fairly long; a kitchen knife perhaps. From the angle of the wound, his killer had probably been a few inches smaller than him. Or perhaps standing on slightly lower ground: the Devon landscape was notoriously undulating. Colin also observed that the murder could have been committed by a man or a woman. That was all they needed, thought Wesley: the entire population of Devon under suspicion.

The only time Colin's stream of social chitchat stopped flowing was when he began to examine the contents of the corpse's stomach.

'He'd eaten a hearty meal just before he died,' he announced after a few seconds of silence. 'Hardly digested. Come and have a look.'

Wesley and Heffernan edged forward reluctantly. Wesley could still taste the sausage and bacon he'd had for breakfast and the last thing he wanted was to throw it up all over the spotless mortuary floor. As Colin waved the bowl containing the dead man's last supper under their noses, Wesley closed his eyes and held his breath. 'I'll send it for proper analysis, of course, but unless I'm very much mistaken, that looks like lobster. Fair amount of wine to wash it down too but we'll know for certain once I've sent this lot to the lab.'

'So he died happy, with a decent meal inside him,' Heffernan observed. 'Homemade or restaurant?'

Colin chuckled. 'Now I'm not a clairvoyant, Gerry. Perhaps a lady friend had gone to a lot of trouble and he failed to appreciate her cooking. That's for you to find out. I'll send samples for toxicology tests. That should tell us if he was the worse for drink.'

'Time of death?' Wesley asked.

'Can't be exact, of course, but I'd say he died about twenty-four hours before he was found, give or take eight hours or so.' He frowned. 'He was found yesterday morning. Monday. But, as I said, he ate a big meal shortly beforehand and nobody I know has lobster washed down with red wine for Sunday breakfast so I'd say he died on Saturday night after a last supper, as if were. I can't be certain, of course but ...'

This theory made sense to Wesley. Evans had enjoyed a slap-up meal. Then for some reason somebody had stuck a knife in his ribs and dumped his body in the river. His dining companion, perhaps? He made a mental note to get someone to check out all the local restaurants with lobster on the menu. It was quite possible that someone saw Evans with his killer. But then again, things weren't usually that easy.

When the postmortem was over and Colin had cleaned himself up, Wesley declined the customary invitation to stay for a cup of tea. He had a long and arduous journey to make. And an appointment with a widow.

*

44

At two o'clock Pam Peterson sat down. Michael, exhausted after a morning at nursery, had fallen asleep and Amelia, worn out from a morning of hearty howling, had done likewise. At first Pam couldn't decide whether to do something about the state of the house or about the state of herself. She had decided on the latter and had showered, washed her hair and changed. Although she knew that Wesley wouldn't be home to appreciate her efforts, the feeling of being cleansed and perfumed lifted her spirits.

After half an hour of pampering she found, to her relief, that the children were still asleep. Freedom beckoned and so did the sightless screen of the computer moniter in the corner of the dining room. It was ages since she'd enjoyed the luxury of doing something unproductive and self-indulgent and the dirty dishes in the kitchen weren't going anywhere.

When she switched the computer on she found there was an email from Neil. He had remembered. In all the excitement of arriving in a new country, he had thought of her.

'Hi Pam and Wes.' He had put her name first. 'Eight-hour flight but no jet lag. Weather fine. Bit warmer than home and good conditions for digging. I'm staying in an apartment near the university, sharing with one of the guys on the dig – Chuck Hanman. He's talked about nothing but baseball so far but apart from that he seems OK.

'I've had a tour of the dig. It's a big operation and very well funded. It's a long time since I saw such good conservation facilities and the site itself is interesting. In 1605 sixty-five settlers came across from England in a ship called the *Nicholas* which sailed from Tradmouth. They built a fortified settlement at Annetown (named after James I's queen) and they intended to trade with the local Indians until they could grow their own food. Everything went fine for a while, until the *Nicholas* sailed for home. Then people started dying of some mysterious illness. Life must have been tough.

'Chuck told me they'd found an adult male skeleton with

a musket ball lodged in the skull. He'd been buried in a wooden coffin which means that he was a gentleman rather than a peasant (they were buried in shrouds). I assumed he'd been killed by the natives who must have resented the settlers pinching their land but I was told this was unlikely because he'd been killed by a European weapon. Bit of a mystery, eh? One of his teeth has been sent away for analysis but I'll tell you more about that next time.

'As for the other thing I mentioned, I don't really know where to start. How do you track someone down in a strange country? I almost wish Gran hadn't asked me because I can see I'll have my hands full at the dig. Don't work too hard, Wes – give those villains a break, eh. Be in touch soon. Neil.'

Pam smiled to herself as she hit the button that would print the email out. Then the smile disappeared when she remembered that Wesley wouldn't be home until late tomorrow. And then he'd probably be too tired to read it. As she stood up, Amelia began to cry. There were times when she envied Neil, when she wished she too could cross the Atlantic without a second thought for her responsibilities.

London was just as Wesley remembered it. Big, crowded, dirty and fast. The traffic on the M25 crawled along at the pace of an elderly snail and on the ordinary roads drivers cut in, drove too close and sounded their horns impatiently. Aggression and frustration hung in the air like mist. Wesley felt he was in alien territory, even though he had been brought up there and had worked there with the Met's élite Arts and Antiques Squad. He had become accustomed to the pace of life in Tradmouth and now he was here in the capital sitting at a busy junction waiting for traffic lights to change with a taxi cab half an inch from his bumper and a lycra-clad cyclist leaning on his wing mirror, he found himself counting his blessings. Things could be worse.

Kirsty Evans lived south of the river. Deptford wasn't far

in geographical terms from Dulwich, where he had lived and attended school, but it was a social world away. Or rather it had been while he was growing up. It was a bad area but the tentacles of gentrification reached everywhere these days. The main thing Wesley remembered about Deptford was that the playwright Christopher Marlowe had met a violent end there in a low tavern, probably at the hands of Queen Elizabeth I's equivalent of MI5, and he wondered to himself how much things had really changed in four hundred years of human existence. As he came to a halt at another set of red traffic lights, he took the opportunity to consult the A to Z that lay open on the passenger seat and discovered that he didn't have far to go.

His first port of call was Evans's local police station where he was told Pete Jarrod was out investigating yet another local shooting. He spoke briefly to the policewoman who had broken the bad news to Kirsty Evans the previous evening. She was a thin DC with spiky peroxide hair and a personality to match – a no-nonsense sort who was probably more at home questioning the local prostitutes than dispensing tea and sympathy to grieving widows – and he was rather relieved when she told him bluntly that, as they were fully stretched with muggings, shootings, murders and robberies, the likes of Mrs Evans weren't high on their list of priorities. Wesley would have to deal with her alone.

He left the station with the feeling that he had been brushed aside as an annoying distraction from the real business of urban policing, and after driving round for a while he found a free parking space outside an office building just one street away from Kirsty Evans's flat, if his A to Z was to be believed. He climbed out of the car and breathed in deeply. Diesel fumes and dust. The pavements were piled with plastic bin bags awaiting collection and some of their contents had spilled out. His foot came into contact with a plastic tray that had once been the temporary home of some takeaway cheeseburger. He could smell a rancid odour

47

rising from the litter and he felt dirt permeating his pores, his hair, his very soul.

As he walked towards Kirsty Evans's apartment he noticed that at least half the people he passed were black. In Tradmouth he was generally in a minority of one but here he was just one of a crowd. A shaven-headed white man was approaching him, staring boldly. He wore a Millwall football shirt over a stocky torso bulging with gym-honed muscles and his hairy arms bore some fine examples of the tattooist's art. As this human pit bull terrier passed, he brushed against Wesley's arm and shot him a hostile glance before spitting on the ground. Wesley averted his eyes and hurried on. Trouble was something he didn't need right now.

Kirsty Evans lived in what appeared to be a converted industrial building. Wesley could see the walls of the foyer through the plain glass front door: they were rough bare brick, featureless and functional. Like some kind of prison. Or a monastery where the brothers lived particularly austere lives. He pressed the button marked Evans and a weak voice wafted from a stainless steel speaker. Kirsty Evans sounded like a frail old woman, but grief can drain the life force from even the liveliest personality.

When the door lock was released, Wesley made his way slowly up the cold concrete stairs and found Kirsty Evans waiting at the open door to her apartment – a tall steel door, double her height. Wesley's first thought was that she looked like a lost little girl. She wore no make-up on her pale face and her fine blond hair was scraped back into a makeshift ponytail. Her eyes were large, blue-grey and bloodshot. She had been crying, which was hardly surprising in the circumstances. Wesley hovered on the threshold for a moment, lost for words and wishing Rachel Tracey was there with him to shoulder the burden.

Once he had introduced himself, Kirsty led him inside and invited him to sit down on a long low, black leather sofa. It wasn't comfortable but Wesley hardly noticed: his mind was on other things.

48

The interior of the apparment was as bare as the rest of the building. This was minimalism. And although the chaos in Wesley's house constantly irritated him, he preferred it to this place with its white walls, floor to ceiling windows and stainless steel. It would be like living in an operating theatre – or Colin Bowman's mortuary. But he knew that such clinical surroundings didn't come cheap.

'I'm very sorry about your husband,' he began.

'You're sure it's him?'

He glanced at a photograph in a stainless steel frame that stood on a sleek beech sideboard. A wedding photograph, taken outside a picturesque country church that looked somehow incongruous in these starkly urban surroundings. Kirsty smiled out at the camera, elegant in her simple ivory gown, while the dead man beamed by her side in his morning suit.

'We're pretty certain, yes. But we'd like you to come to Devon to identify him, if you're feeling up to it. Unless there's someone else you'd like . . .'

She sank down into a deep leather armchair, hugging a suede cushion as though it were a baby. 'No. I want to see him.' She suddenly looked up, her eyes red and moist with unshed tears. 'When the policewoman came last night to tell me, I thought it couldn't be Paddy. He's been all over the place. He can take care of himself. He's lived round here for five years and he's never even been mugged. And he's been in bloody Bosnia, for God's sake. He knew the score. Nothing could happen to him in a place like Devon. The policewoman said he'd been found in a river. Is that right?'

'Yes but . . .'

'Do you know what happened? Did he fall in or . . .'

'We don't know what happened yet, I'm afraid. But we are treating his death as suspicious. I'm sorry.'

She shook her head. 'That's impossible. It must have been an accident.'

Wesley opened his mouth to say something but the right

words evaded him. 'What was he doing in Devon?' he said after a long silence.

'Research, he said. He's been writing a series of books on notorious murder cases. Hack work really. People love true crime. There's nothing like a good conspiracy theory.'

'What did he plan to do in Devon? Did he go there to see a particular person?' His murderer perhaps.

'He didn't discuss it with me. He does . . . did . . . his job and I do mine. I work in finance.'

That explained where the money for the apartment had come from: freelance writers were generally an impecunious breed.

'Do you know what case he was writing about?'

'I haven't a clue.' She frowned. 'Sorry I'm not being much help.'

'His notes and papers, where would they be?'

'He kept all his stuff at the office. He didn't bring it home.'

'The office?'

'He rented a place not far away – in an office block that's due to be redeveloped.'

'So he didn't work here?'

She shook her head. 'He likes – liked – to spread out when he was working. There just isn't the space here.'

Or Kirsty Evans was pathologically tidy and didn't want her partner making a mess all over her white, minimalist surfaces and mucking up her pristine lifestyle, Wesley thought.

'Had he any enemies? Anyone you can think of who might want to harm him?'

She looked up sharply, as if he'd just said something offensive. 'Nobody would want to harm Paddy. Everybody liked him. He was a wonderful bloke – very popular. Life and soul of the party – not that we've been to many parties recently.'

Wesley sensed there was something behind this last remark, some hint that all wasn't quite as perfect as Kirsty wished it to seem.

50

'Would you mind if I had a look at his office?'

Kirsty stood up. 'I'll find the key.' She disappeared into what he assumed was the bedroom and he waited, twisting his wedding ring round and round, wondering whether to offer to make a token cup of tea as Rachel would have done. But then Kirsty Evans didn't really look like the tea type.

Kirsty returned after a few minutes with a Yale key on a key ring in the shape of a bullet. 'Do you want me to come with you or . . .?'

'Yes please,' he replied quickly. For some reason, he didn't fancy looking round the dead man's office on his own. Perhaps he was afraid of what he might find.

Emma Oldchester stood beside her stall at the Ingleham Village Hall craft fair feeling rather pleased with herself. She had sold the Georgian house with the pale striped wallpaper and the tiny marble fireplaces to a lady from Millicombe who had just become the grandmother of a baby girl. It was to be a christening gift – an heirloom the child could enjoy as she grew. Emma had put a lot of work into that particular house and was relieved that the customer hadn't baulked at the three-figure asking price. The money would go towards her stay at Potwoolstan Hall.

She bought the undecorated doll's houses from a retired joiner who made them as a hobby and a means of earning a little tax-free cash. The miniature furniture came from a wholesaler in Morbay. But it was Emma who put these raw materials together and created something magical with her paint, fabrics, her carefully chosen wallpapers and her delicate touch.

Doll's houses had fascinated her since she was small. She remembered her first quite clearly. It wasn't as big or elaborate as the one in the old nursery, that dusty room with barred windows at the top of the main house. Emma had sneaked upstairs to see it often, hardly daring to touch the forbidden treasure – the magnificent Georgian mansion in

51

miniature, made for some wealthy Victorian daughter of the house – that drew her like a magnet. But although her first small dwelling was considerably humbler than the one in the old nursery, at least it had been her own. It had been a birthday present and her mother had left it for her to find on her birthday morning: an intriguing shape at the bottom of her bed in the moonlight, swathed in thin wrapping paper covered with flowers. The paper had torn and a small chimney poked out. She remembered the rustle of that brittle paper, loud as gunfire in the silence, as she touched the big square package. She had asked for a doll's house but never, in her most optimistic dreams, had she expected one to appear. Her mother had always made it clear that they couldn't afford luxuries. But that birthday, her seventh, she had received her heart's desire. It had been the last birthday she had spent with her mother and a few weeks later she had left that doll's house behind, along with her past and her name.

She began to pack away. A few late stragglers hung around the stalls as if they were killing time. But Emma didn't want to be late home. If Patrick Evans had left a message on the answerphone, she wanted to be able to ring him back that day. She would tell him once and for all that she knew nothing; that she couldn't remember. She wouldn't mention her plans to visit Potwoolstan Hall. That was none of his business.

Perhaps she wouldn't hear from him again, she thought hopefully as she placed the houses gently in their cardboard cartons. With careful fingers, she put the delicate miniature furniture in separate boxes, padding them with bubblewrap to prevent her handiwork from being damaged. The houses were her lifeline to the outside world and she treated them like precious things. Like the children she didn't have.

She carried the boxes out to the old blue van. As she opened the doors she could smell paint and white spirit and her eyes began to water a little as she stacked her wares in the back. She had bought the van secondhand from a painter and decorator and it was the best she could afford. But now that orders were coming in over the Internet and she was making a healthy profit at last, she had dared to dream of buying herself something smarter sometime in the distant future.

She'd expected Barry to be pleased about her modest business success but all he did was complain that she was wasting the money she earned on Potwoolstan Hall. He didn't understand: it wasn't a question of money. It was something she had to do. She needed to remember.

Once her precious load was secure, she slammed the van doors shut. It was time to face Barry again and she hoped she wouldn't have to spend the evening listening to his list of reasons why a stay at Potwoolstan Hall was wasteful, stupid and liable to lead to disaster.

As Emma opened the driver's door she looked up. He was there again. The same man, leaning against the rusty railings that flanked the entrance to the village hall. He was a lean man with a shaved head and a sallow complexion. He looked as if he'd been sleeping rough. And he looked ill. Or perhaps under the influence of drink or drugs. His face looked somehow familiar and Emma had the feeling that last time she had seen him he had been much younger – and healthier. And she knew that all those years ago she had been afraid of him for some reason.

A name popped into her head. The name of a singer – Bob Dylan. Dylan. Then the brief flash of memory disappeared.

Her heart began to beat faster. As she stared at him, he looked up. She wanted to call out to him, 'Who are you?' But fear kept her silent.

As soon as their eyes met he took off like a frightened animal, a hunted creature fleeing its pursuers. Emma felt sick as she sank into the driver's seat and gulped in deep breaths to regain her composure.

She had seen a face from the past, from the time shrouded in the mist of blood. If she went to Potwoolstan

Hall she might remember who he was. But in the meantime she wouldn't say anything to Barry. He would only worry.

When Wesley Peterson reached the semi-derelict office building – an aberration in grey concrete and grubby glass, constructed in architecture's darkest years – he studied the façade and felt mildly depressed. These were hardly ideal surroundings for a creative soul, for any soul, come to that. But maybe it hadn't bothered Patrick Evans.

'The rent's cheap,' said Kirsty Evans by way of explanation, as if she had read his mind.

She pushed the door open and walked up the litter-strewn concrete stairs. There was a lift but it bore an 'out of order' notice scrawled in black felt tip pen and the area around it smelled strongly of urine. To Wesley's surprise most of the battered sapele doors bore the names of grand-sounding companies: Jetalife International Leisure PLC, Merchantalia Bond Promotions Ltd, P. J. Worthrope Holidays Ltd. The names sounded respectable enough but the signs were made of paper and stuck on the doors with Blu-tack. The signs were temporary. And Wesley suspected that, once they'd extracted money from unsuspecting clients, the companies were too. This was a fly-by-night sort of place, with few facilities and a short shelf-life. But it had obviously suited Patrick Evans.

Evans's office was on the second floor, a hard climb up the cold stairs. The only indication that they were in the right place was a small piece of paper bearing the words 'Patrick Evans – if it's not important, piss off,' sellotaped to the centre of the door.

Wesley's eyes were drawn to the whiteness of the paper first, then he noticed that the wood around the lock was splintered. Either Patrick Evans had forgotten his key recently or somebody had broken in. He caught Kirsty's eye. 'Did Patrick do this or . . .?'

'It's been like that since he started renting it. He said he was going to get it fixed but . . .'

Wesley unlocked the door with Kirsty's key and stepped inside. It was a shabby little room with dirty magnolia walls and grey carpet tiles dotted with dark stains and cigarette burns. Mildew covered the bottom of the vertical blinds that hung limply at the dusty window and there was a nasty patch of mould where the wall met the ceiling just above the window frame. A battered metal filing cabinet stood in the corner. There were papers and files strewn all over the cheap teak-effect desk. Patrick Evans hadn't been a tidy man.

Wesley turned to Kirsty and noticed that there were tears in her eyes. He knew he had to get her out of there. He should take her back to her flat, away from the memories. He ushered her out and shut the door carefully behind him. They walked back to the flat in silence as Wesley could think of nothing to say. He would have to leave her on her own: he had no choice. Back in Devon there was usually a neighbour, a friend or a relative who could be called upon in times of crisis but Kirsty said there was nobody. She didn't know the neighbours; her friends were at work; and her family came from Worcestershire. She was quite alone. But she assured Wesley that she could cope. And she didn't mind if he took anything from the office that he thought might be of use. He promised he would return in an hour or so to make arrangements for her journey to Devon the next day. But there was something he had to see to first.

He wasn't looking forward to dealing with the local station again, especially the spiky DC who, frankly, scared the life out of him. So he was relieved when he found Pete Jarrod had returned from investigating his latest shooting. As Pete's teenage gunman had just been caught in a raid on a nearby council flat and was now safely locked up in the cells, he was in a remarkably good mood and provided the tea that Wesley had been craving for the past couple of hours. After ten minutes exchanging news, Wesley felt he could get down to business. He requested help to pack Patrick Evans's papers into boxes so that he could take them back to Devon to go through at his leisure.

A young constable was sent to help with the packing and after half an hour two cardboard boxes containing Patrick Evans's papers were carried through the streets and loaded into the boot of Wesley's car.

Wesley looked at his watch, wondering how long it would take to get to his parents' house. It was five o'clock already but his mother wouldn't be home until her surgery finished at half past six. And his father's full list of patients at the hospital usually ensured he wasn't home until seven these days. He sat in his car contemplating his next move and feeling guilty; guilty that he couldn't do more for Kirsty Evans; guilty that he couldn't spend more time with his parents. And even more guilty that he couldn't be there for Pam.

He returned to Kirsty's apartment and let her talk about Patrick. He'd started off his working life as a journalist and moved on to freelance investigative work. In between assignments he had written a couple of books about real-life Victorian murder cases and found he'd enjoyed the excitement of making fresh discoveries in dusty archives. Then he had begun work on books about more recent cases; cases she'd never wanted him to share with her. Somehow, when he left an hour later, he felt that he knew the dead man better. And he was aware that he'd performed a service for Kirsty as well. He'd given her somebody to talk to.

Wesley left Kirsty's apartment just after six o'clock and prepared himself for a long battle with the London traffic as he drove slowly through the littered streets towards Dulwich.

Normally, Gerry Heffernan jumped at every chance to get out and about, to put distance between himself and his boss, Chief Superintendent Nutter – whose idea of a fun afternoon was a budget strategy meeting followed by an appraisal of the latest Home Office equal opportunities initiative – but today he was stuck in his office, dealing with the investigation into Patrick Evans's murder. The routine of going through statements from the hotel staff – all of whom had seen nothing, heard nothing and knew nothing – depressed Gerry Heffernan. He had pushed his paperwork to one side and had gone into the main CID office in search of something constructive to do.

He looked round the office, searching for Wesley, until he remembered that he'd gone off on his jaunt to London ... or 'the Smoke' as Steve Carstairs insisted on calling it, usually referring to it with loving reverence, as if the capital of England was some sort of eldorado.

He passed Steve Carstairs's desk just as he was finishing a phone call. 'Anything new on that theft at Potwoolstan Hall?' he asked.

Steve shook his head. 'Nothing. I think our best bet is to wait for the thief to flog the jewellery. Mind you, none of it's turned up yet, which means that whoever's nicked it probably knows better than to risk selling it to reputable jewellers. I think we should be looking at local fences. Or jewellers who aren't so reputable, if you know what I mean. I'll get on to it, shall I?'

Heffernan nodded. It was as good a strategy as any.

'And I nearly forgot, sir. There's just been a call. A kid's been picked up for twocking by the Neston Traffic lads. He was carrying some interesting ID.'

The chief inspector looked at Steve, exasperated. Why couldn't he be more specific?

'What do you mean exactly?'

Steve took a deep breath. 'This kid nicked a car.'

'I know twocking means taking without the owner's consent, Stephen. What's this about ID?'

'He had a driving licence and credit card in his pocket. Name of Patrick Evans.'

Heffernan rolled his eyes to heaven. 'And did he say how they came to be in his pocket?'

'Said he found them.'

'Where?' Heffernan didn't think for one minute that Steve would have thought to ask.

'Er, not sure, sir. I told the lads at Neston you'd be in touch.'

'I hope the kid in question's still at Neston nick.'

Steve nodded wearily. 'I think so, sir.'

'OK. You can drive me over.' Gerry Heffernan's navigational skills were kept for the river. He was an experienced sailor but he'd never learned to drive on dry land. Wesley's insistence that it was never too late to learn was always greeted with a dismissive grunt.

Fortunately, they found the young culprit at Neston police station when they arrived. His name was Leigh Bolt; a small, shaven-headed creature with the face of a malevolent pixie. Leigh didn't look as if he had seen more than fifteen birthdays but his immature years didn't stop him from loudly demanding his rights and the services of his brief. The chubby, middle-aged PC given the thankless task of looking after him, wore a patient, long-suffering expression that Gerry Heffernan had only seen before on the faces of painted martyrs in church. Heffernan reckoned a good clip round the ear would do Leigh Bolt no harm whatsoever. But he wasn't going to risk legal action and his career by administering it.

The newly decorated interview room still smelled of paint and Leigh lounged on a brand-new chair, his feet, encased in pristine white trainers, up on the table. Heffernan was in the habit of putting his feet up on his desk so he felt a hypocrite for telling the boy off. But he did it all the same and an affronted Leigh obeyed.

'I hear you've been nicking cars.'

Leigh began to study his fingernails. 'So?'

'And I hear you've got a driving licence.' The boy glanced at him impatiently then looked away. 'Trouble is, it's not yours, is it? And the man who owns it was found dead yesterday. In fact he was murdered. That makes you a suspect, doesn't it, Leigh?'

This produced the reaction Heffernan expected. Leigh jumped up, knocking his chair over. 'I never did nothing.

I found it, that's all. This wallet was just lying there and I picked it up. Honest.'

'Where did you find it?'

'In some woods near the river. We was messing about. I just saw it lying there.'

'Have you still got the wallet?'

Leigh shook his head. 'Took the money and the cards out, didn't I? Chucked the wallet in the water.'

Heffernan stood up. 'Show us where you found it.'

Leigh looked confused for a second then he stood up. 'OK. Fine.'

Half an hour later Steve, following Leigh's directions, turned the car into a gate Gerry Heffernan recognised from many years ago. He could hardly forget it. And the brash new sign told him that his memory served him well. This was the drive leading to Potwoolstan Hall.

'What are we doing here? This can't be the way.' He looked at Leigh accusingly as though he was playing some sort of practical joke on him. One that wasn't very funny.

'Yeah, it is. We come here sometimes. Have a laugh. Nobody stops us.'

Heffernan could see the bulk of the Hall looming up on his left. It was an attractive building; built in Tudor times with stone gables and pretty mullioned windows. A manor house, not too big and not too small; cosy enough to be a home as well as a statement of wealth. But to Gerry Heffernan the sight of it conjured images of blood and violent death. There had been talk of witchcraft at the time of the massacre. Dead crows had been nailed to the kitchen door and the front door and over-imaginative journalists had dug up some old tale about murdered virgins and a curse.

But there had indeed been an atmosphere of evil in that house, so strong that it was almost palpable. And Gerry Heffernan wondered whether it still pervaded the place twenty years later.

When they'd passed the building, he was tempted to look back, to allow his eyes to be drawn to the scene of horror like

59

a ghoulish spectator at a road traffic accident. But he kept his eyes focused forward. He had a job to do. He wondered whether Leigh knew about the grim events that had happened there before he was born. Perhaps he did. Perhaps that was the attraction: the vicarious thrill of being near the murder house.

They had reached the stretch of woodland behind the Hall that led down to the river, and when the track petered out into a clearing, Steve stopped the car.

Heffernan said nothing as Leigh led the way down the narrow track leading to the water's edge. Oak trees with budding branches rose up on either side of their path; the stunted oaks fringing the River Trad that gave it its distinctive beauty. In the summer, when the foliage was dense, the Trad could almost be mistaken for some steamy tropical river – if it weren't for the English climate.

On this particular section of bank a narrow strip of grass lay between the trees and the river. Gerry Heffernan noticed that somebody had had a fire there recently. He also spotted charred white twists of paper dotted around the ground. The lads had come here to smoke cannabis. Hardly unusual in the countryside.

'Show me where you found the wallet.'

Leigh strolled over to the remains of an old lime kiln. 'Just here.' He pointed to the ground. Heffernan squatted down and studied the place. He could see dark stains on the grass that might have been blood and two narrow parallel lines of churned-up earth led down to the water's edge; possibly marks made by the heels of a body that had been dragged over the soft ground.

'And you threw the empty wallet into the river? Where?'

'About there.' Leigh pointed vaguely at the water.

Heffernan looked up at Leigh. 'When was this?'

'Sunday night. Look, I didn't do nothing. I just found it. Honest.' He stood there, his eyes wide and innocent. Heffernan believed him.

'Come here to smoke a few joints, do you? Pop a few

pills? Build a fire and have a jolly Boy Scouts' picnic?'

Leigh gave Heffernan a sideways look and sniffed. 'Something like that.'

'I'll need the names of the mates who were with you. They won't be in any trouble. We just need your story confirmed, that's all. You weren't around here on Saturday night, I don't suppose?'

Leigh shivered. 'No. We were in Morbay. I'm bloody freezing. Can we go?'

'No stamina, the youth today.' Heffernan turned to Steve, who was shifting from foot to foot, his hands thrust in his pockets. 'Call the station, will you. I want this place sealed off as a crime scene and tell SOCO to get over here pronto. I want the river bed near here searched too. I want the dead man's wallet and the murder weapon.' The scene of crime officers wouldn't relish the thought of getting wet. But, Heffernan thought, that was their problem.

As Steve made the call, the chief inspector leaned against a tree trunk for a while, watching as the twigs Leigh was idly chucking into the water were snatched by the current and disappeared downstream. If the body had gone in here then it would have been swept away by the Trad's strong undertow until it became caught up in the overhanging branches of a fallen tree half a mile downstream.

Colin Bowman had assessed the time of death as being late Saturday night and Heffernan found himself wondering what would bring a man to a place like this after enjoying a good meal on a Saturday night. It was an isolated place used by local youths up to no good; a strange place to meet someone. Perhaps there was a woman involved. It had been a dry, clear night on Saturday, a suitable night for a romantic stroll on the river bank with a lady friend: a lady friend who carried a knife. Perhaps when they had asked around the restaurants they might have a clue to his companion's identity.

Exactly what had Evans been doing in the grounds of Potwoolstan Hall? It was private property, and too out of the

61

way for somebody to wind up there merely by chance to admire the view. Gerry Heffernan knew that his next move would stir up unpleasant memories. He was going to have to call at Potwoolstan Hall to ask a few questions.

What does a thief look like? Serena Jones supposed that a thief – a successful one – looks much the same as anyone else. Much the same as Charles Dodgson in fact.

Serena, with her degree in English Literature from one of the country's newer universities, had sussed out the *Alice in Wonderland* connection almost at once. And now that Dodgson was in one of the endless meditation workshops, she decided to put her investigative talents to good use. What were the chances, she asked herself, that Mrs Jeffries's stolen ring and cash would be somewhere in his room? Quite high, she reckoned. After all, his room was next door to the victim's and he hadn't been at breakfast that day. The police had made a token search but she didn't have a high opinion of Steve Cairstairs's powers of observation.

Serena emerged from her room, trying her best to look casual. After ensuring there was no one about, she tried Dodgson's door and it opened smoothly. She experienced a rare tingle of nervousness. But with the fear of discovery came the thrill of taking a risk. She shot inside the room and closed the door behind her.

She was looking for something, anything, that would link the man she suspected was a phoney, to the theft. She began to search the pockets of the clothes hanging in the wardrobe, her heart pounding as she listened for approaching footsteps.

Her hand crept into the inside pocket of a jacket and came into contact with a wallet. Stupid to leave it there with a thief about. Unless he himself was the thief. She pulled it out and opened it. There was a driving licence in the name of Anthony Jameston. And charge cards – Diners Club and American Express – as well as two platinum cards, all in the name of Anthony Jameston. No mention of Charles Dodgson. And nothing belonging to Mrs Jeffries as yet.

Then Serena struck gold: at the back of the wallet was a House of Commons pass in the name of Anthony Jameston, MP. Either her man had stolen Anthony Jameston's wallet. Or the Member of Parliament was at the Hall under a false name. She still wasn't quite sure which.

She replaced everything carefully, trying to recall where she'd heard the name Anthony Jameston before. But the more she thought about it, the more the answer eluded her. After checking the room was exactly as she found it, she let herself out, thanking some unspecified power – Serena wasn't a religious young woman – that she hadn't been caught.

She walked nonchalantly down the staircase and out of the front door. Mobile phones were forbidden at Potwoolstan Hall but she'd smuggled hers in: there were some necessities a girl just couldn't do without and there was no way she was going to be cut off from the outside world while she was working.

Once outside, she made for the shelter of some bushes where she punched out the number of her office. 'Can you run a check for me on an MP called Anthony Jameston?'

She waited half an hour, sitting on a damp bench in the garden, soaking up the weak spring sun that trickled out between the clouds. And when the answer to her enquiry finally came, she sat back with a satisfied smirk.

This had the smell of a good story.

Chapter Four

We came upon a plot of ground where we found a good store of mussels and oysters and we found pearls in many. I would I could return to Devon with great riches from this new land but when I think on my father's death and the curse laid upon our house it fills my heart with grief. I must put Potwoolstan Hall from my mind.

It is of the greatest importance that we establish good trade with the natives for soon our ships sail for England (and with them our hopes of safety and escape). This Virginia is a goodly and fertile place but we arrived too late in the season for the sowing of seed so we will have no harvest this year.

Captain Radford and Master Joshua Morton will meet with the Chief of the Natives to trade the goods we have brought with us for food for we cannot sustain ourselves. As yet we have no church but an old sail from the Nicholas *gives us shelter for our worship.*

Captain Radford, Master Morton and others have departed a day since to explore the river and meet with the Chief. We prayed for their safety beneath our sail. We begin work on a church as soon as the fortifications are complete.

In Master Morton's absence Penelope came to me. She confided that she fears her husband and his

choleric bouts of anger. I assured her that I would give
her my especial protection and comfort her in his
absence. Last night I dreamed about Penelope . . . and
my dream was shameful. I must put such thoughts from
my mind and not yield to lust as I once did. Her
brother-in-law, Isaac, watches her always. I must take
care.

Set down by Master Edmund Selbiwood, Gentleman,
at Annetown this twenty-first day of July 1605.

Neil Watson stood beside Professor Keller, watching a group of archaeology students from the local university scraping away at the soil, their faces serious. This was a wonderful opportunity for them, Professor Keller explained. The sites they studied were mostly Native American and any archaeology involving the early European settlers was regarded as a rare treat. Perhaps, Neil thought, that accounted for the careful, almost reverent, way in which they worked.

A new trench had been marked out near the newly uncovered foundations of the settlement's earliest church. Neil asked when the mechanical digger was arriving but his question was greeted with disbelief. They never used mechanical means to open up trenches, the astonished professor replied, looking at Neil as though he had suggested carrying out delicate restoration work on the Mona Lisa with a paint roller and can of emulsion. Every spade of soil from the surface downwards had to be sieved carefully before the next shovelful was dug. It was becoming all too clear that this was another country and they did things differently here. Differently and more slowly.

They watched for a while, then Professor Keller spoke again. 'You've not seen the reconstructed settlement yet, have you?' Something in his manner told Neil he wasn't exactly welcome with open arms. Perhaps he regarded the archaeologist from Devon, England – from the very place those early settlers had embarked on their voyage to the

65

new world – as an intruder, as someone who was going to criticise his working methods. And Neil's remarks about mechanical diggers hadn't helped.

At that moment a young woman appeared. She was small, blond and a little on the plump side with the pretty face and wide blue eyes of a Barbie doll with a high IQ. She smiled at Neil and the professor. She looked friendly. And Neil felt he needed all the friends he could get.

The relief on Keller's face was obvious. 'Dr Gotleib. This is Dr Neil Watson from the Devon County Archaeological Unit in England. Would you be good enough to show him around the settlement?'

He didn't wait for a reply. He hurried away, leaving Neil with the newcomer, feeling rather awkward.

But the young woman wasn't fazed by the professor's rudeness. She held out her hand. 'Hannah Gotleib. You're from Devon, right? Where the *Nicholas* sailed from?' She didn't wait for an answer. 'You're staying with Chuck, that right?'

Neil nodded. He looked around. 'You can see why they settled here, can't you?' The early settlers had certainly chosen a lovely spot. The site was fairly level and he could see the glistening waters of Anne River through the tall trees. The vegetation was lush and green and the sun was shining in a blue spring sky.

'You sure can,' said Hannah with a sudden smile. 'Although some people reckon they'd have been better off on the higher ground a mile upstream.' She turned. 'Come on, I'll show you the reconstructed Annetown settlement. It'll give you a good idea what life was like back then. The costumed volunteers there pride themselves on their authenticity, right down to the last detail.'

Neil allowed himself to be led up a neat pathway through a line of tall cypress trees. This was good, fruitful land. The land of tobacco – that abundant crop that had probably seemed like a good idea at the time.

'I guess you've been given a plan of Annetown,' Hannah

66

continued as they walked. 'We've excavated the original fort, most of the early settlers' village and part of the earliest church. We're working on the land surrounding the church now.'

'Many burials?'

'Quite a few. We've also begun work on the later phase of the settlement to the west.'

'Chuck told me about your murder victim.'

Hannah stopped and swung round to face him, her wide eyes fixed on his. 'That's right. A guy with a musket ball through his brain. He'd been buried in a wooden coffin, which means he must have been a gentleman. Our research indicates that the lower classes were buried in shrouds. Class distinction, I guess.'

Neil smiled. 'I thought these guys left England to get away from that sort of thing.'

'Oh, this lot weren't your idealistic Pilgrim Fathers fleeing from religious persecution: they came later, in the 1620s. The Annetown settlers came here in search of land and wealth. Purely here to exploit the natural resources. King James I of England himself sent them a letter telling them to dig for gold, silver and copper.'

Neil sensed disapproval in Hannah's voice so he made no comment. 'Chuck said something about the skeleton's teeth.'

'That's right. The bones have been sent to the Smithsonian Institute for examination. And one of the teeth was sent to England: a place in ...' She hesitated. 'Yorkshire?'

'Yorkshire. Bradford University. We sometimes send stuff there for analysis. The technique they use there can pinpoint exactly where a person spent his early childhood by measuring the elements in the environment where he grew up.'

Neil was gratified to see that Hannah looked impressed.

As they left the shelter of the trees, the scene before them made Neil stop in his tracks. There was a group of

67

small, wooden houses, topped with thatched roofs and people in the costume of the early seventeenth century seemed to be going about their daily business. Women sat outside the doors, spinning yarn on wooden spinning wheels or kneading dough. Men carried water, chopped firewood or wove cloth on rough wooden looms. They were all dressed in homespun cloth and they really looked the part. It was as though he'd stepped back in time.

Hannah was watching him. She probably expected him to talk to these people, to ask them about the tasks they were performing so dutifully. There seemed to be none of the good-humoured banter he'd observed in historical re-enactment groups in England. It was as if once they had donned the costumes, these people had become the early settlers of Annetown. They were living it.

'Where to next?'

Hannah led him on down a track past the houses and soon they reached a quayside. There before them was a sailing ship – late sixteenth or early seventeenth century by Neil's reckoning – bobbing at anchor at the end of a wooden jetty.

'A replica of the *Nicholas*,' Hannah said proudly. 'You can go aboard someday if you like.'

Neil, unsure what to say, made a few complimentary comments about the historical accuracy of the operation and turned to go. He had sensed that Keller had been trying to get him out of the way and that made him determined to get back to the site and see what was going on. Besides, he wanted to get his hands on a trowel and do some digging. He began to walk back the way he came and Hannah fell in by his side.

'Don't you want to have a look around?'

'Another time maybe. I think I should get back to the excavation. I'm sure they could do with another pair of hands.'

Hannah looked doubtful. She'd had her unspoken instructions to keep him away. But there was nothing she could do against Neil's steamroller determination. She trotted by his side, lost for words.

As they walked, he turned to her. 'Have you ever heard the name Selbiwood? Max Selbiwood?'

There was a spark of recognition in Hannah's eyes. 'Edmund Selbiwood was one of the original Annetown settlers. His name's on the list of the passengers who came over on the *Nicholas*.'

Somehow this news surprised Neil. He had only asked about Max Selbiwood on the off-chance that Hannah, being local, might have heard of him. His grandmother had told him that Selbiwood came from Annetown, Virginia and that was all he had to go on. He had hardly expected a connection with the site.

They walked beneath the shade of the cedars and eventually reached the expanse of bare earth and interesting holes that was the site of the excavation. A group of diggers had gathered round one spot and seemed to be chattering excitedly. Something was happening.

Ten minutes later Neil heard that another skeleton had been unearthed about a hundred feet away from the church. Another skeleton whose skull had been penetrated by a musket ball.

Breakfast at the Petersons' Dulwich home wasn't quite as Wesley remembered from his childhood. Nowadays his parents were busy people with little time to sit around the breakfast table and chat first thing in the morning. His mother was due at her surgery two miles away at eight thirty and his father had a long list of patients to see at the hospital that morning before a heavy afternoon of operations. They assured him that they were delighted to see him: they only wished they had more time.

At seven in the morning Wesley sat at the kitchen table with a bowl of cereal in front of him. His mother bustled in. Dr Cecilia Peterson had gained a little weight in middle age but she was still a good-looking woman. She stopped

69

suddenly and looked at her son.

'Are you OK, Wesley? You look tired. Are you sleeping well?'

Coming from a doctor this was bad but he resisted the temptation to rush to the mirror. He told himself that she was his mother. And mothers always worry. It goes with the territory.

Before Wesley could answer, his father came in. He was a tall, distinguished-looking man with greying hair and a small, neat beard. He hurried to the mirror and adjusted the sky blue bow-tie he was wearing.

'I'm just off, honey,' he said to his wife, kissing her on the cheek. He looked at Wesley and smiled. 'Good to see you, son.' Mr Joshua Peterson, Fellow of the Royal College of Surgeons, grasped Wesley's hand in both of his. 'We'll be down soon to see that little granddaughter of ours. And young Michael. You take care now.'

Wesley stood up and threw his arms around his father. It had been too long since he had last seen him. The man who had seemed a towering presence as he grew up was now the human being – the equal, not the god. When Wesley thought about all the feckless and absent fathers he came across in the course of his work, he had come to appreciate his own parents. By the standards of the modern day his upbringing had been strict, with the emphasis on good manners, church attendance and academic effort. They were immigrants in a new country and they had to try just that little bit harder. Luckily, Wesley and his sister, Maritia, had gone along with it. They had never been natural rebels: perhaps things would have been very different if they had been.

When his father left the house, Wesley experienced a sudden wave of sadness and wished he could preserve the moment. Ten minutes later he and his mother left the Victorian villa overlooking the park, Cecilia chattering about Michael and Amelia, Maritia's looming wedding and commenting on the fickleness of the weather. After a warm hug, mother and son went their separate ways. It had been a pleasant interlude. But it faded like a distant dream once he started to face the crawling traffic to Deptford.

As he drove towards Kirsty Evans's apartment, he realised he had left the papers from Patrick Evans's office in the boot of his car overnight. He had forgotten all about them; in fact he'd put the whole case out of his mind as soon as he'd arrived at his childhood home. It had been careless of him. And Wesley wasn't usually a careless person.

He was relieved to find that Kirsty was waiting for him, her coat on and her overnight bag packed. He hadn't fancied staying a moment longer in London than necessary and he had a long journey ahead. He thought of the traffic on the M25 and his heart sank.

It took them almost five hours to reach Tradmouth and Wesley was glad they'd set off early. As he had feared, it had been a journey of gushing confidences and uneasy silences. But by the time they reached Devon he felt that he knew Kirsty Evans – and her husband – better.

After studying economics at university Kirsty had landed herself a job in the City and she had met Patrick in a bar when she was out with friends. He had been a journalist, a few years older than her and with a worldly charm she'd found irresistible. To Wesley's embarrassment she spoke of their physical attraction to one another; how they'd ended up in bed the first night they met and stayed there all the following day. The instant lust hadn't lasted, of course, but had settled down into something more tranquil. The wedding in the country church in her parents' home village had followed. Then the grand passion had dulled into companionship with a few storms along the way. Patrick had wanted children and she hadn't, which had been a major cause of disagreement. And recently, thanks to their respective jobs, they hadn't really seen much of each other.

But she was grieving for Patrick, hurting. And, after hours closeted alone with her, Wesley didn't think he could take much more. He would ask Rachel to accompany her to the mortuary if she was available.

It was almost two o'clock when they reached Tradmouth and Wesley drove straight to the police station car park. To his relief, Rachel was in the office and she hurried down the stairs to the foyer where Kirsty was waiting. Wesley watched Rachel as she left the room. She wore a knee-length denim skirt and a tight black T-shirt and she had allowed her straight blond hair to fall to her shoulders today instead of sweeping it up in the usual ponytail. To a man who had just spent a morning suffering grief and heavy traffic, she looked beautiful. When she'd gone he made for Gerry Heffernan's office, wondering how soon he could get home to Pam.

He found Heffernan sitting at his desk with a glum expression on his chubby face. But when he saw Wesley standing there he grinned.

'You got out in one piece then?'

Wesley looked at him, puzzled.

'That London. You managed to escape?'

Wesley laughed. Gerry Heffernan had always had a low opinion of the capital – unlike his native Liverpool which he spoke of as if it were some north-western Shangri-La – his Land of Lost Content. 'I brought Kirsty Evans back to identify her husband's body. Rachel's with her.'

'What's she like?'

Wesley shrugged. He still felt he didn't really know what made Kirsty Evans tick. She was the hard modern career woman with the minimalist apartment who fell in love with a freelance writer and opted for a romantic white wedding in a pretty country church. There was a contradiction there somewhere. But then he supposed most people were full of contradictions.

'Learned anything useful?'

'He was working on a book about a famous murder case but she doesn't know which one. He did his work in a rented office in a run-down block, probably as cheap as you can get in London, and he kept all his work stuff there. I've brought most of his files back and I'll go through them as soon as I get a chance. Any progress this end?'

'Indeed there is. Thanks to a little toerag called Leigh Bolt, it looks like we've found the place where Evans was killed.' He grinned. 'When Master Bolt, aged fifteen, was caught twocking in Neston, Patrick Evans's driving licence and credit card were found in his pocket. He showed me where he'd found them.'

'Where was that?' Wesley asked patiently.

Heffernan leaned forward. 'The grounds of Potwoolstan Hall. In the woods that stretch down to the river.'

'Accessible to outsiders?'

'There's nothing to stop anyone from walking or driving in. In fact, Leigh and his mates have been using the river bank as their own personal playground by the looks of things. The drive leading to the Hall branches off into a track that goes down to the river and there's a clearing where you can park a car.' He looked sheepish. 'Mind you, I think our patrol cars have probably obliterated any tyre prints.'

Wesley nodded philosophically. Another possible cockup amongst many. Life in the police was full of them.

'So Evans and his murderer might have driven to the Hall then walked down to the river from this clearing. Evans's car's still in the hotel garage so he must have met someone who gave him a lift.' Wesley thought for a moment. 'The murderer must have been someone he trusted.'

Heffernan shrugged. 'I want to ask some questions at the Hall. Maybe Evans met someone who's staying there. Or perhaps someone saw something. Fancy another trip out?'

This was exactly what he wanted. Something to get the smell of London out of his nostrils. Rachel could look after Kirsty Evans. He was going for a walk by the river and a visit to a healing centre. Just what the doctor ordered.

Wesley grabbed his jacket from his chair on the way out

and followed the chief inspector out of the office.

Potwoolstan Hall was getting Serena Jones down. All that earnest New Age psychobabble made her want to wipe the smug expression off Jeremy Elsham's smooth, lightly tanned face. He was a charlatan – she recognised one when she saw one. She had avoided his regression sessions so far, choosing instead a diet of meditation, giggle-inducing chanting and the art therapy sessions led by a local artist called Gwen Madeley; a nervy, solemn woman with sly eyes, long brown hair and a genuine talent. And surprisingly expensive clothes.

Steve Carstairs had nearly ruined everything. It was a good thing that she had never told him what she really did for a living. If she had, he would have betrayed her for sure. Their half-hearted relationship had begun when he'd picked her up in a club and they had arranged to meet a few days later at a karaoke bar on the Morbay waterfront. He was good-looking and splashed his money about but when their less than memorable rendezvous had been followed by several more nights of clubbing and pubbing she had discovered that Steve only had a place for one person in his heart – and that person was Steve. He had boasted that he was the scourge of the local villains, but somehow Serena hadn't believed a word of it. He was a pathetic specimen who got off on playing the hard man, the tough cop. And after enduring a fortnight of his company, she had begun to make excuses.

When he'd turned up at the Hall she had been gratified to see that the young woman sergeant who was with him seemed to have him where she wanted him but Serena cursed Mrs Jeffries for not taking better care of her valuables. Steve's appearance might have blown her cover. And that would never do.

They had just had lunch – vegetarian of course – in what used to be the Hall's library, now converted into a refectory with long pine tables and walls painted in a restful shade of pale green. It was a pleasant, sunny room and the food was edible, if rather strange: nuts, mushrooms and pulses seemed to feature highly on the chef's list of ingredients but Serena didn't mind. Perhaps, she thought optimistically, a week off the fast food would make her lose some weight.

Serena sat on a wicker armchair in the entrance hall, pretending to be engrossed in an improving book. She was booked in for an aura workshop but nobody would ask questions if she didn't turn up. Jeremy Elsham insisted that the Beings each controlled their own programme of enlightenment. Which meant that she could come and go as she pleased.

The theft of her fellow Being's money and ring had never been mentioned at the Hall. It had been hushed up like some dreadful family secret. She wondered how the police investigation was going. No doubt Steve would be able to enlighten her. But after what she had just discovered, all thoughts of the theft had been pushed to the back of her mind.

She sat with one eye on her book – a worthy Booker Prize winner that was a little hard-going for her taste – and the other on the staircase. The woman in the wheelchair passed by with a cheery good afternoon and a comment about the weather but Serena didn't reply. The Mrs Carmodys of this world weren't of any use to Serena Jones. Not like the man who called himself Charles Dodgson. Her heart began to thump in her chest as she watched him coming down the wide oak staircase. He hurried down, trying to make himself inconspicuous, and shot out of the front door.

Serena abandoned her book gratefully and followed after him, careful to keep her distance. Dodgson was definitely up to something and there was no other entertainment on offer.

She had half expected him to make for the car park but instead he was heading for the woods. He walked quickly, his progress heralded by the cries of the crows nesting in the dark trees. She followed, keeping close to the tree trunks. A twig cracked beneath her trainers and she froze. But her quarry hadn't heard the sound above the crows' raucous noise. She had a fleeting wish that someone would come along and shoot the evil-looking birds and stop their din once and for all.

Dodgson stopped in a clearing and Serena flattened herself against a tree and waited, trying to ignore the nettles stinging her bare legs and the twigs digging into her back.

Serena heard hushed voices. Someone had been waiting for Dodgson. Serena crept closer and peeped round a fat tree trunk. Gwen Madeley, the art therapist from the Hall, was talking to Dodgson, her face close to his. Dodgson looked anxious, as though the conversation wasn't a happy one. A lovers' tiff perhaps. If he was indeed Anthony Jameston, he wouldn't be the first Member of Parliament who had difficulty keeping his trousers on.

As Serena began to tiptoe back towards the Hall her mobile phone began to ring. She cursed and pressed the button that would silence it before uttering a hushed 'Hello'.

Her heart sank when she heard Steve Carstairs's voice on the other end of the line. This was the last thing she wanted. He asked her if she was still at the Hall and when she answered that she would be there till Monday morning he lowered his voice, as though he feared he would be overheard.

'I thought I'd just tell you that my boss is coming to interview everyone at the Hall today. I won't be there but ...' He hesitated as though he was unsure what to say next. 'Just wondered if you fancied coming out one night next week. I've looked at my shifts and I'm free on Monday night or ...'

'I'll be washing my hair,' she snapped.

'I need to talk to you. It's important.'

Serena hesitated. Her curiosity had been aroused. And Steve might provide some useful inside information.

'OK then. Come to my flat at seven on Monday.' Before
he could say anything she pressed the button that ended the
call. Steve Carstairs would dance to her tune. Or there
would be no dance at all.

Rachel Tracey was back in the office. As soon as she sat
down, Wesley shot out of Gerry Heffernan's office,
anxious for news.

'How is she?'

Rachel looked puzzled for a second. Then she realised
Wesley was talking about Kirsty Evans. 'She checked into
the Marina Hotel last night when we got back.'

'How did the identification go?'

'As you'd expect. I said I'd go to see her later.' She
picked up a piece of paper on her desk. 'There's a message
here from the Tradmouth Castle. The manager's asking
when he can clear out Evans's room and relet it.'

'I take it SOCO have finished with it?'

Rachel nodded.

'Tell him it's OK to go ahead then. If they pack up his
possessions then we'll make sure they're returned to his
wife.'

Rachel smiled. 'Sure.'

'How's the flat-hunting?'

'Still looking.' She hesitated. I've seen a few places but
it's difficult to decide. I could do with taking someone
along. Getting a second opinion.'

Wesley said nothing as Rachel blushed and pushed her
hair back off her face. He returned to his desk and tried to
focus his mind on the reports lying in a neat pile in front
of him. But when he failed, he stood up and strolled over
to the chief inspector's office.

He found Heffernan by his coat stand reaching for the
disreputable anorak he always wore. It hung there in the
cooler months like a royal standard, a sign that he was in
residence. Wesley wished he would buy himself a new one;
something more in keeping with his position as a senior

investigating officer who was likely to encounter press, public and the likes of Chief Superintendent Nutter. But such sartorial considerations meant nothing to Gerry Heffernan. When his wife, Kathy, had been alive, there had been someone to curb his natural sloppiness. But now there was nobody: he was on his own.

'Let's get down to Potwoolstan Hall, Wes. Get it over with.'

'That place bothers you, doesn't it?'

Heffernan didn't reply. Wesley had never seen him silenced by anything before. Whatever he had seen at Potwoolstan Hall had made a lasting impression.

As they walked to the car park, Wesley remembered that Patrick Evans's papers were still in his car boot. He wavered for a few seconds, wondering whether to take them upstairs to the office and delay their journey for a few minutes. But he glanced across at Heffernan who was waiting to be let in to the passenger seat and decided against it. The things would be safe enough where they were. And besides, he might get a chance to go through them at his leisure at home that evening.

They drove up the steep hill leading out of the town and then houses gave way to open, hilly countryside, to rolling green fields dotted with sheep and cattle. Wesley kept his eyes open for the road to Derenham which forked off beside a large pub with wooden tables and children's climbing equipment in its wide front garden. The sun was attempting to shine on the patchwork landscape but once they turned on to the narrow lane the view was blocked by high budding hedgerows. These lanes had been created when the fastest mode of transport around was a decent horse and they were mostly single track. Wesley found himself following a tractor at a snail's pace. But he consoled himself with the thought that it was preferable to being trapped in the snarled-up traffic of London. At least the air was fresh and the scenery was good.

For some reason, Wesley had imagined Potwoolstan Hall

78

to be some brooding gothic pile straight out of the cornier variety of horror film. But the reality was a pretty, mellow stone house, probably dating from the sixteenth or early seventeenth century. The frontage boasted a series of ornate gables that reminded Wesley of the ones he'd seen on a trip to Amsterdam, no doubt added to impress the neighbours all those years ago. It was an attractive house. And if Wesley hadn't known its history, he would have said it was probably a friendly house. But he knew from long experience how appearances can deceive.

'Is this it? Your house of horrors?'

Gerry Heffernan didn't answer. He was staring ahead.

Wesley parked on the gravel in front of the house, ignoring the numerous 'No Parking' signs that sprouted from the flower beds. He was sure they didn't apply to police vehicles, even unmarked ones. He got out and stretched his legs. He had had enough of driving that day. Heffernan stayed in the passenger seat for a while before unfastening his seat belt. Last time he had been inside this house he had been confronted with the aftermath of a massacre and some things were hard to forget.

The studded oak door stood open and Wesley led the way into the entrance hall. Again he had expected gloom and was surprised to find the place bright and cheerful. He glanced back at Gerry who had stopped, as though reluctant to go any further. Wesley looked round. The sign on a door to his right said 'Strictly Private' and he had a sudden urge to rush over and push it open to see what was on the other side.

He didn't have to wait long to have his curiosity satisfied. The door opened and a tall man emerged. Wesley thought that he looked like a distinguished member of the dental profession with his short white coat and greying temples. When the man smiled, Wesley noticed that his teeth were as even and dazzling white as any Hollywood film star's and he had the pinched and polished look of a man who had undergone a face lift or two.

79

'Jeremy Elsham. I'm the facilitator. Welcome to Potwoolstan Hall.' He held out his hand and the obsequious smiled remained fixed. Wesley found himself wondering whether he knew who they were. Perhaps he had mistaken them for clients.

Wesley produced his warrant card and introduced himself while Gerry Heffernan hovered some way behind him, uncharacteristically silent.

As Elsham opened the door marked 'Strictly Private', Wesley glanced at his boss. From the expression on his face he suspected that the entrance to Elsham's well-appointed office brought back bad memories. But to Wesley it bore no resemblance to a scene of carnage: it was more like the office of the chief executive of a multinational company. The thick beige carpet on the floor concealed any stains that might have remained on the floorboards and the walls were covered with a subtly patterned wallpaper, the colour of parchment and cream.

The first thing that caught Wesley's eye was the picture on the wall behind the desk: a dark portrait of two thin, bearded young men in Jacobean costume sitting stiffly in their ruffs and padded doublets. They bore a striking resemblance to each other – brothers perhaps – and there were faint, yellowed words between the two figures, rendered illegible by the dirt and varnish of centuries. Wesley stared hard but at that distance he couldn't make out what they said.

Although Gerry Heffernan had overcome his misgivings and entered the room, Wesley sensed his discomfort. It would be up to him to do all the talking.

'You're aware that teams of officers have been searching the section of river bank belonging to this house?'

Elsham nodded earnestly. 'Have they found anything?' The question was casual and Jeremy Elsham sat back in his black leather chair, his hands clasped together in an attitude of prayer.

'There's evidence that a serious crime took place there.'

'I don't see what that has to do with me, Inspector. This is hardly a high security establishment. I said that to the officers who came about the theft, anybody can walk in to the house or grounds. It's a place of healing, not a prison.' He smiled. It was a smug, superior smile and Wesley found himself disliking Jeremy Elsham.

'You'll appreciate that we need to check out every avenue of enquiry in a case of murder ...'

Elsham's eyebrows shot up. 'Murder?'

'A man was found dead in the river on Monday morning and we've found evidence that he was attacked on your land. I'm afraid we'll have to speak to all your staff and guests. Someone may have seen something suspicious.'

Elsham put his head in his hands for a few seconds, a gesture of weary resignation. Then he looked Wesley in the eye. 'Is it really necessary? The Beings have come here for rest and healing. Most of them were questioned about that theft. Some have even had their rooms searched. The last thing they need is the stress of more police questioning.'

'This is a murder enquiry, sir,' said Wesley stiffly. 'If we could have a word with your staff. And the ... Beings. May we use this office?'

'Anywhere'll do,' Heffernan said quickly. He didn't like being in that part of the house. And after what he must have witnessed there, Wesley could hardly blame him.

Elsham offered them the use of the conservatory. It was quiet in there. Good energy, he added earnestly. Wesley wondered how much Elsham really knew about the Hall's gruesome history. If he was as sensitive to atmosphere as he claimed, surely he would have picked up evil vibrations in a place were six people had been slaughtered.

'That's an interesting painting,' said Wesley, pointing to the dark portrait behind the desk.

Elsham turned round. 'It was hanging at the top of the stairs when we bought this place. Someone said they're the two sons of the man who built the Hall. I've been meaning to get it valued.'

81

'Yes. I'd do that if I were you,' Wesley said, glancing at Heffernan who was standing by the door, eager to be gone.

They decided to call for back-up. Many hands make light work, as Wesley's grandmother back in Trinidad was fond of saying, and the presence of a couple more officers would ensure that they got through the interviews quickly.

There were eleven Beings in residence. A Mrs Beatrice Carmody who was confined to a wheelchair; a Mr Dodgson; a Serena Jones who was, according to Rachel, acquainted with Steve Carstairs; Mrs Jeffries, the victim of theft; then there was a Mr and Mrs Jackson who had only arrived a couple of days before; a pair of gay advertising executives seeking refuge from London stress; a middle-aged actor undergoing a crisis of confidence; and an elderly couple from Manchester who had come to recharge their spiritual batteries.

According to the booking details provided by Elsham's wife, Pandora, Serena Jones was due to leave on Monday, and would be replaced by a Mrs Oldchester. Gerry Heffernan hadn't been able to keep his eyes off Pandora's pneumatic charms but Wesley found her easy to resist. He also suspected that she was probably brighter than she looked. And considerably older.

Charles Dodgson and Serena Jones couldn't be found and it was hardly worth speaking to Mr and Mrs Jackson, who had arrived after the murder. They looked at the list and decided to start with Mrs Carmody, Mrs Jeffries, Elsham himself and Pandora, together with the cook – a Mrs Webster – and her assistant – a sixteen-year-old school leaver called Donna Louise, who lived in the nearest village. The back-up could deal with the rest of the Beings; together with the reflexologist who worked at the Hall on weekday mornings; the yoga teacher; the acupuncturist from Morbay who came in two days a week; and Gwen Madeley, a local artist, who provided art therapy for the Beings. There were also three cleaners, local women, who came every morning and a gardening firm who visited once a week to keep the grounds in order.

They began with Jeremy Elsham himself, who claimed that he hadn't been down to the river since last summer when he had taken the Beings there for a vegetarian barbecue. The river bank was available to any Being in search of solitude and meditation by the water, but as far as he knew nobody had been down there recently. It was mainly visited in the summer months. He hadn't been aware of local youths using it. If he had been he would have taken steps to prevent it.

Pandora echoed her husband's statement. She knew nothing. Neither did Mrs Geraldine Jeffries, who spent most of the interview complaining loudly about police incompetence and demanding that they retrieve her money and ring without delay. Wesley promised to check how the investigation was progressing but it seemed that this wasn't good enough – she expected instant results. Mrs Jeffries was a difficult woman, rendered even more difficult, he guessed, by her discovery during a regression session that she had been an Egyptian princess in a former life. She'd been a demanding woman before she'd established this tenuous royal connection, but now she was ten times worse.

That just left Mrs Beatrice Carmody, who propelled her wheelchair awkwardly into the conservatory. She answered Wesley's questions eagerly enough but, as he expected, she told them nothing they didn't know already.

As there was no sign of Charles Dodgson or Serena Jones, there seemed to be little point in staying. They could leave it to the other officers to interview the rest of the guests and the Hall's staff. But Wesley felt he wanted to see Dodgson for himself. Of course he had no reason at all to suspect that Dodgson wasn't his real name. But, on the other hand, he could be a thief or a con man with a knowledge of literature and a sense of humour. Was Potwoolstan Hall his own personal wonderland where he could steal at will? And if he had robbed Mrs Jeffries, what else was he planning?

Wesley said nothing of his suspicions to Heffernan. They

83

were unformed, nebulous. And they were probably just a figment of his over-active imagination.

They returned to Tradmouth and as Wesley parked in the police station car park he glanced at the clock on the dashboard. It was six o'clock but the day wasn't over yet. Wesley yawned. It was only that morning that he was having breakfast with his parents but it seemed like weeks ago.

'Keeping you awake, are we, Wes?' It was the first time Gerry Heffernan had spoken since they had left Potwoolstan Hall.

Wesley didn't answer. As they walked up the stairs to the CID office on the first floor, his legs felt heavy. Hoping that a cup of coffee would wake him up, he got one from the machine before joining the chief inspector in his office.

He noticed that Rachel Tracey was sitting at her desk. He stopped and rested the plastic cup of scalding coffee on a filing cabinet before it burned his fingers.

Rachel looked up at him. 'Kirsty Evans has been asking for you.'

'You mean she's got something to tell me?'

Rachel smiled and shook her head. 'Don't think so. She kept saying how nice you were. How you understood what she was going through. I think that if you're not careful the grieving widow is going to start clinging to you.'

He said a soft 'Oh dear' and retreated into Heffernan's office with his coffee. Maybe Rachel was exaggerating. Or maybe Kirsty had misinterpreted his natural sympathy. But whatever the truth was, he was glad she'd be returning to London shortly.

He closed the door of Heffernan's office behind him and slumped down in the worn office chair.

'You look knackered,' was the closest Gerry Heffernan got to sympathy. 'I'd get off home soon if I were you.'

The mention of home prompted him to look at his watch. It was half past six. He had promised Pam that he'd phone her from London but he'd forgotten. And he'd vowed to be home at a reasonable time. Another broken promise.

'So what have we got so far?' he said, trying to take his mind off matters domestic.

'Our victim was a freelance writer from London and he was writing a book about some crime, presumably one with a Devon connection. According to his wife he was down here doing research. He has a lobster dinner then goes for a walk with his murderer in the grounds of Potwoolstan Hall and gets a knife in his ribs.' Heffernan thought for a moment. 'Any chance he could have eaten at the Hall? With Jeremy Elsham and the lovely Pandora perhaps? Then a little after dinner stroll by the river and ...'

'I thought of that. Apparently Jeremy and Pandora always eat with the guests. And the food's strictly vegetarian.'

'And lobster hardly counts as vegetarian. Aren't they boiled alive?'

Wesley nodded.

'So have we any idea what Evans was writing his book about?'

'He was killed in the grounds of Potwoolstan Hall. Could he have been investigating those murders?'

'Hardly. It was an open and shut case. The housekeeper went crazy. No mystery there.'

Wesley frowned. 'I've got his files in my car boot but I haven't had a chance to look through them yet.'

Heffernan raised his eyebrows, leaning back in his chair. It gave a creak of complaint and looked as though it was about to collapse under his weight. 'And his wife didn't know what he was up to?'

Wesley shook his head. 'She says he never took his work home. Unlike some police officers. His hotel room was searched, which suggests someone was after something he had. Maybe new evidence in an old murder case he was proposing to write about.'

'A local case?'

'Not necessarily. He might have come down here to see

someone involved in a crime that happened in a different part of the country. And that someone took exception to his questions.'

'But did his killer find what they were looking for?' Heffernan picked up a report on his desk and began to read it. 'Report's come back – no fingerprints found in Evans's hotel room that match any of our records. Dead end.' He threw the report down again.

Wesley looked at his watch. He couldn't put if off any longer. It was time to go home.

Anthony Jameston didn't know why he'd decided to use the name Charles Dodgson but it had seemed like a good idea at the time.

He sat on his bed and looked out of the window at the view across the river, wishing the door would lock, wishing for privacy. Gwen Madeley had misled him when she'd said the place was filled with healing energy. It was a place full of hostility and pretence: it seeped from the walls.

He should never have come to Potwoolstan Hall. He had chosen it as his bolt hole because Evans had made him curious, anxious to see the place his wife would never talk about. He didn't know what he had expected to find there. Perhaps some answer to why he had never really been able to get close to Arbel.

He buried his head in his hands. Parliament was in recess and he had booked a fortnight's stay at the Hall. But he had been there six days already and he was still no nearer understanding the truth.

The police were asking questions about Evans. But how could he tell them about his dealings with the dead man?

Maybe it would be better to say nothing. To keep silent.

Wesley pushed the front door open and called out. He had seen Della's car parked in the drive. That was all he needed; a visit from a thoughtless, feckless mother-in-law. After the day he'd just had all he wanted was peace and a quiet night by the television. In fact that was exactly what he wanted after most days.

A cry of 'Here he is at last. I bet he's got another woman he's not telling you about,' followed by a high-pitched giggle, came from the the living room. Della had had a glass or three of wine again.

Pam emerged from the living room. 'I thought you said you wouldn't be late.'

Wesley stepped forward and kissed her on the forehead. 'Sorry. How are the kids?'

'In bed. Don't disturb them,' she replied, watching his face. 'My mum's here.'

'So I heard. How much has she had to drink?'

Pam turned away, annoyed. 'You make it sound as if she's an alcoholic.'

Wesley thought he'd better change the subject. 'What have you been doing with yourself?'

'Apart from sharing a bottle of wine with my drunken mother, you mean?' Her lips twitched upwards in a smile. 'Neil's sent an email. I printed it out for you. Hang on.' She rushed into the dining room and came out again holding a sheet of paper. He had waited in the hall. He wasn't in the mood to face Della right now.

His dinner awaited him in the kitchen, cold and congealing. He looked at it. Cauliflower covered with cheese sauce that had solidified into unappetising lumps. But he was hungry and it was better than nothing so he placed the plate in the microwave. It was his own fault for being late.

He sat down at the kitchen table and began to eat, trying to ignore Della's irritating giggles from the adjoining room. When he had finished he picked up Neil's email and started to read. Somehow he hadn't expected him to get in touch so soon.

As he read, he felt envious. While he had been struggling through the London traffic and fighting losing battles against criminals who seemed to be getting smarter and more vicious by the day, Neil had been uncovering

America's early history. And when Neil came across a skeleton that had met its end under suspicious circumstances, nobody expected him to catch the culprit who, in any case, would have died centuries ago. Neil had no hostile witnesses to deal with; no lawyers doing their best to convince juries of the blameless innocence of sadistic villains and – more often than not – succeeding; no criticism by public and politicians; no risk of serious injury or even death. There were times when Wesley asked himself why he hadn't stuck to archaeology.

He put his dirty plate in the dishwater, longing to put his feet up and drink a couple of glasses of wine in front of an undemanding TV programme. But Della was there, and she'd probably stay for the rest of the evening, making him feel like an intruder in his own home.

He preferred to be exiled to the peace of the dining room with a good book than to suffer Della when she started to spout the half-baked anti-establishment and anti-police rehetoric she usually came out with when she'd had a few drinks. And besides he had just remembered that Patrick Evans's files were still in the boot of his car.

After tidying up a little in the kitchen to appease Pam, he opened the front door and sneaked out to the car. Once back in the dining room he took the files from their boxes and began to arrange them neatly on the table. He always felt more able to deal with things when they were tidy and organised. He picked up the first file, which was full of notes and cuttings. They concerned a case back in the 1970s. A notorious East End gangster called Toothless Terry who had links with the Flying Squad. Wesley scanned the file and put it to one side. He had heard of similar cases before: at one time many professional villains liked to have tame policemen in their pockets.

The next file concerned a case of arson in an East End factory. Several bodies had been found, probably those of illegal immigrants who were forced to work there for a pittance. Again it seemed that there was an underworld connection. But no mention of Devon as yet.

He opened another file, then another. Most of the crimes that Evans had investigated seemed to have taken place in London. Eventually, he found a case of a woman up in Glasgow who had been acquitted of the murder of her husband's mistress but still nothing connected with Devon or the south west.

Patrick Evans specialised in reviewing old cases with fresh eyes and seeking out evidence that had either been ignored or unavailable at the time. It occurred to Wesley that he would have made a good policeman if he hadn't chosen to be a journalist and author. And at least the police force would have given him a regular income every month.

Wesley had emptied the first box and found no mention of any Devon connection, ancient or modern. He replaced everything neatly before emptying the second box and laying the files out on the table in an orderly manner. When he examined them he found more of the same. There were the murders of several prostitutes in Cardiff, possibly linked to a local dignitary, and a kidnapping in Leeds. At least things were moving further afield.

The fourth file Wesley picked up was much slimmer than the others. In fact, when he opened it up he found that it was completely empty. Wesley stared at it for a moment before turning it over to look at the name on the front.

His heart began to beat faster and he was hardly aware of Della's irritating laughter drifting in from the living room. This file had been emptied: Evans had probably brought its contents to Devon with him. All his instincts told him that this was what whoever had searched Evans's hotel room had been after.

And the name printed on the front in neat black letters was 'Potwoolstan Hall'.

Chapter Five

This river we have discovered ebbs and flows a hundred and threescore miles where ships of great burden may harbour in safety. Wheresoever we land upon this river we see the goodliest woods of beech, oak, cedar, cypress, walnut, sassafras and vines. There is an abundance of food and we dine most commonly on fish, turtles, raccoons, birds and oysters.

The Chief of the Savages sent more men with gifts of tobacco and fruits. Master Joshua Morton set up a target against a tree and willed one of the savages to shoot. The savage took from his back an arrow and drew it strongly in his bow and shot the target a foot through and yet a pistol could not pierce it. Then, seeing the force of this bow, Master Morton set him up a steel target which burst the next arrow all to pieces. The savage flew into a great rage and Master Morton made to fire his pistol at him. Yet I stopped him, fearing he would anger the natives who would come to do us harm.

It is Penelope's habit to gather fruits in the woods in the mornings so I sought her out. I fear her husband greatly. He is a choleric man with murder in his heart, yet Penelope doth deceive well and plays the meek and dutiful wife. It may be that I should have nothing to do with her. But I fear she hath bewitched me.

Set down by Master Edmund Selbiwood, Gentleman, on the twelfth day of August 1605 at Annetown, Virginia.

Neil Watson was disappointed to find that there was no email from Pam. But it was early days, and besides, she probably wouldn't have much to say. Life would be carrying on as normal back in Tradmouth. Wesley working long hours while Pam was stuck with the kids was hardly news.

He squatted in the trench and gazed up at the tall cedar trees outlined against the blue sky. The early settlers must have thought this place was paradise. But this paradise had to be defended and Professor Keller's team had found what remained of their defences against the natives – and presumably that old enemy of the English at that time, Spain.

Neil was impressed by what he had seen of Virginia so far; the green, wooded landscape, the kind weather and the pretty clapboard houses, white and well kept with manicured gardens enclosed by neat picket fences. It seemed like a good place. But it hadn't been good for the two men with musket balls lodged in their skulls who had died there hundreds of years ago. He wondered what had led to their deaths. An accident? A quarrel? He'd probably never know but it was intriguing all the same.

The favourite topic of conversation of his new flatmate, Chuck, was still how his favourite baseball team was doing. The analysis of each game the Yankees had played and the performance of each player was beginning to get on Neil's nerves. He had never really been one for team sports and the unfamiliarity of the game's rules and characters seemed to make matters worse. He'd known a lot of men back home in England who had a similar obsession with football, chewing over every tackle, every foul and every offside decision in tedious detail, and he'd always tended to avoid their company. But as he and Chuck were sharing a small apartment there was no escape. And no time off for good behaviour.

91

Chuck, however, did have his uses, local knowledge being one of them. And he was eager to help Neil in his search for Max Selbiwood, even promising to search for his name in lists of local residents. Neil didn't enquire too closely about how he was going to tackle this onerous task: he was just glad to have someone to do it for him. Chuck reminded him of an over-enthusiastic dog, a Labrador perhaps, enjoying a game of fetch. But he wasn't complaining. It could save him a lot of work.

As Neil scraped away carefully at the palisade trench, a remnant of one of Annetown's earliest fortifications, he thought of Hannah Gotleib. She hadn't turned up at the dig that day and he wondered where she was. And what she was doing that evening. He hadn't even asked her if there was a significant other in her life: somehow it had seemed inappropriate, too personal.

He could always ask Professor Keller if he knew her phone number. But he knew in his heart of hearts that he wouldn't have the courage. It would be another cosy night in with Chuck listening to the ins and outs of the baseball season.

Easter weekend came and went. Gerry Heffernan disappeared from the office for an hour on Good Friday to sing with the choir at St Margaret's Church and returned looking subdued. Wesley felt an unexpected pang of regret that he hadn't gone with him.

They spent most of Saturday going over everything they knew about Patrick Evans's death and making sure that there was nothing obvious that they'd missed. All the staff and guests at Potwoolstan Hall had now been interviewed and Wesley took a particular interest in Charles Dodgson's statement. But, like everybody else, Dodgson claimed to have seen nothing suspicious. Patrick Evans's murderer was either very clever or very lucky. Or someone was lying.

On Sunday morning, Wesley caught up with domestic

chores, salving his conscience and trying to ignore the joyous clamour of church bells carried on the cool spring breeze. In the afternoon, he and Pam walked on the quayside at Tradmouth with the children, licking ice creams and watching the boats scuttle across the river.

When it was time to head home, Wesley said that he had something to do and promised he wouldn't be long. The thought of Kirsty Evans sitting alone in her hotel room was making him uncomfortable.

Kirsty seemed pleased to see him and grateful for the opportunity to talk about Patrick as they lingered over a cream tea in the bright hotel lounge. In the weeks to come people would probably avoid the subject for fear of opening up raw wounds. Kirsty was quite adamant that she had never heard Patrick mention the name Potwoolstan Hall. And Wesley had no reason to disbelieve her. She had already assured him that Patrick had never brought his work home.

Monday was a bank holiday, as damp and depressing as only a British bank holiday Monday can be. But Wesley went into work early that morning and requested the files on the Potwoolstan Hall case. They were kept in the archives – case solved – and Wesley's demand to see them produced a flurry of activity before a young uniformed constable brought them up to the CID office and deposited them on his desk.

Gerry Heffernan arrived in the office late, pleading a faulty alarm clock. He lurched past Wesley's desk, still apparently half asleep, then he stopped and swung round. 'What's new?'

Wesley told him about his cream tea with Kirsty Evans the previous day. 'Someone from Uniform is taking her back this morning. Said he was glad of the trip to London. There's no accounting for taste.'

Heffernan raised his eyebrows. He wasn't so unsentimental about his home town. There was times when he waxed very lyrical about the virtues of Liverpool, wallowing in nostalgia after a few pints in the Tradmouth Arms. He looked at the files piled up on Wesley's desk, normally kept so neat, unlike his own. 'What's all this?'

'The Potwoolstan Hall murders. I told you the papers were missing from the file I took from Evans's office. It must have been the case he was investigating or else why would he be down here? I'm seeing if anything was missed at the time.'

'You're wasting your time, Wes. It was the housekeeper. She had a history of mental problems and her employers, the Harfords, had been giving her a hard time. They accused her of stealing. In the end it turned out that she hadn't done it but it still caused a lot of ill feeling.'

'So she killed the whole family? Seems a bit over the top.'

Heffernan sighed. 'The psychiatrist who gave evidence at the time said Martha Wallace was like a pressure cooker ready to explode at the slightest provocation.'

'Hindsight is a wonderful thing. I wonder if he'd have reached that conclusion if he'd examined her before it happened. What sort of mental problems did she have?'

Heffernan shrugged. He wasn't well up on medical matters. 'Heard from your mate Neil?'

Wesley looked up, surprised at the sudden change of subject. 'He sent us an email when he first arrived to say he'd got there OK.'

They were interrupted by the arrival of Rachel Tracey. She was holding a piece of paper. She was grinning and she looked as though she had news to impart.

'You know Steve and Paul have been checking out fences and dodgy jewellers? Well it seems they paid a surprise visit to a jeweller called Jack Wright in Morbay first thing and they found a bracelet and earrings that fit the description of the stuff pinched from the Dukesbridge health spa.'

'Jack Wright? He's been warned before about not being too particular about who he buys jewellery from. What about the rest?'

94

'He admits he's sold some stuff on to a contact in London – necklace and ring that could be the ones pinched from a woman on that creative writing course near Neston.'

'So he's owning up?'

'He says he'd no idea they were stolen and he wants to co-operate.'

Heffernan grinned. 'The old old story. He thinks he might get away with it if he pleads ignorance. With his track record he's pushing it. So did he say who it was who took advantage of his better nature?'

'A man called Mr Smith, who claimed to have found the jewellery in a house he's clearing out belonging to an old aunty who's just passed away.'

'How touching. Description?'

'Vague. Could fit a thousand balding middle-aged men.'

Wesley frowned. This description didn't fit any of the guests or staff at Potwoolstan Hall. Charles Dodgson was definitely in the clear. 'Any sign of Mrs Jeffries's ring?'

Rachel shook her head. 'It seems the "aunty's" house is taking a long time to clear out and that's why the stuff's being offered for sale in dribs and drabs. According to Wright, Mr Smith is very convincing.'

'We'd better see if he can tell us any more,' said Wesley, ever hopeful.

'It's on my list.' She gave a small, smug smile. This one would be easy to crack. It was only a matter of time before the thief was in the interview room confessing all.

Emma Oldchester had never been so determined about anything before. Her father had pleaded with her not to go. So had Barry. But for once she would defy them. She knew she had to go through with it. She had no choice.

She had been working all weekend to finish the houses that had been ordered. Mrs Bartlet's and Miss Pinson's were ready but she would finish off the other two – Mrs James's and Mrs Potts's – when she got back. Emma felt calm, organised, as she knelt down before the house she would never sell. The special house. Her house.

The façade was split in two, like double doors. She opened the right-hand side. It was all there, the dark, heavy furniture, the green wallpaper and the fine oak staircase. She had taken so much care; put into it every detail she remembered, large and small. The small drawing room to the left of the entrance hall had been painted a dark mustard shade, she remembered that. And she remembered the blood that had splashed on to the walls as if someone had thrown pots of red-brown emulsion paint around. There had been a horrible smell; a vaguely metallic odour, the same as she had smelled once in a butcher's shop. Blood. The smell of the slaughterhouse.

She looked at the miniature room and touched one of the figures that lay on the ground near the doorway. It lay there dead, its blue dress splashed with rusty-red paint. There was another, male figure, also splattered with blood. The colour of the blood was exactly right, just as she remembered it. It was on the other two figures too, another male and female who lay on the landing just outside the frilly bedroom upstairs. The russet paint had splashed up the landing window. She hadn't wanted to leave any detail out.

But the hallway was the worst. A doll lay on the floor between the front door and the stairs, a mass of red-brown gore where its head should be and the walls and floor around it bathed in blood.

She opened up the other half of the frontage to reveal the left-hand side of the house's interior. Inside, she could see the dining room with its dark glossy furniture and striped red and white walls. The table was set for five with tiny cutlery and plates, and wine glasses, small as a thumbnail, stood by each place setting. But no figures sat on the little Sheraton-style chairs. The meal had been eaten already and the diners had departed.

The room to the left of the dining room was furnished as a kitchen complete with a dresser, stove and scrubbed pine table. A small doll sat at the table, not upright but slumped.

The doll wore an apron that had once been white but was now stained with rusty brown and the head looked as though it had been dipped in paint the colour of dried blood. Something lay beside the doll's right hand: the tiniest of guns. Emma had put so much care into getting everything right.

She stared for a while before shutting the front of the house, concealing the scene within. Then she bent and picked up a tiny doll, dressed all in black, that had rolled under the table. She put it in the pocket of her cardigan. It was time to go.

Barry wouldn't be home until six. He would have to get his own meal that night. Emma would be at Potwoolstan Hall, eating her vegetarian supper. She wondered if they'd use the dining room and if they'd left it how it was: after all, nobody had actually died in there. Her hands began to tingle with nerves and excitement at the thought that she would actually be there. She would see it again. She wanted to know the truth so badly. And Jeremy Elsham would help her to find it.

Emma shut the door of the spare bedroom that served as her workshop behind her and made her way downstairs, her footsteps muffled by the thick carpet, the best quality they could afford. Barry said it didn't do to skimp. She picked up the case that stood near the front door. She had packed it first thing that morning, impatient for the moment.

After making sure the burglar alarm was switched on and the door was shut properly, Emma Oldchester put the case in her van and drove off towards Potwoolstan Hall.

Chuck had come up trumps. He had found the address of a Max Selbiwood who lived in the leafy suburbs on the other side of town from the university. Chuck had even offered him the use of his pick-up truck that evening. Neil was grateful for Chuck's boundless generosity and enthusiasm, but he wasn't sure that he was ready to face Max Selbiwood just yet.

He had given the matter a great deal of thought that day while he was working at the dig. If it were indeed the right Max Selbiwood, then he would be a very old man, the same age as his own grandmother. Or perhaps the Max that Chuck had found was the son of the man he was looking for. In which case it would be difficult to explain the reason for his visit.

In a moment of cowardice he almost convinced himself that he should leave well alone; that he should concentrate on doing what he was over there for: excavating an important site where settlers from England, mainly from the West Country, had landed all those centuries ago. Neil had never been one for sentiment but he felt that it would be wrong to let his dying grandmother down and abandon his search for Max Selbiwood. He pictured her in the nursing home, her body giving up the fight for life while her mind was still so alert to everything that was going on around her, every pain, every indignity brought on by dependence on others. She had asked him to do this one last thing for her and he could hardly back out now.

'Hi, how are you doing?'

Neil was crouched in a trench, scraping the earth gently from around the outline of a section of stained soil left by the decayed timbers of an early wooden building. He looked up from his lowly position and saw Hannah Gotleib standing there on the edge of the trench.

'We're uncovering some armour and weapons in trench five, probably discarded by the early settlers. Come and take a look.'

Neil straightened himself up. Why was it everyone else's trench seemed to contain all the most exciting finds? It was the story of his archaeological life. He followed Hannah across the site, distracted by the sight of her shapely rear. When he looked back at the dig where the archaeologists were working, concentrating on their work with earnest faces, he could see the footprint of the original Annetown fort quite clearly; the traces of the ditches dug by the earliest colonists to support their protective timber walls.

He quickened his pace and caught up with Hannah. She looked at him and smiled; a dazzling white-toothed smile.

'You know you said that one of the early settlers was called Selbiwood?'

She nodded.

'Do you know anything about him?'

She looked at him curiously, as though she was surprised by the sudden question. 'He was described in contemporary documents as a gentleman of Devon but that's all I can remember.'

Neil followed her to the trench where the armour was being unearthed with painstaking concentration. Hannah stood beside him, watching and, after a decent interval of ten minutes or so, he summoned the courage to ask if he could look at the archives. Hannah led the way to the large wooden building on the edge of the site. This was no glorified garden shed. This was a permanent research facility housing archives, conservation laboratories, computer rooms and even an exhibition space. Neil entered this veritable palace of archaeology with envy. What he wouldn't give for something like this back home.

Hannah knew exactly where to look for Edmund Selbiwood. As she had said, he was indeed a gentleman of Devon and his place of abode in England was listed in the old records as Potwoolstan Hall near to the town of Neston.

Neil was silent as he made his way back to the trench where he was working. He was racking his brains, trying to recall where he had heard the name Potwoolstan Hall before.

He had contemplated asking Hannah out for a meal that evening, but with Chuck's offer of the use of his pick-up, he would be otherwise occupied. At least the snippet of interesting knowledge he had just gleaned would give him something to tell Max Selbiwood. If and when he found him.

As she walked up the drive to the hall, Emma Oldchester was shaking. She wondered why they insisted on their guests parking so far away. Perhaps they thought arriving on foot, dragging your suitcase behind you, was some sort of preparation, a lesson in humility. Like someone going the last few hundred yards of a pilgrimage barefoot or on torn, bleeding knees. Her wheeled suitcase trundled behind her like an obedient dog until she rounded the corner. When she caught her first full view of the Hall she halted suddenly and let the handle drop but she was hardly aware of the thud as the case toppled over behind her. She was here at last. This was it. The killing ground. The place of her nightmares.

She stood there, frozen with terror. It was just as she remembered it. The crows sitting in the tall trees shrieking their coarse, mocking derision; the solid stone house with its gables and dark windows. The ancient oak front door. There had been a back door too. There had been two crows: one nailed to the front door and one to the back. She would never forget the blood and the bedraggled black feathers. Witchcraft. Evil. She could still sense it, smell it.

She forced herself to pick up the case. 'I will fear no evil,' she whispered under her breath. 'Even though I walk through the valley of the shadow of death, I will fear no evil.' Her heart was pounding as she walked forwards.

She stumbled the last few yards to the front door. Once it had always been kept closed but now it stood open, welcoming. She wavered on the threshold, her mouth dry and her palms damp with sweat.

A man appeared in the hallway. He wore a white jacket and he was smiling, showing a set of even white teeth. His arms were outstretched in welcome.

'Ms Oldchester? Emma? I'm Jeremy Elsham, the facilitator.' His voice was deep and resonant. A hypnotic voice. 'Welcome ... welcome.' He took her hand in both of his and held it for a full half minute as he gazed into her eyes.

'You are afraid,' he said in velvet tones. 'You have lived with this fear for a long time. That's why you've come to us.'

She gave a small nod and felt tears prick her eyes. It was as if he knew, as if he could see into her mind. He put his arms around her and drew her towards him until her cheek was pressed to the crisp cloth of his white jacket. He smelled of cleanliness with a whiff of expensive aftershave. He smelled good. He held her and she stood there stiffly as he moved his hands slowly up and down her back.

100

'I sense that you've suffered a great tragedy in your life,' he whispered in her ear.

Emma felt his warm breath on the side of her face and experienced a feeling of helplessness, as though she were drowning in honey.

He planted a small, almost reverent, kiss on her forehead. 'We can help you, Emma. We can release you from the prison of your past and . . .'

'Jeremy.' The voice was female. Calm but with an unmistakable touch of anger.

Jeremy Elsham released Emma from his grasp and turned round slowly. He was smiling with his mouth. But his eyes were expressionless.

'Ms Oldchester? Welcome to Potwoolstan Hall.' The woman with the collagen lips spoke in a curt, businesslike manner.

'This is my wife, Pandora,' Jeremy Elsham said smoothly. 'She'll show you to your room. We don't lock doors here. Locked doors are a symbol of locked minds.'

Emma turned her wide-eyed gaze on Pandora and sensed the woman's disapproval. But the fact that she'd found her in Jeremy's arms was hardly her fault. She had assumed that it was just the way he greeted all the Beings. As she followed Pandora up the staircase, she had an uneasy feeling that the past might not be the only thing she would have to wrestle with at Potwoolstan Hall.

At least her meeting with Jeremy and Pandora had distracted her from her surroundings. In fact, her encounter with Jeremy had left her rather dazed. The way he had held her close had excited her in a way she didn't quite understand.

When she was halfway up the stairs she stopped and looked back over her shoulder into the spacious entrance hall. Apart from the dark, Jacobean staircase, it had changed beyond all recognition and bore no resemblance to the doll's house she had so painstakingly constructed. Then it had been a place full of gloom, blood and shadows but now it was modern and light. If Emma had been taken into the building blindfold, she wouldn't have recognised it. She wondered what the drawing room and the kitchen looked like now and whether the events still remained there somehow, recorded in the bricks and plaster. Surely it was unthinkable that such violent actions would leave no trace behind. Surely the place was haunted by the ghosts of the dead crying out for vengeance.

She was about to follow Pandora when she spotted somebody crossing the hall below. She closed her eyes for a second and opened them again and when she glanced down into the hall again that face from the past had disappeared.

As she followed Pandora to her room, her mouth was dry and she was beginning to shake. Perhaps it had been a ghost she saw. A ghost who had aged with the years.

Wesley flicked through Jack Wright's statement. Wright had made a great show of cooperation, emphasising Mr Smith's plausibility and his own horror that stolen goods had passed through his hands. But at the same time he had told them very little.

It was, however, a fairly trivial matter compared with murder and it was only Patrick Evans's connection with Potwoolstan Hall – whatever that connection was – that made him take any interest at all in the disappearance of Mrs Jeffries's money and ring.

He was starting to build up a picture of what had happened at Potwoolstan Hall on that March day back in 1985.

The Hall was owned by a family called Harford. Great-great-grandfather Ebenezer Harford had made his fortune from brewing in the nineteenth century, owning four thriving breweries in Devon and Cornwall and accumulating enough wealth to purchase Potwoolstan Hall, a farily modest late Tudor manor house in a spectacular setting near the banks of the River Trad. The place had been built by the Selbiwood family, who had suffered a slow descent into genteel poverty some years before and were forced to sell their ancestral home to make ends meet. Thus the brewer became lord of the manor and he made improvements to the old place that would have been way beyond the Selbiwoods' shallow pockets.

The Hall, with its Victorian conveniences, had been handed from father to son and had been inherited by Edward Harford in 1968. Edward lived at the Hall with his wife Mary and his three children Jack, Catriona and Arbel, the youngest and the only one of the three to have been adopted. Edward had sold the Harford breweries to a large national brewer for a handsome sum in the late 1970s, staying on as a director.

To the outside world, the Harfords had it all. But then in 1985 tragedy stuck. Edward Harford was fifty-four when he died and his wife, Mary a year older. The twins, Jack and Catriona were aged twenty-five: Catriona was engaged to be married to Nigel Armley, a naval officer, and Jack was working for the large brewer that now owned the family firm. Jack and Catriona had both been sent away to boarding school but now lived at home, as did the youngest child, Arbel. Reading between the lines of the detailed report it seemed that Arbel was the rebel, the one who liked to do her own thing. In fact this had probably saved her life. She had been staying in London when her family was murdered and she had discovered the bodies when she returned home to Devon the next day for a family party to celebrate Mary Harford's birthday. If Arbel hadn't been in London, if she'd been the home-loving type, she would almost certainly have died with the rest of her immediate family.

Wesley read on. He wanted to get a clear picture of what had happened on that fateful day. And he wanted the main players clear in his head. He wanted to know what had driven the Harfords' housekeeper, Martha Wallace, to wipe out the entire family like that. Was it some catastrophic event? Or was it a slow drip, drip of resentment that had ended in fury?

A month before the murders, Mary Harford had discovered that some of her jewellery was missing. He smiled to himself. Funny that history should repeat itself in the same place. But then jewellery was high value and portable – irresistible to the light-fingered. And coincidences happen more often than most people think. The most obvious suspect was the housekeeper, Martha Wallace, who had been experiencing financial difficulties and suddenly appeared to have come into money.

Wesley flicked through the papers, wanting to find out more about Martha Wallace: her background; the type of woman she was. And what had made her kill the family she worked for. At last he found the information he was looking for. Martha was thirty-five years old and even though she came originally from the Manchester area, she had relatives in the south-west. She was the widow of an able seaman, based at Plymouth, who had died in an accident aboard his ship and she had a seven-year-old daughter who lived with her in the staff flat at Potwoolstan Hall. Martha had worked in a hotel before her marriage and it had been Catriona Harford's fiancé Nigel Armley, the naval officer, who had recommended her for the job of housekeeper at the Hall as her late husband had been under his command.

Wesley looked at the photograph that had been attached to her file with a paperclip; a snap of a smiling woman, fair-haired and a little plump, wearing a low-waisted floral summer dress, a style fashionable in the 1980s. She was smiling at the camera, screwing her eyes up against the sun. She had a wide, generous mouth, wavy hair and freckles. Wesley turned the photograph over. Her name was written on the back: Martha Elizabeth Wallace. He studied the face. It was an open face, a healthy country face that might have belonged to some laughing Victorian milkmaid. To Wesley Peterson, it hardly looked like the face of a thief or a mass murderer. But then appearances can often deceive.

He read on. There was a report in the file of the police investigation into the theft of a sapphire necklace and a diamond brooch. Mrs Mary Harford had called in the local police and had virtually accused Martha of stealing them on the grounds that she had been buying herself new clothes and her daughter had new toys. When interviewed, Martha, understandably, was very upset at the accusations and explained that she had inherited the money from a recently deceased uncle in Manchester. She had paid off her debts and treated herself and her seven-year-old daughter to a few little luxuries. This story checked out and her innocence was established, but the ready accusation soured relations between Martha and her employer.

The only other member of the Hall's indoor staff was an eighteen-year-old girl called Brenda Varney who came in to help with the cleaning each morning. Brenda was a girl who talked big and she boasted that one day she'd escape her humdrum life to make it as a actress or a model. When she failed to report for work a couple of weeks after the theft of the jewellery, nobody was really surprised. And when a Tradmouth jeweller reported that a girl answering Brenda's description had tried to sell Mary Harford's stolen jewellery, the police went to pick her up. Only they were too late. Brenda had left home, seemingly disappeared off the face of the earth, and all efforts to trace her and the jewellery failed. This was the week before the Harfords were killed. But the police didn't link the two events at the time.

The strangest aspect of the case was the fact that dead crows had been nailed to the front door and the kitchen door. It was possible that someone had wanted to unnerve or frighten the occupants of the Hall with a spot of amateur witchcraft. But would Martha really nail such an unpleasant and unhygienic object to the door of her own kitchen, her domain? But if Martha hadn't done it, then who had?

Wesley scratched his head. In the weeks leading up to the murder of the Harford family it seemed that the only unusual event that had occurred was the theft of Mary Harford's jewellery from the box she kept on her dressing table. He found himself wondering about Martha Wallace's behaviour at that time. Statements said that she had been quiet, that she had been brooding and resentful and had said little to the family. But then, Wesley thought, most people wouldn't be happy about being falsely accused of theft by their employer. He was sure that if Martha Wallace had had somewhere to go, she would have walked out on the Harfords there and then. But shooting them all dead? Perhaps the accusations, the lack of trust had hurt that much.

It seemed that on the fateful night, between nine o'clock and ten o'clock, Martha had taken Edward Harford's shotgun and a rifle from their locked cabinet and loaded them. She must have come across Catriona's fiancé, Nigel Armley, first in the hall, where she emptied both barrels of the shotgun into his face. Then she threw the shotgun down by his body and shot Jack and Catriona Harford with the rifle as they emerged from the drawing room to investigate the noise, before climbing the stairs to the master bedroom where she killed their parents, Edward and Mary, who had just come out onto the landing. She had aimed for her victims' heads and Wesley flicked through the gruesome photographs of the crime scene quickly, his stomach lurching at the sight of the bleeding corpses, especially that of Nigel Armley, whose face had been shot away.

After her shooting spree, Martha Wallace had taken the rifle, sat down at the kitchen table amidst food she had been preparing for the party the following evening and shot herself in the neck. When the crime was discovered the next day, Martha Wallace's seven-year-old daughter was discovered kneeling at her mother's feet, rocking to and fro, stuck dumb with terror. According to the file the unfortunate child had been taken to stay with relatives, too traumatised to be questioned.

It had seemed like an open and shut case. The radio that might have masked the sound of the shots in the kitchen was switched off, which also pointed to Martha's guilt. If she had heard shots, surely she would have left the kitchen to investigate. But as Wesley closed the file, certain things worried him. Even if Martha Wallace had resented the Harfords enough to murder them, would she have done it with her young daughter in the house? And she had been preparing food for the following day. Why start making party snacks that were never going to be eaten? And, if it came to that, why not just add a little something to the Harfords' dinner and poison them?

106

As far as Wesley could see, the police had accepted the easier explanation. But there were things about the case that didn't add up and he wondered if Patrick Evans had reached the same conclusion. Patrick's file on Potwoolstan Hall was missing and somebody had killed him in the grounds of the Hall. Everything pointed to a connection. And if there was one, then the whole case would have to be looked at again.

Wesley glanced towards Gerry Heffernan's office. The boss was inside, bent over his paperwork, frowning. He would be glad of a bit of distraction from the monthly crime figures.

It had been a long day but Steve Carstairs managed to escape from the CID office just after six, saying that he had things to follow up. It was well known that Steve had a string of tame informants, or snouts as he preferred to call them, in many of the less salubrious pubs in the Tradmouth and Morbay area, so Wesley Peterson hadn't asked too many questions. But then Peterson seemed to have something on his mind, something to do with the Potwoolstan Hall files he had asked for. Peterson was a bloody graduate, always playing Sherlock Holmes and showing off his superior knowledge. And he was black so he got all the promotion going. Steve Carstairs didn't have a high opinion of black people – or graduates, come to that – and he regarded Wesley Peterson's calm ordered manner as some sort of personal affront. There were times when he contemplated transferring to the Met. Perhaps he would one day. But he had a nice motor and a decent flat in Morbay. And Serena Jones had invited him to her place so his luck might be in.

He stood in the hallway of his flat and examined his appearance in the mirror. He was pleased with what he saw; pleased with the slim body honed by regular trips to the gym. He ran his fingers through his thick, dark hair, styled at the best unisex salon in Morbay, and took his soft leather jacket from the coat stand. It had cost a week's wages but it had been worth it. He turned heads, particularly female ones.

Steve made his final inspection and concluded that

Serena Jones wouldn't be able to resist him. He tossed his car keys up in the air and caught them before picking up the bottle of wine he'd bought from the off licence on his way home. It wouldn't do to keep the lady waiting.

He drove to Neston and parked in a vacant space marked 'residents only'. The building was by the river, once an old warehouse but now converted beyond recognition into luxury apartments with wrought-iron balconies. A nice place. Serena had never actually told him what her job was, but if she could afford a place like this it must be a good one.

He caressed the bonnet of his car absentmindedly before touching the pocket that contained a newly bought packet of condoms. Serena Jones was a fortunate lady.

When Serena opened the door of her apartment to him, he stepped inside without waiting to be invited and handed her the bottle of wine before making himself at home on his hostess's low black leather sofa.

'How about opening the wine?' Steve suggested.

'Aren't you driving?'

It wasn't the answer he'd expected. Perhaps he'd misread the situation. But he wasn't one to give up that easily. 'That's up to you,' he said softly, with more than a hint of suggestion in his voice.

Serena Jones slumped down on the chair opposite and pulled down the hem of her short skirt. 'I suppose you were expecting to stay the night.'

For once Steve was lost for words. He opened and closed his mouth but no sound came out.

'Let's get one thing straight, Steve. I invited you here because I wanted to talk to you as a policeman. Not because I want to take up where we left off. OK?'

Steve sighed. 'If that's how you want it.'

There was a lengthy silence and Steve found himself longing for the glass of wine he'd expected, if only to relax him and give him something to do with his hands now that other options had been closed to him. He stood up and went to the kitchen, returning with a corkscrew and two glasses.

He poured the wine out and handed a glass to Serena.

'I never told you what I do for a living, did I?' she said, playing with the stem of her glass.

'Why? Is it something illegal?'

'Not exactly. I'm a journalist on the *Neston Echo* but I've been working on a story I thought might interest the nationals. That's why I was at Potwoolstan Hall. I was undercover.'

'Undercover? For the *Neston Echo*?' Steve found it impossible to keep the sarcasm from his voice. The *Neston Echo* usually confined itself to dog shows, petty crime and town councillors' speeding offences. Somehow he had never thought of its reporters going undercover.

'I'm doing a series of articles on alternative healing and I wanted to see if Jeremy Elsham was a fraud.'

'And is he?'

'I'm not sure. But I was a bit concerned about this regression business ...'

'Regression?'

'He hypnotises people and takes them back to their childhood, recovers memories. It could be dangerous stuff in the wrong hands, playing with people's minds.'

Steve took a sip of wine. This all sounded like rubbish to him.

Serena leaned forward. 'I asked you here because I wanted your advice. I booked into the Hall because I wanted to see the setup for myself.'

'Did you let him hypnotise you?'

She snorted. 'Come on, Steve, I'm not stupid. I was there under false pretences and I wasn't going to risk giving myself away. Not that I think anyone'd be able to put me under, but I wasn't taking any chances. I just went to the spiritual healing and meditation workshops. And when Elsham was conducting one of his regression sessions and his wife was out, I had a quick look through the filing cabinets in his office.'

Steve looked uncomfortable. 'I don't think you should be telling me this. We have to have a warrant to do that sort of thing.'

'You could say I was being a public-spirited citizen. Trying to point you in the right direction.'

'Did you find anything?'

She leaned forward, pulling her top down to display more cleavage. 'I wondered if you'd do me a favour. In the public interest of course.'

Steve stiffened. He thought the invitation had been too good to be true. 'What?'

'It wouldn't be hard for you to look Jeremy Elsham up on the Police National Computer, would it? If I can say that he's had convictions for this and that . . .'

Steve edged away. Even he knew when he was being used. 'I don't know.'

'It can't do any harm, Steve. And nobody'll know where I got the information. If Elsham's a fraud, the public should be warned.'

'We've already checked out the names of everyone at the Hall. Unless he's using an alias, Elsham hasn't got a record.'

She looked disappointed but still managed a smile. 'There, that wasn't too difficult, was it? There was a lot of police activity in the Hall's grounds.'

'They think that's where that Patrick Evans was killed.'

'What else can you tell me?' She looked at him as though he were the most fascinating man in the world.

He swallowed hard. 'Nothing much. The press have had a statement.'

'I hear the widow's been staying at the Marina Hotel. Any chance she'll talk to me?'

He took another drink. 'Doubt it. Any ideas about who pinched that old girl's ring and cash? My boss seemed to think there might be something dodgy about that bloke Charles Dodgson but there's nobody of that name and description with a record.'

Serena stood up and walked to the window, a secretive smile on her face. 'Charles Dodgson's no thief.'

'How do you know?' Her smug expression was starting

to annoy him. He hated someone knowing something he didn't.

'I know because his name's not Dodgson. It's Anthony Jameston MP and he's a rising star in the government, tipped for big things in the future. What he's doing at a place like Potwoolstan Hall, I've no idea but he seems to know the art therapist up there rather well. Secret meetings in the woods. How corny can you get? If they want to screw each other why don't they just get on with it?'

'Don't suppose you found out why he's using a false name?'

Serena shrugged. 'Probably doesn't want his wife to know where he is.' She smiled smugly, as though she knew a juicy secret.

'I suppose it'll be all over the papers tomorrow.'

She snorted. 'It's hardly the *Neston Echo*'s cup of tea. But I know some of the nationals are going to be interested. It might be my lucky day.' She sat down on the sofa beside him and edged closer. He could smell her perfume, heavy and sensual. She put out her hand to touch the front of his shirt and her fingers lingered. 'I've heard a whisper that Patrick Evans was an author who wrote books about true crimes. Any chance he was planning to write about those murders at the Hall?'

Steve didn't answer but he sensed she could read his mind.

'Why don't you have another drink?' she said.

'I shouldn't if I'm driving.'

'Who said you'd be driving tonight? A woman's entitled to change her mind, isn't she?'

Steve refilled both their glasses before Serena had a chance to rethink her decision. It looked like his luck was in after all.

Serena came closer and kissed his ear softly. He could smell the warmth of her breath on his face as she whispered. 'And you will keep me posted about the murder enquiry, won't you?'

111

Steve drained his glass. Everything came at a price.

Wesley arrived home at seven. The brown paper bag he carried contained a Chinese takeaway from the Golden Dragon. A peace offering.

Pam took the bag without a word and started to arrange the containers on the kitchen table. She didn't speak. Wesley knew she was annoyed.

'Is something the matter?' He knew as soon as the words were out of his mouth that it was a silly question.

'No.' The plates landed noisily on the table, followed by the cutlery.

Wesley put his arm around her but she shrugged if off. 'I'm back at school in a couple of weeks and I'll have to cope with the kids as well as all the work I'll have to bring home.' She looked him in the eye. 'You're never here.'

'I'm sorry,' was all he could think of to say. It was useless to make promises he couldn't keep, to say that he'd be home by five thirty every night and spend all his weekends being the model father. As much as he'd like to do these things, the criminal fraternity had other plans. 'We're in the middle of a murder enquiry. When things quieten down . . .'

'But they never do, do they?' There were tears in her eyes.

Wesley took her in his arms and held her. 'We'd better eat up. It's getting cold.'

They ate the meal in virtual silence but by the time they'd finished, Pam looked a little calmer. There had been no noise from upstairs so, presumably, the children were fast asleep. If either of them awoke during the night, Wesley resolved to see to them, to do his bit. He would make more of an effort from now on. He cleared the dishes away and opened a bottle of wine, pouring a glass for Pam. She was instructed to go to the living room and sit down. By the time the dishwasher was on, Wesley was feeling quite virtuous, almost smug.

As he settled down beside her on the sofa she was looking more relaxed. Maybe she'd just had a bad day.

'Neil's sent another email,' she said, retrieving a sheet of A4 paper from the coffee table, which she handed to Wesley. He poured himself a drink before he began to read.

'Hi Pam and Wes,' it began. 'You should see the facilities they've got here. Conservation labs, archives. You name it, they've got it. There's an amazing reconstruction of the settlement too and even a replica of the ship the settlers sailed over from Devon on. I'm also learning a lot about baseball but I won't go into that. Do you remember I said I needed to trace someone for my grandmother? Well, I've found the address and I'm going to see him. Sorry to be so mysterious but I want to see how it goes first. Be in touch soon. All the best, Neil.'

Wesley handed the email back to Pam. 'Sounds as if he's enjoying himself.'

'Glad someone is.'

Wesley took a gulp of wine, wondering if he was going to spend all his life feeling guilty. Had Gerry Heffernan felt like this when his wife, Kathy was alive? Had she given him those reproachful looks when he arrived home? Had she made him feel bad about the hours he put in at work? Perhaps when the time was right, he'd ask him.

At nine o'clock the next morning, Emma Oldchester entered the regression room. It was a small chamber with midnight-blue walls and thick red velvet drapes at the windows; warm and dark, like a womb. And Emma was afraid. More than afraid. She was terrified.

Jeremy Elsham was sitting in the big leather armchair. He wore a black polo neck sweater instead of his customary quasi-clinical jacket. He stood up when Emma entered, stepped towards her and took her hand.

'You're sure about this, are you, Emma?' he asked, his eyes studying her face intently.

Emma nodded. She wanted to get it over with.

'Lie back. Make yourself comfortable. Put everything out of your mind.' He spoke smoothly, hypnotically. She lay on the chaise longue, trying to forget her feelings of terror, forcing herself to relax, clenching and unclenching her hands. It was working. She closed her eyes and tried to tell herself she was in bed, ready to drop off to sleep.

'You're on a beach. The sun is warm on your body and all you can hear is the sound of waves and sea gulls. You're safe and happy. There's nothing to worry about and you feel calm.'

Emma could feel the tension leaving her body as Elsham's honeyed tones droned on in her ear. His voice had become deep and muffled, like a sound heard through a wall. She was on her tropical beach, her body relaxed, listening to the gentle rhythm of the waves.

She didn't know how, but suddenly she was at Barry's side. She was wearing her wedding dress. They were getting married. She didn't feel particularly happy, just safe and secure. Her father, Joe, and her mum, Linda, were standing there beside her, posing for a photograph. They were smiling. Perhaps with relief.

Then Barry disappeared and she was with her parents in their back garden. She was about eleven years old and she was holding Flopsy, her rabbit, and Dad was taking a photograph, a happy family snap. It was a sunny day and she was laughing. They had just come back from a holiday in a caravan and a neighbour had been feeding Flopsy. The rabbit had put on weight while they'd been away and Dad said that she might be having babies. The prospect of having lots of little rabbits around made her happy. She was laughing.

But then suddenly everything went dark and she heard herself screaming.

She wasn't in the garden any more. She was younger still – about seven years old – and she was sitting on the floor rocking to and fro while Mum and Dad watched her from the door, their faces anxious, frightened. Mum took a step forward and held out her arms. Only she wasn't Mum. She was Aunty Linda. And Dad was Uncle Joe. Emma didn't want to be there. She wanted her mum. Her real mum.

Then she experienced a terror that paralysed her limbs.

114

She felt sick. And she didn't dare cry in case he heard her. She'd been going upstairs to see the big doll's house in the old nursery. She wasn't supposed to be there but she'd slipped out of bed while her mother was working in the kitchen. She'd hidden behind the big oak chair in the hall and watched as he climbed the staircase, taking the stairs two by two, carrying the gun. She'd heard the bangs from upstairs and stayed there for what seemed like hours, frozen with terror. Then she had run out into the hall and seen a thing without a face. It was covered in blood and so was she. She ran past it though the dining room to her mother. She wanted her mother.

She began to sob, pleading with her mother to wake up, to stop playing. But she didn't move. She was slumped, open-eyed, over the kitchen table, surrounded by uncooked cheese straws and vol-au-vent cases. Then Emma heard footsteps and she knew she had to hide. She crouched in the pantry, surrounded by bottles and tins, and peeped through the grille in the door. As she watched, holding her breath, a dark figure wiped the gun on a tea towel and placed it in her mother's dead hand, carefully, almost lovingly, arranging the scene. Emma could feel hot tears were rolling down her cheeks and any moment she feared that she would let out a sobbing cry that would bring the figure to the pantry. She prayed. 'Please, God, let me be quiet. Let Mum be all right.'

Then the kitchen door closed softly. The bringer of death had gone.

Emma waited a long time before she gathered the courage to push the pantry door open and run to her mother. 'Wake up. Please, Mum, wake up.' She slipped down to the floor, sobbing, and rocked to and fro on the hard stone floor. The fluorescent light above them had flickered and died and the kitchen was plunged into darkness. But she could see the moon through the window, a dim sphere peeping over the bare branches of the trees outside. The moon seemed red. As if it were stained with the blood seeping from her mother's neck.

Emma threw her head back and screamed.

Chapter Six

The savages have a great reverence for the sun above all things. At the rising and setting of the same, they sit down, lifting up their hands and eyes. Then they make a circle on the ground with dried tobacco and pray, wagging their heads and hands.

Yesterday I walked with Penelope and she confided much to me. She told me of her parentage; that she is the bastard daughter of a great lord who did seduce her mother and abandon her in her trouble. She desires her rightful position above all things and it seems the want doth eat at her soul. She confided that her husband hath a great fortune but that she bears him no love as he is uncouth and most violent towards her. She showed me marks and bruises about her person then she let me kiss her but broke away for fear of discovery.

I desire her yet she is married woman and I must pray for strength, adultery being a grievous sin.

I think of my brother at Potwoolstan Hall, left to bear the burden of the sins of which my father stood accused. Penelope says that one day I shall return to Devon with great riches. I told her not to speak of such things.

Set down by Master Edmund Selbiwood, Gentleman, on the fifteenth day of August 1605 at Annetown, Virginia.

Neil was having trouble with Chuck's pick-up. It was automatic for a start. It was also more than twice as big as the Mini he was used to driving.

He drove slowly down the unfamiliar roads, past white colonial houses with large front porches and fluttering American flags, wondering if he was doing the right thing.

The green of the trees and gardens seemed more vivid than back in Devon. The air was warmer and even the bird-song sounded different somehow here, where those West Country men and women had settled all those centuries ago. The early settlers must have thought they'd hit paradise. But at the dig they'd found the bodies of two murdered men. For some, paradise had contained a rather large serpent.

Modern-day Annetown, some mile and a half from the site of the original settlement, was a small town of some thirty thousand souls and large signs welcomed visitors to 'Historic Annetown'. Following Chuck's detailed directions, Neil drove down wide avenues past the neo-classical façade of the university and eventually arrived in the western suburbs. Here there were more flags and more white clapboard houses set in pristine green lawns. This was middle America, prosperous and proud and maybe, Neil thought, just a little smug.

As he drew up outside Max Selbiwood's address he wondered why he felt so worried about meeting an old man – someone his grandmother had known – but he couldn't come up with an answer. He stared at the house, set back behind its white picket fence and its manicured green lawn. It was a colonial house, gleaming white clapboard with windows set in the mansard roof and a swinging double seat hanging in the front porch. But there was no sign of anyone at home.

Neil's grandmother had known nothing of Max Selbiwood's life. He had been a student when she met him – or rather a student who was serving in the US Army, stationed in England during the Second World War. After he'd left, she had never heard from him again so his life after 1944 was a mystery to her. She didn't even know whether he was alive or dead. Neil sat in the pick-up, biding his time. This wasn't something he could just rush into. If he went about it the wrong way, he might give the old boy a heart attack. If indeed he had found the right Max Selbiwood.

He had the sudden, uncomfortable thought that in this community, one of the neighbours might mistake him for a wrongdoer and either call the local cops or come after him with a loaded firearm. It was probably unwise to sit there in Chuck's scruffy pick-up like a burglar on a reconnaissance mission. He would have to face Max Selbiwood now or never.

He climbed out of the driver's door and walked slowly up the neat path to the front porch. The seat was swinging gently in the breeze but there was no other sign of movement. Neil knocked on the door, a firm confident knock. He had always found that it was best to sound confident even if you were reduced to quivering jelly inside.

When he heard slow footsteps shuffling towards the front door he cleared his throat and stood up straight. The door opened slowly to reveal a tall, elderly man wearing a check shirt and pale slacks. His hair was snowy white above his long, deeply furrowed face and his intelligent blue eyes and thick white eyebrows gave him the look of a benevolent bird of prey. He regarded Neil suspiciously, waiting for him to state his business.

'I'm sorry to bother you, but are you Max Selbiwood?'

The man studied him, curious. 'Say, are you English?'

Neil nodded eagerly.

'I thought so from your accent.' Selbiwood visibly relaxed.

Neil decided to come right to the point. 'You were stationed in Somerset during the war?'

'That's right.'

'I don't know if you remember a Jean Thomas ...'

The old man smiled warily. 'Sure I remember Jean.'

Neil shuffled his feet, suddenly nervous. 'My name's Neil

118

Watson. I'm an archaeologist and I'm over here for a few weeks working on the Annetown settlement. I'm Jean's grandson and she asked me to look you up while I was here.'

'I'm glad you did. Come in, why don't you? I remember your grandmother well. We sure had some good times back then.' He sounded quite pleased that this woman from his distant past had remembered him. 'So how is Jean after all these years?'

Neil ignored the question and didn't move. He watched the old man's face. 'The thing is, Mr Selbiwood . . . This is a bit awkward.' He paused and took a deep breath. It was best to get it over with. 'She told me that you might be my grandfather.'

Jeremy Elsham sat in his office at Potwoolstan Hall. His hands were shaking as he lifted the coffee Pandora had brought him.

The words Pandora's Box popped into Jeremy's mind. He'd opened Pandora's Box. Let out demons that should have been safely shut away. He had taken Emma Oldchester back to her childhood. At first it had been fine, the usual memories of family life; holidays and pet rabbits. Then things had gone horribly wrong. When Emma was seven she had witnessed something truly terrible, so horrifying that she had curled up into a terrified snivelling ball. She had even wet herself during the session; an embarrassment to all concerned. Hardly good for the Hall's image.

Jeremy had never met anything like this before. He usually took the Beings on a quick trip through infancy before getting on to the more sexy stuff; the past lives – the Egyptian princesses or the Tudor courtiers, with perhaps the occasional First World War soldier killed in the trenches thrown in for good measure. But he had never had the chance to reach back as far as Emma's past existences. Her current one had been eventful enough.

When Emma had woken up distressed and wet he had done his best to stay calm. Then Pandora had taken her up to her room to shower and change and had reported half an hour later that Emma was feeling better but she wanted to stay in her room.

But Jeremy was worried about the demons he had unleashed. And whether Emma or her family would sue for any psychological damage the session had caused.

Perhaps it had been a mistake to include the regression therapy in the Hall's menu of attractions. Many years ago he had studied the techniques of hypnotism and he even had a framed diploma to prove it, although he never put it on display. He had hypnotised people many times with no mishaps. But now, for the first time, he feared that he was out of his depth. He stared at the portrait of the two dark, Jacobean men that hung behind his desk. They seemed to be smirking at him. Mocking him. Saying 'We told you so.'

As he sipped his coffee, preparing to go out and be charming to the Beings over afternoon tea and vegetarian snacks, he felt an uncharacteristic reluctance to face a world that had suddenly turned sour. He would be glad when Emma Oldchester left. The sooner the better.

There was a soft knock on his office door and he shouted 'Come'. He hoped that it wasn't another problem. He wasn't in the mood. The door opened slowly and Emma Oldchester stepped into the room. She looked around, her eyes large and fearful.

'Can I talk to you?'

Jeremy assumed his best avuncular expression and glanced at his watch. 'Of course. Please sit down.'

'Look, I'm sorry about ...'

'Don't worry,' he said smoothly. 'It happens from time to time ... when Beings encounter overwhelming emotions during their regression.' This was a lie, of course, but he supposed it would make Emma feel better that she wasn't the only one whose bladder had given way in all the excitement. He noticed that she was looking around the room, nervous.

'Was this ... Did this use to be the drawing room?'

'I'm not sure,' he replied, watching her face.

She pointed at the painting of the two men. 'I remember

120

that. It used to be at the top of the stairs.'

Elsham swallowed, wondering what was coming next.

'The thing is, when I was hypnotised I hoped I'd remember.'

Elsham shifted in his seat, uncomfortable. 'Remember what?'

'Who killed them. Since my regression it's been coming back ... like flashbacks.'

Elsham sat forward, his heart pounding. 'What are you talking about?'

'The murders. Here in this house.'

'When we took over this place we had it cleansed of all hostile energy.' He spoke smoothly, trying to hide the agitation he felt inside. He knew the history of the Hall: that was why he had managed to buy the place so cheaply. 'Our other Beings have sensed nothing amiss and ...'

Emma shook her head. 'You don't understand. I was living here. They said my mother killed them but she didn't. I know she didn't.'

Elsham stared at her for a few moments in horror before his curiosity got the better of him. 'Who did kill them then?'

Another shake of the head. 'I can't see his face yet.' Her eyes started to fill with tears. 'That's why I came back here. I need to remember.'

Elsham's hand crept towards the button that would summon Pandora. 'I'm so sorry, Emma. If I'd known all this, I would have advised you not to come here. You obviously find the experience of returning to Potwoolstan Hall very distressing and I'm sure it would be best if you left us. For your own good. The kind of healing we offer here isn't suitable for your particular case and ...'

'No.' Emma was surprised at how firmly the word came out. 'I want you to hypnotise me again. Just once more. Please.' She hesitated. 'A man's been telephoning me, wanting to talk to me about what happened. I said no at first but now I want to see him. I have to prove my mother didn't kill those people. Please. I'm booked in for five more days. I'm not going home.'

Jeremy Elsham assumed a fixed smile as he pressed the button that would summon his wife. Perhaps a complimentary massage would keep Emma Oldchester out of his hair for a few hours.

Wesley noticed that Steve Carstairs was looking rather pleased with himself. But then Steve was an easy man to please: a sexual conquest; a juicy snippet of information from one of his criminal contacts in a smoky Morbay bar; or a member of the ethnic minorities brought in for some petty offence. It was all the same to Steve.

It wasn't until Rachel Tracey placed the newspaper on his desk that Wesley understood that day's reason for Steve's good mood. It was a red-topped tabloid paper – the *Daily Galaxy* – and the headline read 'Police probe murder Hall link.' There was a large photograph of Potwoolstan Hall underneath.

He began to read the article. According to the author, the police were working on the theory that there was a connection between the massacre at Potwoolstan Hall in 1985 and the murder of Patrick Evans. This might well be true. But it certainly wasn't something that they wanted to be public knowledge just yet. Then Wesley glanced at the name of the article's author and everything became clear.

'Steve,' he called across the office.

Steve looked up, resentful.

'This Serena Jones who wrote this article about the Evans case. Is it the same Serena Jones who was staying at the Hall? Friend of yours, wasn't she?'

Steve's face went bright red. 'I know her.'

Probably in the biblical sense, Wesley thought, although he didn't say it. Steve's education probably hadn't included scriptural references.

Wesley turned his attention back to the article. Something had caught his eye.

'Staying at the hall at the moment is Anthony Jameston

MP, a junior minister in the Home Office, whose wife, Arbel, lived there in 1985 and discovered the bodies of her family, murdered by their housekeeper, who had later committed suicide. Is it a coincidence that her husband, tipped as one to watch in the world of politics, chose to spend Parliament's spring break at the scene of this tragedy, now reborn as an alternative healing centre?'

The question was left hanging. And it had achieved its objective of whetting Wesley's curiosity.

'Steve, what's all this about Arbel Harford's husband?'

Steve looked smug. 'It's that Charles Dodgson's real name.'

'And you didn't think to share this with your colleagues?'

Steve's face turned red. 'I was going to. Serena must have found out the stuff about his wife.'

'We could do with her here,' Wesley muttered under his breath, annoyed with himself for not checking Charles Dodgson out more thoroughly himself, embarrassed that Serena Jones had succeeded in discovering something that he should have known from the start.

When he had studied the case files he had wondered what had become of Arbel, the eighteen-year-old who had made that terrible discovery that would scar most people for life. Now he knew. She was no doubt a very wealthy women in her own right: she would have inherited the lot.

Wesley couldn't help wondering how Arbel had coped with the trauma of her family's slaughter over the years. He would like to have known where she was now and if Patrick Evans had spoken to her. And whether she was aware that her husband was staying at the scene of her darkest hour.

He sat at his desk for half an hour feeling restless, his mind on Potwoolstan Hall. Then he walked over to Rachel's desk, earning himself a sly look from Steve Carstairs. But one glance told him that she was busy. She was sifting through statements and Wesley hardly liked to interrupt her.

He scanned the office and spotted DC Darren Wentworth talking to Trish Walton. As he had only recently transferred to CID from Uniform, it was about time he had a bit more experience of CID work. Wesley summoned him over and when he told him he was going to interview a possible witness in the Patrick Evans case, Darren's eyes lit up. At least it was a change from paperwork.

Darren drove them out to Potwoolstan Hall – gaining yet more experience – or rather, giving Wesley a break. Wesley had telephoned the Hall to make certain Anthony Jameston – alias Charles Dodgson – was still there, and an irritated Jeremy Elsham had complained that there were reporters prowling the grounds. Word had got out about the Evans connection and it had the smell of a juicy story.

Wesley told Darren to put his foot down. As they drove, Wesley felt obliged to make conversation. 'How are you liking CID?'

'Very much, sir,' Darren replied, rather stiffly.

'Better than what you did before? What was it?'

'Crime prevention . . . sir.'

'Was it you who came to our house . . . told my wife to have window locks fitted?'

'Don't know, sir. Might have been.'

Wesley had run out of things to say. So he broached the more comfortable subject of work, of Patrick Evans's connection with the Potwoolstan Hall case.

'He might have been down here for a different reason,' Wentworth said, in Wesley's opinion unhelpfully.

Wesley frowned. 'Well, his hotel room was searched so his killer must have been after something he had. He wrote about famous murder cases. And an empty file on the Potwoolstan Hall case was found amongst his papers.'

'But if it was empty we can't know for certain, can we, sir?'

Wesley didn't answer. He felt mildly annoyed that Darren Wentworth, the newest recruit to Tradmouth CID was pouring cold water on his precious theories. Or perhaps he was merely voicing the doubts that were in the back of his own mind.

Wesley suddenly remembered something: something he

124

hadn't done that he had intended to do. A sin of omission. He hadn't yet contacted Evans's publishers. Perhaps they had a proposal or synopsis for the book he was working on. He cursed himself for being so inefficient.

They drove in silence until they swung into the gates of the Hall and saw a group of people by the gate. They were warmly dressed as if they were in for a long wait. Some of the bolder ones – a man with a weasel face and two young women, their hair dyed an identical shade of blond – ran alongside the car, knocking on the windows.

'Ignore them,' Wesley instructed. 'Elsham told me when I rang him that all hell had broken loose since that piece appeared in the *Daily Galaxy*. The fuss'll die down soon.'

'You think it will?' Wentworth sounded doubtful. Wesley began to regret his choice of companion. Wentworth wasn't the most cheerful and encouraging of souls.

'They'll be after another story tomorrow with twice the scandal and three times the sex,' Wesley said with a confidence he didn't feel.

He instructed Wentworth to ignore the signs that said 'No cars beyond this point' and carry on to the Hall. But, as he parked, Wesley noticed that there were yet more journalists hanging about, some with tape recorders, some with cameras. All with the keen expressions of hounds on the scent. They gave nothing away as they ran the gauntlet of questions and snapping cameras and they were relieved when a young woman in a starched white dress opened the door and took a swift look at their identification before allowing them to slip inside.

'Jeremy's expecting you,' she said with a slight lisp. She looked terrified.

The young woman seemed quite alarmed when Wesley told her they wanted to talk to Mr Dodgson. She led them to the conservatory and told them to wait.

They sat down on a pair of wicker chairs set around a low table, making sure there was a third chair for the man who was about to join them. Wesley made no attempt at conversation with his colleague. He was thinking about the coming interview and getting the facts straight in his mind. If a man uses a false name then it's a fair assumption that he has something to hide.

It wasn't long before the man who had been calling himself Charles Dodgson appeared in the doorway. He hesitated for a second then, like an actor assuming a role, he straightened his back and strode in, his hand outstretched.

'This is really most embarrassing,' he said as he shook Wesley's hand firmly. 'I suppose you know by now that Charles Dodgson's not my real name.' He took a business card from his pocket and handed it to Wesley. 'I'm Anthony Jameston. I assure you I'm not in the habit of using a false name, but I thought that it would allow me more privacy under the circumstances. The last thing I expected when I came here for some peace and quiet was to become involved in a police enquiry. All these reporters . . .'

'One of your fellow guests here was a journalist. She was investigating Mr Elsham's rather unorthodox healing methods but once she realised there was a connection between this place and the recent murder . . .'

Anthony Jameston nodded, resigned. 'Bad luck really.'

'You lied to my officers about your identity when they talked to you about the recent theft.' Wesley watched his face.

Jameston spread out his hands, a gesture of admission. 'I'm sorry about that. I didn't really know what to do for the best. I knew I hadn't stolen anything so I saw no reason to complicate matters. You do understand, don't you?'

Wesley gave him a businesslike smile and signalled him to sit. 'I believe your wife was involved in the tragedy here back in 1985. The man who was killed in the grounds was called Patrick Evans: he was a freelance writer and we think he was proposing to write a book about the case. Have you ever had any contact with him?'

Jameston took a packet of cigarettes from his pocket. 'If

126

those bastards from the press weren't there I'd suggest that we took a stroll in the grounds. They don't allow smoking in here. Or meat. Or alcohol. Bit of a hell hole really. All lentils and chanting.' He smiled and Wesley, in spite of his initial suspicions, began to warm to the man.

Jameston walked over to the nearest window and opened it. Then he pulled out a gold lighter and lit a cigarette, inhaling deeply. 'That's better,' he muttered. After a few moments he turned to Wesley. 'I suppose I'd better come clean. I did meet Patrick Evans. He rang me and said he wanted to talk to me about a book he was writing. And you're quite right; he was investigating what happened at this place.'

Wesley's heart began to beat a little faster. 'What can you tell me about him?' He felt he knew very little about their murder victim's professional life. Every little snippet of information and every impression helped to complete the jigsaw.

'He seemed a pleasant enough chap. He specialised in raking over old murder cases, especially ones he thought might have involved a miscarriage of justice.' He shrugged his shoulders. 'But we all have to make a living, don't we, Inspector?'

'Why did he contact you? Why not ring your wife?'

Jameston thought for a moment. 'I rather liked him for that actually. You see it was my wife's family who died here. And she found the bodies. She was only eighteen at the time and she's never talked about it in all the time I've known her. Evans thought it might distress her if he contacted her directly. He thought if he went through me . . .'

'I understand,' said Wesley quickly. 'So the newspaper was right? Your wife is Arbel Harford?'

Jameston nodded.

'Tell me about your meeting with Evans.'

'We met for a drink one lunchtime. He said he'd been examining the case and certain things didn't add up. The police had accepted the obvious explanation at the time but

127

he thought the housekeeper was innocent, that she had been murdered along with the family.'

'Had he any evidence?'

'He said he was getting close to the truth.'

'So who did he think killed the Harfords and Martha Wallace?'

'He didn't say. Presumably I'd have had to buy the book to find out. You know what these authors are like . . . never take kindly to giving away their endings.'

'Did Evans speak to your wife?'

Jameston shook his head. 'I told her what he'd said but she didn't want to cooperate. She said she didn't see the point in picking at old wounds.'

Wesley looked him in the eye. 'So Patrick Evans was writing about the Potwoolstan Hall case and, lo and behold, you turn up at Potwoolstan Hall. Why?'

Jameston turned towards the window and threw his smouldering cigarette end outside. Then he turned back to face Wesley. 'I've been under a lot of pressure recently. I don't want to go into details. I just needed to get away. Somewhere discreet. That's why I hit on the idea of using an alias. I needed my privacy.'

'And you're a fan of Lewis Carroll?'

'Ten out of ten, Inspector. Didn't think anybody would twig.'

'You didn't answer my question. There are a lot of exclusive health farms and clinics around. Why Potwoolstan Hall?'

'I'd heard the place had become a healing centre and after talking to Patrick Evans . . . Well, I suppose my curiosity got the better of me.'

'Did your wife know you were coming here?'

'No. I told her I was staying at a health spa in Hertfordshire. I saw no reason to upset her. But I've confessed all now. Didn't want her finding out from the papers. She took it very well, actually. I suppose I should have left when the police started sniffing around when that

128

silly woman had her money stolen.' He sighed. 'I came here for peace and quiet.'

'And because you were curious about the Hall.'

'That too.'

'Any other reason? Serena Jones told one of my officers that you had a private meeting with one of the staff here in the grounds.'

Jameston walked slowly back to his chair and sat down. 'If I could get my hands on that Serena Jones I'd cheerfully strangle her – and don't go writing that down.' He looked straight at Darren Wentworth, who was sitting, notebook in hand, waiting to note down the pertinent points of the interview. 'I thought she was a hard-faced little minx when she was staying here. I should have guessed what she was up to. But she's got it all wrong. Gwen Madeley is an old childhood friend of my wife's. I met her years ago when she called to see Arbel in London and she recognised me at once. I had no idea she worked here and I thought I ought to have a word with her in private away from the Hall. I wanted to make sure I could count on her discretion.'

'What does this Gwen Madeley do here?'

'She's an art therapist. Not that I've tried it myself. Can't draw a straight line. Gwen's known Arbel since they were children. They were inseparable until Arbel went away to school and they saw a lot of each other in the school holidays. In fact Arbel went to stay with Gwen's family after the tragedy.'

'Did Gwen say if Evans had been in touch with her?'

'As a matter of fact he did call round to see her but she wasn't able to tell him much.'

'You do know that Evans was murdered in the grounds of this Hall, down by the river?'

'Yes. I was questioned by a young constable a couple of days ago and I'm not changing my story.'

'But you didn't mention in your statement that you'd met the dead man?'

'I was only asked if I'd seen or heard anything suspicious

on a particular night. I hadn't. I told the truth.'

It was a real politician's answer. And Wesley was reluctant to let him get away with it. 'But you didn't tell the whole truth.'

'Look, Inspector, I met Patrick Evans a few weeks ago in a pub in London and I've not seen or heard from him since.' He looked Wesley in the eye. 'I can't prove that, of course. How can you prove a negative? But I swear to you, it's true.'

Suddenly Wesley found himself believing every word. But then he asked himself why. This man was obviously a consummate actor. And possibly a consummate liar. And yet his instinct told him that he was telling the truth.

'What are your immediate plans?' Wesley asked.

Jameston took the cigarette packet out of his pocket again and played with it, opening and closing the lid, taking a cigarette out then putting it back again, as though trying to fight temptation. 'Arbel said she might come down here; maybe stay with Gwen. The press soon latched on to her connection with the massacre case and when I spoke to her on the phone this morning she said she's been pestered by journalists. I offered to drive straight back but she said she wants to get away from London.'

'Gwen Madeley . . .'

'What about her?' he snapped, suddenly defensive. Perhaps they were more than old acquaintances after all.

'If we can have her address.'

Jameston hesitated. 'I believe she has a cottage near here but I've never been there so I can't tell you the address. Surely Elsham will have it.'

'She's not here today by any chance?' Wesley asked, hoping he'd be saved a journey.

'I haven't seen her. If that's all, Inspector . . .'

Wesley knew when he was being dismissed. No doubt on the way back to Tradmouth a dozen more vital questions to ask Anthony Jameston would pop into his head, but now he couldn't think of any more. He watched as Jameston left the

130

conservatory, wondering whether he had been hiding anything. Probably. Most people he interviewed had something, perhaps something quite innocent or irrelevant, that they'd rather the police didn't know about.

He looked at Darren Wentworth, who was sitting awkwardly on the edge of the flimsy wicker chair. 'Gwen Madeley next, I think.'

Wentworth said nothing. He followed Wesley out of the conservatory. When they reached the entrance hall they were met by Jeremy Elsham. There were dark rings beneath his eyes and the lines on his face, hardly visible before, were now deep furrows. The facilitator was feeling the strain.

'Is there any news on the theft, Inspector? Mrs Jeffries is talking about legal action and . . .'

Wesley put on his smoothest smile. 'I'm sure it won't be long now till we have sufficient evidence to make an arrest.' It was always best to sound confident, even when you had no idea where the next arrest was coming from. Elsham provided Gwen Madeley's address without comment and, as they left, Wesley wondered why he seemed so worried. Was it the theft, the discovery that Patrick Evans had died on his land or the recent press intrusion? Or was it something else entirely?

As they drove out, the more intrepid reporters thrust their faces against their car windows and some even made a futile attempt to run after their car. At least, thought Wesley, it would give them some exercise. Some of them looked as if they needed it.

'Now we know what it must be like to be a film star pursued by the paparazzi,' Wesley said, trying to lighten the mood. Darren Wentworth, sitting in the driver's seat, didn't smile.

Gwen Madeley's cottage was easy to find. But when they arrived there was no sign of life.

He put Gwen Madeley on his mental list of people to visit and told Wentworth to head back to the station.

*

Emma Oldchester watched from the landing as the two policemen left, hidden by the banisters, just as she had stood so often as a little girl. She wondered what they were doing there. Was it something to do with all those reporters outside? Something to do with that sleek, rather pompous man who called himself Dodgson? Or maybe they had come about her?

She had pleaded with Jeremy to regress her again but he had spoken smoothly about her not being a suitable subject. He had been afraid, she could sense it. And he had tried to fob her off with offers of massages and meditation sessions. But that wasn't why she was here. She had to know the truth about what had happened when she was seven: the truth she had erased from her memory.

As she stared down into the hall someone emerged from the door of the Beings therapy room on the right. Emma crouched down behind the banisters, hoping she wouldn't be seen.

The woman's face was so familiar. She had aged considerably, of course. And the hair was completely different. But she recognised the snub nose and the small, watchful pale blue eyes.

But was it really her? And if it was, why had she returned to Potwoolstan Hall?

Rachel Tracey slammed a copy of the local paper down on Wesley's desk. Her cheeks were flushed with righteous anger. 'Have you seen this?'

Wesley picked the paper up and read the headline. 'Police clueless.' He sighed and began to read the story beneath. 'A source close to Tradmouth CID revealed yesterday that the police are baffled by the death of author Patrick Evans whose body was found in the River Trad a few days ago.'

Wesley looked at Rachel. 'What do they mean by "a source close to Tradmouth CID?" What source?' He looked at the name at the end of the article. 'Serena Jones again.

Now why doesn't that surprise me?'

He marched to Gerry Heffernan's office, holding the paper out in front of him as though it was something dirty. He handed it to the chief inspector without a word and watched as he read. Wesley had expected a rise in the boss's blood pressure accompanied by a stream of colourful naval oaths but instead Heffernan just handed the paper back to Wesley with a sigh.

'Well, you can't fault it for accuracy, can you? It's true, Wes, we're nowhere near making an arrest. There's been no luck with local restaurants: Evans didn't eat lobster or anything else for that matter in any of them on the night he died. Nobody at the Tradmouth Castle saw anyone even remotely suspicious near his room.' He turned the cheap biro he was holding over and over in his fingers. 'Mind you, this headline could work in our favour.'

'How do you work that one out?'

'This could lull his killer into a false sense of security. Make him careless. If he thinks he's running rings round us then he might start making mistakes.'

Wesley gave a weak smile. 'You do realise who this "source close to Tradmouth CID" is, don't you?'

Heffernan grinned. 'Shall I have a word with our DC Carstairs? Tell him I'm going to roast his balls over a slow fire? Or worse still get him to sit in on one of the chief super's budget strategy meetings?'

'I think a lecture on keeping your mouth shut will suffice. He was probably trying to impress Ms Serena Jones with his inside knowledge.'

'What inside knowledge?'

'Precisely. I'll send him in, shall I?'

Heffernan nodded. 'How's it going?'

'My trip to Potwoolstan Hall with Darren Wentworth proved quite fruitful. I confirmed that Anthony Jameston MP – alias Charles Dodgson – is married to Arbel Harford, the girl whose family were murdered at the Hall back in 1985.'

'Go on.'

'Patrick Evans made contact with Jameston and they met in London. Jameston was determined not to involve Arbel. He didn't want to upset her, which is understandable. An old friend of Arbel's works at the Hall, an artist called Gwen Madeley. Jameston met her in the grounds to ask if he could count on her discretion, so he says. We haven't managed to see her yet but Jameston claims that Evans spoke to her – says she told him nothing. He swears he hasn't seen Evans since London and that he knows nothing about his death.'

'Believe him?'

'I did when he said it,' Wesley replied. 'I want to see what this Gwen Madeley has to say. It looks as if Evans was thorough. So, if Martha Wallace didn't kill the Harfords and Evans was getting close to finding out who did, we've got our motive. Whoever killed the Harfords killed Evans.'

Heffernan scratched his head. 'You've had a look at the Harford files. Any thoughts yet?'

'A few. But it would help if we knew where Evans's researches were taking him.' Wesley looked at his watch. 'I've got a call to make.'

He walked back to his desk and picked up the phone. Kirsty Evans had provided the number of Patrick's publishers. But when Wesley got through he was told that his editor was away at a book fair. He left his number and told himself that he would just have to be patient.

He heard a shuffling behind him and looked round. Darren Wentworth was standing there, looking at him expectantly. 'Did you say we were going to visit that Gwen Madeley, sir?'

Wesley looked at his watch. He wanted to study the files on the massacre again and see if there was anything obvious he'd missed. 'First thing tomorrow, Darren.'

A couple of hours later Wesley was no wiser. He felt overwhelmed by the details in the files: the players that were names without faces. It was six thirty when he left the office.

As soon as he arrived home, the front door opened to reveal Pam framed in the doorway with Amelia in her arms, striking a Madonna and Child pose for a second until Michael came dashing out from behind her, hurtled down the drive and hurled himself into Wesley's arms, chattering.

Wesley hauled the child upwards until he was sitting on his shoulders and walked into the house.

Pam smiled. 'Twenty to seven ... you're early tonight.'

Wesley detected a hint of sarcasm in her voice. 'Anything to report?' He hoped she'd have something to tell him that would take his mind off police work for a couple of hours.

'We've had yet another email from Neil.'

Wesley followed her into the kitchen with Michael still on his shoulders, hitting the top of his head and urging him to move faster. He swung the child to the floor but Michael started to complain, clinging to his legs. Pam handed Amelia to him while she turned on the heat under a pan.

'What did he say?' he asked, trying to keep hold of the wriggling baby.

'See for yourself. I've printed it out. It's in the living room ... unless Amelia's eaten it or Michael's scribbled all over it.'

It wasn't until after they'd eaten and put the children to bed that Wesley finally managed to find his way into the living room and sit down. He looked at his watch. It was eight thirty. He glanced at the telephone, praying it wouldn't ring that evening, that the station would leave him alone, before picking up Neil's email from the coffee table. He started to read.

'Hi Pam and Wes,' it began. 'Things are fine over here. Weather beautiful and scenery likewise. The dig is going well. I told you about the skeletons they found, didn't I? Both died the same way, musket ball through the head. I think I told you they

135

sent a tooth from the first skeleton off for analysis? Well the results came back today. They use this amazing technique: they direct a high intensity laser beam at a powdered sample of the tooth which vaporises and releases atoms which can identify the geology of the place where the tooth's owner was raised. Our first corpse was definitely brought up in the south-west of England and that makes it pretty certain that he was one of the first settlers who sailed from Tradmouth on the *Nicholas*. Fantastic what you can tell from just one tooth.

'You remember my grandmother asked me to find soneone for her? It was a man from Annetown who she met during the war when he was stationed over in Somerset – wartime romance, I suppose. His name's Max Selbiwood and as Selbiwood's not a common name it was quite easy. He says he wants to visit England and see my gran but I haven't told him how ill she is. Maybe I should. I'd hate him to have a wasted journey at his age.

'Max turns out to be a direct descendant of one of the first settlers, an Edmund Selbiwood who's named on the passenger list of the *Nicholas*. He was the younger son of the family who lived at Potwoolstan Hall, not far from Neston. (Isn't that the place where all those people were murdered years ago?) Max has some old family letters and documents and he's going to let me see them.

'Must go now. Got to be at the dig. We're still excavating the palisades of the original fort. Have a nice day, as they say in these parts. Neil.'

Wesley stared at the sheet of paper. Somehow he never associated Neil with touching reunions between old wartime sweethearts, Neil being the most unsentimental creature he knew. Perhaps it was something in the Virginia air.

It was strange that Selbiwood had a family connection with Potwoolstan Hall but then coincidences happen from time to time. Wesley wondered whether it was significant in any way. But how could it be? Selbiwood's connection went back centuries, a lot further back than the massacre. He was aware that he was thinking like a policeman. And he told himself to stop. He was off duty.

Pam came into the room and flopped down on the sofa. 'You've read it then? What do you think?'

'All this long-lost wartime sweetheart stuff seems a bit out of character.'

'He's always been close to his grandmother and she is very ill. Cancer, he said. Apparently she asked him to contact this man for her while he was over there.'

Wesley looked at his wife and wondered how much Neil had confided in her about his plans. And how it was that she seemed to know far more about Neil's life than he did.

Gerry Heffernan had no reason to go home. Now both his children were away at university he lived alone, answerable to nobody. But he hated the emptiness of his cottage on Baynard's Quay every time he let himself in at night. That was why he had bought himself a takeaway that evening after most of his team had returned to the bosom of their families, and went back to the office to go over the case.

It was eight o'clock and he could hear the sweet sound of the church bells wafting over the river. Practice night. As he was in the choir at St Margaret's he knew most of the bell-ringers: perhaps he would join them in the Star for a pint when they'd finished. The companionship of acquaintances in a smoky, crowded pub was better than being alone.

As he read the files he wished Wesley was there. Wesley had an irritating habit of pointing out the loopholes in his most prized theories but in spite of that, Heffernan valued his analytical mind.

He'd noticed that Wesley always made lists. Perhaps it was time he followed his inspector's example and became more organised. He spread a sheet of paper out in front of him and began to write: Massacre: where are people who featured in the original investigation?

Arbel Harford – Daughter of Edward and Mary Harford, aged eighteen. Just left boarding school.

137

Staying with friend in London at time of shootings. Travelled down to Devon next day for her mother's birthday celebrations and discovered bodies. Now married to Anthony Jameston MP, junior minister in the Home Office (he's just turned up at the Hall. Why?)

Victor Bleasdale – head gardener. Left for new job in Yorkshire the morning before shootings. Interviewed by North Yorkshire police and eliminated from enquiries. Current whereabouts unknown.

Richard Gibbons – undergardener at Potwoolstan Hall now living in Tradmouth (conviction for shoplifting). Interviewed and eliminated. Address on the Tradmouth Council Estate.

Brenda Varney – cleaner. Probably stole jewellery from the Harfords. Disappeared a couple of weeks before the killings and couldn't be traced at the time. Current whereabouts unknown.

Pauline Black – daughter of Harford employee killed in industrial accident. Dispute with Jack Harford. Alibi for time of killings. Current whereabouts unknown.

Gwen Madeley – childhood friend of Arbel Harford. Interviewed in case she'd witnessed anything unusual (she hadn't). Arbel stayed with her after the murders. Art therapist working at Potwoolstan Hall.

Dylan Madeley – Gwen Madeley's elder brother. Interviewed but never serious suspect. Numerous convictions for drugs and petty crime. He'd left home a few weeks before the murders and was living in Morbay at the time. Current whereabouts unknown.

Heffernan frowned. Dylan Madeley had a record. That's why his name rang a bell. But he'd been in Morbay at the time of the murders and he had never been considered as a serious suspect.

Heffernan flicked through the files, concentrating on the people they hadn't encountered yet. Brenda Varney had disappeared, whereabouts unknown and no alibi for the time of the shootings. Head gardener Victor Bleasdale had left Potwoolstan Hall to take up a new job in North Yorkshire the morning before the murders and had been interviewed by the police up north and eliminated from enquires. Richard Gibbons, likewise, had been interviewed and eliminated. But now he wanted to talk to them both.

It had been assumed at the time that Martha Wallace was guilty – an open and shut case – so nobody had bothered digging too deeply into alternative possibilities.

He closed his eyes and saw the blood-soaked scene that had confronted him at the Hall all those years ago. Why the dead crows? Was it to muddy the waters? Or did it hold some significance?

Then there was Martha Wallace's seven-year-old daughter. According to the files she had been taken in by relatives, far too traumatised to give any sort of statement. Heffernan found himself wondering what exactly she had witnessed. And whether those memories had ever resurfaced. Surely Patrick Evans would have tried to find her. And he wondered if he should do likewise.

But tomorrow they would pay Gwen Madeley a call. It was about time they had a clearer picture of what they were dealing with.

Gwen Madeley slumped down behind the front door of her cottage, her back braced against the wood. She had thought it was reporters at first, wanting to ask her about Patrick Evans. And about her connection with Arbel.

But now she knew who had been knocking and rattling at her windows. She had never been able to cope with

139

Dylan when he got himself into this state. And if she didn't do something about it, she knew he'd be back. He always came back.

Gwen thought about ringing Anthony Jameston. But then she hardly knew him. She had only met him once before briefly when she had called at the London house to see Arbel. When she had met him at the Hall the other day, she had found him attractive. But Jameston hadn't responded to her signals. Perhaps she had been too subtle. Perhaps that was her trouble. There had been so many times when Gwen had yearned to have someone to confide in; someone to take care of her and help her to deal with Dylan, to get him off drugs and back on his feet. A man to protect her. Even if he was Arbel's man.

Anthony had told her that Arbel was planning to come down to Devon again. It was difficult to tell what Anthony and Arbel's exact relationship was, but she did know that they inhabited a different world from the one she moved in. Theirs was the big, rich world of the wealthy and powerful and she was a small-time, small-town artist struggling to get a man in her bed and make ends meet.

But there was a bond between her and Arbel. A link that could never be broken. And Patrick Evans had wanted to dig up the past again.

Evans had asked question after question. Pushing and pushing as though he knew he was on the brink of discovering the truth.

Now Patrick Evans was dead. Perhaps he had asked one question too many.

The kitchen at Potwoolstan Hall had changed out of all recognition. It was now a therapy room, plain and white. The pantry where Emma Oldchester had hidden a few yards from her mother's dead body had been opened up and made into an alcove. At half past ten, when the occupants of the Hall had retired for the night, Emma crept downstairs and crouched there in the dark, on the exact spot, trying to remember.

140

The tension in her head, born of her frustration, had developed into a constant nagging headache. She had tried so hard to make Elsham understand why she had come. That she was there to lay the ghosts that haunted her and to clear her mother's name. But he had merely smiled: that irritating, patronising upward curve of the lips. She'd felt like punching him.

Hiding there in the pantry all those years ago, she had heard the killer switch off the radio that had masked the sound of the shots in the main house before arranging her mother's body carefully, almost lovingly. Then he had wiped the gun and placed it in her hand. It had had to look like suicide. It had needed to be right. Sometimes the killer's face swam into blurred focus for a split second, only to retreat again into the darkness. It was no good. She returned to her room on tiptoe, unsure what to do next.

The fact that there was no lock on the door of her room made her uncomfortable but there was nothing she could do about it. Unable to settle, she opened the door again and stepped out on to the landing. It was almost midnight and all the Beings were tucked up for the night but a light was still visible underneath the door of Jeremy Elsham's office. He was working late.

As she stood looking over the oak banisters she spotted someone moving across the hall towards the front door and froze. There was something furtive, yet also something familiar about the way the man moved and she watched as he opened the heavy oak door, just a cautious crack at first, then much wider to admit a woman who clutched the front of her jacket defensively as if she was nervous and afraid.

Emma's hands went up to her mouth and she took a step back. Even though she hadn't set eyes on the woman in the hall for almost twenty years, Emma recognised her at once. Arbel Harford had been beautiful then. And the years had been kind to her.

Chapter Seven

Today I walked with Penelope near to the place where the Nicholas *is moored. The captain is to set sail for England soon and I was sorely tempted to sail with him. I think often of my home at Potwoolstan Hall and of my brother yet I know that I cannot return. I must make the best of my new life in this good and fertile land of Virginia and I pray the Lord that I will have strength to endure any trials and hardships that lie ahead in the winter season.*

I think not only of the trials of the body but also those of the soul. Penelope did tell me that her husband used her ill last night, taking her against her will and beating her most grievously. She showed me her wounds and I longed to kiss the bruised flesh, to kiss away her pain. I fear where the madness of my desire for her might lead me.

Set down by Master Edmund Selbiwood, Gentleman, on the twenty-fifth day of August 1605 at Annetown, Virginia.

Wesley felt a tingle of excitement as he approached Gwen Madeley's cottage. He was about to come face to face with someone directly concerned with the massacre. And anybody with a connection with the massacre had a connection with Patrick Evans.

He was gradually forming a mental picture of what had happened at Potwoolstan Hall all those years ago. Martha Wallace had shot the elder daughter's fiancé, Nigel Armley, first with a shotgun. The noise had brought the two Harford children, Jack and Catriona, to the door of the drawing room where they had been shot with a rifle. Then the housekeeper, distraught at false allegations against her, had climbed the stairs to the main bedroom at the back of the house where she surprised Edward and Mary Harford, who were on the landing, preparing to investigate the noise, and killed them before going down to the kitchen and committing suicide. This version of events meant that Martha must have taken the trouble to steal the key to the gun cupboard from Edward Harford's desk. Then she must have taken the two firearms, realised that one wouldn't be enough to carry out the job, located the ammunition and loaded them, even though there was never any suggestion that she was experienced in handling firearms. In the circumstances, would she really have been so calm and calculating?

The more Wesley thought about the Harford case, the more he was convinced that the police had gone for the easy solution; the one the real killer, whoever that was, had wanted them to swallow.

And now the dead case had been resurrected by Patrick Evans's murder. Which meant he must have been close to the truth. Whatever that was.

'Bit quiet round here,' Heffernan observed cheerfully as they pulled up outside Gwen Madeley's cottage. 'You wouldn't think a woman on her own would want to live so far from civilisation, would you?'

Wesley didn't answer. He switched off the engine and climbed out of the car. Heffernan was right. The cottage was isolated, set back on a narrow lane surrounded by ploughed fields that would soon be full of growing crops. There were no other houses in sight. But then some people liked solitude.

The two men strolled slowly up the short path to the front door. The tiny garden was paved over, not a budding flower in sight. Perhaps Gwen Madeley was no gardener, which was something Wesley could sympathise with. Sometimes a few slabs of concrete are the only solution.

Wesley pressed the doorbell but the sound of the bell ringing inside the cottage was followed by silence.

'Looks like she's out.' Heffernan began to stroll back to the car.

Wesley walked round to the back of the house, shielding his eyes and staring into the windows. But he saw no sign of life.

The back garden was more of a courtyard, paved over like the front. At the back stood a wooden outbuilding that resembled an over-large garden shed. Wesley peeped in the large picture window and saw that it was an artist's studio: Gwen Madeley's place of work.

Wesley studied the cottage, looking for any telltale movement in the upstairs windows. He tried the handle of the back porch and when the door swung open, he stepped back in surprise. He was more surprised when he found the inner door unlocked and thought it strange that Gwen Madeley was so cavalier with her home security. As he hesitated on the threshold, he felt a knot of dread in the pit of his stomach.

Welsey decided to return to the car to report his findings and he found the chief inspector slumped in the passenger seat listening to a discussion about Liverpool's prospects in the football league on the car radio. 'She'll have gone out and forgotten to lock up, Wes,' he announced with authority. 'Don't worry about it.'

'But Anthony Jameston said she'd talked to Patrick Evans. And Evans is dead.'

Reluctantly, Heffernan switched off the radio and heaved himself out of the car, saying that he supposed it would do no harm to check, just in case. But if he shared Wesley's misgivings, he hid it well. He was going along to humour his over-anxious colleague, like a parent checking under-

144

neath a child's bed to make sure there were no monsters lurking there.

When the two men reached the back porch, Wesley drew a pair of plastic gloves from his pocket and pulled them on before opening the door. Heffernan rolled his eyes and followed him over the threshold. Once they were inside, Wesley stopped and the chief inspector almost collided with him.

Wesley looked around, noting every detail of the low-beamed, open-plan room with its inglenook fireplace at one end and its shabby rustic pine kitchen at the other. The place was clean and tidy but a pine dining chair lay on its side next to a smashed white mug with brown liquid oozing from its base. He bent down to examine it. Judging by the state of the cottage, Gwen Madeley was house proud. Surely she would have cleaned up the mess. Unless something had stopped her.

Upstairs, there were two bedrooms and a small, neat bathroom with clean, white-tiled walls. The smaller of the bedrooms contained a double bed, a chest of drawers and wardrobe but no visible detritus of habitation: a guest room. The bed was freshly made up with a blue and white gingham quilt and there was a vase of fresh daffodils on the windowsill.

The second, slightly larger, bedroom was obviously Gwen's own. The door of a large stripped pine wardrobe stood slightly ajar to reveal a colourful collection of clothes, floaty floral prints mainly. An array of bottles and lotions stood on the antique dressing table, arranged with neat precision in order of size. Bright beads hung from the mirror and a trio of old flower prints hung on the wall above the bed. It was a pretty room, a feminine room. And Wesley found himself wondering whether there was a man in Gwen Madeley's life. Apart from Anthony Jameston, that is.

'Nothing up here,' Heffernan said, making his way down the stairs. 'What about the shed at the back?'

'Studio,' Wesley corrected. 'She's an artist.'

Heffernan grunted.

'I looked through the window. No sign of her.'

145

They trailed across the back garden and Wesley tried the studio door. It was firmly locked.

Unexpectedly, Heffernan produced what looked like a set of keys from his pocket: or rather a set of long thin metal instruments of varying shapes and sizes. Wesley recognised them at once.

'Where did you get those?'

'From a burglar I arrested once. I said I'd look after them for him till he finished doing time. Funny how he never came and asked for them back.' He grinned and began to work away at the lock on the studio door, trying one after the other, jiggling the metal in the lock until it turned with a satisfying click.

'You've missed your vocation, Gerry,' Wesley said as the studio door swung open.

They stepped into the spartan, whitewashed space, well lit by a skylight and the large window that faced out on to the courtyard. There was a portable Calor Gas heater in the corner beside a paint-stained steel sink. Canvases, both finished and bare, were propped up against the walls.

A finished canvas stood on an easel in the centre of the room. The style was Impressionist, with bold brush strokes and indistinct images. The two policemen recognised the subject immediately – Jeremy Elsham seated on his black leather executive chair like a king upon a throne. Gwen worked at the Hall and the intimate style of the painting suggested that she knew Elsham well. She had captured the essence of the man.

Wesley wandered over to a large cupboard. It was locked but the chief inspector obliged with his skeleton keys. There were more canvases stacked inside. Wesley drew one out and his stomach lurched with shock. It was a vivid image of a woman slumped across what looked like a kitchen table, surrounded by the detritus of food preparation; broken eggs, flour, baking trays and wooden spatulas. Her face was turned sideways and her eyes were wide open but they were dead eyes; eyes that no longer saw. The large

146

scarlet wound on the woman's white throat had been lovingly depicted in various shades of red oils and a long black object lay on the table by her hand. A rifle.

It was an image he'd seen before in the scene of crime photographs from Potwoolstan Hall. This was Martha Wallace ... dead. He glanced at the others. More portraits of the dead, the most horrific being the depiction of Nigel Armley, the Harfords' elder daughter's fiancé, whose face had been blasted away with the shotgun.

Wesley was just about to hand them to Heffernan when he heard a voice.

'What the hell are you doing?'

Wesley swung round to face Anthony Jameston, who had the grace to blush. 'I'm sorry, Inspector, I didn't know it was you.'

Heffernan shielded Wesley from view as he pushed the pictures quickly back into the cupboard and shut the door.

'Where's Ms Madeley?'

Heffernan opened his mouth then closed it again, lost for excuses.

Wesley came to the rescue. 'We found her door unlocked. We were concerned so we thought we'd better have a look round.'

The woman standing behind Anthony Jameston stepped forward. She was probably around forty; slim with brown hair swept back off her long face in a neat ponytail. She wore an expensive leather coat over jeans and a cashmere jumper which matched her watchful blue eyes. She had aged about twenty years but Wesley still recognised her from photographs. The doe-eyed vulnerability he had noted in those old images hadn't diminished with the years.

'This is my wife, Arbel,' Jameston said, rather formally. 'We've come to see Ms Madeley. She's not at the Hall so we thought we'd find her here.'

Wesley shook Arbel's hand. It was soft and warm and her grip was firm. 'You and Ms Madeley are old friends, I believe?'

147

'That's right. I'm supposed to be staying with her for a few days.' Arbel looked anxious, as though she sensed something was wrong.

Wesley hesitated, wondering how to phrase the next question. This woman had lost her entire family under bizarre and tragic circumstances and he didn't want her to catch sight of the gruesome pictures in the cupboard. He wondered why Gwen Madeley had painted them in such bloodthirsty detail.

'I'm sorry to resurrect painful memories, Mrs Jameston, but we're investigating the death of a man called Patrick Evans. He was writing a book about the murder of your family. Your husband met him, I believe. And I'm told that he talked to Ms Madeley.'

Anthony Jameston stepped in, the protective husband. 'I really don't think we should be raking this up again, Inspector.'

But Arbel interrupted, placing a firm hand on her husband's arm. 'The police have a job to do, Tony. Patrick Evans wanted to see me but Tony put him off. I'm quite willing to help the police but talking to someone who wants to rake up the whole thing again to make money is a different matter. I didn't want to see Evans and I never met him. End of story.' The uncertainty in her eyes didn't match the confidence in her voice.

'Did your friend, Gwen, mention his visit?'

'No. She probably didn't want to upset me.' The confident mask slipped and her voice wavered a little.

'Have you any idea where Ms Madeley might be?'

'I expected her to be here. Is her car in the garage?'

Wesley glanced at Heffernan. They hadn't thought to look.

The garage was a rickety wooden structure, about ten yards away from the cottage, standing next to the entrance to a field. Wesley left the studio, leaving the boss to lock it up, hoping the Jamestons wouldn't notice his unorthodox set of keys.

148

There was a dusty window in the side wall of the garage and it didn't take long to discover that it was empty. Wherever Gwen Madeley had gone, she had gone there in her car.

The Jamestons had followed him out to the garage and were standing there expectantly, awaiting the verdict.

When he said the car was gone, Arbel looked relieved. 'She's probably gone shopping. Anthony insists on finishing his course of therapy up at the Hall.' She didn't sound pleased about her husband's stubbornness. 'But I couldn't bring myself to stay there so Gwen offered me a bed.' She looked Wesley in the eye. 'You've got to understand, Inspector Peterson, that my husband needs privacy and . . .'

'You must be upset by the recent press intrusion.'

She pressed her lips together and didn't answer.

'I understand, Mrs Jameston, I really do,' he said with unfeigned sympathy. Nobody who had lost her family like Arbel Harford had could come out unscarred by the tragedy. For all her apparent self-possession she must live with demons.

'Is it all right if I take my things into the cottage? I'm sure Gwen will be back soon.'

Heffernan spoke. 'We had a look in there, love. There's a mug smashed on the floor and . . .'

Arbel looked worried.

'Perhaps she had to go out in a hurry and didn't have a chance to clear up,' said Wesley. He looked at Gerry Heffernan, who gave an almost imperceptible shrug of his large shoulders.

Arbel put a hand on Wesley's arm, her touch gossamer light. He noticed her hands were small and pale and she wore three rings set with large diamonds that seemed too heavy for her slender fingers. 'Would you like me to look round to see if Gwen's left any hint of where she might have gone or . . .?'

'Thank you. That would be helpful.'

As they walked back towards the cottage, Wesley noted the new black Mercedes convertible parked outside. Arbel's presumably. And there was a small car parked behind it, a little red Fiat with the driver still behind the wheel. As soon as they came into view, the driver of the Fiat emerged from the car and Wesley recognised her immediately.

Serena Jones almost ran over to them, small tape recorder in hand and eager as a hound on the scent. 'Mr and Mrs Jameston. Could I have a quick word . . .?'

But Gerry Heffernan had other ideas. 'Look, love, why don't you leave these people alone?'

Serena ignored him. 'Just a quick statement, Mrs Jameston. Did you meet the murdered man? Did you meet Patrick Evans?'

Arbel Jameston hurried away, her eyes fixed ahead. Anthony Jameston's face was like thunder as he linked his arm through his wife's. It was a protective gesture. Wesley found himself wondering whether the pair had children. Somehow he thought not.

Wesley left the chief inspector to deal with Serena. He would soon get rid of her. There were times when Wesley wished he possessed Heffernan's bluntness.

He followed the Jamestons into the cottage. 'Sorry about that. It must make it very difficult for you.'

'You can say that again,' Arbel said. 'Tony's been under a lot of stress recently. There's that immigration enquiry and . . . The last thing we needed was this Evans business.'

'I understand,' Wesley said, wondering how Arbel really felt about her husband's choice of bolt hole. And how Jameston had felt when he had to tell her where he was.

'They'll lose interest soon,' Jameston said confidently, sounding as though he believed it.

Wesley hoped he was right but he suspected that a juicy story like a Member of Parliament using a false name and turning up at the very place his wife's family had been murdered had a lot more mileage in it yet.

He looked at Arbel. 'If Ms Madeley doesn't turn up by tonight, where will you stay?'

'I'm sure she'll turn up soon.' She suddenly looked

150

worried. 'I booked into a hotel last night so I could always stay there.' She thought for a moment. 'Perhaps I'd better take her spare keys, just in case there's a problem. I noticed them hanging in the kitchen. But I should stay around: if Gwen comes back and I'm not here ...' She hesitated. 'Tony wanted me to stay at the Hall. He reckoned it would do me good to lay a few ghosts but I couldn't face ...' A spasm of pain passed across her face.

Looking around Gwen Madeley's cottage for the second time, Wesley began to notice things that had eluded him on his first inspection: fresh flowers in the vases; the bright postcards pinned to the fridge with twee magnets. Wandering through into the kitchen area he noticed that a huge steel pan – the type used in restaurant kitchens – stood on the worktop. Arbel, standing behind him, saw him looking at it.

'She cooks lobsters in that. I don't know how she can do it ... boil the poor things alive. You can buy them in Bloxham still walking along the quayside.' She shuddered. Wesley supposed that Arbel Jameston, née Harford, had had enough of suffering and death to last her a lifetime.

Anthony Jameston rolled his eyes. 'Arbel's rather squeamish, I'm afraid.'

'So Ms Madeley doesn't share Jeremy Elsham's vegetarian principles?'

'Obviously not.'

Wesley wondered how long it would take Gerry Heffernan to get rid of Serena Jones. He had something to tell him. If Gwen Madeley was fond of lobster it was likely she'd cook it for guests. Patrick Evans had eaten lobster shortly before he died in the grounds of Potwoolstan Hall.

And Gwen Madeley was missing.

'That cheeky madam, Serena whatshername's confirmed that Steve's been telling her all our little secrets. I'm going to have him in my office as soon as he gets back and ask him how he fancies going back to handing out parking tickets.' Heffernan grinned wickedly. 'She kept trying to change the subject. Kept asking me if we're any nearer finding Evans's killer.'

'And are we?'

Heffernan didn't answer. The police were clueless – just like in Serena Jones's headline.

'Any word on the Madeley woman yet?'

Wesley shook his head. 'As Arbel Jameston said, it's far too early to panic. She's probably out shopping. But as she's had dealings with Evans I've circulated her description and her car registration number ... just in case.'

Heffernan slumped in his chair. He looked tired. 'Do you understand what's going on yet, Wes?'

'I think Patrick Evans's death is linked to the murders at Potwoolstan Hall. Which, presumably, means that Martha Wallace was murdered too and it was made to look like suicide. Was there any suspicion at the time that she might have been innocent?'

Heffernan shook his head. 'Not really.'

'I've been looking through the file and there were a few people at Potwoolstan Hall at the time we should be having a look at. There's Brenda Varney, the cleaner who stole the jewellery from Mary Harford and promptly disappeared. It was rumoured at the time that she had some pretty unsavoury friends. And the dead crows nailed to the doors is just the sort of theatrical touch that would appeal to a girl like that.'

'You're being very judgemental today, Wes,' Heffernan laughed.

Wesley smiled. 'Then there are the two gardeners, Richard Gibbons and Victor Bleasdale. We have an address for Gibbons – he's got form for shoplifting – but Bleasdale's whereabouts are unknown.'

'Bleasdale left the morning before the murders.' He grinned. 'You're not the only one who's been reading those files.'

'He might still be worth talking to. Who else is there?'

'Well, there's Gwen Madeley. She was Arbel Harford's mate but I can't see her having a motive, can you?'

'She might still know something; something she told Patrick Evans over a cosy lobster dinner.'

152

'What about Arbel herself? She inherited the lot, didn't she?'

'She couldn't even stand the thought of boiling a lobster alive so I can't see her cold-bloodedly wiping out her family and their housekeeper. Besides, she has a cast-iron alibi for the time of the murders. She was staying with a friend in London. She went to a party and drove back to Devon first thing the next morning: it was her mother's birthday and they were having a family party that evening. She arrived at the Hall about eleven, which is the exact time of the 999 call from the murder scene. The victims had died between nine and ten o'clock the previous night so we can safely rule her out. What about enemies of the family? Disgruntled employees?'

'Gwen Madeley has an elder brother, Dylan, who has convictions for robbery and possession of drugs. Wouldn't surprise me if he's done a bit of dealing too in his time. He left home a few weeks before the killings.'

'I wonder if he's still in touch with his sister?'

'Unfortunately, the computer doesn't tell us that so we'll just have to ask her when she turns up. A young woman called Pauline Black gets a mention in the files. Her dad died in an industrial accident at the brewery the Harfords owned. Pauline took them to court but lost the case. The Harfords' lawyer managed to convince the court that the victim had been careless and hadn't followed safety proce- dures. She'd been to the Hall to confront Jack Harford and there was a row. She was interviewed at the time but she wasn't a serious suspect.'

'I'll ask Rachel to see if she can trace her.' He sighed. 'I can't see any other likely suspects. Maybe we should be digging deeper.'

'The killer knew where the guns were kept so he'd have had to be close to the household.' Heffernan turned a pen over and over in his chubby fingers. 'There's someone we haven't mentioned yet. Not that she'd be a suspect. But she might be a possible witness.'

'Who?'

153

'Martha Wallace had a little girl. She was seven at the time and she was found in the kitchen with her mother's body. She was too traumatised to say anything. Poor kid.'

'Do we know what happened to her?'

'She was taken in by her mother's cousin and his wife.'

'Local?'

'I believe so. She'll be in her twenties now. If she's made a new life for herself I don't want to rake it all up again, but it may be necessary.' Heffernan sighed. 'Can't make an omelette without breaking eggs.'

'I'd like to leave her out of it if at all possible.'

'So would I, Wes. But, who knows, she might hold the key to this whole business. We'll have to talk to her.'

Wesley couldn't argue with that. He'd ask Rachel to see to it as soon as possible. If little Emma Wallace had stayed in the area, it shouldn't be hard to find her. But for all they knew, she could be on the other side of the world by now.

Wesley left the chief inspector's office. He had things to organise, things to check up on. Reports to write. When he came to a natural break, he looked at his watch and saw that it was almost six o'clock. How time flew when you were overworked.

His brain was spinning. He'd had no luck contacting Evans's elusive publisher and they were still waiting for Gwen Madeley to turn up. Rachel was attempting to trace Martha Wallace's daughter and Pauline Black, and she had delegated the job of finding the gardener, Bleasdale and Gwen Madeley's brother, Dylan, to Steve and Darren Wentworth. Something was bound to turn up soon.

As it was now almost certain that Patrick Evans didn't eat at any local restaurant on the evening of his death, it was just possible that Gwen Madeley had provided him with his last lobster supper. They knew Evans had spoken to her. Perhaps she'd had more to tell him so he went back. He couldn't imagine why Gwen would want to kill Evans. But he still couldn't get her criminally inclined brother, Dylan, out of his mind. Wherever he was.

154

He reached for his coat. It was time he went home. If he wanted to be any use tomorrow he needed some rest.

He was about to leave the office when Rachel caught his eye. 'I've traced Emma Wallace's foster parents – a Mr and Mrs Harper. Joe Harper was Martha Wallace's cousin and he and his wife couldn't have children of their own so the arrangement suited everybody. Mrs Harper died a couple of years ago but I've spoken to Joe Harper on the phone and he's given me Emma's present address. He's asked us not to bother her unless it's absolutely necessary. He said they never talked to Emma about what happened and she never spoke about her natural mother or her life at the Hall. He and his wife reckoned it was best that way.'

'He could be right. If she's erased the memories, I'd be reluctant to stir them up again.' Wesley knew when he was out of his depth. It would be best if Emma, when they found her, was interviewed by an expert – someone who knew how to handle such delicate situations. 'Did Harper mention Patrick Evans?'

'Yes. He said Evans phoned him a few times but he refused to meet him. And he told him to stay away from Emma.'

Wesley raised his eyebrows. 'In that case I'd better have a word with Mr Harper. When I've got a minute.

When the telephone on Wesley's desk began to ring he hesitated, wondering whether to leave it and make his way home or answer it and risk being home late ... again. He flung his coat down and picked up the receiver. For all he knew it could be important. It could be the breakthrough he was waiting for.

He was surprised to hear Kirsty Evans's voice on the other end of the line. He had almost forgotten her existence.

'Inspector Peterson? This is Kirsty Evans.' She spoke tentatively, as though she wasn't quite sure whether she was doing the right thing.

'How are you, Mrs Evans?'

'OK.' From the tone of her voice this was a lie.

155

'What can I do for you?' He put on his most sympathetic voice, the one he knew instinctively that his parents used when dealing with their patients, particularly the ones that had been through a bad time.

'I've been sorting out Paddy's clothes. I'm sending the good ones to Oxfam. I thought it was the right thing to do.' The words came out quickly, as though she'd been rehearsing what she was going to say. Then there was a pause while she collected her thoughts. 'I looked in all his pockets to make sure he hadn't left anything ...'

'You found something?' Wesley tried not to sound too eager.

'Yes. A list of names and addresses. Just scribbled. I don't know if it's any use but I thought I'd better tell you.'

Wesley took a deep breath, telling himself to be patient. 'Thank you. You did the right thing. Have you got the list there?'

Kirsty recited the contents of the list her late husband had made, her voice shaking slightly. The experience of clearing out his most personal things had clearly upset her. Wesley wrote quickly, stopping Kirsty in mid-flow from time to time so that he could catch up and to check spellings.

'Are you all right?' he said gently when she had finished.

'Yes. Of course I am.' Her confident words didn't convince Wesley. 'Look, I have to come down to Devon again tomorrow to make some arrangements ... about Patrick's body and ... I'll see you then, shall I?'

Wesley heard himself saying yes, he'd meet her for lunch. They could have a long talk. It wasn't until he put the phone down that he started to doubt the wisdom of acting as a shoulder to cry on. Perhaps he should have passed her over to Rachel. His sister, Maritia, had always accused him of being too soft. Probably not a good trait in a policeman.

He looked down at the names and addresses he had copied down and felt a glow of satisfaction. Patrick Evans

156

had traced the gardener, Bleasdale, to an address in North Yorkshire. Mr Joe Harper, Martha Wallace's cousin, was on the list and there was an address for an Emma Oldchester on an estate of new houses on the outskirts of Neston. Emma: Martha Wallace's daughter.

Richard Gibbons was there too, as was Gwen Madeley. Dylan Madeley's name was there but there was no address for him. Arbel Jameston, he noticed, didn't feature on the list at all.

There were a few more names without addresses; names which, according to Kirsty were followed by a large question mark. The first was Brenda Varney, the light-fingered cleaner: her whereabouts were still a mystery. And the second was Pauline Black, the dead employee's daughter. There was also a Jocasta Childs. Her name was followed by a large tick. What this meant, Wesley hadn't the faintest idea.

He looked at his watch. If he headed for home now, there was a chance that his supper wouldn't be congealing in the microwave. He left the office, giving Rachel Tracey a shy smile on his way out.

'I've seen an advert for a flat,' she said when he was halfway out of the door.

He turned. 'Where is it?'

'Above an art gallery on Armada Street. Two bedrooms.'

Wesley noticed that Darren Wentworth was watching him. 'I'd better go,' he said quickly, avoiding Rachel's eyes.

'Are you ready, Max?' Somehow Neil couldn't bring himself to address Max Selbiwood as Granddad.

The old man donned his baseball cap with a flourish and grinned. 'Ready as I'll ever be.'

They climbed into Chuck's pick-up and drove through the suburbs of New Annetown, past white clapboard houses and a little white colonial church, straight off a picture postcard. Everything appeared ordered and polished in this green and white landscape. Even the reconstructed first settlement with

157

its little thatched houses had seemed tidy and well organised and Neil wondered how accurate this was. In the seventeenth century there would have been dirt, disease and fear. And social envy as the artisans did all the work and the gentlemen did all the talking in their brave new world.

The sun was shining down as usual as they reached Old Annetown. Coming from England, Neil regarded constant good weather as a novelty and he said as much to Max. But Max didn't reply, he was too busy looking out of the window, as excited as a child about to pass through the gates of Disneyland.

Neil led Max past the exhibition centre and laboratories and on to the site of the main excavation. He would save the reconstructed settlement and the replica of the *Nicholas* till last.

Hanna Gotleib was taking photographs but when she spotted Neil she raised a hand in greeting and Neil waved back.

'Friend of yours?' Max asked with a twinkle in his voice.

'Colleague.'

But Max was grinning. He was a perceptive old boy and Neil knew that he was in danger of underestimating him. 'Yeah, right. Sure she is.'

Neil turned the conversation to archaeology. 'They found two skeletons; both shot with musket balls. Seems that life in old Annetown wasn't all hymn singing and growing vegetables. You all right, Max?'

The old man's face had turned so pale that Neil was worried for him. Perhaps he had some underlying illness he hadn't mentioned.

'Have you seen enough here? Do you want a coffee or something?'

Max turned to him. His blue eyes were watering and the frown lines on his face had deepened into furrows. He had seemed sprightly for his age before. But now he seemed as old as Neil's grandmother, his old sweetheart. And her life was ebbing away slowly and painfully.

158

'Something the matter?' Neil asked, fearing the answer.

Max began to walk away from the area of the dig, away from prying eyes and ears, towards the woodland that stood between the dig and the reconstructed settlement. He stopped and sat down on one of the wooden benches provided for visitors. Neil sat down beside him, waiting for some explanation. It was a few seconds before Max spoke.

'Maybe I shouldn't have come.'

'Why? What is it?'

When Max didn't answer, Neil turned to face him, wondering if everyone who discovered a close long-lost relative felt like this; the urgent desire to know them better; to know for certain where you came from. Neil had never been one for family. He kept his parents happy by regular appearances at Christmas and landmark occasions but he knew he wasn't a particularly devoted son. He had always found his work more satisfying than human relationships. But his grandmother was an exception: he had always made time to go and see her. Now he had found her old lover for her; the man whose child she had borne, and he suddenly felt that he was out of his depth.

'Let's walk.' Max stood up and made for the reconstructed township. Neil walked by his side in silence. Eventually they reached the Anne River and the wooden jetty – or dock as Hannah Gotleib called it – that jutted out into the water. Moored there was the replica of the *Nicholas*.

They stood side by side on the jetty staring at the ship. By modern-day standards she was small, but she had made it across the Atlantic Ocean. It couldn't have been a comfortable voyage and the people on board wouldn't have known what awaited them when they landed. They had either been incredibly brave or incredibly foolhardly and Neil wasn't sure which.

Neil was so engrossed in his own thoughts that the sound of Max's voice beside him made him jump. 'You know I'm descended from one of the guys who came over on this ship – Edmund Selbiwood?'

159

'Yeah.'

There was a long silence, as if Max was making some sort of decision.

'What is it?'

But Max shook his head. 'Nothing. Forget it.'

'I'd like to know. I'm interested.'

But Max had turned away.

Just before breakfast Emma lay fully dressed on her soft bed, so much more comfortable than the one she shared with Barry back home. Vague details were returning now, like things viewed underwater in the dark. The figure with the gun swam in and out of focus. And the shadowy, half-perceived face didn't make any sense.

Jeremy Elsham was still refusing to hypnotise her again, instead placating her with various therapies: massages and meditations which left her feeling pampered and relaxed, almost as if she was in a deep, dream-filled sleep. But she needed to know what happened. Somehow she had to persuade Jeremy to take her back again to that day. She couldn't leave the Hall without proving her mother's innocence once and for all.

Seeing Arbel there the previous night puzzled her. One of the other Beings had said that the smooth-spoken man who called himself Charles Dodgson was really Arbel's husband who was a Member of Parliament. It was a strange coincidence, she thought, that he should choose to stay in the place where his wife's family died and she wondered why he was really there. Perhaps he, like her, was on a quest for the truth. Perhaps hers weren't the only memories Patrick Evans had awakened.

She toyed with the idea of speaking to him. But if she told him who she was – that she was the daughter of the woman everyone thought had slaughtered his wife's family – she wasn't sure how he'd react. It was probably best to say nothing.

She wondered how Arbel had felt when she entered the

front door again after all those years. Had she experienced the terror Emma had felt?

But it wasn't only Arbel who occupied her thoughts at that moment. There was the impostor to consider. She had waited long enough. It was time to face her.

Emma swung her feet down on to the thick carpet and walked slowly to the well-appointed en suite bathroom with its glossy white surfaces and soft fluffy towels. She stared at her face in the mirror. Emma Wallace, daughter of Martha Wallace and an able seaman called John Wallace who had died on a training exercise when Emma was still a baby. She had suppressed the memories until now; seen herself as the child of her devoted foster parents, her mother's cousin and his wife who had loved and cherished her as if she had been their own. But now it was time to face the truth.

She crept out of her bedroom, shutting the door behind her, slinging her handbag over her shoulder – with a thief about she wasn't taking any chances – before making her way downstairs.

She knew where the impostor's room was. As there was no lift, some of the ground-floor rooms had been set aside for people who couldn't manage the stairs. Emma raised her hand to knock, but then thought better of it. She turned the handle and opened the door.

The woman inside the room looked up, an expression of horror on her face, as if she been discovered naked in the shower by a stranger. But Mrs Carmody was fully dressed. She was sitting in her wheelchair by the dressing table at the far side of the room, next to an open suitcase. White underwear spilled out of the drawer and she appeared to be packing.

'Brenda?' Emma said, her eyes fixed on those of Brenda Varney, one-time cleaner to the Harford family . . . and for so long vanished off the face of the earth.

Chapter Eight

She has bewitched me. It must be so for I desire her beyond reason. I fear what would befall us if her husband discovered our passion, and yet I must think on it. All our sins have grave consequences and we cannot escape the Almighty's wrath on the Day of Judgement. But it may be that my soul is already lost to Satan.

Penelope speaks wildly, saying that her husband's brother, Isaac, has sworn love for her. There is no love between the brothers and she talks of Isaac's threats to kill her husband. And if he will kill Joshua Morton, his own blood, it may be that he would kill me also.

I tell her not to entertain such foolish fancies. And yet I am afraid for it is a simple matter to disguise murder as accident in this perilous land. Perhaps it must be that I return to England when the ship comes again with supplies and seek my fortune in some part of England far away from Potwoolstan Hall. But how can I leave Penelope to the mercy of violent men?

Set down by Master Edmund Selbiwood, Gentleman, on the third day of September 1605 at Annetown, Virginia.

*

At the age of seven Emma had been fascinated by the clothes and make-up Brenda Varney wore; by her boasts of an exciting future in London with pop stars and models. Brenda had taken her up to Mrs Harford's bedroom when the family were out and caked her face with grown-up make-up. When Emma's mother had seen the finished result she had been furious: she had shouted and made her scrub the make-up off.

Brenda looked so different now from that hard, sly, glamorous creature who had flashed through her childhood like a bright firework through a dark sky.

The woman stared at Emma. The armpits of her red blouse were dark with sweat and her eyes were wary.

'I'm Emma, Brenda. Remember? Martha's little girl. I must have been seven when you last saw me.'

'You're mistaking me for someone else. My name's not Brenda.'

'How come you're using the wheelchair, Brenda? What happened?'

'I had a car accident. And my name's not Brenda. You've made a mistake.' The woman spoke slowly, patiently, as if humouring a child.

'My mum nearly got the sack because of you. She lay on her bed crying her eyes out. She never stole anything in her life. And she never lied.'

Emma closed the door behind her and as she stepped further into the room, Mrs Carmody backed her wheelchair away slightly, as if she feared Emma was deluded and might do her some harm. Emma felt suddenly powerful: nobody had ever been afraid of her before. It was strangely liberating.

'Jeremy regressed me. He took me back to when it happened. Did Patrick Evans find you? Did he talk to you?'

The older woman had regained her composure. 'I don't know what you're talking about, love. My name's Beatrice. Beatrice Carmody. Not Brenda.'

Emma twisted her wedding ring round, suddenly

163

confused. Perhaps she'd got it wrong. Perhaps this wasn't Brenda after all.

Mrs Carmody smiled patiently. 'Look, I'm just here for a bit of peace and quiet like everyone else. Why don't you just go and get some rest, my love. You're mistaking me for someone else. Sorry,' she added as Emma started to cry.

Barry Oldchester looked uncomfortable. But then most people would if the police turned up unannounced. He sat on the sofa and stared at Wesley and Rachel, his forehead wrinkled with concern.

'Your wife's name's come up in one of our enquiries, Mr Oldchester.'

Barry Oldchester frowned and played with his wedding ring. 'How do you mean?'

'Can we speak to her?'

'She's not here. She's gone away for a few days.'

'Have you heard of a man called Patrick Evans?'

He straightened his back, suddenly alert, like an animal scenting danger. 'He kept ringing Em. Said he wanted to speak to her.'

'What about?'

'No idea.'

'Could it have been about the murders at Potwoolstan Hall in 1985?'

Oldchester didn't answer.

'The woman who murdered the family at the Hall before committing suicide was called Martha Wallace and she had a seven-year-old daughter called Emma. Emma was adopted by relatives called Harper who lived in the area. Was your wife's maiden name Harper?'

Oldchester nodded and took a deep breath. 'OK. Evans, kept calling Em's dad, Joe, but Joe wouldn't talk to him and he told him not to bother Em. Not that he took much notice.'

'Did your wife ever talk about what happened at Potwoolstan Hall?'

164

'No.'

'Did she meet Patrick Evans?'

Oldchester shook his head. 'No. Like I said, he kept ringing up, pestering her, but she never met him. Didn't want to.'

'Did you meet him?'

'No. I spoke to him on the phone but I never saw him. I just wanted him off our backs.'

Wesley could understand this. But he wondered how Oldchester would have reacted if Evans hadn't taken no for an answer. 'We'd like to speak to your wife, Mr Oldchester. Can you tell us where she is?'

Barry Oldchester took a deep breath. 'Potwoolstan Hall. It's a healing centre now.' He said the words with heavy irony. 'She's spending a week there. Costing a bloody fortune.'

Wesley sat for a few seconds, stunned. 'So she's actually at the Hall now?'

'I kept telling her it was a stupid idea. Mad.' He hesitated. 'There's something you should see.' He stood up and walked to the door. Wesley and Rachel followed, curious.

Oldchester led them upstairs and opened one of the bedroom doors. 'It's in here,' he said, standing aside to let them in.

Wesley and Rachel stepped into the room. Doll's houses stood on deep shelves around the walls and a long trestle table along one wall was cluttered with tiny paint pots, brushes, sandpaper and small squares of wallpaper. The houses were of all styles; modern, Georgian, thirties suburban, country cottages; some finished and some in various stages of decoration. But one, set low down near the door, was different from the rest. The exterior was painted to look like ancient stone with Dutch gables and Tudor windows. It was Potwoolstan Hall in miniature.

'Go on. Open it up,' Oldchester said, almost in a whisper.

Wesley obeyed. But when the front of the house swung

open he stepped back, shocked. It was all there, right down to the wallpaper and furniture. The small bodies lay slumped in the appropriate rooms and the blood was splashed up the walls, just as it was in the gruesome photographs Wesley had seen. Emma Oldchester had made a miniature reconstruction of the crime scene.

She had been found clinging to her dead mother's body. Perhaps she had felt compelled to make this reconstruction, to keep re-enacting the events until she hit on the truth – whatever that was. That was why she had gone back, to discover what had really happened. But Wesley's instincts told him that she might be playing a dangerous game.

'I see what you mean,' Wesley said.

'Since that Evans started ringing it's become like an obsession. I'm worried sick about her. They do something called regression at that place: hypnotise them to make them remember their childhood and that. She's desperate to remember, you see. She wants to know what really happened: she wants to know that her mum didn't kill all those people. I tried my best to stop her going but short of imprisoning her, what could I do?'

'I'm sure she'll come to no harm there, Mr Oldchester,' he said with a certainty he didn't feel. Evans had met his death in the Hall grounds so perhaps he needed to speak to Emma Oldchester sooner rather than later.

Wesley spent ten minutes trying to persuade Oldchester that it wouldn't be a good idea to go to Potwoolstan Hall and drag Emma home. Eventually, he seemed to acquiesce but as he and Rachel took their leave, the man looked as if he had all the troubles of the world on his shoulders.

'What did you make of that doll's house?' he asked Rachel as they drove.

'I don't know. Emma was traumatised at the time and, according to the files, the psychologists who saw her said that she'd blotted the whole thing out. But she must have witnessed something.'

'And now she's gone back to Potwoolstan Hall. You'd

166

imagine that wild horses wouldn't drag her back into that place.'

'I think we should make sure she's all right; the sooner the better.'

Rachel said nothing.

'So how's the flat-hunting?' Wesley asked, making conversation. 'Did you go for the one in Armada Street?'

'I'm still trying to decide. Why don't you help me make up my mind?' A smile played around her lips. 'Come with me and have a look at it. There's a café next door. We can have a coffee before we go to see Emma.'

'That'd be nice,' Wesley stuttered, feeling like a man who's just about to dive into deep and treacherous waters and doesn't know how to turn back. He decided a sudden change of subject might save the situation. 'Did I tell you Neil Watson's in the States? He's looked up some old wartime sweetheart of his grandmother's. And it turns out this man's a descendant of the family who built Potwoolstan Hall.'

'The Harfords?'

'No, not the Harfords. They didn't buy it until the nineteenth century. This was a family called the Selbiwoods. One of the younger sons went off to seek his fortune in Virginia in the seventeenth century, hence the connection with Neil's Mr Selbiwood.'

Rachel smiled. She had learned to treat Wesley's interest in things historical with polite indifference. 'I'm looking forward to that coffee,' she said meaningfully.

Wesley didn't reply.

Wesley made an excuse not to visit the flat with Rachel. It might have been quite an innocent invitation but he sensed a bat squeak of danger. Just to be on the safe side, he told her he'd have to forgo the coffee because he needed to check on something back at the station before they talked to Emma Oldchester. He was relieved when he found Gerry Heffernan in his office, eager to impart some fresh information.

'Our trusting jeweller, Jack Wright, rang to say that "Mr Smith" has been to see him again. Offered him a very nice ring, which fits the description of the one stolen from Mrs Jeffries, and left it with him for valuation. Smith's coming back.' He grinned. 'And when he does, we'll be waiting for him.'

'That should improve our clear-up rate. I've just been to see Emma Oldchester's husband. Patrick Evans was trying to make contact with her but the husband claimed that he never met him and neither did she. Oldchester showed us a doll's house Emma had made: only this was no ordinary doll's house. It was a reconstruction of the crime scene at Potwoolstan Hall.'

Gerry Heffernan scratched his head, lost for words.

'Emma was on the list of people Evans intended to see while he was down here. She's Martha Wallace's daughter. And she's at Potwoolstan Hall right now. She's signed in to Elsham's healing centre.'

Heffernan caught on quickly. 'Patrick Evans died in the Hall grounds. And if it wasn't Martha Wallace who killed those people ... if it was somebody else and they're still around ...'

'If the killer thinks Emma witnessed the murders, she could be in danger.'

'We'd better get down there, make sure she's OK. The Nutter's just summoned me to his office.' Heffernan looked at Wesley and winked. 'Mind if I come with you?' He stood up, knocking a pile of papers to the floor.

The two men hurried from the office, Heffernan getting his coat into an undignified tangle as he struggled to find the correct sleeves, and as Wesley drove to Potwoolstan Hall, he hoped they'd find Emma Oldchester safe and well so that his mind would be put at rest. But he had an uneasy feeling as he passed through the gates that things might not be quite that simple.

Jeremy Elsham's wife, Pandora, greeted them at the front door, her face stiff with plastic surgery and disapproval.

'This is starting to feel like police harassment,' she said, indignant. 'I don't know what else we can tell you. Nobody here knew that man who died. Anybody can get to that river bank . . .'

Wesley stopped her. 'We want a word with one of your guests. Can you let Mrs Oldchester know we're here?'

Pandora stared at him as if the request was some terrible affront. 'The Beings come here for healing and quiet. They don't pay good money to be disturbed every five minutes by . . .'

Gerry Heffernan stepped forward. 'Look, love, this is a murder enquiry. Just get her, will you?'

This did the trick. Pandora, her face taut, strutted off towards her husband's office, her heels clicking angrily on the hard wood floor.

Wesley and Heffernan followed her into the office uninvited and found her consulting a chart on the wall. 'She's in the meditation room for one of Jeremy's workshops at the moment.'

'Thanks, love,' said Gerry Heffernan cheerily. 'Just point us in the right direction.'

Wesley peered at the chart. He noticed that Emma had been down for aromatherapy first thing that morning. Then two hours later, meditation. The Beings had a busy and organised schedule.

'I'll come with you,' Pandora said frostily. 'You can't just barge in there.'

She shut the office door firmly behind her and strode through the hallway into a comfortable sitting room that would grace any country house hotel, then she led them out into a wide corridor where one of the closed doors bore the legend 'Meditation Room in use. Please wait.'

But Gerry Heffernan had never been one for obeying orders. Before Pandora could stop him he flung the door open. When he stepped inside he was greeted by the curious stares of a trio of cross-legged Beings who appeared more uncomfortable than serene. Jeremy Elsham, seated in the lotus position on a raised dais, untangled his limbs and stood up, managing somehow to maintain his dignity.

'What is the meaning of this?' he hissed in a voice that made Wesley suspect he might have been a headmaster in some previous incarnation.

'We're looking for Emma Oldchester,' said Gerry Heffernan, scanning the upturned, perplexed faces. 'Anyone know where she is?'

'How dare you disturb our meditation. This intrusion has completely disrupted our positive energy. I've a good mind to complain to your superiors.'

But Heffernan was unrepentant. 'We're investigating a murder. Now I'll ask you again. Does anybody know where Emma Oldchester is?'

Jeremy Elsham had been put in his place. Obviously unused to being crossed, he fell into a silent sulk. The three Beings on the floor, all identically dressed in what looked like blue towelling pyjamas, looked at each other and after a few seconds of silence one of them stood up.

'I saw her going out about half an hour ago. She was walking towards the woods.' The man who spoke was small with red hair and an earnest frown. He glanced nervously at Jeremy Elsham as if afraid he'd earned himself a detention from the headmaster for speaking out of turn.

'Was she alone?' Wesley asked.

The man nodded.

'And this was half an hour ago?'

Another nod.

Wesley addressed Jeremy Elsham, who was fuming silently on the dais. 'Were you expecting her at this session?'

'Yes. Her name was down.' Elsham looked uneasy, as though the subject of Emma Oldchester worried him in some way.

'Then we'd better find her.' He turned to leave the room, then turned back. Just one more thing, Mr Elsham. Did you hypnotise Mrs Oldchester?'

There was no mistaking it. Elsham was frightened. 'She wasn't a suitable subject. She became disturbed.'

'What happened?'

'I have my Beings' confidentiality to consider, Inspector,' he said, glancing at the trio whose meditation had been so rudely interrupted.

Wesley knew he was holding something back. He would talk to him in private once they'd made sure Emma was safe.

'Let's get some uniforms over there,' Heffernan whispered as they walked back to the entrance hall. 'I want her found.'

'Maybe she's decided to do the sensible thing and go home,' said Wesley. 'Or perhaps she's decided to go shopping and take a break from all that earnestness.'

'It'd get on my nerves ... especially with Sir in charge. That Elsham reminds me a bit of my old headmaster,' Gerry Heffernan added as he marched towards the entrance.

Emma Oldchester leaned against a tree. She had vague, pleasant memories of these woods. Her mother had brought her here for a picnic once. And further on, by the water, was the little shingle beach where they had spread the tartan blanket. She had dipped her bare toes in the water and her mother had told her to be careful. The currents were dangerous.

Emma left the shelter of the trees and walked to the river's edge, where she stood gazing at the far bank, warmed and comforted by the memories of her early childhood. When she closed her eyes she saw a fleeting image of her real mother: her face, the way she smelled of lavender polish and cooking; the impatient tone of her voice when she told her off.

But the day her world had collapsed was still a dark blur. Her mind had blocked out the horror but snatches were emerging bit by bit from the shadows. She had a vague half-memory of wandering amongst the dead and tripping over a man in the hall who had no face and of her feet and nightdress being covered in his sticky, warm blood.

Then there was the man with a gun; the man she had to hide from. She had glimpsed his face when Jeremy took her back. But what she had seen was impossible.

Someone was calling her name. She turned slowly. It was a policeman and she could see the relief on his face.

'We've been looking all over for you, my lover,' the plump young constable said, his Devon accent warm and somehow comforting. 'Our chief inspector's worried about you.'

Emma Oldchester allowed herself to be led back to the Hall, to the bright conservatory where the young constable had told her the chief inspector was waiting.

She entered the conservatory, experiencing a sudden feeling of panic but she walked on, her hands clenched by her side, staring at the two men who had just stood up to greet her. One was a good-looking young black man with gentle, intelligent dark brown eyes. The other a rather overweight and shabby middle-aged man who looked as though he had dressed in the dark that morning, pulling shirt and trousers from a heap on the floor. Neither man looked particularly intimidating. But the fact that they were policemen made her nervous.

When they invited her to sit down, she perched on the edge of a wicker chair, as if preparing for a swift escape. The shabby one, who introduced himself as Chief Inspector Gerry Heffernan, told her they'd spoken to Barry about Patrick Evans. Quietly, unemotionally, Emma confirmed her husband's statement, rather surprised at how relaxed she was beginning to feel. Patrick Evans had rung her several times but she'd refused to see him. She added that Evans had also rung her father and that he too had refused to get involved with his research. Let the past remain buried.

'You are Martha Wallace's daughter?' the younger man

172

asked softly, almost in a whisper.

Emma nodded, still outwardly calm but now experiencing slight feelings of panic. 'And before you ask, I don't remember what happened. The psychologist I saw at the time told my parents that I'd probably never remember. That it was something my mind couldn't deal with so I blotted it out. It's common in cases of trauma, he said. But now I want to remember, that's why I came here.'

'Do you think that's a good idea?'

She looked Wesley in the eye. 'I won't change my mind. I can't go through life wondering whether my own mother was capable of murdering all those people like that. They say bad blood runs in families, don't they? I've got to know. Do you understand?'

She stood up, straight-backed, with the tragic dignity of an aristocrat going to the guillotine in the French Revolution. 'I have to go for my massage now.' Without another word she left the room. Wesley had wanted to ask her about the doll's house. But that could wait.

He would be keeping an eye on Emma Oldchester.

Wesley began to walk to the car, Heffernan following behind.

'That Emma didn't tell us much.' The chief inspector sounded disappointed.

'I didn't really expect her to. I'd like to talk to this Joe Harper, her foster father: he's Martha Wallace's cousin and, presumably, he knew her well.'

'Shall we pay him a call next?'

'I don't really want to turn up unannounced.' He looked at his watch. 'And there's someone else on Evans's list I want to see. We've got an address for Richard Gibbons. He was under-gardener at the Hall at the time of the killings. And it's not far.'

They found Gibbons's house nestled amongst the huddle of cream-painted council houses on the outskirts of Tradmouth. As they pulled up outside, Wesley noted the

173

neat and colourful front garden behind the fancy wrought-iron gate and the round black satellite TV dish stuck to the front of the building like a medal on a military chest. The council had recently put in new plastic windows and painted the pebbledashed exterior so the place had a neat, well-cared-for look. Perhaps Gibbons was house proud.

Gibbons himself answered the door. He was an unprepossessing man with receding, greasy hair and a shiny face. His short-sleeved grey T-shirt revealed a pair of pale, spindly arms and Wesley found it hard to imagine him wielding a spade. He also had sly, watchful eyes and a brief flash of apprehension passed across his face as they introduced themselves.

Gibbons led them through into the living room where the floral three-piece suite clashed alarmingly with the orange swirls on the carpet. Interior design obviously wasn't Gibbons's strong point. Wesley sat down.

'I didn't know if you'd come,' said Gibbons. 'They said on the news he'd been murdered.'

Wesley and Heffernan looked at each other. 'You're talking about Patrick Evans, I presume?' said Wesley.

The man nodded.

'So you met him?' Heffernan asked impatiently.

'Er, not exactly. I arranged to meet him in the Fisherman's Arms last Saturday night. Then he rang again – on the Saturday morning it was. He said could we change it 'cause he was meeting someone that night and it was the only night they could make it. I said I'd meet him on Monday instead. I went there, only he never turned up.'

'How did you arrange the meeting? Presumably you didn't know what he looked like?'

'He described himself and said he'd be carrying a copy of the *Guardian*.'

Wesley smiled. 'Very cloak-and-dagger. Did he say what he wanted to talk about?'

There was a slight, almost imperceptible, hesitation. 'He said he wanted to talk about the killings at Potwoolstan

174

Hall. I told him I couldn't help him but ...'

'What is it, Richard? Who are these people?' The voice was female, surprisingly deep while Gibbons's had been high.

Wesley turned round. An old woman was standing in the doorway. She was small, under five feet tall, with curly grey hair and the face of a malevolent monkey. Her body was rotund and she reminded Wesley of a barrel in the loose brown dress and cardigan that stretched across her chubby frame.

She glowered at Wesley. 'I don't want any of your sort in my house. Get out. Go on. Get out.'

Gibbons at least had the grace to look embarrassed. 'You can't say that, Mother. They're policemen. They've come to see me. Go back upstairs.'

'He's never no policeman.' She pointed at Wesley like some wicked fairy issuing a curse. 'He's a bloody ...'

Gibbons cut her off. 'He's a policeman. Now go upstairs,' he said, giving Wesley an awkward sideways glance as he hustled his mother out of the door and up the stairs.

'Sorry about that,' he said when he returned. 'She's a bit senile these days and ...'

'I understand,' said Wesley coolly. He encountered racism from time to time but the directness of the old woman's hatred had shaken him a little. He glanced at Gerry Heffernan, who was standing there with his mouth hanging open, unsure how to react to the situation.

Wesley took a deep breath. He was there to do a job and it was time he got on with it. 'I understand you were under-gardener at Potwoolstan Hall at the time the Harford family were killed.'

Perhaps it was the embarrassment Gibbons obviously felt about his mother's behaviour that suddenly rendered him more cooperative.

He leaned forward eagerly. 'Yeah. That's right.'

'According to your statement you were working in the

grounds when you heard Arbel Harford scream. You ran into the house and found her there in a state of shock. And then you saw the bodies.'

'Yeah. It was horrible. Like something out of a film.'

'And where had you been the previous night, when the murders took place?'

'I was out at the cinema with a mate till ten thirty then I went straight home. The police checked it out at the time.'

'Do you remember a girl called Brenda Varney who cleaned at the Hall?'

A shadow of panic passed over Gibbons's greasy face for a split second, then disappeared. 'There was someone called Brenda – used to clean. Didn't know her very well.'

'Any idea where we might find her now?'

He shook his head. He was lying. And he wasn't very good at it.

'What about the other gardener, Victor Bleasdale?'

'He left just before it happened. Went up north.'

'Do you know where he is now?'

'No idea.'

They questioned Gibbons for another five minutes but he didn't tell them anything they didn't already know. But at least he had told them that Evans had arranged to meet someone on the Saturday night, the night of his death. And that somebody had been worth breaking his appointment with Gibbons for. But then, Wesley thought, most people would be.

He looked at his watch. Lunchtime. Kirsty Evans was meeting him at the police station. And he planned to take her for a pub lunch. But it wasn't something he was particularly looking forward to.

Pam Peterson didn't recognise the woman who was walking so close to her husband, glancing at him from time to time with what looked like affection. Pam could tell from the woman's body language, from the way she kept touching his sleeve, that this was no professional encounter ... at

176

least on her part. And they were making for the Tradmouth Arms. A lunchtime tryst. If Pam hadn't been encumbered by Amelia's pushchair, she would have followed them.

The woman was blonde and she wore a short skirt under a leather coat that must have cost a fortune. Pam had never seen her before and she suspected that maybe she was someone he worked with, someone new that Wesley hadn't seen fit to mention to her. She experienced the first feelings of raw jealousy she'd had in years and felt decidedly dowdy – the mother of two young children, harassed and permanently tired with dark rings beneath her eyes.

As she made her way back home, pushing Amelia's pushchair up the steep, narrow streets that led upwards away from the river, she paused from time to time to catch her breath, and she began to think of Neil. Before he left for the States he had started saying things, paying her clumsy compliments. With Wesley so wrapped up in other things, she had rather liked the thought of being a desirable woman again, even though she had known Neil for years and had learned long ago not to take him too seriously.

When she opened the front door she manoeuvred the pushchair up the front step before switching off the bleeping burglar alarm.

Amelia was fast asleep so Pam left her in her pushchair and made her way to the computer in the corner of the living room. She just had time to check her emails before she had to fetch Michael from nursery. She was pleased to find that there was another one from Neil. She printed it out and sat down to read it, still wearing her coat.

'Hi Pam and Wes.' He was still putting her name first, she thought with satisfaction. 'Things going well here. We've almost finished excavating the palisades of the original fort and everyone seems very excited about it. Remember those two skeletons I mentioned with musket balls in their heads? They're trying to extract DNA at the moment to see if they're related. There must be a story there somewhere but it's all a bit of a mystery at the moment and precious little to go on. Even Wes would be stumped by this one.

'I've seen a lot of Max. We're getting on quite well and at least it gets me away from Chuck's perpetual baseball commentary. He says he wants to donate some old family papers dating back to the early settlers to the museum at Old Annetown. I said I'd help him sort through them. He wants to visit England and it'd be good if he could see Gran again. I must be turning sentimental in my old age. He wants to see Potwoolstan Hall when he comes over – the ancestral home. You wouldn't be able to email me some pictures of the place, would you? Max'd be thrilled if you could. Must finish now. I've got to be at the dig in half an hour. Neil.'

Pam sighed. She was missing Neil. And her husband was lunching with an attractive blonde.

Kirsty Evans took a sip of her vodka and orange before placing the notebook on the table.

'Where did you find it?' Wesley asked.

'His editor had it.'

'I've been trying to contact her.'

'She's been away at a book fair. Only just got back. She rang me yesterday just after I'd spoken to you. Paddy went to see her the day before he left for Devon. She thinks he must have left it on her desk by mistake and it became hidden under a rather large manuscript. It was only when she got round to reading the manuscript that she found it.'

Wesley stared at the dull green school exercise book, hardly liking to touch it. Kirsty took a piece of paper out of her pocket and set it down beside the notebook.

'This is the list of names I read out to you. Most of them are mentioned in the notebook too. Brenda Varney, for instance. There's a section about her going to prison for theft and it says that she's used other names.'

Wesley raised his eyebrows. Patrick Evans had done a lot better than the police.

'And Paddy went up to North Yorkshire to find Victor Bleasdale, the gardener. He says in the notebook that he hit a dead end. He even checked the records in case he'd died but he found nothing. He wonders if Bleasdale changed his identity.'

Wesley said nothing. Gardeners don't usually go round swapping identities like international criminals. But there were always exceptions.

'Pauline Black gets a mention. Her father died at the Harfords' brewery and Pauline blamed Jack Harford for his accident. She was working at a hotel in Morbay at the time of the murders and she had an alibi. Said she was at her aunt's house but I don't know if anybody checked it out at the time.'

Wesley didn't comment on the police's implied incompetence. 'Where is she now? Any idea?'

'Paddy's notes say she married someone from Somerset – Glastonbury. But he doesn't say if he managed to trace her.'

'She could be anywhere.'

'There's a Jocasta Childs mentioned as well; no address apart from the name Trecowan: there's a village in Cornwall called Trecowan; or it might be the name of a house or even the name she uses now.' She smiled. 'The only note against her name is "checking Greg". Can't think what that means.' Kirsty drained her glass. 'Can I have another?'

He took the empty glass from her reluctantly. She'd had three already. 'Where are you staying?'

She looked into his eyes. 'Are you married, Inspector Peterson?'

'Yes.'

'Shame,' she said softly as he walked over to the bar.

When Wesley returned to the office after seeing Kirsty back to the Marina Hotel, he felt uneasy. She had been quite drunk. Perhaps he should have been firmer with her. But

179

she was an adult and she wasn't breaking any law so he was hardly in a position to tell her what to do. She had wanted to meet him later – for dinner. He had pleaded a previous engagement, not mentioning that it was with his wife. But he felt for Kirsty Evans. There was an almost childlike vulnerability behind the confident, professional façade. The country bride had taken over from the big city girl. Perhaps we all return to our roots in times of crisis.

He had spotted Arbel Jameston at the hotel and out of courtesy he had said hello and asked whether she'd had any word from Gwen Madeley. But the answer was no. It was so unlike Gwen, she said, to go off like that and she felt she ought to stay in Devon until she had turned up safely. Anthony had agreed: she and Gwen were old friends after all.

Arbel had looked strained and he had hardly liked to ask her how seeing the Hall again had affected her. The sight of the bodies had disturbed hardened police officers so it would hardly have left an eighteen-year-old girl unscarred.

The more Wesley tried to concentrate on his present-day problems, the more the scene of crime photographs of the Hall kept returning to his mind. Those shocked, staring eyes; Nigel Armley's missing face; Martha Wallace sprawled amongst the half-prepared party food, her throat ripped out by a bullet.

He wondered what had made Gwen Madeley paint those dreadful scenes. He had looked at the files and there was no mention of her having been there. She had painted something she wasn't supposed to have seen. And she still hadn't turned up. Perhaps it was time they put more effort into tracking her down.

He looked up and saw Rachel standing there. 'How's it going?' she asked.

'Kirsty Evans found her husband's notebook. He'd made notes about some of the people on his "must see" list. I've already had a word with Richard Gibbons the under-gardener. He said he arranged to meet Evans on the night he died but Evans put him off: said he had an important meeting with someone.'

'His murderer?'

'Possibly. There were a few more names as well. Emma Oldchester's adoptive parents; the gardener, Victor Bleasdale – but he left the morning before the killings; Brenda Varney, the cleaner who pinched Mrs Harford's jewellery. There's Gwen and Dylan Madeley but no address for Dylan. There was also someone called Jocasta Childs but I'm not sure where she comes into it. And there was a woman called Pauline Black, daughter of a man who died at the Harfords' brewery.'

'So he was working on the assumption that Martha Wallace was innocent?'

'Looks like it. And the fact that someone murdered him and searched his hotel room means that he was probably on the right track.'

As Rachel returned to her work, something nagged at Wesley, making him restless. He walked over to Steve's desk and asked him if there was any word on Gwen Madeley yet. All patrols had been asked to look out for her car but there'd been no reported sightings. In view of the fact that she was expecting Arbel to stay with her, Wesley was growing more worried. Nobody invites an old friend to stay then disappears into thin air. Steve, however, seemed quite unconcerned.

'Did I mention the tapes?' Steve said unexpectedly.

'What tapes?'

'When Elsham hypnotises people he makes tapes. One of the other guests told Serena. She had a look in his office but she couldn't find them.'

'Why didn't you mention this before?'

'Forgot.'

Wesley decided it was best to say nothing. To stay calm. 'Emma Oldchester might have said something under hypnosis that Elsham hasn't told us about. The DCI might want a word later,' he added ominously. Heffernan would be livid. Perhaps it would be better not to tell him about Steve's memory lapse. But why should he do Steve a favour?

Most days Neil called at Max's house when he had finished at the dig for the day. He usually stayed an hour or so before returning to Chuck's apartment. Somehow he felt it was the right thing to do. The old man was on his own and they had a lot of catching up to do. Max had ordered his plane ticket to England but Neil hadn't contacted his grandmother yet: things were complicated by the fact that her daughter, Neil's mother, as far as he knew had no idea of her true parentage. Things like that out of the blue could come as a shock. He would have to take things slowly.

But that day it wasn't Max who was waiting for him on the front porch. The man putting a considerable strain on the swinging rocking chair was big in every direction. As soon as he spotted Neil he stood up.

'You Neil Watson?' The way he said it told Neil that this was no friendly greeting. The man took a step towards him. He was probably in his forties or early fifties. His ginger hair was cropped short and he wore a bright Hawaiian shirt over a pair of baggy beige slacks. He had bright blue eyes, the colour of Neil's own, and a mouth that didn't smile.

'Yeah. That's me. Where's Max?'

'In the back yard. I wanted to speak with you in private. You know who I am?' There was contempt and just a hint of a threat behind the question.

Neil shook his head, puzzled by this stranger's hostility.

'I'm Brett Selbiwood. I'm Max's son. He's told me all about you.'

Neil automatically held out his hand. 'Pleased to meet you. I suppose that makes you my uncle. You know all about my grandmother and ...?'

Brett ignored Neil's outstretched hand. 'You do know you have no claim on him? Or his property?'

'Of course not. I never thought ...'

182

'There's not even proof that your ... mother, is it?'

Neil nodded.

'There's not even proof that she is who she says she is. And even with DNA evidence I'll fight this through the courts ...'

'Hang on. I think there's been a misunderstanding here.'

Brett Selbiwood took another step towards him. Neil backed away. 'There's no misunderstanding. If you've gotten it into your head that you can get anything out of my pa, you're mistaken. Now get out of here.'

Neil stood his ground. 'At least let me see Max. He's coming over to England with me and ...'

Neil was quite unprepared for the sharp pain of the punch when it came, and as he drove away fast in Chuck's pick-up, his nose dripping blood, he thought of all the brilliant things he ought to have said. And wondered what to do next.

As Wesley and Heffernan parked outside Potwoolstan Hall for the second time that day, a cloud of black crows rose, screeching, from the tops of the trees. Something or someone had disturbed them. The sky was an ominous shade of grey, laden with rain.

In the entrance hall they almost collided with a woman in a wheelchair: Mrs Carmody. She was wearing a coat and there was a suitcase by the front door. It looked as if she was leaving. She fluttered apologies and made a feeble joke about being a bad driver before Pandora appeared, relieving them of the need for further pleasantries. After assuring Mrs Carmody that her taxi was ordered, speaking in a tone people usually reserve for backward children, she showed them into Jeremy Elsham's office. As he stepped over the threshold, Wesley glanced back over his shoulder. Nigel Armley, Catriona Harford's fiancé, had been found in the hallway with his face blown away.

He forced himself to concentrate on what Jeremy Elsham was going to tell them ... whether he wanted to or not.

183

Elsham sat behind his impressive desk. The bags beneath his eyes had grown deeper and darker and he turned a pen over and over in his fingers, staring at the unmarked pink blotting paper before him.

'Sorry to bother you again, Mr Elsham. But I believe you have some information for us,' said Wesley.

Elsham looked puzzled. 'I've told you everything I know.'

'You make tapes when your clients are regressed to their childhoods.'

'Do I?'

Heffernan banged his fist on the table. 'Don't mess us about. We know you do.'

Elsham reddened. 'There's nothing sinister about it, Inspector. It helps to have a record, that's all.'

'May we hear Emma Oldchester's tape?'

'Not without her permission.'

'This is a murder enquiry,' Heffernan growled.

Elsham hesitated. Then he walked over to the wall opposite the window and swung a seascape in oils to one side. Behind it was a safe. He unlocked it and took out what looked like a cassette tape which he handed to Wesley who passed it to Heffernan.

'Do you always lock the tapes in your safe?'

Elsham nodded. 'These things are highly confidential.'

Heffernan leaned forward. 'I bet you hear some juicy bits of scandal, eh. You're never tempted to pass anything on to the Sunday newspapers?'

Elsham bristled with righteous indignation. 'That's an outrageous suggestion. Do you want my cooperation or not?'

'Of course we do, sir,' said Wesley quickly in an attempt to smooth Elsham's ruffled feathers. Sometimes tact wasn't Gerry Heffernan's strong point. 'If we could hear the tape ...'

Elsham put the cassette into the machine and pressed the button. Wesley could tell he was seething inwardly. Maybe

184

the boss had gone too far.

First they heard Elsham's voice, soothing, hypnotic. He was putting Emma under, telling her that she was feeling drowsy and peaceful and that she would soon be asleep. The voice seemed to be having a similar effect on Heffernan, who had closed his eyes.

Emma's voice was fairly high-pitched with a soft local accent. Elsham prompted her from time to time, moving her backwards in time gently. It was about five minutes into the tape that Emma began to relive the events of 1985. It was no longer her voice but the voice of a terrified child, hidden in the pantry, peeping through a grille in the door, paralysed with fear. A child who had watched someone place a gun in her dead mother's hand.

They heard Jeremy Elsham's voice, soft and coaxing through Emma's distressed sobs, asking who it was. Did she see the killer's face?

There was a short period of held breath, of expectation, before she answered.

'He's in the kitchen.' The child was crying now, almost incoherent.

'Who's in the kitchen, Emma?'

'Mr Bleasdale,' she sobbed. Then she seemed to waver. 'No. The other man. He shot my mummy.' With that Emma Oldchester had begun to weep uncontrollably.

'And you were going to keep that from us, Mr Elsham?' Wesley asked.

Jeremy Elsham hung his head and said nothing.

Chapter Nine

Joshua Morton is dead, perished in a grievous misadventure. He was hunting with his brother, Isaac, when they came upon some wild creatures, strange birds that some call turkeys. Isaac fired upon the birds but his brother had stepped between him and his prey, quite unaware of the danger.

Penelope keeps to her quarters as befits a widow and the whole settlement met together beneath our sail to pray for her.

Isaac Morton is said by all to be half mad with grief but I have reason to doubt the truth of this. I was walking near the river when I heard a sound in the bushes. Thinking it was some creature, I stepped softly towards it but the sight that met my eyes made the bile rise in my throat. Penelope was there, lying on the ground, her skirts lifted while Isaac Morton had his pleasure of her, enjoying her body after murdering her husband, his own brother. I watched them from the shelter of the bushes ... watched while Isaac grunted above my beloved like a beast.

The next day Isaac Morton was found dead, his life ended by a musket ball. Some say he shot himself out of remorse for his brother's death. But I say he hath been punished for his unnatural lust.

Set down by Master Edmund Selbiwood, Gentleman,

on the sixth day of September 1605 at Annetown, Virginia.

Wesley stared at the wall of the CID office, at the two images of Patrick Evans. Alive and dead. He wasn't sure when Kirsty planned to go back to London. Perhaps he should make another effort to see her. To make sure she wasn't left alone in a strange town. But, on the other hand, it might be a mistake to become too involved.

As the Senior Investigating Officer, Gerry Heffernan had planned their tasks for the next day; who they were going to interview and what lines of enquiry they were going to follow. He told the team to get an early night because he wanted them in the office first thing. Wesley decided to go home. He needed a change of scene. And he might think better slumped on the sofa with a glass of wine in his hand.

As he walked home, up the narrow streets, he couldn't get Emma Oldchester's voice out of his mind. She had said a name – Mr Bleasdale; no doubt her mother had encouraged her to call the gardener that, to show some respect. Then she had come out with the strange utterance about the 'other man'. But which other man? And why Bleasdale? Bleasdale hadn't even been there at the time. He had gone up north to start a new job.

He had decided against questioning Emma again for the moment. He was terrified of upsetting her. If she was to relive the events of 1985 it should be in the presence of an expert, a psychiatrist perhaps, who knew what he or she was doing. Unlike Jeremy Elsham. There were some officers who'd risk Emma Oldchester's sanity to get a result. But Wesley Peterson wasn't one of them.

At least they knew that Evans hadn't talked to Emma. Her husband and father had fended him off. But was Barry Oldchester just over-protective? Or was he afraid of something? He was considerably older than Emma – fifteen years or so. A middle-aged man wedded to a waif-like girl. He must have been in his early twenties at the time of the shootings – old enough to kill. Had he been involved somehow? Had he his own reason for making sure Evans's book never saw the light of day? He resolved to check out Oldchester's background. There were so many possibilities. And none of them made the slightest bit of sense.

And another thing that didn't make sense was the witchcraft element: the dead crows that had been nailed to the doors. Had the murderer put them there for some twisted reason? Perhaps the killer had some connection with the occult. He was keeping an open mind. But he was sure of one thing. Patrick Evans had been getting near the truth. And that meant the Harfords' killer was close at hand.

These thoughts made the journey home seem short. When he reached home he put his key in the lock, wondering what domestic chaos awaited him.

Pam didn't rush to the door. She rarely did these days. Once she would have come running into the hall to greet him with a kiss.

She was upstairs, putting Michael to bed. He opened the door to Michael's room and crossed the threshold on tiptoe. Pam was sitting on the old wooden chair she kept by the cot. She glanced up when he entered but carried on reading from a large story book in a low, hypnotic tone; something about a lazy teddy bear. Wesley crept out. If he disturbed Michael just as she was getting him off to sleep there'd be hell to pay.

A few minutes later she joined him downstairs. He noticed she was wearing lipstick and the perfume he'd given her for her birthday.

'I saw you in Tradmouth at lunchtime,' were her first words.

Wesley felt slightly uncomfortable. 'Really.'

'Who were you with? Someone from work?' The question was more than casual. If Wesley didn't know better, he would have said that she was jealous.

'It was the widow of that man who was killed: Patrick Evans. She's come down from London to make some arrangements.'

Pam muttered something about food and hurried off into the kitchen, leaving Wesley sitting awkwardly on the sofa with no option but to pick up the TV remote control and flick through the channels in search of something interesting. He happened on a travel programme extolling the virtues of visiting Virginia USA. It was always odd how places one had hardly given a thought to keep popping up once some connection is established.

Neil was lucky, he thought. The place looked attractive with its white colonial houses, its sandy beaches and blue water and its old tobacco barns set in the lush green wooded landscape. He started to watch the programme and soon a reconstructed early settlement appeared on the screen with people in seventeenth-century costume re-enacting the bygone minutia of everyday life. A disembodied voice informed the viewer that it was here near the Anne River that the early settlers had landed, some years before the arrival of the Pilgrim Fathers. Wesley stared, fascinated, searching each face, looking for Neil but telling himself that the programme had probably been filmed months ago, long before Neil set foot on American soil. After five minutes Pam called out to tell him that the food was ready and he immediately felt guilty that he hadn't helped her. But he was tired, exhausted by turning all the possibilities over in his mind. He needed some time out to think. But he had as much chance of getting it as he had of taking off on a Caribbean holiday the next day. Zero.

'Neil's asked me to send him some pictures of Potwoolstan Hall,' Pam said as soon as they had finished eating. 'I found a book on local history in the library this afternoon and I scanned in some pictures of the hall and emailed them to him. Did you know there's supposed to be a curse on the place? The man who built it, Josiah Selbiwood, killed a local girl and buried her somewhere in the grounds. Legend has it the villagers found out and murdered him. Then they cursed the Hall by hanging dead crows on the doors: quaint local custom, apparently.'

She suddenly had Wesley's full attention. 'Crows?'
'Dead ones.'

He smiled to himself. That explained a lot. Whoever had murdered the Harfords knew about the Hall's history.

'Why's Neil so interested in the Hall?' It struck Wesley as strange that Neil was demanding pictures of the epicentre of their enquiries.

'Max is a descendant of one of the Selbiwoods who settled in Virginia and the Selbiwoods built Potwoolstan Hall. Max is trying to discover his roots.'

She stood up and started clearing the dishes away noisily. 'I'll do that,' said Wesley gently, touching her hand. 'Go and put your feet up.'

She left the kitchen without a word and Wesley packed the dishwasher, his mind only half on what he was doing. Emma Oldchester's voice kept echoing through his head. Where was Bleasdale, the gardener, the man she had named before apparently changing her mind?

For the first time he even wondered whether the murder of Patrick Evans had anything to do with Potwoolstan Hall at all. Perhaps it had just been a mugging that went wrong. Perhaps he'd disturbed some youngsters high on drugs and they had robbed him on the river bank and stuck a knife in his ribs. Perhaps they should be questioning the kids who found his wallet again. Or perhaps pigs were developing aviation skills. If his murder was unconnected with the Harford case it was carrying coincidence too far.

Wesley suddenly longed to talk the case over, not in the chaotic bustle of the office but over a leisurely drink. To try on ideas and theories like clothes and discard any that didn't fit. He looked at his watch. It was eight o'clock already.

He had been out of the house since first thing that morning and he hadn't returned till late. If he went out now, Pam wouldn't exactly be delighted. But it was worth a try.

'Do you mind if I go out for an hour or so?' he asked

sheepishly. 'I just want to have a word with Gerry. We'll probably just pop into the Tradmouth Arms and . . .'

'You see him all day at work. Why don't you just move in with him?' But then she looked at him and realised that if he stayed at home, he might be there in body but not in spirit. 'Go on if you must. But don't be late.'

He left the house, eager as a newly released prisoner walking out to the freedom of the outside world. It was a cool and drizzly evening so he drove to the waterfront, not intending to drink.

He parked the car and cut through the narrow cobbled street lined with overhanging medieval houses which led to Baynard's Quay. When he reached the quayside he stood for a few seconds looking out across the dark water, shot with slivers of gold from the reflected lights of the town. He could see the lights of Queenswear on the opposite bank, the coloured lights of the pub by the landing stage, giving the place a strangely festive look. Dark boats bobbed at anchor: it was high tide. A fishing boat chugged purposefully along the river towards the sea. Wesley breathed in and smelt seaweed and a whiff of diesel blended with the faint smell of cooking from one of the nearby restaurants. He liked Tradmouth at night.

Gerry Heffernan owned a small, whitewashed cottage at the end of the quay, separated from the Tradmouth Arms by a short, steep alleyway. The cottage nestled up against its larger, grander neighbours like a child against a row of grown-ups. Wesley knocked at the door and waited. When the chief inspector answered, Wesley saw that he had discarded his rather shabby working clothes for a pair of old jeans and a cream roll-neck sweater, the kind favoured by submarine captains in wartime movies. When he saw Wesley his face lit up with a beaming smile. He was glad of the company.

'Come in, Wes, come in. What brings you here? Gwen Madeley hasn't turned up, has she?'

'No. I just fancied throwing a few ideas around.'

Heffernan rubbed his hands together eagerly as though he couldn't think of a better way to spend an evening and led the way into the cottage. Wesley could never get over how neatly he kept it: a place for everything and everything in its place, a habit he claimed to have picked up from his days as an officer in the Merchant Navy. For a man with the most chaotic desk in the station, the state of his home came as rather a surprise.

They walked the few yards to the Tradmouth Arms. It was a warm, convivial pub, serving good ale and specialising in sea food. The bar staff had already been asked if Patrick Evans had eaten his last lobster there. But lobster had been off the menu that Saturday night.

'So what do you make of it all?' Heffernan said when he was settled with a full pint of best bitter in front of him. Wesley, stuck with orange juice, wished now that he had left the car at home. 'Has anybody seen Emma Oldchester's foster father yet?'

'He's on my list. When Rachel phoned him he told her that he and his wife had never discussed what happened at the Hall with Emma. According to the psychologists she saw, she'd blotted the whole thing out and he thinks it's best that she's not reminded. Who knows? Maybe he's right. Evans contacted him but he refused to meet him.'

'What about the husband? Barry Oldchester?'

'Ditto. Refused to see Evans. He's much older than Emma, you know.'

'Perhaps her foster parents thought he'd be a safe pair of hands, as it were. Someone sensible who'd look after her.'

'You could be right. Emma must have been desperate to remember what happened if she let herself by hypnotised by Elsham.'

'I expect Evans's phone calls brought it all back to the surface.' Heffernan thought for a few moments. 'I've been wondering about this hypnotism business. I was talking to one of the bellringers at St Margaret's the other night – turns out he's a psychiatrist at Tradmouth Hospital. He'd know about that sort of thing, wouldn't he?'

'I expect so.'

'If I could ask him to see Emma Oldchester ...'

Wesley smiled to himself. In the Met it had been the Masons and the golfing fraternity who provided each other with favours. Gerry Heffernan's network of contacts was rather less conventional but no less effective. 'Worth a try,' he said, draining his glass of orange juice. He'd been thirsty. He went to the bar to buy another round and when he sat down again, things were a little straighter in his mind.

'I think we can safely assume that Martha Wallace didn't kill the Harfords. But someone made it look as though she'd done it. Someone who knew they might be suspected? Did you know there was an old legend about the Hall being cursed hundreds of years ago? The local peasants nailed dead crows to the doors.'

This captured Heffernan's attention. 'The killer must have known about it.'

'According to Patrick Evans's notebook, he went up to North Yorkshire but he didn't find the gardener, Bleasdale. I've looked at the file and Bleasdale was interviewed by North Yorkshire police just after the murders but as he'd left Devon before the Harfords were killed, he was eliminated from the enquiry. According to Gibbons's statement in the file he was telling the truth. Do you trust Gibbons?'

Heffernan shook his head. 'Not as far as I could throw him. What about all this stuff Emma said about Mr Bleasdale shooting the Harfords then changing her mind and saying that they were shot by "the other man"? Was she just rambling or what? Perhaps by the other man she meant the other gardener – Gibbons.'

'Gibbons had an alibi. It was checked at the time. And what was his motive?' Wesley sighed. They were getting nowhere. 'I'm concerned about Gwen Madeley. Surely she wouldn't take off when she's expecting a friend to stay and leave her place unlocked.'

'Maybe her brother, Dylan, knows where she is. He's on Evans's list.'

'If we can find him. And where do Arbel and that husband of hers fit into all this?'

'Maybe they don't. But I still think it's funny he should choose to stay at Potwoolstan Hall. Decidedly odd if you ask me.'

'He said Patrick Evans had made him curious about the place. But I'm wondering whether Gwen Madeley was the attraction. Does he know her better than he's admitting? He met her in the woods.' Wesley took a long drink and thought for a few moments. 'Those paintings of the murder scene in her studio; how could she have known the details? She must have been there at some point but there's nothing in the files about her having been on the premises between the time Arbel reported it and the police arriving. As far as I can see she was only told about the murders afterwards when they were looking for a place for Arbel to stay.'

'Odd. Unless she went to the Hall before Arbel got there. But if that's the case, why didn't she raise the alarm?'

Wesley sighed. 'If we could find her we could ask her. She can't have vanished into thin air. Perhaps we should have another go at Richard Gibbons. If we can get past his mother. He was around the grounds the morning the bodies were found.'

'Mmm. Brenda Varney had a reason to resent the Harfords.'

'And again we don't know where she is. Anyway, Emma implied they were shot by a man. The other man,' Wesley took another drink and leaned forward. 'Let's make a list of all the men connected with the case.' He took a diary out of his pocket and turned to the blank pages at the back. 'Right. We've got Richard Gibbons, the under-gardener who said he was at the cinema with a friend at the time of the murders, then he went home to his old mum. The cinema alibi checked out and the mother backed his story all the way, of course, but that's what mums are like. However, we only have his word for it that he didn't meet Patrick Evans that Saturday night. Then there's Anthony Jameston.'

'He wasn't even around at the time of the murders. He didn't meet Arbel till later on.'

'Do we know that for sure? He talked to Evans.'

'Only because Evans was trying to get to Arbel.'

'What about Barry Oldchester? Did he have any link with the Hall?'

'Not that we know of.'

'Emma's foster father, Joe Harper?'

'There's no evidence of a link between him and the Harfords.'

'Jeremy Elsham?'

'The same. No link. He's not even from Devon.'

'But why choose Potwoolstan Hall?'

'He probably got the place cheap. Why don't you ask him if you think it's important?'

But Wesley wasn't to be discouraged. He wrote down the names as though he was on the verge of an exciting discovery. 'There's Dylan Madeley, Gwen's brother. Convictions for drugs and robbery. We need to find him. And Victor Bleasdale?'

Heffernan nodded. 'Now Emma has named him he's worth a second look. Maybe he didn't go up north the day before the murders. And maybe Evans did manage to trace him and that's why he was killed. If Bleasdale's the killer, he must be somewhere nearby.'

'What did he have to gain from killing the Harfords?'

'Perhaps it was revenge. Perhaps he was due to get the sack like Brenda and they had a row.'

'Gibbons would have known about something like that.'

'That's why I want another word with him. He worked with the man. He must have known him better than most.'

'Is there a photograph of Bleasdale anywhere in our records?'

'No, Wes. And he had no form so there's no fingerprints either. Shame.'

195

They sat there for a few moments contemplating their drinks. Wesley was instinctively against fingerprinting and photographing the entire population, but he had known times when it might have come in useful.

He looked at his watch then at Heffernan, who was sitting there expectantly with an empty glass. 'Look, Gerry, I really should be getting home. Pam . . .'

'Yeah, off you go. I think I'm going to stay and have another.' He stood up to go to the bar. 'See you tomorrow, eh? First thing.'

Wesley left, feeling uneasy, torn between keeping a lonely man company and his duties as a husband and father. But you can't please all the people all the time. He climbed into his car and drove back home, shifting into second gear to tackle the steep gradients of the streets leading up from the waterfront.

It was ten fifteen when he reached the house but the place was already in darkness. Pam had gone to bed and he took this as a signal of disapproval. He suddenly regretted his impulsive visit to Baynard's Quay. Maybe he was becoming obsessed with work, letting it take over his life. He had seen it happen so much in his job, especially with his colleagues in the Met. He climbed the stairs wearily. When they had caught the killer of Patrick Evans and Gwen Madeley had turned up safe and well, he would make it up to Pam and the children.

He crept into the bedroom and found Pam reading. She said nothing as he sat on the bed and kissed her cheek.

'Sorry I'm late. I think Gerry needed some company.'

'And I didn't.'

Wesley didn't have an answer for that.

'You left your mobile in the hall.'

'Yes. I realised when I got to Gerry's.'

'You had a call while you were out. A Kirsty Evans. She wants to know if you can meet her for lunch again tomorrow.' Pam pressed her lips together in disapproval.

'I won't be able to. I'll get one of the others to look after

196

her. Trish maybe.' He looked at Pam hopefully. 'The woman's husband's just been murdered. She just wants a sympathetic person to talk to, that's all.'

Pam didn't look convinced. That night Amelia woke up twice. And Wesley's guilty conscience made him get up to see to her both times.

Jeremy Elsham walked slowly down the landing and stopped outside Anthony Jameston's door. He hesitated for a few moments before walking on, continuing the night patrol just as he did every night, just to make sure that all was well and that none of the Beings were in need of any sustenance, spiritual or physical. They expected attentive service for their money and, in the absence of live-in staff, it was his and Pandora's duty to provide it out of normal hours.

He had wondered about approaching Jameston. But Pandora had counselled against it. And it was her affair after all. He made his way back to the bedroom where he knew she would be waiting for him.

Sure enough she was there, propped up on one elbow, a slight smile of invitation on her face. Jeremy slipped his dressing gown off and got into bed beside her.

'All quiet?' she asked, just as she did every night.

'No problem. They've been swilling down the camomile tea all day.' He lay down and pushed a straying strand of hair off her face, thinking that the last stay in the cosmetic surgery clinic had done wonders for her appearance. 'I wanted to talk to Dodgson ... sorry, Jameston. Now we know who he is, I think we should say something.'

Pandora turned away from him. 'No.'

'Why not?'

'Because we should keep out of it, that's why not. That man was murdered here in the grounds. And Gwen's still not turned up. But then Gwen's always been an awkward bitch.' Jeremy ran his fingers over her naked back and she turned over again to face him. 'Promise you'll say nothing?'

197

'I'm not stupid,' he said before turning out the light.

Pam Peterson was in a much better mood after a good night's sleep. She woke up before Wesley and watched him sleeping, regretting that she'd been such a bitch the night before. Wesley awoke when Michael rushed into the room and flung himself, laughing on to their bed.

'Why have they got to be so bloody lively in the mornings?' Pam muttered rhetorically as she shuffled downstairs in her dressing gown to make some tea and toast.

She returned ten minutes later to find father and son cuddled together and she stood in the doorway with the breakfast tray and smiled. Michael's bowl of cereal was waiting for him downstairs. But Wesley might as well have breakfast in peace.

She ate her toast, watching Michael spoon the sugary cereal into his mouth, then she switched on the computer. Since Neil had left for the States she had carried out this ritual every morning, awaiting his emails with eager anticipation. And this morning she wasn't disappointed. There was a long one waiting. She printed it out, read it through then ran up the stairs to show it to Wesley.

'Hi Pam and Wes,' it began. Wesley knew he hadn't long so he scanned the details of the dig and the latest forensic tests on the skeletons they'd found. It seems the two skeletons shot by musket balls were related, according to DNA tests. Possibly brothers. But it was the third paragraph that caught his eye. 'I've been in a bit of a fight. Well, not a fight exactly because I didn't punch him back – it was only me who ended up with a bloody nose. Max's son has got it into his head that I'm after the old boy's money. He's warned me off in no uncertain terms and I'm wondering what to do next. Max intends to donate some old documents to the museum and he wants me to help him go through them. I'll let you know how I get on.'

'Sounds like he's in trouble,' Pam said. She sounded worried.

'I'm sure Neil can take care of himself.' Wesley's mind was on other things. On automatic pilot, he dressed and left the house, kissing Pam goodbye and promising to be home at a reasonable hour. He only hoped it was a promise he'd be able to keep.

He arrived at the office before Gerry Heffernan. Punctuality had never been the chief inspector's strong point.

As soon as he'd sat down at his desk Steve Carstairs swaggered over, still wearing his leather coat over a black shirt and a pair of well-cut jeans. 'I've been checking on Jeremy Elsham. In 1992 he bought a garden centre in Glastonbury. Then he set up a small healing centre, specialising in regressions and auras, whatever those are. Then five years later he bought Potwoolstan Hall at a knockdown price and went upmarket. The place is doing quite well, apparently.' He grinned, as if he was saving the best until last. 'Anyway, I did a bit more digging and it turns out that Elsham married a lady called Pauline Black back in 1989. Wasn't there a Pauline Black connected with the Potwoolstan Hall case?'

'You're right.' Wesley thought for a moment. Elsham's wife was called Pandora. Did he trade Pauline in for a newer model? If so, where was Pauline now?

'No record of a divorce or a remarriage. What if Pandora is Pauline ... sort of repackaged?'

It was certainly a possibility. If Pauline had reinvented herself with plastic surgery then it was quite likely she'd have wanted to change her name along with her image. It was something he'd look into – when he had the time.

'Have you found out what Elsham did before Glastonbury?'

Steve shook his head. 'Haven't been able to find a thing.'

'A man with no past, eh? Well done. Keep on digging. Rachel in yet?' he asked, trying to sound casual.

'She's somewhere about.'

'Can you run a check on Pauline Black? See what you

199

can find under the name Pandora Elsham ... or Pauline Elsham. If you can do it as soon as possible ... please.' He looked at Steve and gave him a businesslike smile, as though he had no doubt that he would carry out his orders there and then. It was like training a dog, he thought: act confident and you'll earn their respect.

As Steve wandered away, Rachel appeared at the office door.

'That theft at Potwoolstan Hall – Jack Wright's just called to say "Mr Smith" rang and he's happy with Jack's valuation of the ring. He's coming into the shop some time this morning to pick up his money. The boss isn't in yet. Will you let him know?'

Wesley looked at his watch. 'Sure. With any luck we might get this one cleared up today,' he said with some relief. He wanted the team's full attention on Evans's death and Gwen Madeley's disappearance. Distractions he could do without.

As Rachel walked away, he opened the file on the desk in front of him, hoping for inspiration. The Potwoolstan Hall case: the brutal murders of six people on the 29th March 1985. He had read it over and over again, dreamed about it: he knew it so well he felt he could recite some of the witness statements off by heart. There must be something there in that file he'd missed. He began to read it again.

It was all there. Martha Wallace had met Nigel Armley in the hall where she had shot him with a shotgun that was normally kept in the gun cabinet, before going on to shoot the rest of the family with a rifle, then shooting herself. He sat back and stared at the words on the page. She had taken two weapons from the cupboard: the shotgun, holding two cartridges, and the rifle that held ten bullets. She emptied both barrels of the shotgun into Nigel Armley's face before using the rifle on the others. Had she worked it all out? If she used two weapons then she wouldn't have to reload. It seemed very calculating for a woman in an agitated mental

200

state. But then who knows what goes through people's minds in extreme circumstances?

He read on, flicking through statements until he came to Victor Bleasdale's. A local constable up in North Yorkshire had interviewed Bleasdale in his small tied cottage in the grounds of his new place of work, a stately home that opened its doors and its gardens to the public five days a week. Bleasdale had expressed shock at what had happened but he had been able to tell the constable very little. He had left the morning before the killings and stayed the night at a motel in the Midlands, arriving in North Yorkshire early the following afternoon. Nobody had bothered to check out his story at the time, and Wesley feared it was too late to correct this omission now. Bleasdale had described Martha Wallace as rather unstable – Wesley wondered if those were his exact words or if the constable had paraphrased his description to sound more formal. He had expressed concern for Martha's little girl and had hinted that the tragic events didn't exactly come as a surprise, considering the state Martha had been in over the past weeks. He had asked what had happened to Emma but the constable obviously hadn't been able to tell him.

Wesley wriggled in his chair. There was something wrong here but he wasn't sure what it was. He asked Trish to find him the number of the nearest police station to the Yorkshire stately home: he would ask someone there to check out whether Bleasdale still worked there. Or, if he'd moved on, where he had gone. But if Patrick Evans had been up to Yorkshire, that's where he would have started. And as far as he knew, he hadn't found him. Or perhaps he had.

Maybe Victor Bleasdale was closer than they thought. Who was to say he wasn't back in Devon? Who was to say he hadn't killed those people all those years ago and had returned to cover his tracks, alerted by Evans's enquiries? After all, Emma Oldchester had named him under hypnosis.

201

He hadn't seen a picture of Bleasdale: all he knew was the little Richard Gibbons had told him. Bleasdale could be anyone. Or anywhere. He had to speak to Gibbons again. He was their only link to Bleasdale. Albeit a tentative one.

He heard a familiar voice. Gerry Heffernan had arrived, pleading a faulty alarm clock. Wesley stood up so quickly that for a few seconds he felt light-headed, and hurried to Heffernan's office, arriving just as the chief inspector was taking off his coat.

When Heffernan heard what Steve had discovered about Jeremy Elsham's marriage to Pauline Black, his eyes lit up. He had that hound on the scent look again.

Then he gave him the news about Jack Wright's call. The thief was on the move.

'Tell Rachel to see to it, will you?' He peered out of his window into the CID office. 'And she can take Darren. He looks as if he could do with some fresh air.'

There was a single knock on the office door, heralding Steve Carstairs' arrival. 'I've run a check, sir,' he said breathlessly. 'Pandora Elsham used to hold a firearms licence. She was a member of a shooting club.'

Heffernan grinned. 'Let's go and open Pandora's box, eh? But before we do, let's have a word with Emma Oldchester's dad. I want to see what he has to say about Patrick Evans.'

He took his anorak off the coat stand and marched out of the office, Wesley behind him. No time for leisurely musings about the whereabouts of Victor Bleasdale over a cup of station tea.

Jack Wright's jewellery shop was on the wrong side of the large seaside resort of Morbay. When Jack's grandfather had begun the business in the era of late-Victorian optimism, it had been a rather classy establishment and the name V. Wright and Sons had been engraved in boastful gold above its glittering window displays. Blushing Edwardian brides had selected their wedding rings in its plush interior and guilty husbands had bought diamond bracelets to appease their suspicious wives.

The district had been a haven of bourgeois respectability back then. But after the Second World War the world had changed and the grand Victorian villas were divided into flats and bedsits. With the opening of Morbay's university, the students moved in beside the recent immigrants, the single mothers, the hostels for the homeless and those far too poor to afford Devon's rising house prices.

The engraved name still stood proudly above the shop but, like the area, V. Wright and Sons had gone down in the world and its grimy plate-glass windows displayed rows of skinny silver chains and cheap digital watches. Times were hard. And sometimes Jack Wright was tempted to ignore the warning bells that sounded in his head when someone who came in trying to sell quality items was prepared to accept a fraction of their true value. Desperation can blur the lines between honesty and dishonesty. And as far as his business was concerned, Jack Wright was a desperate man.

But today he was all cooperation. Especially since the detective sergeant they sent was a rather attractive young woman: a natural blonde with a no-nonsense manner. Rachel Tracey was the stuff of Jack Wright's fantasies.

Jack himself was in his fifties but he still wore his greying hair long, thinking it made him appear younger. When Rachel entered the shop, followed by Darren Wentworth, he greeted her with an obsequious leer, assuring her that he was anxious to do anything he could to help the police. Rachel wondered whether he'd have been so keen to aid the fight for law and order if he hadn't been caught in possession of stolen goods in the first place. But she decided to give him the benefit of the doubt and smiled sweetly as he cleared a place for them to sit in the cluttered office behind the shop, a dusty room dominated by an imposing oak desk that was a relic of a more prosperous age.

Promising to give a discreet signal when "Mr Smith" arrived, Jack left Rachel and Darren alone, sipping strong tea from chipped mugs in awkward silence. Rachel didn't feel like making polite conversation. And besides, she said to Darren, they should be trying to listen to what was going on in the shop. Perhaps Rachel's years in CID had made her suspicious, but she didn't altogether trust Jack Wright: he seemed just a little too eager to please.

Being closeted in the small office with Darren Wentworth, whose anti-perspirant wasn't as effective as the advertisers claimed, was hardly Rachel's ideal way to spend the morning: if she'd been with Wesley Peterson, it might have been a different matter. And when Jack Wright finally gave his signal – three soft knocks on the office door – she was relieved that the boredom was over. When Wright resumed his place behind the counter, making a great show of examining a ring through an eye glass, Rachel bustled out from the back of the shop, trying to look as though she worked there and was going out for a break. But she positioned herself at the shop door as Darren emerged from behind the counter.

The couple in the shop glanced at Darren nervously.

The man, short with thinning, greasy hair, was a stranger but Rachel thought she had seen the woman somewhere before but she couldn't quite remember where. She was average height, slim with short brown hair and she might once have been pretty in a chocolate-box sort of way. She was well dressed but her clothes were from chain stores rather than designer boutiques. The couple looked ordinary, hardly like thieves. But then this was probably the secret of their success.

Then it suddenly came to Rachel why the woman was so familiar. 'They obviously work miracles up at Potwoolstan Hall,' she said. 'You were in a wheelchair last time I saw you.'

Mrs Beatrice Carmody swung round, and gaped.

*

Joe Harper's small semi-detached house on the outskirts of the village of Stokeworthy boasted a bright white UPVC front door and a fine display of daffodils in the immaculate front garden.

Wesley rang the doorbell and waited.

'Nice garden,' Heffernan commented, shifting from foot to foot.

Wesley didn't reply. As he raised his hand to ring the bell a second time, the door was opened by a man in his sixties: well built with a thick shock of grey hair, a neat grey beard and a complexion that suggested he had spent most of his working life out of doors.

The two detectives showed their ID and Wesley asked politely if they could have a word. Harper stood aside to admit them, his eyes downcast. But Wesley was used to people being nervous when the police turned up on their doorstep.

'I believe you've had contact with a man called Patrick Evans,' Wesley said as soon as they'd sat down in the neat, old-fashioned front room.

Harper nodded. 'He rang me. Wanted to talk about my Em – my daughter. I told the policewoman on the phone.'

'Can you remember exactly what Evans said?'

Harper looked from one to the other as if he suspected it was a trick question. 'He asked me about what had happened at the Hall – about my cousin, Martha. I told him I never believed she'd done it. She'd been upset about Mrs Harford thinking she'd took that jewellery but that was all cleared up. She talked about looking for another job but Em was settled there. They had a nice flat, you see.'

'So you thought Martha was innocent?'

'No doubt about it. She'd never have done that. Specially not with Em in the house. She was murdered with the rest of 'em. I told the police at the time but no one took no notice, and me and Linda were too busy caring for Em to make a fuss. Em came first – always has, poor little maid. We never had no kiddies of our own. Just Em.'

Wesley smiled. 'And you loved her like she was your own?'

'More. She needed us, you see. It damaged her, all that business: affected her mind. She needed a bit of love.'

'Terrible thing for a kid to go through,' Heffernan said. 'Can't have been easy for you and your missus. What did you tell Evans?'

'Not much I could tell him. All I knew was that Martha was innocent and I told him that. I said I hoped he'd set the record straight, clear her name.'

'But you didn't meet him?'

'No point. I told him everything I knew over the phone. But I did ask him to leave Em alone. I didn't want her bothered and reminded of it all.'

'Did you know Emma's gone back to the Hall? She wants to remember what happened.'

Harper's big face clouded. 'Barry told me. I hoped he'd be able to talk some sense into her.'

'I take it you don't approve?' Wesley said softly.

'You can say that again. God only knows what that load of cranks'll do to her. She's not strong. Not strong in her mind.'

Harper offered tea. Like many of his class and generation, he had the habit of hospitality. But Patrick Evans had never received any. Or much information, come to that.

On their return to the office Gerry Heffernan greeted the news of Mrs Carmody's arrest with a wide grin. 'One down, a couple of hundred to go,' he said cheerfully, as if their workload was a welcome challenge rather than a relentless tide.

'So why the wheelchair?' Wesley asked. He was perched on the edge of the chief inspector's desk, listening intently.

'Who'd suspect a respectable middle-aged lady in a wheelchair? If something was stolen on the top floor of a building without a lift, she'd have the perfect alibi.'

Rachel took her notebook from her bag. 'I've been doing

206

a bit of research. Someone who might fit her description stayed at the health spa outside Dukesbridge – said she was blind and asked for a ground-floor room. And at the residential creative writing course at that arts centre near Neston, there was a woman on crutches who'd broken her leg and couldn't make it up the stairs. Then there was a woman recovering from a hip operation at the residential cookery course in Morbay and a woman with a broken ankle at the residential art course near Exmouth. She changed her name, her disability and her appearance every time. That's why it took so long for us to get on to her, especially as everything was stolen from the upper floors. Quite clever really. And those are only the cases in this police authority. She could have been doing it all over the country for all we know.'

Gerry looked at Rachel in admiration. 'Good work, love. You couldn't get us a cup of tea, could you? I'm parched.'

Wesley glanced at Rachel. Instead of her usual righteous feminist fury, she smiled. 'I'll see what I can do,' she said before leaving the chief inspector's office.

'You're a brave man, Gerry,' said Wesley.

'Who dares wins, Wes. Now where were we up to?' Heffernan sounded hungry for activity, an antidote to the paperwork he was always complaining about. Wesley sympathised.

But they were interrupted by Rachel. There was no sign of the tea they'd asked for but her eyes were shining with triumph. She looked as if she was about to impart a juicy piece of news. 'We've just identified "Mr Smith", Carmody's accomplice. Richard Gibbons – Tradmouth address. Isn't there a Richard Gibbons on Evans's list?'

Heffernan beamed. 'There certainly is. Thanks, Rach. Kettle on, is it?'

The smile disappeared from Rachel's lips and she made a rapid retreat.

'It'll do Gibbons and Carmody no harm to stew for a while. Meanwhile, let's go and see what Pandora Elsham has to say for herself. And I think it's time we had another word with Emma Oldchester.'

'I couldn't agree more. Do you think Pandora's really Pauline Black?' Wesley sounded doubtful.

'You know what, Wes, you're a natural pessimist. Of course it's her. But why did she want to buy Potwoolstan Hall? That's what I want to know. Did you see that newspaper on Steve Carstair's desk?'

'No.'

'"MP Husband of Tragic Heiress in Murder Quiz." Written by our own Ms Serena Jones.'

'Steve's been warned not to talk to her. Surely he wouldn't be so stupid.'

'I think he got her started and now she's just keeping her eyes and ears open and making lucky guesses. I read what she'd written. All speculation.'

'Let's face it, Gerry, that's all we've got ourselves. Speculation.'

When Wesley and Heffernan arrived at the Hall everything seemed quiet. The press had lost interest and moved on, but there was still a police presence in the form of a single patrol car, detailed to keep an eye on the scene of Patrick Evans's death but also to provide a modicum of protection for Emma Oldchester, who had been due to leave the next day but had insisted on extending her stay. For one so apparently fragile, Wesley thought, she was being remarkably stubborn.

Jeremy Elsham himself came out on to the front steps to greet them. Behind the fixed smile and the smooth gloss of his tan and steel-grey hair, he looked worried. And Wesley was about to add to his problems.

'We'd like a word with your wife, sir, if that's convenient.'

The fixed smile disappeared but they were invited to wait in Elsham's office. Wesley looked round, remembering Emma Oldchester's doll's house. The tiny figures lying on the floor by the door, their hands touching. At some point

208

Emma must have emerged from her hiding place and wandered round the house. She must have seen it all to remember it so accurately. Arbel had found her clinging to her mother's body, rocking to and fro: she must have returned to Martha's side, seeking some sort of solace. And now she was back in that house, determined to clear her mother's name. A quote from the Bible popped into Wesley's head, half remembered from his devout childhood. Something about letting Justice flow down like waters ... Perhaps all Emma wanted was to give Justice a little push. Understandable in the circumstances. But he still wished she'd go home.

Pandora entered the room, an innocent, inquisitive expression on the stretched, cat-like face. Heffernan told her to sit down.

'We've been doing a bit of checking,' he began. 'I believe you're a good shot. Member of a gun club, weren't you?'

Pandora stared at him blankly.

'Why didn't you tell us you knew the Harford family?' Heffernan tilted his head to one side, awaiting an answer.

'I didn't know them. Not really,' she said quickly.

'You took Harfords Brewery to court over your father's industrial accident. Harfords won. The court found that your father had been careless and that it hadn't been his employer's fault.'

Pandora's face had turned red beneath her make-up. 'They got people to lie for them. They made sure everyone told the same story – that my father had climbed over the barrier, taking a short cut. But that barrier was dangerous. It collapsed. They mended it afterwards.'

Wesley looked her in the eye. 'It's natural to be angry, Pauline.'

She stared at him, sullen.

'You'd have done anything to get justice for your father. You came here to the Hall back in 1985, didn't you? You came to have it out with the Harfords. There were witnesses.'

209

'Yes but . . .'

'Then you came back here on the 29th of March 1985 and took your revenge for what they'd done to your father?'

'No,' she shouted.

'Would you rather we continued this conversation back at the police station?' Wesley asked softly.

She looked alarmed and shook her head.

'You changed your name.'

'It's not a crime. Just before I met Jeremy I decided to reinvent myself. I swapped Pauline for Pandora, went blonde.'

'Jeremy was running a healing centre in Glastonbury when you met him. What did he do before that?'

She looked at him as though the question had surprised her. 'He ran a garden centre. Why do you ask?'

'Why did you buy the Hall?' Wesley asked.

'Jeremy wanted to expand. I knew this part of Devon and . . .'

'But why Potwoolstan Hall?'

'It was perfect for what we wanted and it had been empty for years. Nobody wanted to buy it because of what happened, so it was ridiculously cheap.' The corners of her lips turned upwards in a triumphant smile. 'And besides, I liked the idea that I would own the Harfords' house. They'd treated my family like shit and I ended up owning their house.' She leaned forward. Wesley could smell her perfume: something expensive and French. 'But do you think I could live here if I'd killed them? That'd be sick.'

Wesley refrained from saying that he'd known sicker things happen; that murderers were often compelled to return to the scene of their crime. He glanced at Heffernan, who was watching the woman like a cat watches a mouse.

'So where were you when the Harfords died?'

'I told the police at the time. I was at my aunt's house in Morbay. I was trying to sort out my dad's affairs. I couldn't have done it.'

'According to our records your statement was never

confirmed. You had a car. You could easily have left your aunt's and ...'

'Maybe I could, but I didn't. Killing that load of smug bastards wouldn't have brought my dad back.'

'You know that your guest Charles Dodgson is really Anthony Jameston – Arbel Harford's husband?'

'Yes. I saw Arbel briefly a couple of days ago. For the first time actually: she wasn't here when I came to see her brother. She's not a bit like him, you know; there's no family resemblance. But then there wouldn't be, would there? I read in the papers that she was adopted.'

'You must have really hated the Harfords.'

'Whatever I thought of the Harfords, I wouldn't wish it on anybody to lose their entire family like that. Honestly. I lost my mother – she died of cancer – then I lost my father. If I feel anything for Arbel Harford, it's sympathy. What happened to my father was hardly her fault, was it?'

'Did you ever meet the housekeeper, Martha Wallace?'

She shook her head. 'No. Surely that proves I didn't kill them. I'd hardly have killed an innocent woman, would I?' She hesitated. 'And she had a kid. She had nothing to do with what happened to my dad so why on earth would I want to harm her?' She looked into his eyes, anxious to be believed. But Wesley was keeping an open mind.

'Did you ever meet either of the gardeners? Man called Victor Bleasdale and the under-gardener, a lad called Richard Gibbons?'

'No. Of course I didn't.' She looked genuinely puzzled. Wesley found himself believing her. 'I came here to talk to Jack. His sister and her fiancé were there but I didn't see anyone else. Jack Harford was a conceited little shit, full of himself. My dad was just another number on the balance sheet to him, not a human being. Dad said that his father had been different when he ran the brewery. Jack was full of all this management speak and I could see he'd fight me all the way about the compensation.'

'So you gave up?'

211

'This was before the days of the compensation culture and no win no fee. Jack won the case once and I couldn't afford to take it any further. End of story.'

'And his sister, Catriona? What was she like?'

'She didn't say a word; wouldn't even look at me. Her fiancé seemed OK though. I bumped into him in the hall on my way out and he said he was sorry about my father. I thought that was nice of him. Don't know what he saw in that snooty cow. Pity he died too,' she added as an afterthought.

'Does Anthony Jameston know about your connection with his wife's family?'

Pandora shook her head. Then she looked at Wesley, suddenly worried. 'That Emma Oldchester – Jeremy told me that she's that woman's daughter. And the man who died in the grounds – wasn't he going to write a book about what happened?'

Wesley glanced at Heffernan. 'Your name was on the list of people he wanted to talk to.'

Pandora frowned. 'Was it?'

'Did he ever get in touch?'

Pandora shook her head vehemently. 'Absolutely not. I never saw him. Never.'

Heffernan stood up. He'd heard enough for now. 'Any chance of having a word with Mr Jameston, if he's free?'

She walked across the room and consulted a large wall chart. 'He's having his aura healed at the moment,' she said, matter-of-factly.

Heffernan grinned. 'Another time maybe. It wasn't important. Is there anything else at all you can tell me about the Harfords?'

Pandora shook her head again.

As Wesley told her she could go, his mobile phone began to ring. After a brief conversation he turned to Heffernan. 'Looks like our luck's changing. As soon as the Carmody woman's fingerprints were taken they were checked against the computer. Her real name's Brenda Varney, alias June

212

Wheeler, alias Beatrice Carmody, alias Wendy Felton, alias Mary Thorpe. Brenda Varney. Recognise the name?'

Heffernan grinned smugly. 'The cleaner who stole Mary Harford's necklace and brooch. She's on Evans's list.'

'Looks like her fondness for jewellery hasn't faded with the years. I wonder if Emma Oldchester recognised her.'

'We can ask her.'

They walked out into the hall, where Jeremy Elsham was hovering anxiously, whispering to his wife. 'By the way, Mr Elsham,' Heffernan spoke at full volume, 'remember your guest, Mrs Carmody? We've just arrested her for theft. It was her who pinched Mrs Jeffries's money and ring. Paid her bill in cash, did she? Or has she given you a bouncing cheque?'

Jeremy Elsham's mouth fell open. 'But ... but she couldn't walk ... she was in a wheelchair. How did she ...?'

It was Wesley who answered. 'The wheelchair was her alibi. How could she possibly steal anything from upstairs when she had no way of getting up there?' He paused while this sank in. 'Interestingly enough she used to work here as a cleaner when she was young.' He addressed Pandora. 'Perhaps you met her, Mrs Elsham. Brenda Varney?'

Pandora shook her head. 'I've never seen her before in my life.'

'Can we have a word with Mrs Oldchester?'

'She's meditating,' Elsham said protectively.

'And we're investigating a murder,' Heffernan hissed. 'Just get her, will you.'

They spoke to Emma Oldchester in the conservatory again and she admitted that she had thought she recognised Brenda Varney and had tried to speak to her. But the woman had told her she was mistaken so that had been that. Emma had withdrawn before she made a fool of herself.

Wesley noticed that Emma looked pale and drawn but she wore a stubborn expression that told him she wouldn't change her mind: she was determined to stick it out at the

Hall, probably in the hope that Elsham would agree to take her back once more to her childhood. Wesley didn't know whether she was brave or foolish. In view of Evans's death, possibly the latter. But she was breaking no law so there was nothing they could do.

Before they left, Wesley gave her his business card, with strict instructions to ring any time if she was worried.

'Think she'll be OK?' he asked Heffernan when they were out of earshot.

'I reckon she's tougher than she looks.'

Wesley said nothing. Somehow he couldn't share his boss's optimism. If the killer knew that Emma was on the verge of remembering that dreadful day, she would be in grave danger.

'What do you make of our Pauline-Pandora then?' Heffernan asked as they walked to the car.

'I think she's telling the truth.'

Heffernan was keeping an open mind. 'We'll have a word with Gibbons when we get back. And there's another person on Evans's list we need to see. Dylan Madeley, Gwen's brother. Nobody's been able to find him yet. He's a familiar face at Morbay nick apparently. In and out of drug treatment centres and several convictions for robbery and possession. Not like his sister, eh?'

'I've got a bad feeling about her, Gerry. If she was expecting Arbel, she'd hardly just take off like that. I think we should make finding her a priority.'

Wesley drove back to the station. He wanted a word with Dylan Madeley himself. He had a nagging suspicion that when they found him, they might find Gwen. But where were they hiding?

When they walked into the CID office Trish Walton was on her way out, heading for the ladies. The sight of her reminded Wesley of the phone call he had received the previous night.

'Trish, can you do me a favour?'

Trish looked at him warily. Favours usually involved

extra work. And she was busy enough already.

'Can you meet Patrick Evans's widow this afternoon? Take her for a cream tea and have a chat. Can you ask her whether she's remembered anything else her husband mentioned about the trip he made up to North Yorkshire? Anything at all, however trivial it seems.'

Trish grinned. This one would be easy.

As soon as they had checked whether anything new had come in, Wesley and Heffernan headed down the stairs to the interview room, disappointed with their lack of progress.

As he drew up outside Max's house, Neil Watson's heart was beating fast. The Stars and Stripes still fluttered from the gleaming white flagpole and the birds still sang in the tall trees surrounding the house but somehow things seemed different now. Spoiled. And he wasn't sure whether he was still a welcome visitor.

At least there was no sign of Brett's car. If there had been he would have driven straight past. Neil had never been one to court trouble.

The door opened slowly and Max said nothing when he saw Neil standing there on the threshold. He walked back into the house, as though he expected Neil to follow.

'I didn't know whether to . . .'

The old man slumped down in his rocking chair. He looked tired – and somehow older than he had done when he and Neil had first met. 'Now don't you go paying no heed to Brett. He's always been one to punch first and ask questions later, even when he was a kid. Nasty bruise. You OK?'

'Got a few funny looks down at the dig. Nothing I couldn't handle,' Neil said bravely, trying to make light of it for Max's sake. He didn't like to mention that Hannah Gotleib had avoided him since Chuck had mentioned in passing that someone had landed a punch on him. Hannah probably didn't go for the type of man who gets involved in brawls.

215

He rummaged in his pocket and drew out a couple of pictures. 'A friend in Devon emailed these pictures to me. It's Potwoolstan Hall. The Selbiwood family seat.'

Max donned the spectacles that were lying on the table beside the rocking chair and studied the pictures Pam had sent. He nodded earnestly, as though they confirmed something he already suspected. 'So that's what Edmund left behind.'

He said nothing for what seemed like a long time and Neil waited patiently. He felt that Max had something momentous to say . . . some dreadful knowledge that he had never shared with anyone. 'You know about history, stories from the past and . . .' He paused, as though weighing up what Neil's reaction was likely to be. 'If you found out that you were descended from a murderer, how would that make you feel?'

Neil stared at the fireplace. There were logs in the grate, although the weather was too warm for a fire. Photographs stood on the mantelpiece: Brett and presumably Brett's children in graduation robes: one of them, a boy, looked rather like him. It was almost like seeing a slightly altered version of oneself in the mirror. There was a woman too, a black and white studio portrait. Probably Max's late wife . . . the girl he had left Neil's grandmother behind in England for. She was pretty . . . probably prettier than Jean.

For the first time Neil wondered what he was doing there digging up old loves, old pain. And for the first time he looked at Max and saw a man who'd betrayed his grandmother; who'd left her pregnant and alone while he went back home and got on with his life. He tried to push this thought to the back of his mind.

'You've not answered my question. How would that make you feel?'

Neil shrugged. 'I suppose there are villains in every family. People hanged for stealing sheep, highwaymen, murderers. I don't think it would bother me that much. Unless it was recent, of course.'

From the look on Max's face he knew he'd given the

right answer. The old man stood up stiffly. 'Those papers I mentioned. The ones for the museum. You will hand them over for me, won't you?'

Neil nodded. If he had his hands on old family documents he'd find them hard to resist. Max swayed slightly and steadied himself.

'Are you OK, Max? You look a bit tired.'

The old man managed a weak smile. 'I didn't sleep too good last night, that's all. Come back here tomorrow, won't you? Same time. I'll have everything ready.'

'You're still planning to come over to England, aren't you?' Somehow Max's words seemed so final, as though he was trying to say goodbye.

'Sure. Brett can't stop me.' The words were defiant but the voice sounded weaker somehow. 'Next time you call England, tell Jean I'll be there soon. Will you do that?'

Neil touched the old man's hand, noticing the skin stretched like thin parchment over the bones and protruding veins. 'Sure,' he said before taking his leave.

Richard Gibbons had given cigarettes up long ago on his mother's insistence. But he longed for one now.

He remembered police interview rooms from the times he'd had his 'little spot of bother', as he always thought of it. The small matter of a few CDs stolen from a record shop in Morbay. The police had been quite unreasonable. And they'd no business coming round and upsetting his mother.

'You're entitled to have a solicitor present,' the young black man said politely. Richard Gibbons hated him, not so much because of the colour of his skin but because of his well-spoken voice and his educated manner. Gibbons had the feeling that Wesley Peterson was looking down on him. But then he had that feeling about a lot of people. Even Brenda at times.

'You remember me, don't you, Richard? I came to your house to ask about a man called Patrick Evans. Do they call you Richard?'

217

'Of do you prefer Dick ... or Ricky?' the big Scouse one said. He was nothing like his colleague. He had twinkling eyes that had seen it all. No airs and graces. Gibbons wondered how these two got on together, working so closely.

'Richard.'

'That what your mother calls you?' the big man said with a grin.

Gibbons didn't answer. He was being laughed at. It always happened.

The younger man leaned forward, looking him in the eye. 'You might as well give us a full statement about the stolen jewellery. Brenda's been very cooperative. I must say it was a clever scam. Brenda goes to a residential course or health spa pretending to be unable to use the stairs for one reason or another. Then she steals from the upper floors and hands the goods over to you immediately to dispose of so if her room's searched she's always clean. Do you split the proceeds fifty fifty or ...?' Wesley Peterson tilted his head to one side, awaiting an answer.

Gibbons took a deep breath. 'Brenda gets most 'cause she does most of the work, takes the risk. I get my cut.'

'How did you and Brenda meet?'

'I knew her from when we both worked at the Hall. I used to be sweet on her then she upped and left. They said she'd nicked some jewellery but I never knew nothing about that. I met her again in a pub in Morbay about a year ago. I recognised her at once. She asked me if I wanted to make a bit of money. Said she had this idea.'

'And you just couldn't say no,' Heffernan muttered.

'Brenda can be very persuasive,' Gibbons said earnestly. 'And she's a very attractive woman.'

'So it was sex as well as greed,' Heffernan observed with a wide grin. 'Why go back to Potwoolstan Hall?'

Gibbons shrugged. 'We looked for places where Brenda could keep track of the guests – not just hotels where they could come and go. And places without lifts.'

'So the Hall fitted all your requirements?'

'Something like that. Brenda did all the research. She's very thorough.'

'Didn't it bother her going back to Potwoolstan Hall?'

'Brenda's not superstitious,' he answered, almost proudly.

'Did you and she ever talk about what happened there ... the murders?'

'Sometimes.'

'And?'

Gibbons shrugged. 'Nothing much to talk about really. That housekeeper killed them. She was a funny woman. Stuck-up. Mad eyes.'

It was funny how, with hindsight, all murderers have mad eyes, Wesley thought to himself.

'Brenda had a lucky escape, leaving the Hall before it happened. If she'd been there, Martha Wallace might have killed her as well.'

'Suppose so.'

'What about Victor Bleasdale, the gardener? You must have known him quite well.'

'Not really. We only ever talked about work.'

'He left just before the killings, didn't he?'

'He got a job up north.'

'And nobody saw him again after that?'

'I think the police saw him ... interviewed him, like.'

'What was Bleasdale like?'

'He was a hard worker; liked to keep me on my toes.' He gave a sly grin. 'And he was one for the girls. Good-looking bastard,' he added with envy.

'How did he get on with the Harfords?'

'OK, I suppose. Mrs Harford used to come down to discuss the garden with him and he used to be all "Yes, Mrs Harford, no, Mrs Harford, three bags full, Mrs Harford." The Harfords were OK as long as you knew your place.'

'Did he talk about the job in North Yorkshire?'

Gibbons screwed up his face, trying to retrieve a half-forgotten memory. 'I can't remember. It was a long time ago. But I think he left quite sudden, like.'

Gerry Heffernan had been watching Gibbons intently but now he leaned forward and stared him in the eye. 'Would you recognise him if you saw him now?'

'Dunno. People change.'

'What about Brenda? Would she recognise him?'

'You'd have to ask her.'

'Is there any chance Bleasdale could have shot the Harfords?'

Gibbons snorted. 'Nah. He'd left by then. He was miles away. No, you can count him out. And the same goes for me and Brenda before you try and fit us up.'

He sniffed loudly. He was an unpleasant little man, Wesley thought. But that didn't mean he was a murderer.

'Is there anything else you can tell us about Bleasdale? Anything at all? Did he have a girlfriend or ...?'

'There was someone,' Gibbons said with a twinkle in his small eyes. 'I never saw them together, mind, but she left messages for him in the shed and that.'

'Who was it?' Heffernan growled.

Gibbons grinned, revealing a row of uneven, yellow teeth. 'That friend of Miss Arbel's was always hanging around the Hall and the grounds. She even used to come when Miss Arbel was away. Now why would she want to be doing that?'

'Because she fancied Bleasdale?'

'Got it in one. Want to know what her name was?'

Wesley sat back and said nothing. Richard Gibbons wasn't the only one who could play games.

After a few moments, Heffernan spoke. 'Could it be Gwen Madeley?'

The disappointed look on Gibbons's face told Wesley all he wanted to know.

Brenda had nothing to say that they hadn't heard before.

220

Her favoured tactic was to plead ignorance and Wesley knew that she was unlikely to give them anything worthwhile. Besides, she had been nowhere near Potwoolstan Hall at the time of the murders. On her own admission, she had been investigating the possibilities of London at the time.

Wesley particularly wanted to talk to Arbel Harford. According to Trish Walton she had checked out of the Marina Hotel and was staying at Gwen Madeley's cottage, saying that it was nearer the Hall, where her husband was staying. And that she felt she ought to be there for Gwen in case she returned. But even though the move seemed sensible, Wesley wasn't happy about it. Gwen Madeley had already disappeared. And he had an uneasy feeling that Arbel might be in danger.

He and Heffernan were about to set off but just as the chief inspector was leaving the office he received a call from Chief Superintendent Nutter, who wanted a progress report on the Evans murder. Heffernan took off his coat and slouched out of the office with a hangdog expression on his chubby face. There was little to report. Little that was positive anyway.

Wesley drove to Gwen Madeley's cottage alone. Perhaps Arbel might be more willing to talk one to one, he thought. When he arrived he was glad to see her Mercedes parked outside. She was in.

Arbel Jameston, née Harford, seemed smaller, more vulnerable, than when she and Wesley had last met. She was dressed simply but expensively in well-cut black trousers and a silk shirt and there were dark rings beneath her eyes as though she hadn't slept. She wore no make-up and there were no diamonds on her fingers. But then Wesley had come unannounced: she hadn't been expecting visitors.

'Any news of Gwen?' she asked anxiously as soon as he'd crossed the threshold.

'Sorry. But we're doing all we can,' he said, trying to

221

sound convincing. 'I'd just like to have an informal chat if that's OK.'

Arbel didn't seem to resent the intrusion, if anything she seemed grateful to have somebody to talk to. She invited Wesley to sit down while she put the kettle on for coffee but he followed her into the kitchen.

'I'm sorry to descend on you like this, Mrs Jameston. Hope you don't mind.'

She turned with the full kettle in her hand and looked at him with curiosity for a second before rearranging her features into an expression of helpful gratitude. 'Of course I don't. If there's anything I can do to help you find Gwen, anything at all, I'm only too pleased to help. Not that I can add anything to what I've already told your colleagues.' She looked Wesley up and down. 'You don't seem like your average country policeman.' She immediately became flustered, as though she'd just realised that the comment might be misinterpreted as some sort of racist remark. 'Please don't misunderstand me ... I don't mean ...' She was blushing now.

Wesley took pity on her. 'I didn't start off as a policeman. My degree's in archaeology.'

Arbel tilted her head to one side, a mannerism Wesley found attractive. 'But you didn't become an archaeologist?'

Wesley smiled. 'I suppose archaeology has a lot in common with police work: gathering the clues, interpreting evidence, fitting that evidence into a likely scenario. They say inside every archaeologist there's a detective waiting to get out and my grandfather was a chief superintendent back in Trinidad so law and order must run in the family.' It was time to steer the subject back to Gwen Madeley. 'I believe you and Gwen have been friends for a long time?'

'Yes. We both went to the local school.' She hesitated and her face clouded, as though she was remembering something painful. 'Then I was sent away to boarding school when I was seven. But I saw Gwen in the holidays.'

'Gwen has a brother.'

222

Arbel turned her head away. 'Dylan. He fell in with a bad crowd and became involved with drugs. He comes to Gwen when he wants money.'

'Have you seen him recently?'

She shook her head. 'Not for years.'

'How often do you see Gwen?'

'Not often. You know how it is. Busy lives.'

'Where do you think she could be? Is there anywhere she'd be likely to go?'

'I've really no idea. If I knew, I'd tell you.'

'She wouldn't be with Dylan?'

'I shouldn't think so.'

'Do you mind talking about your family?'

There was no reply for a few moments, then she gave a slight shake of the head.

'Do you remember a young woman called Pauline Black? Her father died in an industrial accident at your family's brewery.'

'I heard something about a man dying and his daughter turning up at the Hall. But I was away at school at the time. I never saw her.'

Wesley wondered whether to tell her about Pandora but decided against it. It would serve no purpose. 'Do you remember the under-gardener, Richard Gibbons?'

She smiled. 'I remember some gormless lad who used to hang around the grounds with a rake, staring at my legs every time I set foot out of doors. Is that who you mean?'

The description seemed to fit Gibbons as he would have been almost twenty years ago. 'Yes, that sounds like him. Tell me about the gardener, Victor Bleasdale.'

She studied her fingernails. 'What about him?'

'He went up to Yorkshire. Why did he leave?'

Arbel didn't answer. She made the coffee and carried the two brimming mugs through to the living room, where she sat down on Gwen's low sofa. Wesley took the chair opposite, watching her face.

'Is there something about Bleasdale I should know?'

223

'Why?'

'You don't seem to want to talk about him.'

She picked her mug up and took another sip. The coffee was good, freshly ground. Pam always used instant these days. 'If you must know,' she said after a few moments, 'there was a bit of a row a few weeks before he left.'

'What was the row about?'

Another hesitation told Wesley that there was about to be an embarrassing revelation. He only hoped it was relevant to their enquiries. 'Vic and Gwen . . .' She let the sentence hang in the air for Wesley's imagination to fill in the blanks.

'Victor Bleasdale was sleeping with Gwen Madeley?'

Arbel nodded. 'Her parents found out and her father went storming up to the Hall. I was there. It was rather embarrassing. Mr Madeley demanded that my father sack Vic.'

'And did he?'

'I think my father might have suggested to Vic that he look for work elsewhere but I don't suppose he saw Vic's inability to keep his trousers on as a reason to dismiss him immediately. It wasn't as if Vic had seduced me or my sister, was it?' She gave a nervous giggle, somehow incongruous in a woman of her age.

Wesley looked her in the eye. 'So Gwen and Victor Bleasdale had an affair. Did she tell you about it?'

'In glorious detail. She thought she was in love.'

'Gwen never married.'

'No.'

'Do you think Victor Bleasdale could have killed your family?'

There was a slight, uncertain pause before she spoke. 'No, of course not. He'd gone up north by then, hadn't he?'

'You seem to have some doubts.'

'Well, Vic had a terrible temper and if my father had spoken to him about Gwen he might have resented . . .' She shook her head. 'I hadn't been home for a while. And I was

224

staying with a friend in London at the time so I didn't really know what went on. But ...'

'But what?'

'Vic did know where the guns were kept. And he probably knew that my father kept the key to the gun cupboard in his desk drawer. I remember him borrowing my father's rifle to shoot crows once. His own was out of action for some reason. And he was a good shot. He used to be in the army.'

She gathered up the coffee mugs and bustled into the kitchen, her mind still on the events all those years ago. Wesley sat quite still on the sofa, cursing himself that he hadn't discovered this information a long time ago. Bleasdale had been having an affair with Gwen Madeley, to her parents' consternation. Bleasdale might have argued with Arbel's father and had access to the guns that were used to kill the Harfords and Martha Wallace. And Bleasdale had disappeared.

Wesley followed Arbel into the kitchen again. There was one question he was longing to ask.

'How did Bleasdale get on with the housekeeper, Martha Wallace?'

Arbel turned around. 'I remember my mother saying that they couldn't stand each other.'

'Did you tell any of this to the police at the time?'

She shook her head. 'Vic was up north by then and they didn't seem interested in what he got up to with one of the local girls. They seemed quite sure that Martha had done it.' She paused. 'But you're not, are you?'

'We think Patrick Evans was about to discover who really killed your family.'

Arbel stood at the sink with her head bowed. 'I really don't want it raked up again, Inspector. I still have nightmares about finding them, you know. Can't everyone leave the whole thing alone?' She spoke quietly, almost in a whisper. Wesley noticed that there were tears in her eyes and he felt like a bully. 'I wish I'd met that man Evans. I

225

wish I'd had a chance to tell him how much pain he was causing.'

'I'm sorry,' he said. 'But we think Evans died because of what he'd found out about the deaths at the Hall.' Wesley paused. 'There's a possibility that the killer might still be around. And that means anybody connected with the case might be in danger. That's why we're worried about Gwen. Has she ever done anything like this before?'

Arbel's eyes widened in alarm. She was a frightened woman. A woman who had met death once and was terrified at the prospect of meeting it again.

'Wouldn't it be best if your husband stayed here with you?' Wesley said, concerned.

'He's only at the Hall for a couple more days. I can manage on my own,' she answered bravely.

'It must have been a shock when you found out where he was.'

She gave a bitter smile. 'Tony was never the most sensitive of people. But I think I understand why he came here.'

There was an awkward silence. She seemed to be taking her husband's stay at the Hall very calmly, almost as though she had long ceased to care what he did.

She looked at her watch. 'Look, it's lunchtime. Gwen's left plenty of stuff in the freezer. You will stay, won't you?' The invitation seemed sincere, not just given out of politeness.

Wesley hesitated. Then he thanked her and accepted. After all, the alternative was only a sandwich back at the office.

She hurried over to the freezer and opened the door, kneeling down to examine its neatly labelled contents. 'There's lobster in mornay sauce here. That OK for you? I can put it in the microwave.'

'Great,' Wesley said with a smile, thinking that Gwen Madeley wouldn't even have had to have made much effort to provide Patrick Evans with his very last supper.

*

Gerry Heffernan was sitting with his feet up on the desk, listening again to the tape Jeremy Elsham had made of Emma Oldchester's journey back to childhood. He had played it so often he felt he almost knew it off by heart. Emma's voice had begun to haunt his dreams.

But although the words had become so familiar, he kept listening in the hope that he'd hear something new. Something that would make everything clear at last. But it didn't work. He heard the words but their meaning was still unfathomable.

When Wesley popped his head round the door, Heffernan looked up and grinned. 'Had a nice lunch?'

Wesley came in and sat down with a sigh.

'What's up?'

'I've had a good talk to Arbel Jameston and she told me some interesting things about Victor Bleasdale.'

'What?'

'She confirmed what Gibbons said about Bleasdale and Gwen Madeley. And she said it was possible that Bleasdale argued with Edward Harford over it. And she also said Bleasdale and Martha Wallace couldn't stand the sight of each other.' He paused, saving the best till last. 'And Bleasdale used Harford's rifle to shoot crows so he knew where to find the keys to the gun cupboard. He also used to be in the army. According to Arbel he was a crack shot.'

The chief inspector scratched his head while he took it all in. 'But he was on his way to Yorkshire when it happened.'

'Did anybody check properly at the time?'

Gerry Heffernan was uncomfortably aware that the answer was probably no. According the records, a constable from North Yorkshire Constabulary had taken a statement to the effect that Bleasdale had left Devon on the morning before the murders to drive up north. He had broken the long journey with an overnight stay at a motel near Nottingham and arrived at his new place of employment just after lunch the following day. Presumably the interviewing officer hadn't asked to see any proof of this stay, such as a receipt, so it was possible that Bleasdale had either doubled back to Potwoolstan Hall or never left that day in the first place; a possibility that nobody seemed to have considered at the time.

'I think our priority is to find Victor Bleasdale. I suppose we'd better start where he was last seen.'

Wesley stood up. 'I think Gwen Madeley knew something and that's why she's gone missing. If she was having a relationship with Bleasdale ...'

'Think she's dead?'

'Let's hope not, eh. But I did discover one interesting thing. Gwen Madeley's freezer is full of lobster dishes. Do you think she might have been the person Evans stood Gibbons up for on the night he died?'

'You think Gwen Madeley killed him?'

'Or he ate there and he met someone else afterwards. Either way, we've got to find her.' He thought for a moment. 'I'm going to have a word with Trish. She took Kirsty Evans for a cream tea and there's something I want to ask her.'

Wesley left Gerry Heffernan staring into space. A few minutes later he returned, finding the chief inspector just as he'd left him. He didn't seem to have moved a muscle during Wesley's short absence.

'Trish asked Kirsty Evans if she could remember anything her husband said about his trip to North Yorkshire. Kirsty said he'd seemed quite excited when he came back but that wasn't unusual if his researches were going well. And apparently he mentioned something about dahlias, but she can't remember what.'

'Dahlias? You mean the flowers? You think he might have found our elusive gardener after all?'

Wesley grinned. 'It's a possibility. Now all we've got to do is find him ourselves.'

Chapter Ten

Penelope came to my dwelling last night, late and in secret. I was resolved not to admit her at first but my best intentions vanished at the sight of her lovely face. She looked to me to be so pure, so innocent, yet in my mind I kept seeing her with Isaac Morton.

When we were alone she kissed me, gently at first then with a passion that aroused me. She told me that Isaac had forced himself upon her and that she had yielded because she feared him, which was as I thought. She said that now Isaac is dead we can be man and wife, as soon as custom and propriety allow and left my dwelling in the guise of a modest widow. She doth dissemble as if it is a thing of ease. I have a great longing for her and yet I know not what to do. It may be that I should not marry for I fear the curse upon our blood.

Today Henry Jennings and Richard Smith – both members of our council – died of the bloody flux. I pray for the health of those living and the souls of those dead.

Set down by Edmund Selbiwood, Gentleman, at Annetown this thirtieth day of September 1605.

The skeleton lay there on the bench. AR 2. Neil Watson

wondered how the man with the musket ball lodged in the cavity where his brain had once been would have felt about being reduced to two letters and a number. Surprised, perhaps. Or angry. He had existed in an age of names, an age of certainties.

Neil stared down at the bones for a while before walking briskly out of the laboratory. He had gone there to seek refuge from the humid warmth of the spring Virginia morning in the lab's air-conditioned interior. Or at least that was the excuse he had made to himself. In reality he had wanted to see the skeleton; out of curiosity perhaps. Or something deeper. Something he didn't understand himself.

After telling Chuck that he had something important to do on the other side of town he made for the pick-up and climbed into the driver's seat. He was accustomed to driving on the right now and it felt quite natural as he steered through the wide streets towards Max's house.

He checked that Brett's car wasn't there before parking up. The last thing he wanted was another confrontation. He felt nervous as he opened the gleaming white wooden gate and walked up the garden path towards Max's front porch. What if Brett was there? What if he had parked around the corner for some reason?

He climbed the wooden steps up to the porch, pressed the bell push and waited. He pressed the bell again and strained to listen. But the only sounds he could hear were birdsong and the distant hum of a lawnmower. Max wasn't in. Neil felt disappointed. He had wanted to discuss Max's trip to England, his journey to see Jean for the last time. He had a sudden vision of them as he had seen people in mono-chrome wartime photographs. Dancing, walking together arm in arm. The young GI who had sailed across the Atlantic to encounter possible oblivion on the Normandy beaches and the pretty Land Army girl who had learned to live for the moment. Sex and looming death must have been a heady combination.

Neil rang the doorbell again, just to be sure. He heard

nothing. But then he touched the door gently and it moved. Cautiously he touched it again and it opened a few inches. It was unlocked.

He pushed the door open further and walked down the hallway on tiptoe, feeling as nervous and furtive as a novice burglar and wondering why the old man had been so careless with his security precautions. He called Max's name, first softly, then louder, walking from room to room, listening to the mellow ticking of Max's clocks.

The room at the back of the house that Max used as a study was smaller than the other downstairs rooms. It was a cosy room with dark red-striped wallpaper, polished furniture the colour of chestnut and a rich Turkish rug on the floor. It was a man's room: Max's territory.

Neil found it empty. But he spotted a package lying in the centre of the neatly ordered desk. His name was on it, written in bold capitals. Dr Neil Watson. Care of the Association for the Preservation of Annetown Antiquities, Annetown Archaeological Project. Neil picked it up and felt it. The packet was bulky and he assumed it contained the documents Max had promised to give him to pass on to the museum. Neil wondered whether he should take them. But, on the other hand, he didn't want Max to find they were missing and panic, thinking they'd been stolen. It would be better to come back another time and do things by the book.

He stood for a while, staring at the packet, before deciding to check the rest of the house. From the kitchen window he could see the garden that Max always referred to as the back yard, even though it was a large grassed area with shrubs and trees. But unless Max was hiding up a tree – difficult at his age – he wasn't out there.

Neil knew that if Brett caught him creeping about the house uninvited, it would confirm all his worst suspicions. But, as he reached the foot of the stairs, he had an uneasy feeling that things weren't right.

The wooden staircase creaked under his weight, the noise loud as a gunshot over the gentle rhythm of the clocks

231

ticking the time away in every room. 'Max,' he shouted, louder this time. Perhaps he was having a lunchtime doze.

Neil looked in the bedrooms. He had never been upstairs before. Like downstairs, the décor was dark and rich in a colonial style that somehow fitted the house. It had probably been Max's late wife's choice: women tended to make the decisions where interior decoration was concerned.

He pushed at the third door off the landing and it opened a foot but no further. Whatever was blocking it gave way slightly with each push and Neil's heart pounded as he managed to open the door far enough to see inside the room.

Max Selbiwood was lying on the red carpet just behind the door, staring upwards with unseeing eyes. And Neil knew at once that he was dead.

When Wesley had broken the news to Pam that he was staying overnight in Yorkshire, she had appeared to take it philosophically and had invited her mother over to keep her company. But Della had pleaded a prior engagement with a man fifteen years younger than herself; a date that couldn't possibly be broken. So much for motherly devotion.

If only Pam understood how important the investigation was. If only she hadn't looked at him as though he was King Herod at a kiddies' party. He felt he was being cast as a villain just for doing his job. And that wasn't fair. As he drove down the hill to the police station he felt a wave of helpless frustration. It had been so different once. Pam had understood ... once.

He picked Steve Carstairs up at the station. He viewed the prospect of a long journey with Steve with some trepidation but he was the only officer working on the case who was available at that moment. Recently the two men had reached an uneasy truce; an agreement to live and let live. But Steve still wasn't Wesley's travelling companion of choice.

'Have you seen anything of that Serena Jones?' Wesley

asked innocently as they turned on to the M1.

'No.'

From the way Steve said the single syllable, it was obvious that the subject was off limits. Wesley suspected that Serena Jones had used Steve for her own ends and he had been stupid enough to supply her with information, probably in an effort to impress her, not realising that she was a journalist with a job to do and ambitions to leave Devon and head for Fleet Street.

'Victor Bleasdale said he broke his journey and spent the night of the murders at a motel near Nottingham. I think we should check whether the place actually exists ... or existed. Fancy taking over the driving soon?'

'Yeah. Whatever.'

Wesley glanced at the clock on the dashboard. It would be another couple of hours before they were anywhere near their destination. Not for the first time Wesley wondered why he hadn't stuck to archaeology when he had the chance.

Somehow Wesley had expected the Earl of Pickrington's estate manager at Gristhorpe Hall to speak with a Yorkshire accent so he had been mildly surprised to find that he was Welsh. David Pugh was a stocky, red-headed man, slightly below average height, and he was one of those people who exude energy, always restless, never still. Even as Pugh sat at the huge oak desk beneath the window of the estate office – a monumental piece of furniture used by their Lordships' stewards for the past two centuries – he fidgeted with pens and straightened papers.

The cavernous office was situated next to the stable block of the large eighteenth-century hall. There was no modern office furniture; no beech filing cabinets or work stations. Instead there were heavy oak cupboards and bookcases built against the cool green walls, reminders of the days when trembling tenants would have shuffled over the stone-flagged floor, touching their caps, pleading for more time

233

to pay their rents. The modern computer on the desk and the photocopier in the corner of the room looked out of place, as did the selection of brochures piled on the table at the far end of the room advertising the joys of corporate shooting weekends and the delights of the main house as a luxury wedding venue. Everybody had to make a living these days, thought Wesley. Even earls.

'You've come a long way to see us, Inspector,' Pugh said. 'Must be something serious.'

Wesley cleared his throat, searching for the right words: something grave but not sensational. 'We're investigating a murder and we believe it may be linked to six killings that took place in Devon back in 1985. One of the people involved in the case travelled up here on the day of those deaths to take up a post here. He was a gardener.'

Pugh sat back with a look of satisfaction on his face, as though he was one step ahead of him. 'You mean Victor Bleasdale? You're the second person to ask me about him.'

'Who else asked you?' He thought he knew the answer but it was as well to have it confirmed.

'An author it was ... name of ... Hang on, I've got his business card here somewhere ...' He began to rummage in a wooden box on his desk. Wesley sat patiently and watched, wondering how much progress Steve was making down at the local police station. He had sent him there to try to find the officer who took Bleasdale's original statement. But he didn't hold out much hope.

'Here it is,' Pugh said, holding up a small rectangle of white card triumphantly. 'Patrick Evans. Author and freelance journalist. Address in London.' He said the name of the capital city with what sounded like contempt.

'Can you tell me what was said at your meeting? You see, Mr Evans has been murdered and we think his death may be linked with what he discovered about Victor Bleasdale.'

David Pugh looked alarmed. 'Oh dear. Of course I'll help in any way I can.' He scratched his head. 'Oh dear.

234

Let me think. Yes, he came here a few weeks ago – rang up to make an appointment like. Asked me all about this gardener Bleasdale, he did. Now I had to tell him that I don't remember much about the man. I was Deputy Estate Manager in those days . . . very much the dogsbody. I seem to remember Bleasdale wrote to us asking if there was a job going. He had very good references and the head gardener had been moaning on about being overstretched for months. We wrote offering him the job. Somewhere in Devon I think he lived.'

'You mean he wasn't coming here to be head gardener? You see, he was head gardener back in Devon and it was assumed that he was coming here for promotion, to be in charge of a bigger garden.'

Pugh chortled. 'Well, if he thought that he was in for a disappointment. Sid Crouch was head gardener. Then there was Geoff Clayton, who took over when Sid retired. Bleasdale was only third in the pecking order. Maybe that's why he left so suddenly. Perhaps there was a misunderstanding and he expected to be top dog.'

Wesley sat forward. 'He left?'

'Like I said to that author fellow, there isn't much to tell. He just upped and left. Cleared his things out of the cottage that went with the job and disappeared into thin air and nobody heard from him again. Sid Crouch was furious. Not that he'd been impressed with his work. He'd had to have words with him on several occasions. Even threatened him with the sack if he didn't pull his socks up.'

'What was wrong with his work?'

'Why don't you ask Geoff. He's in charge of the gardens now. That author fellow talked to him.'

'Where will I find him?'

'I know it's Saturday but I'd try the greenhouses. Very fond of his geraniums is Geoff. We have a fine display here in the summer when the house and grounds are open to the public.'

'And Sid Crouch? Is it worth talking to him?'

235

Pugh assumed a solemn expression. 'Sid passed away a year after he retired. Mind you, he was eighty-three. His Lordship had to let him go in the end. Couldn't be helped.'

Wesley stood up and put out his hand. 'Thank you very much, Mr Pugh. You've been very helpful. If you point me in the direction of the greenhouses . . .'

'I knew there was something not quite right about that Bleasdale, you know, and I pride myself on being a good judge of character.'

Wesley glanced at his watch: he only had just over an hour before he had to meet up with Steve to hear what he had found out from the local police.

He took his leave from Pugh politely but firmly and headed out of the stables, passing beneath the wide arch through which grand carriages had once swept into the cobbled yard. A white clock tower stood above the archway, probably built so that the estate workers would know the time and have no excuse for lateness.

He walked down the path towards the walled garden as Pugh had instructed and saw the greenhouses on his left. Their glass and white framework gleamed in the weak northern sun as Wesley approached the entrance and when he opened the door the smell of damp compost hit him, combined with the sharp, distinctive smell of growing geraniums. It was warm and humid beneath the glass roof and Wesley removed his coat as he looked for a human being amongst the foliage.

He soon spotted a figure moving behind the plants at the far end of the greenhouse. The man swung round, alarmed, when Wesley greeted him. It was clear he wasn't expecting visitors.

'By heck, thou gave me a right turn.' Wesley had found his authentic Yorkshireman at last. He introduced himself and explained the reason for his visit.

Geoff Clayton was a big man with a thick shock of white hair and a large, open face. Probably in his late fifties, he bore the hallmarks of his profession: old corduroy trousers and hands stained with soil. He looked to Wesley like an honest man. And he awaited his assessment of Victor Bleasdale's character with some interest.

'You're the second person who's come asking me about that Vic Bleasdale. What's he gone and done?'

'I'm afraid we're still pursuing our enquiries.'

The gardener chuckled. 'That's what t'police always say. Means nowt. You reckon Vic's a murderer, am I right? T'other one did and all – bloke who called himself an author.' The word was said with some contempt as though this man of the soil had no time for anybody involved in such effete activities.

'Patrick Evans?'

'Aye. That's him.'

'What did you tell him?'

Geoff Clayton ignored the question and started to make for the greenhouse door. 'Come on, lad, I'll mash us some tea. Like geraniums?'

Wesley realised that Geoff wasn't a man to be rushed. 'Yes. My wife took some cuttings last year. They're doing quite well. What compost would you advise?'

This seemed to clinch it. Wesley was now Geoff's bosom pal. As they left the greenhouse and walked towards the neat wooden potting shed nearby, Wesley received a torrent of horticultural advice he knew he'd have no chance of remembering. He nodded gratefully, as if he was taking in every word.

But it was over a mug of tea so strong that Wesley could feel it grating against his teeth, that Geoff's information became really interesting.

'Vic Bleasdale only stayed a couple of weeks before he buggered off without a by your leave. Moonlight flit it were. Cleared out his cottage and nobody saw hide nor hair of him again.'

'What was he like to work with?'

Another chuckle. 'Hadn't a clue. And bone idle. If he hadn't left I reckon old Sid would have given him his marching orders.'

'Do you mean he hadn't a clue about gardening?'

'Aye, that's exactly what I mean. Didn't know his wall-flowers from his daffodils, that one. You wouldn't have thought he'd worked as a gardener before. In fact, I had my doubts. I only just managed to stop him spraying weedkiller on Sid's prize dahlias. Ruddy idiot.'

Wesley leaned forward, excited. Dahlias. Kirsty Evans had mentioned dahlias. 'Did you tell Patrick Evans about the dahlias?'

He thought for a moment. 'Aye. He wanted to know all about Bleasdale so happen I did.'

'You think Bleasdale might have been an impostor then?'

A slow grin lit up Geoff Clayton's face. 'Aye. Happen he could have been. Is that a crime, do you reckon? Impersonating a gardener.'

'If it's not, maybe it should be,' said Wesley as he took another sip of mahogany-brown tea.

The telephone on Rachel Tracey's desk began to ring. She picked up the receiver and recited her name.

The man at the other end of the line identified himself as a constable in the traffic division and asked to speak to Inspector Peterson.

'He's not here at the moment. Can I help?'

'It's just that car we've been asked to watch out for – the one belonging to that missing woman, Gwen Madeley. It's turned up on a lane near Derenham. Near a footpath leading down to the river. The farmer who reported it said it's been sitting there for a couple of days. Just thought I'd let you know.'

The line went dead, leaving Rachel staring at the receiver. Then she dialled the number of Wesley's mobile. This was something he'd want to know at once.

The police station nearest to Gristhorpe Hall was in the small North Yorkshire town of Pickrington. It was a pleas-ant, stone-built town, clustered around a large market

238

square which was blessed with more than its fair share of public houses and restaurants. Wesley imagined that at the weekend people in outlying villages probably descended on the bright lights of Pickrington for a good night out.

The police station was a red-brick Victorian building situated in one of the narrow side streets that snaked off the market square. The exterior stood as it had done for over a century, the community's temple of law and order, but the interior had been stripped of all its original features and transformed into a fine example of bland institutional design, all grey walls and pale-wood office furniture.

Wesley met Steve as arranged in the station foyer. Steve stood up as he entered through the swing door; his hands were thrust in the pockets of his leather jacket as usual.

'How's it going?' Wesley asked. 'Anything new?'

'Yeah. The constable who took the statement is retired but he still lives on the outskirts of the town. Anyway, he doesn't remember much about it. He took the statement and sent it through. Just routine. He can't even remember what Bleasdale looked like.'

'Hardly surprising. Anything else?' He had the feeling that Steve was saving the best till last.

'Oh yes,' said Steve triumphantly. 'There's more. A couple of weeks after Bleasdale made his statement his car was found burned out in a lane leading to some farm cottages just off the Whitby road. Enquiries were made but the police were told that he no longer worked at Pickrington Hall and nobody knew where he'd gone.'

Wesley felt his heart beating faster. 'You say his car was burned out. Bleasdale wasn't in it, by any chance?'

Steve shook his head. 'Apparently not. He disappeared into thin air never to be seen again.'

'Until Patrick Evans woke the dead,' Wesley said quietly.

His mobile phone began to ring, singing out its tinny version of Bach's Toccata and Fugue. After a brief conversation he turned to Steve.

'That was Rachel. They've found Gwen Madeley's car.'

He looked at his watch. They were stuck in North Yorkshire for the night, booked into one of the numerous pubs on the market square, and there was nothing much Wesley could do.

He had hoped that Gwen Madeley was still alive. But now he was beginning to fear the worst.

Steve had disappeared off to what was reputed to be the hottest local nightspot – probably barely lukewarm by big city standards – just when Wesley wanted someone to discuss the case with. Wesley had been left alone in the hotel bar, the focus of curious stares from the locals. He consumed two pleasing pints of Black Sheep bitter before retiring upstairs to his room, hoping that Steve would be in a fit condition to share next day's driving.

At eight o'clock the next morning Wesley was anxious to begin the long journey south. He wanted to retrace Bleasdale's steps and find the motel where he was supposed to have stayed on his way up to Pickrington. He didn't expect anybody there to remember him; he just wanted to satisfy himself that the place existed. He was starting to doubt whether anything about Victor Bleasdale could be trusted.

The back room of the pub had been converted into a makeshift breakfast room for bed and breakfast guests. It was a large, north-facing room and the weak spring sunlight seeping in through the small windows had to be supplemented with artificial light. The wallpaper was the colour of grubby claret and the woodwork was dark and glossy. The remains of last night's coal fire lay grey and dusty in the hearth. It was a room that looked cosy by night but oddly shabby in daylight. An evening room. Wesley breathed in the aroma of beer and stale tobacco smoke as he and Steve sat together at a table for two enjoying a generous full English breakfast that would have sent Gerry Heffernan into a state of ecstasy. The only other residents in the room were a ruddy-faced middle-aged couple, dressed for walking. They studiously ignored Wesley and

Steve as they chewed through their bacon and eggs, obviously believing in the British virtue of keeping oneself to oneself. Wesley found himself wondering how Neil had adapted to the American way of life. No doubt he'd hear all about it when he returned, which wouldn't be long now. Time flew – or perhaps it was a sign he was getting older.

He looked at Steve – who was clearly recovering from a heavy night – and wondered how life would have been if he was still single and fancy-free. Then he put the thought out of his mind.

'Don't you want that toast?' Wesley nodded towards the half-full toast rack.

'Help yourself,' Steve muttered back.

'Good night last night?'

Steve didn't answer and Wesley sensed that the subject was closed. He wished Gerry Heffernan was sitting there across the table. There would be little chance of extra toast but at least he'd be able to discuss the case, swapping speculations and possibilities.

His mobile phone began to ring and Steve looked wary, suspecting that it heralded more work. After a brief conversation, Wesley looked up. 'That was the DS we spoke to at the local nick. He says he's found something else.' Wesley took a swig of lukewarm coffee and stood up, his chair scraping loudly on the stone-flagged floor.

They walked to the police station to the accompaniment of the bells of the parish church near by: Wesley had almost forgotten it was Sunday. At the station, DS Kevin Haslet was waiting for them. He was a big man, sixteen stone at the very least, who shook Wesley's hand with an enthusiastic and painful grip. Wesley tried his best to smile.

'Now then,' Haslet began. 'I've dug out something else that might interest you. When that car your DC was asking about went up in flames an old lass from the farm cottages reported it. She made a statement.' He handed a sheet of paper to Wesley.

Wesley began to read. The old lass, a Mrs Edith

Shawthwaite, had been observant. On a routine walk with her dog she had seen smoke ahead on the quiet lane, hardly used except by locals, farmers and the occasional walker. She had approached cautiously and as she drew nearer she realised that it was a car in flames. Being a practical sort of woman her first thought was to retrace her steps to her cottage to telephone the emergency services – this being before the days of universal mobile phones. Then she spotted a couple walking off in the other direction and called out to them but they hurried away. She didn't get a good look at their faces but she gave the police an approximate description. Which they promptly filed and forgot about.

The description of the man could have fitted the one they had of Victor Bleasdale. And he was with a young woman with brown hair.

Wesley's heart began to beat faster as he asked where he could find DS Haslet's old lass.

But his elation was short-lived. The old lass had been a friend of Haslet's mother. And she currently resided in Pickrington churchyard. She had passed away three years back.

Wesley hardly said a word all the way home, not even when they discovered that the motel where Bleasdale claimed to have stayed was no longer there, having been demolished to make way for a shopping centre fifteen years before. It just wasn't his day.

The corpse floated in the river, swayed gently this way and that by the outgoing tide. At first the skipper of the car ferry took it for a bundle of old clothes. But after a few seconds he was certain that it was a body. A floater. Buoyed up by putrefying gases; swollen and disfigured by days of lying on the river bed, dragged to and fro by the currents. His colleague, Jim, was busy collecting the money from the drivers, weaving between the parked vehicles on the deck and leaning into car windows. The skipper cut the engines and shouted over to Jim, who hurried to the side rail followed by a couple of pedestrian passengers, a man and a woman whose waterproof clothing showed them to be well prepared for Devon's unpredictable weather.

'Looks like a woman,' Jim shouted up to the skipper, with inappropriate excitement. This was a welcome diversion. Something to relieve the boredom of another day spent travelling back and forwards across the river from first light until dusk.

'Hadn't someone better call the police?' the male passenger said with what sounded like authority. Jim stared at him for a second. The police meant more entertainment. He might even be called as a witness. There might be time off work. And a story to impress the girls in the pub of an evening.

By now some of the other ferry passengers had left their cars and were hanging over the rail, staring into the grey water at the body that was floating face down. A bundle of ragged grey clothes and rotting flesh.

An hour later when the police launch had hauled the body out of the cold tidal waters of the Trad, Gerry Heffernan stood on the deck staring down at the dead woman, whose sodden garments clung around her swollen body. He fought the impulse to cover her gnawed and disfigured face. The river's hungry crabs had devoured her eyes and flesh. But she fitted the description all right.

Gwen Madeley had turned up at last.

Chapter Eleven

Lord Coslake observed with his customary bluntness that as Penelope was much in my company and she was a defenceless widow in a new land, we should ask the Lord's blessing on our union. It seems I must take her for my wife for better or for worse.

Penelope has behaved with much modesty of late and forbids me her bed. Yet I cannot help but think of that day when I spied her with Isaac Morton and the look of pleasure and triumph on her sweet face. It may be that I should tell her my true reason for leaving England. We can seek a new life and a new world but the sins of the blood are with us always.

The weather here grows cooler and I fear what the winter holds for us. Henry Barras died of the bloody flux two nights since. It is strange that the Lord has struck down only members of our Council. Perhaps it is a judgement upon us. Lord Coslake and Master Heath go on the morrow to seek out the Chief of the natives. As we have no harvest we must trade for food or go hungry. A Spanish ship was sighted in the bay of Chesupioc. I pray that the Lord will keep us safe from our enemies. And from all other evils.

Set down by Edmund Selbiwood, Gentleman, at Annetown this twelfth day of October 1605.

*

Neil Watson felt a bead of sweat trickle down his brow as he dug and felt a sudden longing for the cool Devon climate. Hannah Gotleib was sieving the small pile of soil bound for the spoil heap and she smiled as he caught her eye.

'Chuck just told me about Max Selbiwood. I'm sorry. I guess you were getting quite close to him.' There was a question in there somewhere but Neil didn't rise to the bait. He hadn't broadcast his relationship with Max around the dig. As far as his temporary colleagues were concerned, Max had been helping Neil with some historical research.

'Yeah. It was very sudden. Probably the best way to go. Have you had a chance to read the documents he gave us yet?'

Her eyes lit up. 'Only some of them. I guess that stuff about the Morton brothers being shot fits with those skeletons we found. What do you say?'

'It's possible.'

'I think we have ourselves a murder mystery,' she said earnestly.

'Not much mystery now we know who did it. Isaac shot his brother then shot himself.'

'Do you really believe that?'

Neil stopped scraping at the dry earth with his trowel and looked up at her. 'I'll tell you when I've had a chance to read all the papers.'

She smiled. 'Having something written by someone who built this place makes the settlers kind of real, don't you think? When you get back home, can you send me more details about Edmund's family home? Potwoolstan Hall, isn't it?'

'I've got some pictures of the place already but I'll see what else I can find.' He hesitated. 'Some people were murdered there a few years ago: the cook went mad with a shotgun or something.'

Hannah put her hand to her mouth in a gesture of horror but before Neil could say more he heard a man's voice behind him. 'Dr Watson. May I speak with you for a moment?'

Neil swung round and saw Brett Selbiwood standing on

the edge of the trench looking down on him. He took a step back, uncertain what to expect. Another punch perhaps. He didn't need this right now.

'If we could speak in private.'

Neil looked at the man, then at Hannah, who was picking tiny shards of pottery from the soil, oblivious to any animosity between Neil and the newcomer. After a moment of hesitation he climbed out of the trench.

He walked away from the main excavation site, taking the path through the trees; the way to the reconstructed settlement that Hannah had shown him when he had first arrived in Virginia. Brett followed a couple of paces behind.

'Look, I want to say I'm sorry for what I did. I guess I thought you were trying to take advantage of my pa and . . .'

Neil stopped and turned to face him. 'That's OK,' he said automatically, wondering what had brought about this change of heart. He was soon to find out.

'I checked out my pa's will. Sorry to tell you that he's left you nothing. Or your grandma.'

'It never crossed my mind that he would. That wasn't why I tried to find him, Brett. I wasn't interested in his money.'

'Then what . . .?'

'My grandmother wanted me to find him. I did as she asked because she's dying. Then I found out that Max was descended from one of the first people to settle here in 1605 and he was interested in local history. We had a lot in common. And in spite of the fact that he left my grandmother pregnant and never contacted her again, I liked him.' He paused, letting the words sink in. 'He kindly donated some documents to the museum before his death.'

Brett opened his mouth as if he were about to protest. Neil could almost see dollar signs in his eyes. The documents so casually given away might have been worth something.

'And before you say anything, it was all his idea, not mine. And the museum's extremely grateful.'

'What were these documents?'

'An account written by an Edmund Selbiwood in 1605 of the first days of the Annetown settlement. As I said, the museum's very grateful to have them.'

Neil carried on walking. They had reached the reconstructed settlement but the place was empty. The modern-day settlers who re-enacted the past – unlike their seventeenth-century counterparts – probably took days off.

'I came here to invite you to Max's funeral,' Brett said after a few moments, as if the words were choking him. 'I guess he would have wanted you there.'

After giving him the date and the venue, Brett hurried back to the car park, leaving Neil to wander back to the dig alone.

When he reached the excavation, Hannah strolled over to greet him.

'The bones we found on the edge of the churchyard site, the other early burials.'

'Seven complete skeletons if I remember right.' He'd been reading up in his spare time, mainly to avoid Chuck's constant baseball commentary.

'We asked a toxicologist to test samples of bone using a plasma mass spectrometer. Now you usually need soft tissue or hair to get a result but the equipment was so sophisticated that . . .'

'What did they find?'

'The results haven't come back yet.' She hesitated. 'But forget hostile natives and wild animals. I've read some accounts of a mysterious illness that was going round the early settlers here and I'm wondering whether the main danger they had to face came from within Annetown itself.'

But before Neil had a chance to reply, Professor Keller appeared, his tanned face a picture of concern. 'There's a call for you from England, Dr Watson. You can take it in my office.'

Five minutes later, Neil had other things on his mind than the past.

*

Wesley, newly returned from Yorkshire in the late afternoon, wished he could have gone straight home but there was no chance of that just yet. As they set off for Gwen Madeley's cottage both men experienced the trepidation that police officers always feel when they are the bearers of bad news, appearing on some unsuspecting person's doorstep like birds of ill omen.

A momentary look of alarm crossed Arbel Harford's face when she answered the door and she led them through to the sitting room in silence.

'I get the feeling this isn't a social call,' she said as she sat down in the armchair nearest the unlit fire.

'Is your husband still at the Hall?'

'No. He went back to London yesterday. I was going to go with him but I didn't like to leave in case ... in case Gwen came back.'

Wesley glanced at Heffernan, who was standing beside him, shuffling his feet. He decided to come straight to the point.

'I'm afraid we have some bad news, Mrs Jameston. A body's been found.'

Arbel sat forward, her eyes large and terrified.

'I'm afraid we're pretty sure it's Ms Madeley. I'm sorry.' Wesley bowed his head respectfully for a moment. He could see tears forming in Arbel's eyes.

Arbel took a deep, steadying breath. 'How did she die?' The question came out in a whisper.

'She was found in the river. We think she probably drowned.'

Arbel looked down at her hands. 'She was very depressed when I last spoke to her on the phone. She was terribly worried about her brother. The situation was really getting her down. She was taking pills – tranquillisers. And when Tony saw her at the Hall she said she was upset about that man Evans dragging up the past again. It was suicide, I take it?'

'We'll know more after the postmortem but we're

keeping an open mind at the moment,' Wesley said softly.

Heffernan spoke. 'Why should she be upset about Evans? Surely you're the one who should have been upset. It was your family.'

'I know. I was. But . . .'

Wesley held his breath, sensing that Arbel was about to make some revelation. Perhaps she hadn't liked to speak freely before but now that Gwen was dead, she felt able to do so.

'There's something I didn't tell you. I didn't think it was something Gwen would want widely known. I told you she was having an affair with Bleasdale.' She hesitated.

'Go on.'

'She was friendly with my sister's fiancé too.' She emphasised the word friendly. 'It started shortly before the murders.'

'You mean Gwen Madeley and Nigel Armley were having an affair?'

Arbel nodded and the two officers looked at each other. After what Wesley had discovered about the gardener, Bleasdale, having been seen with a brown-haired girl near the burning car, he had rather fancied Gwen in the role of his accomplice, especially in view of the pictures she had painted of the scene. But if she had transferred her affections to Nigel Armley then this seemed rather unlikely.

'How did you know?' Wesley asked. 'Did she tell you about it?'

She shook her head. 'I was looking for her one day. She often hung round the outhouse where Bleasdale kept his things.' She bowed her head. 'I found her in there with Nigel. They were . . . Well, I don't have to spell it out, do I?'

'Did you tell your sister?'

Arbel shook her head vigorously. 'How could I? Catriona was besotted with him. I said nothing to her. I didn't even tell Gwen I'd seen her. Least said soonest mended, isn't that what they say?'

'What was your own relationship with Nigel Armley?'

She shrugged. 'I didn't really have one. He fancied

himself. Thought he was God's gift to women. My sister could make her own mistakes,' she added bitterly.

'Did Victor Bleasdale know about Gwen and Armley?'

'I've no idea. I always used to think Gwen only took up with Vic because she was bored. There's not really that much to do for a teenager in these parts,' she observed with a faint smile.

'If Bleasdale found out he might have reacted violently. You said he had a temper.'

Arbel hesitated, understanding the implications. 'It's possible, I suppose.'

'Do you think Gwen's relationship with Nigel Armley could have been serious?'

'Gwen didn't confide in me. But as far as I know she's not had a serious relationship since his death. Perhaps she never got over it.'

'And what about you? Have you got over what happened?'

Arbel took a deep breath. 'You never get over something like that. But you learn to live with it. Take each day at a time. But I still have the nightmares.'

Wesley looked at her hands and saw that they were shaking. 'So when Patrick Evans started raking it all up again . . .?'

'I wasn't happy about it. But then if Martha really was innocent then . . .' She hesitated. 'I suppose it's only right that her name should be cleared. For the sake of her daughter. Poor girl.' She paused. 'Tony mentioned something about her being up at the Hall. Is that true?'

Wesley nodded.

Arbel closed her eyes for a few seconds and shuddered. 'She must be braver than I am, to face staying in that place again.'

'Have you seen her?'

She shook her head. 'I wouldn't even recognise her now. Anyway, what would be the point?'

'Did you have much to do with her when she was young?'

She shook her head. 'She was just some little kid who hung around the place. I was a teenager and teenagers are selfish and self-obsessed, at least I was.'

Gerry Heffernan leaned forward. 'Someone killed your family, love, and I don't think it was Martha Wallace. And a man's dead. Murdered because he either knew the truth or was getting close to it. I reckon if we find out who killed Patrick Evans, we find out who really killed your family. Will you help us?'

A tear began to run down Arbel's right cheek, leaving a glistening track. 'I want to find out the truth as much as you do. And if someone wanted my family dead . . .' She let the sentence hang in the air but Wesley mentally completed it. If someone wanted her family dead then she might be next on the list.

'And Gwen? You don't think she could have been murdered, do you?'

'There were no obvious signs of violence.' He paused. 'I'm afraid we need somebody to identify the body. But after all you've been through, Mrs Jameston, I hardly liked to ask you to do it.'

Arbel bowed her head. She was trying desperately to hold back the tears. 'I've known Gwen since we were small. I'm sorry but . . .'

'Do you know anybody else who could identify her? A relative perhaps. Or a neighbour?'

'There's the people she worked with at the Hall. And there's her brother, Dylan.'

'We've not been able to trace him.'

'Gwen said he was staying in some sort of hostel. I thought he might have visited her the night she went missing. Gwen wouldn't have left that broken mug on the floor like that. He's been violent before when he's desperate. I kept telling her to tell the police. But he was her brother . . .' She looked Wesley in the eye. 'I don't like Dylan Madeley. And I don't trust him. And if Gwen was depressed it was probably because of him.'

251

'What was Dylan's relationship with your family?'

'Not good. My father told him off for trespassing.' She looked up at Wesley. 'And he used to shoot the crows with Bleasdale, the gardener. He gave me the creeps.'

'But you stayed with the Madeleys when your family died?'

'Dylan had left home a few weeks before. I wouldn't have stayed with Gwen if he'd been there.' She paused. 'You don't think he could have ...?'

Wesley said nothing. He wasn't jumping to any conclusions.

'Will you go back to London now?'

Arbel sighed. 'I feel I ought to stay and sort things out. Gwen had no one else.'

They took their leave of Arbel, muttering trite condolences. Nothing they could say would be adequate. Wesley glanced back at the cottage as they climbed into the car and saw that Arbel was watching them from the window, still and pale.

They drove the short distance to Potwoolstan Hall, parking in the forbidden space at the front of the house, their arrival announced by a fanfare of cawing crows in the glowering trees. In the Hall they found Pandora occupying Elsham's office, sitting behind her husband's desk, surrounded by what looked like the Hall's accounts. When they broke the news about Gwen Madeley she nodded wearily, as though death had become a grim, ever-present companion, hardly unexpected. Wesley offered to drive her down to Tradmouth to identify the body and Pandora didn't protest. She left a note for her husband, who was at the moment taking one of their new Beings on a journey back to a former life.

Bookings at the Hall had fallen off since the news about Evans's murder got out, Pandora complained as they drove. People had cancelled, murder hardly being conducive to spiritual peace. The newspapers had seized on the death in the grounds, making the most of the Hall's grim past. 'Murder Hall', one tabloid had screeched. 'The House of

Death' had been another's not too original contribution. Whoever had killed Patrick Evans was also killing Jeremy Elsham's nice little business.

Pandora identified Gwen Madeley's body with no overt show of emotion. She looked down as the crisp white sheet was drawn aside from the dead woman's face and gave a brisk nod. 'That's Gwen Madeley. Can I go back now?'

As they left the room, Wesley glanced back at the white form on the trolley. He was certain Gwen Madeley had known who killed the Harfords. And now she was dead, possibly by her own hand. Rather like Martha Wallace.

They didn't see Colin Bowman at the mortuary. He was in the middle of a postmortem on a road accident victim. But when Wesley returned to the office after dropping Pandora back at Potwoolstan Hall, there was a message from the pathologist waiting for him on his desk. The coroner had given permission for Patrick Evans's body to be released for burial. Wesley picked up the phone, hoping that Kirsty Evans would be home. He didn't fancy leaving such a message on her answering machine: it seemed impersonal somehow. And inappropriate in the circumstances.

He was in luck. She picked up the receiver after the fourth ring. As soon as he heard her voice, his mind went blank as he searched frantically for the right words to say. But after a few seconds of silence he collected his thoughts and broke the news gently before enquiring how Kirsty was.

She told him she'd been staying with her parents for a few days and had only just returned to London. It was best to resume her normal routine, she explained. She had her life to lead and she couldn't mourn for ever. She would travel down to Devon the next day, she said. She looked forward to seeing him then. Wesley sensed that she was putting on a brave face. The reality, he was afraid, would probably hit her later, merciless as a sledgehammer.

Wesley looked at his watch and saw that it was almost eight thirty. It was time to head home.

*

In the doorway of the dry cleaner's Dylan Madeley sat and shivered. The parade of shops had been built in the Sixties to serve the Winterham estate on the outskirts of Morbay: a bleak land where nobody, not even the most courageous police dog, would venture out of choice. The doorway smelled of urine and the strengthening wind made the litter dance in circles on the filthy pavement.

Dylan put a cold hand to his face and felt moisture on his cheek. He needed another fix. It was the only thing that would blot out the fear and the anger. The hostel had insisted that he stay clean. But he had lapsed and they had told him to go; returned him to the streets. It was the rules. No drink, no drugs. Dylan had fallen from grace as he had so many times before. And now he needed money to pay for it.

He stood up, his limbs aching and his mouth parched. He needed the stuff soon and desperation gave him new strength to walk the hundred or so yards to the small convenience shop which stood out like a beacon amongst its darkened neighbours – some shuttered, some boarded up. A gang of hooded youngsters outside the shop were laughing loudly and kicking a can about. Dylan stood and watched as one by one the teenagers ventured inside, only to emerge again quickly, chucked out by the elderly Indian owner whose instincts told him they were trouble. On his return, each adventurer would be greeted with loud cheers as if he had completed some daring feat. Then the spoils would be shared: a purloined packet of crisps or a stolen chocolate bar. Dylan watched this ritual repeated several times.

Dylan waited until the boys had wandered away in search of alternative entertainment before walking in and pushing the old man to the ground as he helped himself to the contents of the till. He had no thought for his victim: he was only aware of his own need for chemical oblivion, of the sweat of his body and the sandpaper dryness in his mouth. And of his own pain.

Once he had tried so hard. But she had spoiled it all and now it was too late. He didn't care any more. Not even

254

when he was running to the lock-up garage where the dealer hung out and the police car drew up alongside him.

'How was Yorkshire?'

Wesley thought for a moment. 'OK. Where are the kids?'

'In bed.' There was a hint of reproach in Pam's voice. 'We've had another email from Neil. Bad news.'

Wesley hung his coat carefully on the hook by the door he always used and placed his car keys in the drawer of the hall table. 'What?'

'Max is dead. Heart attack, apparently.'

'That's terrible.'

'It gets worse. He's just heard that his grandmother's died. He wasn't due back till next week but he's cutting short his visit. He's getting the first plane out.'

'That's a shame.' It was sad but Wesley assumed that Max Selbiwood and Neil's grandmother had had a good innings, unlike Patrick Evans and Gwen Madeley.

'I didn't make you any supper,' Pam said pointedly. 'Didn't know what time you'd be home.'

'Have you eaten?'

'I had some of Michael's fish fingers.' The tone of her voice was calculated to produce guilt in any but the most insensitive of husbands.

Wesley picked up the phone. A takeaway pizza would keep the peace. For the time being.

Wesley knew better than to ask to see the children. According to Pam, a visit from Daddy might wake them up: or worse still make them over-excited. Sometimes he suspected this was Pam's way of punishing him for his long absences from home.

She led the way into the living room. It seemed unnaturally tidy, which made Wesley feel slightly uncomfortable. He sat down in his favourite chair and picked up the TV remote control.

'Want to see Neil's email?' Pam stood in front of him expectantly, waving a sheet of paper. 'He says he wants

255

more pictures of Potwoolstan Hall to send back to the States.'

'The ones we've got of that place down at the station are hardly suitable.'

The subject of Potwoolstan Hall had jogged her memory. There was something she had to show him. She picked up a newspaper that lay on the coffee table.

'I saw this in yesterday's paper. It mentions Potwoolstan Hall. I kept it. Thought you might be interested.' She pointed to the photograph of a woman with a prematurely aged face and dishevelled blond hair. 'She was a friend of that poor girl whose family were murdered.'

Wesley took the paper from her and began to read. Jo Mylcomb, a divorcée living in the village of Trecowan on the Cornish coast, had been involved in an acrimonious dispute with her retired neighbour over the height of his hedge. She had taken the law – and a hedge trimmer – into her own hands and reduced the size of the problem. The litigious neighbour had taken her to court, claiming Ms Mylcomb had been a thorn in his side from the time she had moved in two years ago.

One sentence gave the game away. Pam had done well to spot it. 'Jo Mylcomb,' it said, 'was last in the news almost twenty years ago when her school friend Arbel Harford's family were murdered at Potwoolstan Hall in Devon. Arbel had been staying with Ms Mylcomb – then Jocasta Childs – at the time of the tragedy.'

Wesley smiled, delighted that some diligent journalist had been doing his or her homework. A Jocasta Childs had been on Patrick Evans's list but they'd had no luck tracing her. Now, through Providence and Pam's sharp eyes, he'd found her. And fortunately she wasn't too far away.

He just hoped her recent brush with the law hadn't put her off cooperating with the police altogether.

He put his arm round Pam and kissed her. 'Forgiven?'

'For now,' she said wearily as the pizza delivery man rang the doorbell.

*

256

Steve Carstairs greeted Wesley with his customary morning scowl as he entered the office. All Wesley's hopes that their weekend in Yorkshire would improve matters had clearly been in vain.

'Call from Morbay nick. Bloke called Dylan Madeley was picked up last night for robbery. Gave a Paki shop-keeper a shove and pinched the contents of the till.' There was something in Steve's voice which made Wesley suspect that he thought the robber deserved a medal.

'Dylan Madeley? Gwen Madeley's brother?'

'Well, there can't be too many Dylan Madeleys about, can there?'

Wesley ignored the sarcasm. He had been asking for it: it had been a silly question.

'I'm attending his sister's postmortem this morning. I'll go across to Morbay afterwards.'

'I'll go if you like.'

'Thanks, Steve, but I think I'd like to see him for myself.'

Steve shrugged and returned to his paperwork.

Heffernan looked up as he opened the office door. 'You're late. What's new?'

'Gwen Madeley's brother's turned up. He's enjoying the hospitality of Morbay nick. Robbed a shop.'

'Someone better break the bad news about his sister. And we need to question him. He was on Patrick Evans's list.'

'And he used to shoot crows with Victor Bleasdale.'

Gerry Heffernan shrugged. 'Motive?'

'He argued with Edward Harford?'

Heffernan held a hand up. 'Just remembered. I had a word with Clive Wellings yesterday after church.'

Wesley looked puzzled.

'The psychiatrist. He's one of our bellringers at St Margaret's. He said he's willing to see Emma Oldchester.'

'Now all we've got to do is persuade her. And that might be easier said than done.' He sat down and pushed a pile of papers on the chief inspector's desk to one side. 'I think

I've located someone else on Evans's list. Jocasta Childs: the friend Arbel Harford was staying with in London. She lives in Cornwall and she's been up in court for chopping down a neighbour's hedge.'

'But she wasn't anywhere near the Hall at the time of the murders.'

'She was on Evans's list. And she might provide us with some insights into the Harford family. Something Arbel confided to her but hasn't told us.'

'OK. We can pay her a visit after we've seen Dylan Madeley.'

Wesley managed a half-hearted smile and looked at his watch. They were due to witness Gwen Madeley's post-mortem in just over an hour's time. He was about to catch up on his paperwork but Heffernan had other ideas. 'Want to go over everything we've got?'

The chief inspector was right. It would help to focus their thoughts. He glanced at the office outside: at the officers working busily at their desks and the large notice board which took up most of the far wall, decorated with photographs of the dead and Gerry Heffernan's scrawled comments.

Heffernan took a deep breath that put a considerable strain on his shirt buttons. 'Victim,' he began. 'Patrick Evans. He was writing a book about what happened at Potwoolstan Hall and someone wanted to stop him.'

'What about Gwen Madeley?'

'We don't know if it's suicide, accident or murder yet. No use speculating until after the postmortem.'

'We have to bear in mind her connections with the Harford case. She was a frequent visitor to the Hall and Arbel Harford stayed with her after the killings. And, according to Arbel, she had been having a sexual relationship with one of the victims, Nigel Armley. And with our missing gardener, Victor Bleasdale.'

'Emma Oldchester named Bleasdale under hypnosis. Could he have killed the Harfords?'

'He was supposed to be on his way to Yorkshire when

258

the killings occurred but he could have lain low all day, killed them, then driven up overnight. Nobody thought to check the motel he claimed to have used at the time. Then there's his disappearance. His car was found burned out. And the fact that his job up there didn't go well and he left after a couple of weeks. Why uproot yourself for a job that's not as good as the one you've already got, then leave right away? It doesn't make sense.'

'Maybe he realised he'd done the wrong thing and cut his losses.'

Wesley thought for a moment. 'So who's our chief suspect for Evans's murder?'

'Let's face it, Wes, we haven't really got one. Who was about at the time? Gwen? Brenda? Gibbons? Dylan Madeley, perhaps? Jeremy Elsham? Pandora? And did whoever kill the Harfords kill Evans as well?'

'Pandora had a grudge against the Harfords for what happened to her father.'

'Somehow I can't see Richard Gibbons having the bottle to commit murder. And Brenda Varney. She's a thief but . . .'

'Shooting the Harfords?'

Heffernan shook his head. 'Not her style. I still think Bleasdale's our man. Don't know why but . . .'

'Emma Oldchester named him but what about this other man she mentioned?'

'If it's a man, that rules out Pandora, Brenda or Gwen Madeley. What about Dylan? A criminally inclined drug addict. Used to hang round the Hall and wasn't on good terms with Edward Harford. I'd say he's certainly worth further investigation. He could easily have killed the Harfords, especially if he was high on drugs at the time.'

Wesley looked sceptical. 'That's the point. He's a junkie who's been in and out of trouble and presumably he's been sleeping rough since he was chucked out of the hostel. Evans's murder appears to have been well planned, calculated. It almost looks like he was lured to his death. Don't

259

forget the lobster in his stomach: cosy meal to lull him into a false sense of security. And the killer used the victim's key to break into his hotel room. If Madeley was sleeping rough he might have been a bit conspicuous at the Tradmouth Castle Hotel.'

'Gwen Madeley had lobster dishes in her freezer. Dylan might have used his sister's cottage as a meeting place.'

Wesley sighed. Somehow it didn't seem quite right. But maybe it would when he came face to face with Dylan Madeley. Maybe, in spite of the drugs addling his brain, he was a cunning, calculating bastard, quite capable of disposing of a threat. Just as he had dealt with the unfortunate Asian shopkeeper.

'What if Bleasdale did it? He killed the Harfords then drove straight up to Yorkshire to his new job, not spending the night at the motel as he claimed. Then he destroys his car and disappears. Gets himself a new identity. He was seen with a young woman but the witness is dead and the police didn't take much notice at the time.'

'No reason why he couldn't have met up with a lass while he was up there.' A faraway look came into Heffernan's eyes. 'I knew a girl from Yorkshire once.'

Wesley ignored his boss's romantic reminiscences. 'What if he's living back here under a new identity and he killed Evans when he started getting too close? It would have been so easy to lure Evans to a meeting on the promise of new information for his book.'

'What about that MP who's married to Arbel? Anthony Jameston? Could he be Bleasdale with a new identity? Could Arbel have fallen for the gardener and be in on the plot? She did benefit after all. Inherited the lot.'

'I've checked him out. Anthony Jameston seems to be who he says he is. Went to Charterhouse, read law at Oxford, called to the bar, elected MP for a west London constituency. Lifestyle funded by his wife's considerable fortune. His life's an open book.'

'Which brings us back to Elsham. Didn't his wife

mention he used to run a garden centre or nursery? I think we should double-check his background.'

'He was ready to let us hear that tape.'

'Only after we'd found out it existed.' Heffernan frowned. He'd had a feeling about Jeremy Elsham from the moment he met him. But even if a man's a charlatan, it doesn't necessarily make him a murderer. He looked at his watch. It was time to head off to the mortuary.

The two men walked. It wasn't far to the hospital and it was hardly worth going to the effort of finding a parking space when they got there.

'Heard from your mate Neil?'

'Yes. His grandmother's just died so he's cutting short his visit to the States.'

'Somehow I never think of that Neil as having a family,' Heffernan observed and said no more on the subject.

Chuck had offered to drive Neil the fifty miles to the airport, which was generous of him. He felt almost guilty for not paying more polite attention to Chuck's constant stream of baseball chatter. Maybe he'd have learned something.

First thing that morning he'd attended Max's funeral at a manicured cemetery filled with rows of snowy white head-stones. It was a well-ordered place, unlike some of the old cemeteries he'd visited back home. Unlike the ancient churchyard where his grandmother would be laid to rest with its lichen-coated stones and winding paths in the shadow of the old stone church. Max's obsequies had been a short, solemn affair and Neil was hardly surprised that he hadn't been invited for refreshments afterwards. He'd been there on sufferance. An unwelcome guest. The illegitimate grandson staining the family name.

He was about to shut his suitcase – not a difficult task as he always travelled light – when he noticed the photocopies he'd made of Edmund Selbiwood's 1605 account of his experiences in the New World lying on the bed. He placed them carefully on top of his clothes and locked the suitcase before looking around Chuck's spare room for the last time. 'So long, Virginia,' he whispered to himself.

He heard a shuffling sound and Hannah Gotleib appeared in the doorway. She was no longer wearing her customary jeans and checked shirt. Her denim dress was short and displayed her long, tanned legs to their best advantage.

'I couldn't let you go without saying goodbye,' she said shyly.

He stared at her, hardly daring to do what he longed to do. But he needn't have worried. Hannah walked slowly over to him, stood on tiptoe and kissed him on the lips, gently at first, but when his arms crept round her waist, more passionately. Neil almost forgot the long journey ahead of him until Chuck burst in and Hannah sprang away.

'Time we were heading off,' Chuck said with inappropriate cheeriness.

Hannah was still looking into Neil's eyes as though she hadn't heard the interruption. 'I've something for you to read on the way back to England.' She rummaged in her shoulder bag and produced a sheaf of photocopied papers. 'Some of our early records. Read them and email me. Tell me what you think. And don't forget to send more pictures of Potwoolstan Hall. And anything you can find out about the Selbiwoods.'

'I promise.' He hesitated, wondering if what he was about to say was too much like commitment for comfort. But he said it anyway. 'Why don't you come over to England? You could see the Hall and I'll show you round Tradmouth where your settlers sailed from. You could join one of my digs; see how we do things over there.'

Hannah smiled, showing a set of perfect white teeth. 'Sounds good. I'll examine my schedule and let you know when I can make it. And when we get the toxicology results on those bones I'll email them to you.' She kissed him again, this time a chaste peck on the cheek for the benefit of Chuck, who was hovering by the door impatiently.

'See ya,' she whispered.

Neil raised a hand in farewell and she was gone.

'Turn up for the books,' Heffernan muttered, breaking the silence as they walked back to the police station.

'Colin seemed pretty sure.'

Wesley, who hadn't looked too closely at Gwen Madeley's bloated corpse, had taken the pathologist's word for it that she had been dosed with tranquillisers then her head had been held beneath the water of the River Trad. There was bruising around her head and shoulders as a result of her having been held until she drowned.

'If her brother came to her for money for drugs he might have gone for a drive with her then walked by the river, lost his temper and killed her.' Wesley knew that this was sheer speculation. The presence of tranquillisers suggested planning.

Gerry Heffernan looked at his watch. It was almost lunchtime. 'Don't know about you, Wes, but I fancy one of Maisie's hotpots at the Fisherman's Arms. Coming?'

'I think I'll send out for a sandwich and catch up on some work. I'll meet you there later and we'll pay Dylan Madeley a visit.'

'Suit yourself.' The chief inspector looked disappointed, like a child whose friend wasn't allowed out to play, and lumbered out of the office.

Wesley opened the yellowing file on his desk. The Potwoolstan Hall murders. There were no photographs of Victor Bleasdale or Dylan Madeley. But there were pictures of all the victims, posed and smiling in happier times. There was a small snap of Edward and Mary Harford, standing close together, looking rather surprised. Catriona Harford, a fair, insipid-looking girl wearing a blue sundress, obviously on some foreign holiday. Catriona's fiancé, Nigel Armley, posed, tall, dark and confident, in his naval uniform. There was Jack Harford in tweeds and cloth cap with a shotgun across his arm, every inch the young country squire – the type many would think of as an arrogant young toff.

Finally, he came to a picture of Martha Wallace. She was

263

sitting on a deckchair in a garden with a colander on her knee and there was a pile of what appeared to be pea pods on the floor by her side. A little girl sat on a rug at her feet, grinning up at the camera. Mother and daughter shelling peas together, a picture of contented domesticity. He estimated that the child must have been around seven so it couldn't have been taken very long before Martha had supposedly shot five people before shooting herself, leaving her daughter traumatised and motherless. Looking at that picture he knew for certain that it hadn't happened that way. There was no way that Martha Wallace would have put her child through that. Martha had been murdered like the others. But he was no nearer identifying her killer.

He put the photographs to one side and took the crime scene pictures from the file just as DC Paul Johnson placed the tuna sandwich he'd ordered on his desk. He thanked Paul and paid the money he owed before eating the sandwich. He had always subscribed to the theory that it was easier to think on a full stomach.

He turned over one photograph, then another. Martha Wallace, slumped at the kitchen table, her astonished eyes wide open and the gun held firmly in her right hand. Surely it would be natural for someone to close their eyes if they were about to shoot themselves, Wesley thought before looking at the other pictures. The Harfords lay together, their hands touching in a final gesture of farewell. They must have been only too aware that they were about to die together. Then there was Catriona sprawled across the doorway of the drawing room, the entry wounds caused by the bullets that killed her, standing out red raw on her forehead and her throat. Jack was slumped against the doorframe, staring ahead in amazement, killed just like his sister with a wound to the head and one to the throat.

Then Wesley turned over the final photograph and was confronted with the worst image of all. The mess of blood, bone and brain where Nigel Armley's face should have been. Wesley glanced at it once, then looked away. The very sight of it made him feel sick. Or maybe there had been something wrong with the sandwich he'd just eaten.

He arranged the photographs of the victims as they were living and as they were dead, side by side on the desktop like a macabre game of patience. The juxtaposition of life and death was disturbing. All that smiling cut short in a moment. Life ended on somebody's whim.

Glancing at his watch, he realised that he had arranged to meet Gerry Heffernan in the Fisherman's Arms before visiting Dylan Madeley. Pleasure before duty. He would have preferred it the other way around.

Wesley and Heffernan drove over to Morbay in silence, travelling on the car ferry. The young man collecting the money looked bored, having recovered from the excitement of spotting Gwen Madeley's body in the water. Wesley sat in the driver's seat staring ahead, feeling slightly nauseous, longing to reach the other bank and be back on dry land.

At Morbay police station the desk sergeant greeted Gerry Heffernan like an old friend and when they reached the interview suite Dylan Madeley was waiting for them.

Dylan scowled as they sat down. Hardly a warm welcome. But then they hadn't been expecting one. He was a gaunt, wiry man with a shaved head and he looked considerably older than his years. His blotchy face bore a day's stubble and a sickly pallor and one of his front teeth was missing.

Wesley spoke first. 'I'm sorry about your sister,' he began.

Dylan's expression softened for a moment and he gave a curt nod of acknowledgement.

'We'd like to ask you a few questions about Gwen. When did you last see her?'

Dylan sat in silence, his hands and feet twitching as his eyes darted about, looking for an escape route.

'It's a simple question,' Heffernan growled. 'When did you last see your sister?'

Dylan shifted in his seat. 'I called at her place a few days ago. She usually bunged me a few quid if I asked.' The voice was hoarse, hardly audible.

'And did she this time?'

He focused his eyes on the tabletop and the twitching stopped for a moment. 'Can't remember.'

'When exactly was this?'

'Can't remember.'

'Think.'

'I can't bloody remember. All right.' His lips curled into a snarl as he slumped back in his chair, his arms folded defensively and his right foot beating a rhythm against the table leg.

Wesley sensed that he'd say nothing more on the subject. It was possible that he'd killed Gwen because she refused to give him money. It would be a convenient solution. But had he killed Patrick Evans as well? And had he been the gunman who shot the Harford family? Perhaps a few more well-chosen questions would provide the answer.

'Where were you when the Harford family were shot?'

Dylan Madeley looked wary. 'I'd just got a place in Morbay. I was there.' He paused. 'I was in a pub with a mate that night.'

'Did the police check your alibi?'

Dylan shrugged. 'Can't remember.' The two policemen glanced at each other. If Martha Wallace's guilt had been assumed, perhaps not many questions were asked.

'Do you remember the gardener at the Hall? Bleasdale he was called.'

'Yeah. Why?'

'And Brenda Varney, the cleaner?'

Dylan's lips twitched upwards. 'Yeah. I remember Brenda.'

'She's just been arrested. Had a scam going with Richard Gibbons. You remember him, don't you?'

'Yeah. What was the scam?'

'She booked into health spas and residential courses pretending to be disabled. She stole from people on the upper

266

floors and nobody suspected her because everyone assumed she couldn't get up the stairs.

Dylan leaned forward. 'I'd like to see Brenda again,' he added wistfully. 'Any chance you can arrange it?'

'No chance,' Heffernan muttered. 'We're not a lonely hearts bureau for villains.'

Wesley almost had to admire Dylan Madeley's cheek. But in the state he was in, he was hardly the answer to a maiden's prayer: even one like Brenda who'd been round the block a few times and wouldn't be too choosy. 'What about Arbel Harford?'

The tapping foot suddenly stilled. 'What about her?'

'She was friendly with your sister ...'

'On her terms. As long as Gwen knew her place.' He hesitated. 'Till the tables were turned.'

'What do you mean?'

Dylan looked uneasy. 'Till she had no one. Till she needed Gwen: that's what I mean.' His hands were shaking and sweat was running down his face.

'You didn't like the Harfords, did you? Mr Harford told you off for trespassing, I believe.'

No answer.

'You were a good shot in those days.'

'So?' The tapping foot started up again, faster now.

'You wanted revenge on the Harfords for all those little humiliations. You took a shotgun and a rifle and killed them. Then you killed their housekeeper to keep her quiet and made it look as if she'd done it. You wiped the weapons and put her prints on them. Clever. Did you know her little girl was hidden in the pantry watching?'

A bead of sweat dripped off Dylan's nose and he banged on the table with his fist. 'If that's what you think you'll have to fucking prove it.'

'Did you meet Patrick Evans?'

'Never heard of him. I want my fucking brief.'

But Wesley hadn't finished. 'Evans was writing a book about the murders at the Hall. He was looking for you.'

'Well, he didn't fucking find me.' He stood up. It was his last word on the subject.

As Dylan Madeley was escorted from the room, Wesley had an uneasy feeling that they had just been face to face with a man capable of gunning down six innocent people. Dylan Madeley had just risen to the top of their list of suspects.

When they left Morbay police station, the wind was blowing stronger, swaying trees and sending litter dancing in an untidy ballet across the car park.

'Going to be a gale tonight,' Gerry said as he climbed into the passenger seat of the car.

Wesley drove back to Tradmouth the long way round. There was no way he was going to chance crossing the river again.

When Neil Watson arrived back at his flat, he found that all he wanted to do was sleep. He had spent the flight wide awake, reading the documents Hannah had given him, feeling a warm glow as he read those words that were a link to her.

He had hauled himself off the plane, made his way into London on the Heathrow Express and caught the train to Saint David's Station in Exeter. When he reached the flat he felt like an explorer who had just completed an arduous expedition. And he needed sleep more than anything else. The wind was howling outside but this was one night when nothing would keep him awake.

As he drifted off into sleep, images of Annetown swam into his head and he saw Max sitting in the rocking chair on his front porch. Beside him sat a young woman dressed in the costume of an early settler, her white linen cap framing a small heart-shaped face with large brown eyes. It was a sweet dream. But it wasn't long before it began to turn into a nightmare.

Before the customary breakfast of organic muesli and fresh orange juice it was part of Jeremy Elsham's daily routine

268

to meditate in the woods leading down to the river. But that morning he sensed that the energy emitted by the gnarled stunted oaks had been disturbed somehow, probably by the gales during the night. He had always been sensitive to changes in his special place. His territory.

He placed his waterproof mat on the ground and zipped up the front of his warm fleece top before sitting down and crossing his legs, an action he performed with an athleticism rare in a man of his age.

Once he had arranged his body into his favoured position, Jeremy Elsham closed his eyes. Then he opened them again. Something was wrong with the spiritual energy of the woods. There was something evil here. Something out of place. And suddenly Elsham was afraid.

He rose slowly from his mat and began to wander through the budding trees, stepping over branches that had fallen in last night's high winds. Eventually he reached the clearing near the water where, according to the police, Patrick Evans had met his death.

One of the trees there had been blown over and it still leaned dangerously, supported by its neighbours. The roots, exposed by the fall, protruded like dry bones from the ground, twisted, reaching for the light. Jeremy Elsham stared down at the earth: at the skeletal hand that was pointing up at him, accusing. He closed his eyes. Why did this have to happen now?

He took a deep, calming breath and returned to the place where he had left his mat. His body shaking, he sat down again and tried to meditate. But concentration was impossible.

He had to think. If he said nothing, the skeleton buried beneath the tree might go undiscovered for weeks, months, years.

Silence was the best way.

Chapter Twelve

We were married beneath the sail as our church is not yet built, the fortifications being most pressing.

Penelope urges me to return to England but I tell her this is folly as we have a new life here in this abundant land and as a younger son I have no fortune. I have no desire to tell her of the events at Potwoolstan Hall and the hatred the people bore towards my father who took all blame upon himself.

Penelope urges me also to put myself forward, to be seen to be a leader of men, so that I may be elected to the Council in the place of those who have met with an untimely death, but I have no such ambition. I have resolved to live humbly and in repentance. High office cannot be mine.

My wife thinks she may be with child. It may be that this is the cause of her restless fancies.

Set down by Edmund Selbiwood, Gentleman, at Annetown this twenty-fifth day of October 1605.

The case was giving Wesley sleepless nights and Pam had complained several times about the amount of time he was spending at work. Even her mother, Della, had made her unwelcome contribution, suggesting that Pam provide herself with a fancy man as she saw so little of the man she was married to – which was typical of Della.

270

The one bright spot on this gloomy horizon was Neil's return to Devon. As soon as he'd slept off his jet lag at his Exeter flat, he'd travelled straight to Somerset to attend his grandmother's funeral. But now he was back and Wesley wanted to see him; to hear all about his Virginia experience. But he didn't know when he'd find the time.

It was two days since they had reinterviewed Dylan Madeley in the presence of his solicitor but he had given nothing away. He had been supplied with methadone and Wesley suspected the drug had given him fresh confidence to follow the tried and trusted policy of denying everything and challenging the police to prove it. It was hard to gauge his feelings about his sister's death because he said very little. Heffernan took this as a sign of guilt but Wesley was keeping an open mind.

They had spoken to Richard Gibbons and Brenda Varney again but they had said nothing about Dylan Madeley, apart from the fact that he liked guns and hated the Harfords.

It seemed that Dylan Madeley was now up there amongst their top suspects and Wesley considered the possibilities. Perhaps Gwen had given Patrick Evans his lobster dinner, then her brother had followed him from the cottage and murdered him. Or maybe Dylan had actually been at their meeting. Gwen might have covered up for her brother out of misguided loyalty and then he had silenced her when he feared she might give him away.

The theory fitted. And it was the best one they had so far.

Rachel Tracey passed Wesley's desk and touched his shoulder gently. She looked serene in her crisp pale blue blouse and tight tweed skirt and she was wearing her fair hair loose. The sight of her somehow made Wesley feel wretched.

'Have you made a decision about that flat yet?' He tried to make the question sound casual.

'Why?'

'Just wondered.' Perhaps he shouldn't have mentioned it.

'I couldn't make up my mind so it went to someone else,' she said sadly. 'I'm still looking, I suppose.'

As she walked back to her desk Wesley stood up and strolled over to Gerry Heffernan's office.

'You look like a lost soul, Wes. Come in.' He stood at the door and called into the outer office. 'Trish, love. We could do with some tea in here.'

Trish, engrossed in her paperwork, looked up and frowned.

'Any thoughts on the case?' Wesley asked.

Heffernan shook his head. 'It's that bastard Madeley.'

'None of his prints were found in Evans's hotel room.'

'He wore gloves.'

'Someone's spoken to the people at the hostel Dylan Madeley was living in till he got thrown out. They said he's been in a bad way but he always spoke fondly of his sister. They said he went to see her from time to time and she gave him money.'

'Which he probably spent on drugs.'

'True.' Wesley could hardly deny that Dylan Madeley's addiction had ruled him. It had probably made him desperate and deceptive; hardly the ideal brother. According to a couple of the residents at the hostel who knew him, he usually spent half his time drugged up and the other half looking for a fix. 'Do you really think he's capable of such controlled and calculated murders?'

Heffernan looked at him, disappointed. 'We've got him in custody on a robbery charge. All we have to do is keep on until he tells us the truth.'

'I admire your optimism, Gerry. I don't suppose anyone's managed to persuade Emma Oldchester to leave Potwoolstan Hall yet?'

'She still says she's not leaving till she knows what happened. I've never met such a stubborn ...'

'Has she been told about that doctor? Clive, is it? The psychiatrist?'

'Of course. I've told her he'll see her but, as I said, she's stubborn.'

272

Wesley stood up.

'Where are you going?'

'Arbel Jameston's still at Gwen Madeley's cottage. I thought I'd have a quick word with her. What do these companies call it? A courtesy call.'

'Don't upset her. She has friends in high places.'

'I'll take Rachel with me. We'll be the souls of discretion,' said Wesley as he disappeared out of the office.

They found Arbel Jameston in the garden, burning rubbish on a small bonfire. When they arrived she offered them tea, her manner slightly distant but scrupulously polite. Wesley and Rachel followed her inside the cottage and made themselves comfortable on the sofa while she busied herself in the kitchen.

Wesley decided it was time to break the news. 'We've found Dylan Madeley. He robbed a shop. He's in custody at Morbay police station.'

Arbel frowned. 'I wish they'd lock Dylan up and throw away the key. He's always been trouble. Always turning up on poor Gwen's doorstep demanding money. She was frightened of him, you know. She was even contemplating moving to the Hall: there's a room she could have had in the staff quarters. If she'd moved she might still be alive.'

'Did she mention Dylan when you last spoke to her?'

'We spoke on the phone a couple of days before I came down and she said she was worried about him. Apparently he'd been round and she said she'd tell me all about it when I came down here.' She hesitated. 'But she never got the chance, did she?'

'Do you think Dylan Madeley killed his sister?'

Arbel shook her head. 'I really don't know what to think. If he'd come to her for money and she'd refused . . .'

'She took tranquillisers?'

Arbel nodded. 'Her nerves weren't good. Worry about Dylan, I suppose.'

'What have you been burning?' Rachel asked.

273

Arbel blushed and stood up. 'If you must know I've burned some of her pictures. You might think I've no right to do that but I think it's for the best. They could cause a lot of pain if some idiot tried to put them in an exhibition or ...'

'Do you mean those pictures of the murder scene that were in the cupboard in her studio?'

Arbel raised her carefully plucked eyebrows. 'You know about them?'

Wesley nodded.

'I found them yesterday. I can't think why Gwen painted pictures like that. I mean ...' She moved over to the window and stared out. 'She told me she didn't go up there; that she never saw the bodies. But she painted the scene just as I found it.'

She turned and looked at Wesley with pleading eyes. 'Don't you see? She must have been there before I arrived. Why didn't she mention it to me ... or the police?' She stared at Wesley as though she expected him to have the answer. But he shook his head.

There was a period of silence before Wesley spoke again. 'Is it possible that Dylan killed your family and Gwen covered up for him?'

Arbel thought for a few moments, more tears welling in her eyes. She shook her head. 'She was my friend.'

'And Dylan was her brother. In spite of everything she might have put her loyalty to him above her loyalty to her friends.'

Arbel looked confused. 'I don't know.'

'If there are any pictures you haven't burned yet I'd like to see them if I may.'

She hesitated for a moment then left the room without a word.

'What do you think?' Rachel whispered.

'Must be a shock finding out that someone you'd trusted could have shielded the person who murdered your family.'

Their conversation was cut short by Arbel's return. She

placed two paintings on the coffee table in front of them. The first showed Catriona Harford slumped on the floor in the drawing-room doorway, the bullet wound on her forehead glistening red. The second showed Martha Wallace slumped at her kitchen table. Arbel was right. Some bright spark might have wanted to exhibit these obscene things in the name of art, causing considerable distress to Arbel herself and Emma Oldchester.

'These are different.' Rachel picked up a third canvas. Wesley recognised the subject at once: Dylan Madeley – much younger, before the drugs had ravaged his face. It had been painted lovingly and there was a softness, a vulnerability about the subject that had disappeared with years of chemical abuse. He put it to one side and looked at the one behind it.

It was slightly smaller than the others and was a half-length portrait of Nigel Armley. He was dressed in an open-necked shirt and looked more attractive than he had done in his photograph. Gwen had captured that elusive quality, charm.

'I told you she had a crush on him,' said Arbel.

'Crush?' Wesley thought it a strange choice of word.

'Do you want to take these pictures? Are they evidence?'

'No. You can burn the ones of the Hall if you want,' Wesley said. He saw no reason why the obscene things should exist any longer than necessary. 'But I'll keep the ones of Nigel Armley and Dylan Madeley. Armley reminds me of someone but I can't think who it is.' He stood up to go.

'By the way, do you have an address for Jocasta Childs, the friend you were staying with when . . .?'

Arbel shook her head. 'Sorry. I lost touch with Jo years ago. Why?'

'I believe she lives in Cornwall now. There was a piece in the newspaper about her. Seems she's been having trouble with her neighbours.'

'Well, you know more than I do.' Arbel didn't appear to

be particularly interested. It seemed she had no desire to renew old acquaintances.

She put out a hand. 'I've decided not to go back to London until after Gwen's funeral. I'm her executor so I'll have a lot to do here.'

'Take care of yourself,' Wesley said as he took her hand. 'And if you need anything, you have my number.'

He walked away, wondering when he'd hear from her again. And saying a silent, unformed prayer for her safety.

After attending his grandmother's funeral, Neil had stayed with his parents for a couple of days, recovering from the effects of jet lag. When he could no longer tolerate domestic life he had returned to Exeter, unable to get Potwoolstan Hall out of his mind. He wanted more than anything to see the place for himself and Wesley had agreed to meet him there, saying there was someone he needed to speak to in the line of duty. When Neil drove his old yellow Mini in through the gates Wesley was waiting for him.

'How did the funeral go?' he asked as Neil climbed from the tiny car.

'As funerals do.'

Wesley sensed he didn't want to dwell on the subject. He wandered up the drive towards the Hall and Neil fell in by his side.

Wesley felt obliged to fill the silence with talk and he decided that architecture was a safe subject. 'The house was gutted in the nineteenth century with all the sensitivity the Victorians usually showed to ancient buildings. Then it was messed around again when it was converted into the healing centre. Not many original features left, I'm afraid, except the staircase and the façade.'

When they reached the Hall, Neil stopped and gazed up at the building. He didn't know what he felt. Sadness? A longing for something lost for ever? Or merely disappointment? He thought of Hannah Gotleib, who would imagine the place to be as it was when Edmund Selbiwood sailed for

276

Virginia: all beams, dark floorboards, limewashed walls and sparse oak furniture, heavy and blackened.

'Want to go in? There's someone I have to see. I'm sure I can square it with the owners for you to have a look around.'

Neil shook his head. 'I think I've changed my mind. It's not quite what I expected.' He took a small digital camera from the pocket of his denim jacket. 'But I said I'd send some pictures to Hannah.'

'Hannah, eh?'

Neil turned away. Wesley had miscalculated. His friend wasn't in the mood for teasing.

'I'd better go in. Are you waiting here or . . .?'

'No. I'll see you tonight. You want to hear about Virginia, I take it?'

As he marched off, Wesley felt uneasy. There was something different about Neil. A new hardness, almost a bitterness. And Wesley was curious.

Emma Oldchester was waiting in the conservatory and he thought she looked pleased to see him, which was a good sign. It meant that she might take notice of what he had to say.

'How are you?' he asked as they sat down. He spoke in a whisper. There were others in the room, a pair of clean-cut men in blue towelling pyjamas sipping carrot juice in the corner and a woman in dark glasses reading by the window.

'I'm OK.' Her hand went up to her cheek, a nervous gesture. She leaned forward and spoke in a low whisper. 'But I keep having this dream. I'm running through a stream of blood flowing down the hall and my feet are squelching in the scarlet mess and I keep falling over and getting blood all over me. There's a man and a woman but they don't see me. They've got blank spaces where their faces should be. Sometimes the faces flicker like a faulty TV screen and I can make out an eye or a nose. Then I wake up, sweating, with tears streaming down my face.'

277

'And you still want to stay here?'

'I've got to remember. If Jeremy regresses me again . . .'

'Chief Inspector Heffernan told you about Dr Wellings, didn't he?'

Emma stood up. 'I don't need a psychiatrist. I'm not mad.'

'I never said you were. Dr Wellings would be able to hypnotise you properly. He's an expert, Emma. He knows what he's doing. Go home and we'll arrange an appointment. Please. I don't think you realise how much danger you're in.'

'I'm booked in till Monday.'

'What's the point of staying if Jeremy Elsham won't do what you want?'

Her eyes were moist with tears. 'You don't understand. This is the only place I feel close to her, to Mum. I sometimes go into the room that used to be the kitchen and kneel in the exact spot where she died. And I've found the flat where we lived. It's empty now. I sit in there just trying to remember her.'

Wesley put his hand on hers and squeezed it. 'I do understand. But I still think you should leave.'

She dabbed her eyes with a crumpled tissue. 'I don't know.' She looked at the dainty watch on her wrist. 'I'll have to go. I'm having my aura read.'

As she hurried from the room Wesley watched her go, not knowing what to do for the best.

Gwen Madeley's portraits of her brother, Dylan, and of Nigel Armley stood propped up on an easel designed to hold a flip chart. Wesley had stared at them, studied them, but it hadn't helped. Perhaps he should have let Arbel burn them with the rest.

He wanted to speak to Dylan Madeley again. He was sure he would have been quite capable of killing the Harfords as well as Evans and his own sister.

And then there was Jeremy Elsham, the man whose past

was shrouded in mystery. He didn't trust Elsham: and he hadn't forgotten that his wife, Pandora, had good reason to hate the Harford family. Why had they really bought Potwoolstan Hall? Was it just because it had been cheap? Or had there been some other reason?

He wished Emma Oldchester would go home to her husband. He had tried to persuade her but, for an apparently nervous, fragile creature, she was remarkably strong-willed.

'Starting an art gallery, are we?' said Heffernan when he entered the CID office.

Wesley smiled. 'I thought a bit of art would raise the tone of the place.'

Heffernan glanced at Steve Carstairs, who was talking on the phone. 'And let's face it, Wes, things could do with a bit of improvement around here. I hear you've been to have a chat with Emma Oldchester.'

'You heard right. I tried to persuade her to go home but she seems obsessed with the Hall. And of course she wants to clear her mother's name.'

'Morbid but understandable. You mentioned Clive Wellings?'

'Of course. She said she'd think about it but I'm not holding my breath. And I'm not happy about Arbel Harford being at Gwen Madeley's cottage. I think she could be in danger.'

'Why? She was miles away when the Harfords were killed and she never even saw Evans.'

Wesley shook his head. 'Doesn't matter. She might have seen something when she found the bodies and didn't realise its significance at the time. Gwen Madeley was killed.'

'Yes, but Gwen Madeley was on the spot when the Harfords died. And she knew Bleasdale, our chief suspect. Knew him rather well by all accounts. I wouldn't be surprised if she was involved somehow – or at least saw more than she let on. From those pictures she painted, she must have been on the scene before Arbel arrived and called the police. She knew something and I reckon she was killed to keep her quiet. We've got to find what happened to Bleasdale after he left Yorkshire. What if he's around here somewhere, right under our noses? What if Patrick Evans found him?'

Wesley scratched his head. 'The trouble is, we know so little about Bleasdale. We haven't even got a photograph; just a description that could fit half the male population of Devon.'

'There's no trace of Jeremy Elsham before the early Nineties. And Pandora mentioned he used to run some sort of garden centre.'

'If he's Bleasdale, Brenda Varney would have recognised him.'

'Not if he's changed his appearance, lost his accent.'

Wesley looked alarmed. 'If Elsham is Bleasdale we've got to persuade Emma to leave the Hall.'

'He's refused to hypnotise her again. Perhaps he's afraid of what she'll remember. He didn't know who she was when he first met her ...'

'But he does now. We've got to get her out of there.'

'And persuade her to see Clive.'

Wesley nodded. Emma's memories should be unlocked by a qualified professional who knew what he was doing. The thought of someone like Jeremy Elsham messing with people's minds had always worried him. Now it was just a matter of getting Emma to see things their way.

'Fancy a trip over the border to Cornwall tomorrow?'

'What for?'

'To see Jocasta Childs. She was with Arbel on the night of the murders and she was on Patrick Evans's visiting list. She probably won't be able to tell us much but she might know some useful gossip.'

Heffernan grinned. He'd never been averse to a bit of gossip.

It wasn't hard to get hold of Jocasta Mylcomb's address

from her local police station. There was a pregnant pause at the other end of the line when Wesley mentioned her name to the constable on duty, which made him ask whether she had a criminal record. The answer was no but he still sensed there was something. No doubt he'd soon find out what that something was.

After obtaining her phone number, he rang Jocasta Mylcomb, née Childs, and asked when it would be convenient to visit. Her voice sounded guarded and a little slurred. And he sensed that she wasn't exactly looking forward to her brush with the law.

When Pam Peterson heard the throaty noise of Neil's car engine suddenly cut off outside the house, she rose from the comfort of the sofa. Neil was expected. She had even tidied up in the kitchen in anticipation of his arrival. She trotted into the hall, called up the stairs to Wesley and hovered in the doorway until Neil rang the bell.

When she opened the door she was struck by how tired Neil looked. She stood on tiptoe and gave him a kiss on the cheek.

Neil looked bemused. 'I'll have to go away more often if this is the welcome I get. Wes about?'

'He's just putting Michael to bed. He'll be down soon.'

Neil made for the living room. He was carrying a tattered leather briefcase which he placed on the coffee table after making himself comfortable.

Pam rushed to the kitchen to get a bottle of wine and three glasses just as Wesley appeared at the door.

'I've brought the documents,' Neil said as Wesley sat down beside him. 'Just copies. The originals have been donated to the Annetown Settlement Museum.' He took the papers from his briefcase and sat there quite still, staring at them. Wesley wondered what was coming.

'I never told you about my exact relationship with Max, did I?' he said after a long pause.

'What do you mean?'

'Max and my gran knew each other in the war. They . . . Max was my real granddad.'

Wesley sat for a few moments, not knowing quite what reaction was expected. 'Sorry he died before you could get to know him properly,' seemed fitting.

Neil shrugged. 'I'm just sorry that he never made it over to England. Gran really wanted to see him again.'

'It's a shame,' was all Wesley could think of to say.

'It's funny to think of Max as family – even though he was only involved briefly in my mother's creation.' He gave a bitter smile. 'My mum never knew Granddad wasn't her real father. Still doesn't.' He paused. 'But I suppose he was her real father in a way. He brought her up and did the sort of things dads do. The sort of things you do for your two.'

'When I get the chance.'

Emma Oldchester popped unbidden into Wesley's mind: her foster father Joe Harper's obvious love for the daughter of his cousin, then tainted with the stain of murder. He and his wife had taken her in and cared for her devotedly, as if she was their own.

'Max went off and Gran never saw him again and Ted, my real granddad, picked up the pieces. Can't have been easy for him, bringing up another man's kid in those days. I know it happens all the time nowadays but . . .' His voice trailed off and he sat in silence. 'I got so carried away with meeting my biological grandfather that I forgot about how Ted must have felt. I'm just glad he never knew.'

Wesley didn't really know what to say. Neil had never talked this way before and he had never seen him so subdued.

'If Max was a Selbiwood, that means you have a family connection with Potwoolstan Hall.'

'I suppose I have.' He didn't sound too pleased about the idea.

Wesley suddenly remembered something that had been nagging at the back of his mind, something he'd intended to tell Neil but had forgotten all about till that moment. 'There's an old portrait of two men in Jacobean costume in the owner's office at Potwoolstan Hall. Exactly the right date for your Edmund Selbiwood. It might be worth looking at.'

Before Neil could answer, Pam entered the room bearing a tray. On it were not only the wine and glasses but an assortment of biscuits and savoury snacks. Neil's absence had transformed him from a friend who dropped in frequently to honoured guest. This was Pam's version of killing a fatted calf.

'So what are these documents you've found,' Pam said as she sat down.

'Edmund Selbiwood, Max's ancestor, met a woman called Penelope who was married to another settler called Joshua Morton. She went over on the *Nicholas* with her husband and his brother, Isaac.'

'Women went over?' Pam sounded surprised.

'On some expeditions, yes. The aim was to set up a colony, I suppose. Sir Walter Raleigh set one up on Roanoke Island in the late sixteenth century. The first baby to be born in the New World to English parents was born there in 1587 but three years later all the settlers vanished and nobody knew why.'

'Penelope must have had guts, sailing into the unknown like that,' Pam said admiringly.

'She had guts all right. She started an affair with Edmund Selbiwood – probably knew he came from a rich family. Then Joshua Morton was shot by his brother, Isaac, who claimed it was an accident. Then it appears that Isaac shot himself out of remorse. But I kept asking myself whether Penelope knew how to handle a musket.'

'You should have my job,' Wesley said. 'What happened to her?'

'She married and had a son who seems to be an ancestor of mine. She was a social climber and she kept trying to persuade Edmund to go home and claim his inheritance.

Or, failing that, to get on the ruling council of the colony.'

'An ancestor of yours?' Pam looked puzzled and Neil felt obliged to give her a brief summary of the facts.

'Oh,' was the only thing Pam could think of to say as she poured the wine. Neil didn't sound too pleased about the discovery of his long-lost family. Quite the reverse.

Neil took a long drink of wine. 'Hannah gave me some other records. I'll leave them with you and let you read them for yourself. No reason to spoil a nice evening. Cheers.'

Neil didn't mention Virginia again, except to say that he planned to email Hannah Gotleib the next day. He only drank one glass of wine and left at nine thirty, pleading tiredness and a need to get back to Exeter.

When Pam went to bed, Wesley stayed downstairs to study Neil's photocopied sheets. He sensed that something Neil had discovered in Virginia had disturbed him. And he wanted to know what that something was.

He began to look through the documents, stopping only when his eyes began to ache. Then he read some sections again, with dawning understanding, before placing them carefully on the sideboard.

Pam called down to him but he told her he'd be another ten minutes. This was the first time that day he'd found himself alone. And he wanted some time to think.

He shuffled out into the hall and picked up his briefcase. He took out the crime scene photographs of the massacre and spread them on the coffee table. Something was bothering him, some tiny detail he must have noticed subconsciously but hadn't yet been able to bring to the surface. He stared at the brutal images for a while before he realised what it was. There was something he wanted to check and he had to go back to the station to do it.

When he reached the front door he hesitated, wondering whether to tell Pam he was going out. But he decided against it. He wouldn't be long. And the last thing he wanted was a row.

He drove down to the police station. The place looked

284

different at night: the windows had become rectangles of white fluorescent light and the car park was bathed in the sickly yellow glow of the street lights. After pulling up in his usual parking space, he rushed to the door, where he pushed the button and answered the duty desk sergeant's disembodied voice. The door was unlocked automatically and he hurried in, suddenly aware that he was dressed in jeans and T-shirt rather than his smarter working clothes. The desk sergeant looked him up and down. He was a thin man with hair to match, quite unlike the large, bearded Bob Naseby who usually held the fort.

'This is a bit beyond the call of duty isn't it, Inspector,' the man said slowly. 'Doing a bit of overtime, are we?'

Wesley smiled. He thought it was expected of him. 'There's something I have to check in the CID office. I'll be five minutes.' He didn't want to hang round and exchange pleasantries so he rushed up the stairs. A couple of cleaners looked up, startled as he muttered an apology and switched on the main light.

He made straight for Gwen Madeley's portraits of Nigel Armley and Dylan Madeley and stared at them for a while, aware that the cleaners had stopped work and were watching him, curious.

He drew one of the crime scene photographs from the pocket of his jacket and looked at it, then at the portraits. Then he spun round to face the cleaners and smiled. 'Thank you, ladies.' One gave an embarrassed giggle.

He gave the desk sergeant a cheery wave as he left the station and he drove home, avoiding the merrymakers recently ejected from Tradmouth's many pubs. He almost felt like joining them. But he still had to be sure.

When he crept back into the house, all was silent. Pam must be asleep – or pretending to be. But Wesley was wide awake now. He took off his jacket and flung it over the banisters before turning his attention once more to Neil's documents.

Chapter Thirteen

Account of Captain Ralph Radford, President of the Council, set down at Annetown, December 1605

Mistress Selbiwood, who was Mistress Morton before her late husband's untimely death, hath offended much my goodwife who doth complain of her arrogant manner. She hath airs above her station and liketh not the harsh life here now that we have not found the gold and wealth her late husband and his late brother did expect.

Mistress Selbiwood's new husband is elected to the Council, though he would not be of my choosing. It seems he doth not conduct himself with the devotion of a bridegroom even though his new wife is with child. Rather I came upon them and heard them quarrel, they being quite unaware of my presence. The quarrel became so violent that I feared for the lady's safety. If her husband treats her roughly it may be that I should offer her my protection for she is defenceless in this strange land.

Wesley bounded into Gerry Heffernan's office and placed a photograph on his desk beside one of Gwen Madeley's portraits. 'Have a look at those. Tell me what you see.'

Heffernan looked puzzled. 'What should I see?'

'I've been wondering why Nigel Armley was the only

one to be killed with a shotgun. Why use two weapons?'

'Martha Wallace didn't know how to reload the rifle and hedged her bets.'

'But the rifle took ten bullets – more than enough.'

'Perhaps she didn't trust her aim.'

'If she'd managed to load it once she could do so again. What if the shotgun was used because it could make a body unrecognisable. What if it wasn't Nigel Armley who died but the killer wanted us to think it was.'

'So who was it?'

'Victor Bleasdale. He was the same physical type as Armley. Armley applied for the job up in Yorkshire and took his place. The gardener up there said he was useless at the job. The real Bleasdale had been head gardener down here and there'd been no complaints about his work.'

'Maybe the Harfords gave him glowing references because they wanted to get shut of him. I've heard of that happening plenty of times. There was this DC over in Neston . . .'

But Wesley wasn't listening. 'Have a close look at the hands in both pictures. What do you see?'

Heffernan screwed up his eyes and looked from one picture to the other. 'The rings. He's wearing a ring on his middle finger in the painting and it's on his little finger in the photo. Maybe he'd put on weight. Or his fingers had swelled for some reason.'

'Or it's a different man. We should run further checks on every man involved in this case as a matter of urgency. Starting with Jeremy Elsham.' He picked up the photograph of Armley in his naval uniform. 'He'll have changed in twenty years: he could even have undergone plastic surgery.'

Heffernan grinned. 'Don't you think we're getting into the realms of fantasy here, Wes?' Heffernan picked up the picture. 'I suppose it could be Elsham. Different nose, grey hair, bit of work on the chin. Did Armley have any family?'

'I've checked. He was an only child and his parents had died in a boating accident when he was in his late teens. I'd like to check on that accident. If a man can murder all those people then he could easily bump off his mum and dad to get his hands on his inheritance.'

Heffernan scratched his head. 'This is all speculation, Wes. We've no proof. And if your theory's right, how did Armley get Bleasdale to put on his clothes?'

Wesley didn't have an answer for that one. Perhaps Heffernan was right. Perhaps he had let his imagination run away with him. Perhaps there was some perfectly reasonable explanation for why Armley wore a signet ring on his middle finger in Gwen Madeley's portrait and on his little finger on the night he died. But he was sure he was on to something.

They'd told Jocasta Mylcomb they'd be there by eleven. It was just over the border, not far from the River Tamar, and Wesley found himself wondering why, if Arbel had kept in touch with Gwen Madeley, she hadn't kept in touch with Jocasta, who didn't live that much further away. Jocasta had been at boarding school with her and, presumably, had come from a wealthy family; a far more advantageous contact for a woman married to a Member of Parliament. But then perhaps they had lost touch through sheer laziness and the swift passage of time rather than through any hostility. It had happened to Wesley himself so many times. In fact when he worked in London, he had almost lost touch with Neil.

According to Jocasta's local police station, she lived at Monkey Puzzle Cottage in Trecowan, a village of approximately three thousand souls, about two miles from the coast between Plymouth and Looe. The name was pretty but the reality was a run-down dump with dirty-grey pebbledashed walls stained with green mould and a rusting caravan in the overgrown front garden. Not a monkey puzzle tree in sight and hardly what they'd expected of an old school friend of Arbel Harford's.

288

As they parked outside, a large brown dog of very mixed ancestry bounded round the side of the cottage barking loudly. It didn't sound friendly. The beast was followed closely by a middle-aged woman with long, greying hair who wore baggy black trousers and a pale blue sweatshirt that had seen better days. She had a turned-up nose, an unhealthy pallid complexion and her movements were slow and deliberate.

'Looks like the sun passed over the yardarm early this morning,' Heffernan whispered.

Wesley stared at her. Gerry Heffernan was obviously better at recognising the signs than he was.

'Rascal,' she shouted to the dog. 'Come here, you bugger.' Her voice was well bred but slightly slurred.

The dog obeyed reluctantly.

Wesley got out of the car. 'We're looking for Jocasta Mylcomb.'

'You've found her. You the policemen from Tradmouth?'

Wesley and Heffernan stood for a moment. Jocasta Mylcomb wasn't what they'd expected. She looked considerably older than her schoolfriend, Arbel Jameston, for a start.

She led the way into the cottage. Wesley sniffed. The place smelled of animals, alcohol and decay. A mess of old newspapers and off-licence carrier bags littered every surface.

'Drink?'

'Not for me, thanks,' Wesley said quickly.

'Or me,' Heffernan echoed.

'Suit yourselves.' She picked up a bottle of vodka and poured a large measure into a dirty glass. 'Sit down. Don't make the place look more untidy than it already is.' She spoke tersely, like someone who'd forgotten the social niceties she'd once learned – or just didn't care any more. 'You wanted to talk about Arbel?'

'That's right,' said Heffernan. 'She's had a bit of a bad

time recently. A friend of hers was killed. Have you ever met Gwen Madeley?'

'Arbel and I don't mix in the same circles any more,' she replied bitterly.

'Perhaps Arbel mentioned her when you were at school together? She'd known her since they were small.'

Again Jocasta shook her head. 'Can't say I recall the name.'

Wesley knew this wasn't going to be easy. 'Your name was on a list of people a man called Patrick Evans wanted to talk to about the murders of Arbel's family. Did Mr Evans contact you?'

Unexpectedly, Jocasta's face lit up. 'Yes. Yes, he did. He came to see me.'

'Did you know he was found dead in the River Trad in Devon?'

Her shock wasn't feigned, Wesley was certain of that. In fact he doubted whether Jocasta Mylcomb would make a very good liar.

'No. What happened? Did he drown or ...?'

'I'm afraid we're treating his death as suspicious and we're sure it's connected in some way to the Harford murders. Were you questioned by the police when Arbel's family were killed?' Wesley asked.

Jocasta shook her head and poured another shot of vodka into her glass. 'No. No, why should I be? I didn't know Arbel's family.'

Gerry Heffernan leaned forward. 'You must have been invited to Potwoolstan Hall.'

'No. I was never asked.'

'But you were her mate. She came to stay with you. Why did she never ask you back?'

Jocasta shrugged. She looked uneasy. 'I really don't know. She'd stayed with us in London a few times and I remember asking her when I could come down and stay with her at the Hall – bit cheeky of me but I was like that in those days.'

'What did she say?'

'She made excuses. And she said I wouldn't like it in Devon. She said I'd find it boring after London.'

'You live in the countryside now.'

She raised her glass to Wesley. 'Well spotted. Couldn't afford London these days.' There was a long pause. 'I bet you're wondering how come I went to school with Arbel bloody Harford and I ended up in this dump, aren't you?'

Wesley glanced at Heffernan but didn't answer. He had hardly liked to enquire about Jocasta's social descent. It had seemed like bad manners.

'My family had a yacht in the South of France and a bloody big house in Hampstead. But my father made some stupid investments and lost the lot. Then he died and, to top it all, my mother went off with a salesman who got through what little money she had left, then promptly went bankrupt. I don't know where the old bitch is now.' She took another drink. 'I married a has-been rock musician when I was twenty-one but that lasted all of five minutes. I tried various jobs but ...' She made a vague gesture with fluttering hands. 'Nothing ever worked out. I'm on what is euphemistically known as benefit now.' She picked up the bottle.

'I'm sorry,' said Wesley, hoping the woman wasn't preparing for a long wallow in self-pity. 'We were talking about Arbel. You say you were never invited to Potwoolstan Hall?'

'Maybe that was a good thing.'

'What makes you say that?'

'Arbel said the place was cursed. Some old squire raped and murdered one of the village maidens and the locals cursed him. I thought she was making it up but ...'

'Did Arbel get on with her family?'

Jocasta frowned, deepening the lines on her face. 'I don't think she was ever happy at home. She hated school more though. I suppose I felt sorry for her. I was a soft touch in those days. I think being adopted made her insecure. Her brother, Jack, had taken great delight in telling her she was a cuckoo in the nest. From what she said, he was a right bastard.'

Wesley raised his eyebrows and looked at Heffernan. From the way Jack Harford had treated people, it was surprising that he'd survived as long as he did.

'What happened on the evening before Arbel left for Devon?'

Jocasta hesitated. 'Nothing much to tell. We were invited to this party. I thought Arbel wouldn't want to stay late because she had to go to Devon the next day. Some sort of party for her mother's birthday.'

'Go on.' Wesley was willing Jocasta to come to the point.

'My brother Guy had these friends – students from Imperial College. They were having a party. I assumed we'd take a taxi but Arbel said she'd drive so we went in her car. She met someone so I got a taxi home and she ended up staying the night at the party.'

'That's not in the reports I've seen.'

'Would you admit to the police that you'd had a quick screw with someone you'd just met at a party? Anyway, someone who looks like a prince through the bottom of a wine glass can often look like a frog the morning after.'

It sounded as if Jocasta spoke from experience. Wesley and Heffernan exchanged glances.

'So you went home and left her there?'

'That's right. She must have gone straight to Devon the next morning.'

'Did she drink at the party?'

'Not at first because she expected to be driving. I don't know what she did after I'd gone, obviously.'

'What time did you leave?'

Jocasta frowned. 'It's so long ago I can't really remember. Must have been around eleven. I had to be up early the next day. I was off to the Côte d'Azur with my parents.'

'Who was the young man Arbel met at the party, do you know?'

She wrinkled her nose, a sign of concentration. 'He was dark. Rather good-looking. I think he was studying some sort of science. Physics, something like that.'

'Well that narrows it down,' Heffernan muttered.

'Sorry. I didn't think to ask to see his passport,' she snapped. 'He was just a friend of Guy's. I didn't take much notice.'

'Where can we find Guy?'

'Australia.' She lit a cigarette.

'Did you tell Patrick Evans about this?'

'Yes.' She flicked ash on to the floor impatiently. 'Look, Arbel spent the night in London and went back to Devon the following morning and found her family dead. Does it really matter whether she was with me or screwing some bloke she'd met at a party? And if it's so important, why don't you just ask her? Nobody's going to bat an eyelid about who Arbel Harford had it off with in 1985.'

Jocasta was absolutely right. Arbel probably hadn't considered a one-night stand at a party was relevant. And it probably wasn't.

'Did Arbel ever mention a gardener called Victor Bleasdale?'

Jocasta shook her head.

'What about her sister's fiancé, Nigel Armley?'

She stubbed out her cigarette violently on a filthy saucer. 'The lovely Nigel? She used to keep a photo of him in her locker. I asked her who it was but she wouldn't tell me. But when I saw the pictures of the murder victims in the newspaper, I recognised him. He wasn't bad-looking. Maybe she felt embarrassed about having a crush on her sister's fiancé. I never met him of course.' She sounded disappointed.

Jocasta paused, as though she was making a decision. 'There was something she said once. I think it might be the reason she never wanted me to go to the Hall.'

'What was that?'

'She said someone tried to rape her. I think she said he

293

was the brother of one of her friends. There was a bit of trouble.'

Wesley held his breath. This was something new.

'Did she mention a name, love?' Heffernan asked quietly.

Jocasta frowned. 'I can't remember.' She took a long drag on her cigarette.

'Could it have been Dylan Madeley?'

She tilted her head to one side. 'Dylan,' she said, testing the name. 'It could have been.'

Wesley smiled. It looked as if Dylan Madeley was back in the spotlight again.

Jocasta drained her glass and looked at the dog, who was lying at her feet licking his private parts. She stood up, steadying herself on the back of the chair.

'You OK, love?' Heffernan asked as he stood.

'Course I am.' The answer was slurred and she looked from one policeman to the other with distant eyes.

'Is there anything else you can tell us about your meeting with Patrick Evans?'

She froze for a couple of seconds. Then she raised a shaky hand. 'I showed him the photos. Hang on. Stay, Rascal.'

The dog watched her stumble from the room with mournful eyes, as though he was well aware of the state his mistress had got herself into. Wesley and Heffernan sat quite still until Jocasta shambled back carrying a gaudy box that had once held Christmas cards. She handed it to Heffernan. 'I showed him these. He took one with him. Plenty left though.'

Heffernan lifted the lid. Inside the box lay a pile of snaps. He flicked through them. 'Which ones was Evans interested in, love?'

Jocasta took the box from him and clumsily selected four pictures, dropping a couple on to the threadbare carpet in the process. 'These were taken at the party I was telling you about.'

294

Wesley took the pictures. A group of laughing young people with drinks in their hands. He recognised Arbel and a younger, healthier, happier Jocasta. A dark-haired boy had his arm around Arbel's shoulder with a smug smile that suggested he realised his luck was in. Wesley turned the picture over. There were names scrawled on the back. Jo. Arbel. Greg. Steve. Sue. Olly. He looked up at Jocasta and experienced a twinge of sadness that the laughing girl had become a bitter woman with little reason to laugh any more. And that this was probably the last image of Arbel Harford before her life was blighted for ever by tragedy.

'You say you gave Patrick Evans a similar picture?'

Jocasta grunted as though she was now impatient for them to go. 'You take it. Help yourself. Take them all if you like.'

'Thank you,' Wesley said.

She frowned. 'I wrote to him, you know. I promised that Patrick I'd ask him . . .'

Wesley looked at her, puzzled. 'Ask who what?'

'Guy, of course. My loving brother down under. I wrote to him to ask him if he remembered the boy Arbel was with. Greg, was it?'

Wesley and Heffernan looked at each other. 'And did Guy remember?'

'Hasn't replied yet.'

'Can you let us know if he does?'

'Yeah. Sure.'

Wesley handed her his card. 'Ring me. Please.'

She hesitated for a moment. 'OK.'

As they left, Wesley thanked her. But she didn't reply before shutting the door in his face.

'Sad,' was Gerry Heffernan's only comment.

'At least we know where to find Dylan Madeley,' said Wesley.

'Forgot to tell you, Wes. He's been released on condition he stays at the bail hostel in Morbay.'

Wesley dropped Gerry off at Tradmouth police station before driving to Morbay.

The communal room of the bail hostel stank of smoke and sweat. The hostel itself was a rambling, run-down Victorian house in one of Morbay's direst streets, not far from Jack Wright's jeweller's shop. The stucco on the façade was flaking like diseased flesh, and threadbare curtains hung limply at the grubby windows. It was a place of last resort. A place where hope was in short supply.

Wesley stared at Dylan Madeley with distaste. Madeley stared back for a while then began to chew his nails. Wesley found this irritating. He placed both his hands on his knees and took a deep breath.

'You'll be going to your sister's funeral?'

Dylan nodded.

After a few seconds of silence, Wesley spoke again. 'Do you remember much about Nigel Armley, Catriona Harford's fiancé?'

'Not much.'

'Your sister was having an affair with him.'

Dylan looked up. 'No. You're wrong.'

'She painted him.'

'She painted a lot of people. That's what she did.'

'Armley wore a signet ring on his right hand. Can you remember which finger he wore it on?'

Dylan looked at Wesley as though he was mad and shook his head.

'In the photograph that was taken of Armley's body, he was wearing the ring on his little finger and in a picture your sister painted he was wearing it on his middle finger.' He produced the two images from his briefcase. 'She'd hardly have got something like that wrong.'

'How should I know?'

Wesley put the pictures away carefully. 'Arbel Harford tells me that Gwen had affairs with both Armley and the gardener, Bleasdale.'

296

Dylan gave an unexpected snort of derision. Then he leaned across the stained coffee table, disturbing a few cigarette butts in the overflowing ashtray, and put his face close to Wesley's. Wesley could smell the sour odour of Dylan's breath and he felt the urge to back away. But he stopped himself.

'Arbel Harford told a friend of hers that you tried to rape her.'

Dylan Madeley rose, sending his chair spinning to the ground with a crash. 'That's a fucking lie. I never touched her.'

Dylan Madeley's eyes bulged with fury and the veins on his neck stood out against the grey flesh. He brought his tightly clenched fish down on the nearest wall. Wesley felt uneasy. Perhaps he should have brought back-up.

Suddenly, Madeley picked up his chair and sat down heavily. 'You want the truth. I'll tell you the fucking truth.'

'OK,' Wesley said calmly. 'I'm listening.'

Wesley listened carefully. And when he left the hostel, he felt more confused than ever.

Gerry Heffernan was sitting in his office chewing the end of his pen when Wesley returned.

'How was Dylan Madeley? Uncomfortable, I hope.'

Wesley didn't answer. 'Did I hear that Brenda Varney and Richard Gibbons are out on bail?'

'Yeah. Brenda's staying with a cousin in Whitely – or at least that's what she told the powers that be. Gibbons has gone home to his dear old mum, which is probably punishment enough for anyone.'

Wesley looked out into the main office. Rachel was sorting through reports. She looked as if she needed a break. 'I'll ask Rachel to go and see Brenda. There's something I need to know.'

Heffernan looked puzzled.

'I'm going to have another word with Emma Oldchester. Want to come? I'll tell you what Dylan said on the way.'

297

Gerry Heffernan looked at his paperwork and stood up. He didn't need asking twice.

Jeremy Elsham twisted the gold signet ring on the middle finger of his right hand round and round; a nervous habit that he'd had for years. He looked Emma Oldchester in the eye.

'That's my final answer. I won't do it. If you'll take my advice, you'll go home.'

Emma stared at him.

'This obsession isn't healthy, Emma,' Elsham avoided her eyes. 'You have to move on.'

'But they said my mother killed all those people and I know she didn't do it,' she said slowly, as though she was speaking to a rather dim child, her fists clenched with frustration.

Elsham turned away. 'That's a matter for the police, not me. Now, if you don't mind . . .'

Before Emma could protest, there was a knock on the office door. Elsham shouted 'Come', and sat down behind the desk that stood between him and Emma like a defensive barrier.

Wesley Peterson entered the room followed by Gerry Heffernan, wearing the expression of suspicious scepticism he always assumed in Elsham's presence.

'We'd like a word with Mrs Oldchester. Your wife told us she was with you. If we could use your office, Mr Elsham. We won't take long, I promise.' Wesley smiled expectantly, not giving Elsham a chance to argue. Elsham mumbled something about having a workshop to supervise and made himself scarce.

'In my day the only workshops we had were connected with light engineering,' said Gerry Heffernan, lowering himself heavily on to the soft leather chair that Elsham had just vacated. It was comfortable. He could have stayed there all day. 'Well, sit down, love. And don't look so scared. We don't bite.'

298

Emma Oldchester gave a weak smile as Wesley sat down beside her. His eyes were drawn to the dark portrait of the two men that hung behind the chief inspector's head. He could have stared at those thin, hungry faces all day. There was something desperate about them; something sad.

Heffernan looked Emma in the eye. 'Now, love, do you remember a lad called Dylan Madeley? He lived on the road to Neston about half a mile from the Hall and his sister was friendly with Arbel Harford.'

Emma hesitated then she nodded.

'What can you tell us about him?'

She shuddered. 'He used to tease me. And he used to shoot things. Once he shot a crow and held it over my face. I got blood on my dress and my mother told me off but I never said what happened.' Her breathing quickened.

'You seem to remember a lot.' Wesley was rather surprised.

'I'm starting to remember more now. It's just ... It's just that night I don't remember. I keep seeing flashes but ... I know if Jeremy regressed me again ...'

Wesley and Heffernan looked at each other. The chief inspector leaned forward. 'Look, love, go home. Elsham won't change his mind. There's no point in staying.'

'But I've got to know.' She sounded like a pathetic child.

'Let's think about that another time, eh, love? When you're feeling up to it maybe you could see that doctor I told you about. Your husband wants you home, you know that, don't you? He's worried about you.'

Emma bowed her head, as though she suddenly knew she had lost the fight. She looked at Gerry Heffernan: as her only hope of finding out the truth he looked rather unimpressive.

Wesley leaned forward. 'Let us take you home, eh, Emma?'

'No need. I've got my van,' she muttered.

'Do you want to ring your husband?' Wesley picked up the telephone receiver and offered it to her. She took it with the resigned air of a woman who has no choice.

299

'Well, that's one problem out of the way,' Heffernan said as they walked to the car.

Wesley was deep in thought. 'Did you notice the ring on Elsham's right hand? Don't you think it looks like the one Armley was wearing in that portrait?'

'One signet ring looks very much like another,' Heffernan replied, putting a damper on Wesley's budding theory.

'When's Gwen Madeley's funeral?' Wesley asked as he reached the gates of the Hall.

'Monday. Dylan'll be there. Did you hear what Emma said about him shooting things and about the dead crow?'

But Wesley didn't seem to have heard. 'I want a word with Arbel Harford,' he said. 'She's staying till after the funeral.'

'Still at the cottage?'

'Mmm. It seems she's Gwen's executor and she's sorting out some of her things.'

'Her and Gwen must have been closer than we thought.'

'Or perhaps there's no one else to do it. Dylan's hardly up to the job.'

Wesley drove the short distance to Gwen Madeley's cottage. Arbel's car was parked outside. When Heffernan rang the doorbell she greeted them with a sad smile.

'Come in, please. To tell the truth I'm glad to have some company. I keep coming across things Gwen kept from when we were children. I feel so silly bursting into tears every five minutes but ...' She took a tissue from her pocket and blew her nose before leading them into the living room, now filled with boxes containing the relics of Gwen Madeley's life.

'I've asked a gallery in Tradmouth to deal with her paintings. It's all the personal stuff that's the hardest to know what to do with. Tea?'

Gerry Heffernan ignored the question. 'We've been talking to Dylan Madeley. Why were the police never told that he tried to rape you?'

Arbel's hand went to her mouth.

'What happened exactly? Take your time.' Wesley spoke gently, giving his boss a warning look.

Arbel took a deep breath and began massaging the back of her neck as though to relieve some tension there. 'I'd just got home from boarding school. I was in the garden and he said Gwen was waiting for me in one of the outhouses. I thought nothing of it and followed him there. Only she wasn't there and he came in behind me and closed the door and ... Look, do I have to go into all this? It's something I'd rather forget.'

'Please, Mrs Jameston. It's important.'

'When I started to scream Dylan tried to make light of it, said he was just larking around but ... I told my father and he went mad. He dealt with it himself. We didn't want the police involved. I just wanted to forget it ever happened. That's it really.'

'And how did Dylan react?'

'He was furious with me for telling on him and he made all sorts of threats. He scared me, if you must know.'

'But you stayed friendly with Gwen.'

'Nobody can choose their relatives, can they? Dylan left home straight after that and I never saw him again.'

Wesley said nothing for a few moments. 'This isn't how Dylan tells it. He said that you manipulated Gwen. He said you turned his family against him. He denies he ever touched you. Says you made it all up.'

Arbel looked hurt and puzzled. 'That's absolute rubbish. He's lying. If you don't believe me ask Brenda Varney: he tried the same thing with her.'

'We have asked her.'

'And?'

'She says he tried it on with her but he gave up when she told him to get lost. She doesn't remember anything between Dylan and you.'

'It wasn't something I wanted to become common knowledge.'

'I saw another old friend of yours too,' Wesley said. 'Jocasta Childs.'

Arbel tilted her head to one side and assumed an expression of polite interest. 'Really? How is she?'

'Patrick Evans went to see her.'

She looked surprised. 'Can't think why.'

'You were staying with her when your family died.'

'That's right.'

'But you weren't with her that night, were you?'

Arbel looked puzzled. 'I was. We went to a party.'

'She went home and you stayed.'

Arbel blushed. 'Well, I meant to go home with Jo but I met this boy and I ended up staying till dawn. I drove to Devon the next morning. Does it make a difference?'

Wesley took the photograph Jocasta had given him from his pocket. 'Recognise anyone?'

Arbel took it and stared for a few moments. 'I think this was taken that night. That's Jo and . . .'

'The names are on the back.'

She turned the picture over. 'Greg, that's right. His name was Greg. We all look so happy, don't we?'

Wesley looked into her eyes and knew what she was thinking. If only she'd known what was coming a few hours later. He took the photo back. Arbel had been eighteen. She'd met a boy and decided to stay on at a party that went on till dawn while her friend took a taxi home. Nothing sinister there.

The tea was finished but Wesley felt strangely reluctant to leave. There was something about Arbel's company that he found appealing. He had one more question to ask her, although he feared it would be a futile one. 'I noticed in the portrait Gwen did of Nigel Armley that he was wearing a signet ring on the middle finger of his right hand. When I looked at the crime scene pictures, he was wearing the ring on his little finger. Did you notice what finger he usually wore it on?'

Arbel looked puzzled. 'Sorry. I don't remember. I don't

think I ever noticed a ring. Sorry.'

'Jocasta told us you kept a photograph of Nigel Armley at school.'

Arbel looked embarrassed. 'I don't really remember, to be honest. I might have done.'

Wesley glanced at Heffernan, who was drinking his tea noisily in the corner. 'I know this seems a strange thing to ask but is there any chance that Jeremy Elsham up at the Hall could be either Victor Bleasdale or Nigel Armley?'

Heffernan almost choked on his tea and Arbel sat there, astonished. 'I don't know what happened to Vic but Nigel's dead, Inspector. He was shot. How could . . .?'

'But is there any resemblance?'

She seemed confused. 'I've only caught a brief glimpse of Elsham. I don't really know. What's this all about anyway? Nigel's dead. I saw him there. He was dead.'

Gerry Heffernan stood up. 'We'll leave you to it, love. We can see you've got a lot to do. We'll see you at the funeral, eh.'

He marched out and Wesley had no choice but to follow.

Wesley managed to set off for home earlier than usual that night and as he drove a sudden thought entered his head and buzzed around like an annoying wasp. What if Arbel took it into her head to confront Elsham? If she suspected that he had slaughtered her family, who knows how she might react. Maybe he had been deceived by her calm exterior. Perhaps he shouldn't have mentioned his vague suspicions.

When he arrived home, Pam was busy preparing for her return to school after the weekend. He found her sitting at the kitchen table, surrounded by a sea of charts, reports and books. Michael, she told him, was at a friend's and Amelia was sleeping upstairs. She made no mention of food so Wesley began to search the freezer and cupboards. But he found it impossible to plan a meal while his mind was on the deaths of Patrick Evans and Gwen Madeley and the safety of Emma Oldchester, who, hopefully, was home by now, safe with her husband. He'd sent Trish round to reassure them both.

When the doorbell rang, Pam stayed where she was. 'Forgot to tell you. Neil said he'd pop round.'

'Thanks for the warning.' Wesley muttered under his breath. Interested though he was in what had become of Edmund Selbiwood who had sailed off to found one of America's first colonies, he didn't feel he could give Neil his full attention. If it wasn't for his guilt about neglecting Pam he would probably still be at work. The realisation horrified him as he strolled into the hall.

When he opened the door, Neil bounced in, all trace of jet lag disappeared. 'I'm on the way to the Tradmouth Arms,' he announced. 'Fancy coming?'

Wesley smiled sadly. 'Another time maybe.'

'Suit yourself. Had a chance to look at those documents yet? Bit of a mystery involved.'

'I've had a quick glance at them. But I've been rather busy and ...'

'Pam in?'

'She's working. She's back at school next week.'

'Everything OK?'

'Fine.'

Neil hesitated for a second. 'We're starting a dig near Neston in a couple of weeks: they're building a new extension at Tradington Hall and they want us to see if there's anything down there.'

'Good,' was all Wesley could think of to say.

'Take care, eh?' Neil turned away and walked slowly back to his car.

Wesley walked into the kitchen, where Pam still had her head buried in her paperwork. He put a hand on her shoulder. She looked up and smiled weakly. A do not disturb smile.

He poured himself a glass of wine from the bottle Pam had opened earlier, went into the living room and switched the TV on.

'I didn't want to come home.'

Trish Walton looked at Emma and tried to hide her exasperation. 'DCI Heffernan thinks it's best if you're away from the Hall. And if you want we can arrange for you to see that doctor.'

She had been about to say psychiatrist but she had stopped herself in time. She didn't want to say anything that might upset Emma Oldchester.

'Everything OK?' Barry Oldchester poked his head around the door. Trish could tell he was nervous, like an expectant father reluctant to intrude on 'women's business'.

'Fine,' Trish replied cheerily.

Oldchester entered the room and put an arm around his wife's shoulders. Trish noticed that she stiffened, as though his touch was unwelcome. 'You can go if you like,' he said. 'I'll look after Em. She'll be OK now.'

'I'm sure she will, Mr Oldchester. But ...'

'I'm capable of taking care of my own wife.' He looked at Emma proprietorially and Trish was struck by the fact that their relationship seemed more like that of father and daughter rather than husband and wife. And it wasn't only the age difference.

Trish wavered for a moment. 'If you're sure.' She picked up her bag and stood up. 'If you're worried about anything at all, ring the number I gave you.'

With his assurance that he'd watch his wife every minute of the night and day ringing in her ears, Trish left the house, rather relieved that she wouldn't have to stay any longer in that claustrophobic room.

Monday morning looked promising; a bright Devon spring day with clear blue skies and sunshine. The weather would be fine for Gwen Madeley's journey to her grave.

Gerry Heffernan hated funerals. Each one he attended reminded him of the worst one of all when he had buried his wife, Kathy, in Tradmouth cemetery on the hill overlooking the town. Gwen Madeley was to be interred in that same cemetery, bringing back the old, bad memories. He had left Wesley alone for a few minutes while he visited Kathy's grave. But, as he stood staring at her name on the headstone, he felt guilty somehow. There was nothing he could do for her; he hadn't even remembered to bring flowers. So after picking up a crisp packet that had blown on to the grave and stuffing it into his pocket, he walked away and joined Wesley at Gwen's graveside, his face a neutral mask. He wished it was over.

Once the service began, he and Wesley studied the mourners. Not many had made the effort to come and pay their last respects. There were a few colleagues from Potwoolstan Hall; Pandora Elsham leading the small party dressed, although not in black, in suitably muted colours. Jeremy Elsham was nowhere in sight.

Arbel Harford and her husband stood slightly apart, dressed in seemly black. Arbel dabbed her eyes with a crisp white handkerchief and stood stiffly, close to Anthony's shoulder.

Anthony Jameston kept glancing at Elsham's party bashfully, like one who knows he has behaved foolishly and doesn't like being reminded of it. He stole a sly glance at his watch from time to time, counting the minutes until he could leave without causing offence.

There were several people at the graveside Wesley and Heffernan hadn't seen before. And then there was Dylan Madeley, glowering angrily into the open grave, his hands shaking, clenching and unclenching his fists.

Further back stood a handful of reporters, local and national. Serena Jones was there, conspicuous in their midst in bright red miniskirt and suede jacket. Wesley felt irritated that she couldn't have shown more respect. But then Serena wasn't the respectful type.

The police always harbour the hope that a killer will turn up at his or her victim's funeral. But in Wesley's experience it rarely happened. It almost seemed like the superstition that the dead eyes of a murder victim always reflect back the image of the murderer. A nice thought but not to be relied on in a murder enquiry.

Once the coffin had been lowered into the earth, the mourners began to drift away. Serena made straight for Arbel and Anthony, only to be waylaid by Gerry Heffernan, who told her to have some consideration.

Serena protested that she was only doing her job and by the time she had finished debating the point, the mourners were gone. Only Dylan was left, staring into the grave. Wesley and Gerry watched him for a few moments, deciding whether the time was right to approach him. But as Heffernan took a step forward, Dylan Madeley sprinted away like a gazelle pursued by a lion and disappeared into the headstoned wastes of the cemetery.

Jeremy Elsham locked his office door. If any of the Beings wanted him, they'd have to wait. He sat down at his desk and took a key from the top drawer.

He stared at the key for a while before walking over to the safe, where all his most confidential and sensitive secrets were kept. He unlocked it and took out a tape. When it was in the machine he pressed the button and sat back, his eyes closed.

He listened to her voice, high-pitched and terrified; a child's voice coming from a grown woman. 'The other man killed my mummy.' He listened as she broke down in terrified sobs; a child face to face with worse horrors than she could ever imagine. A child in hell.

After playing it through once, Jeremy Elsham took the cassette out of the machine and pulled at the thin brown ribbon of tape until it spilled out, draping itself over the edge of the bin as he threw it in. He kicked the bin and the loose tape slithered into its depths.

He unlocked the office door, crossed the hall and, once outside, he made for the trees, looking around, scanning the windows of the Hall for watching eyes. But he told himself

307

that, as he often went to the woods to meditate, nobody would think it strange. And if they did, he could rely on Pandora to make some excuse. She was good like that. And she knew what was at stake.

On his way to the clearing he called in at the outhouse where the gardening tools were kept to pick up a spade. It was time to bury the past once and for all.

'Any sign of Dylan Madeley?' Gerry Heffernan asked with a heavy sigh.

Wesley provided the reply he expected. Dylan hadn't returned to the hostel. All patrols were on the lookout for Madeley and his usual haunts were being checked. It was only a matter of time before he turned up.

Trish Walton gave a coy knock on the open door of Heffernan's office. 'Can I have a word, sir?'

Wesley cleared the spare visitor's chair of its veil of papers and files and Trish sat down stiffly on the edge of the seat. 'How's Emma Oldchester?'

'She's OK. Working on her doll's houses: keeping busy. Her husband said he'd make sure she wasn't left alone. I'll drop in again tomorrow.'

'I'll feel much better when she's remembered everything and we have her full statement,' Wesley said. He looked at Trish. 'She knows who did it. It's locked in her head at the moment but she knows.'

Rachel Tracey knocked on the office door and entered. 'I've had a call from North Yorkshire. You know that picture of Nigel Armley we faxed up? That gardener you talked to – Mr Clayton – identified him at once. It was the man who worked there calling himself Victor Bleasdale.'

Wesley shifted in his seat, feeling rather pleased with himself. It looked like his hunch was right. Armley had swapped places with Bleasdale. He was the killer. But where was he now?

Serena Jones had hoped her great scoop would lead to

offers of work from the national papers. But even though the story of a junior government minister booking in for some New Age therapy under an assumed name at the very house where his wife's family had been murdered had made the second page for a couple of days, everything had now gone quiet. Even Steve Carstairs hadn't come up with anything juicy since his initial desire to get into her knickers had tempted him to indiscretion.

But she hadn't finished with Potwoolstan Hall yet. Now that her cover was blown and she had no chance of seeing things from the inside, she had decided to take the direct approach. She would ask Jeremy Elsham for an interview, implying that she was so impressed by what she'd seen at the Hall that she intended to write a favourable article about the place. She would appeal to his vanity. All men are vain.

She parked her car in the Hall's car park and began to trudge up the path. Serena never normally contemplated failure but this time there was the nagging thought in the back of her mind that Jeremy Elsham might send her away with a flea in her ear. Once bitten, twice shy. This would need all the charm that Serena was convinced that she possessed.

As she rounded the bend she spotted a movement, a figure darting towards the trees. Jeremy Elsham was carrying a spade and it was clear that he didn't want to be seen, which, for a self-promoting man like Jeremy Elsham, was odd, to say the least.

Serena stepped sideways into the rhododendron bushes that lined the drive and watched him disappear into the wood. Then, when he was almost out of sight, she followed, treading softly, alert to all movement, jumping at every bird that fluttered in the canopy of branches. Crows cawed in their scruffy nests in the tree tops: great evil-looking things. Birds of ill omen. She carried on, walking on tiptoe, stopping every now and then to listen. For the first time in years she felt nervous. And she hated the unfamiliar feeling of vulnerability.

She could hear the soft thud of spade on hard earth some-where ahead. She moved forward slowly, holding her breath, cursing silently as a twig snapped beneath her feet and the noise echoed like a rifle shot in the still air. The noise of digging stopped and she flattened herself against a convenient tree, hardly daring to breathe.

When the digging started up again, Serena's courage flooded back and she moved forward, using the cover of the trees. The sound was nearer now and she crept towards it, closer and closer, until she came to a small clearing in the trees. Then she froze.

Jeremy Elsham was sweating profusely. His pale blue tracksuit bore dark stains around the armpits and upper back and he stopped from time to time to wipe the perspiration from his brow. He seemed to be digging at the roots of a fallen tree and every so often he placed something carefully in a cardboard box. Serena pressed her body against a gnarled tree trunk and watched.

Elsham lifted something from the ground. A human skull. He held it for a moment, staring into its empty eye sockets like Prince Hamlet addressing the skull of Yorick.

Jeremy Elsham was digging up human remains. He had buried someone in the grounds of Potwoolstan Hall and was now disposing of the evidence. This was possibly the scoop of her career. Her heart beat faster as she began to make plans.

She was first on the scene – a prime witness – and she would be in on the police investigation from the start. She smiled to herself as she began to creep away. Steve Carstair's home number was stored in her mobile. She would ring him, maybe that evening when he'd finished work.

But first she had to get away to safety. Serena Jones wasn't out of the woods just yet.

Barry Oldchester touched his wife's arm. 'You've had an email from Mrs Potts asking if the house is ready. It's her daughter's birthday tomorrow and she'd like to pick it up tonight. She can come straight round after her evening class.'

Emma sighed. She'd been working on her houses every waking hour to take her mind off other things. 'It'll be finished this afternoon,' she said, looking at her watch. 'Can you email her back and tell her it's OK?'

Barry looked into her eyes anxiously. 'You'll feel better once you've seen this doctor that chief inspector mentioned. Closure, they call it. You've got to come to terms with what happened before you can move on.'

Emma said nothing. He'd probably come across that on some daytime TV programme. Sometimes she wished he wasn't there.

He was taking time off work, hovering over her like an irritating servant. And if Barry didn't work he wasn't earning.

He began to read the paper and Emma watched him. Perhaps she had been fooling herself when she'd thought that once she knew the truth about her past she could think about starting a family. She was beginning to harbour the uncomfortable suspicion that once she knew the truth her dependence on Barry might cease.

That afternoon she worked on Mrs Potts's doll's house, papering the walls with tiny floral prints, gluing in the dainty Victorian fireplaces. When it was finished she looked at it with satisfaction. It would give the little girl hours of pleasure. Her own parents, Joe and Linda, had bought her a doll's house for her ninth birthday. But she had upset them by arranging all the little dolls as though they were dead and smearing them with Linda's lipstick to make it look as if they were bleeding. They had taken the house away from her after a few months.

Once Mrs Potts's house was finished, Barry carried it down into the hall, where it sat, waiting to be picked up by its new owner. And after they had eaten he switched on the TV and sat quietly, intent on the screen. Emma, bored and restless, wandered into the kitchen for a packet of crisps aware that she was only eating for something to do. At nine o'clock the telephone rang and Barry answered it – he always did – while she hurried out into the kitchen to make some hot chocolate. Barry liked his hot chocolate before bed.

When she brought the cups into the living room, Barry was standing there with his back to the gas fire. He looked agitated.

'That was a woman in Neston. Her tank's burst and water's pouring through her ceiling. She says she's called about six plumbers already but . . .'

'Are you going?' She was surprised that she felt so excited at the prospect of being alone.

'She sounded in a right state. Said her husband's away and she's got three young kids.'

'You should go. I'll be OK.'

'I won't be long. That lady's coming round for the doll's house in half an hour. You'll be all right if you lock up when I've gone and make sure you ask who it is before you open the door.'

Emma glanced at the clock on the mantelpiece and felt a sudden chill of fear. 'I'll be fine. You go.'

He kissed her forehead, a fatherly gesture with no hint of desire. 'Tell you what, I'll . . .'

'I can't stand all this fussing,' Emma screamed. 'Just go.'

Without a word, Barry Oldchester left the room and Emma slumped into the nearest chair.

Pam was in the bath having a long soak after her first day back at school. From experience Wesley knew she'd be some time: she'd taken the portable CD player up there as well as a bottle of wine. He'd half hoped she would ask him to join her. But there had been no summons from on high as yet so he had to be satisfied with the papers Neil had left him.

He had read the first part of Edmund Selbiwood's account of the early days of the Annetown settlement already but there were also some new documents which came from a different source. Wesley flicked through them and saw that some were official records and some were accounts written by other settlers that mentioned Edmund and the woman he was besotted with, Penelope Morton. The type of woman most mothers would advise their sons to avoid.

He was about to settle down to continue Selbiwood's account when the telephone rang. He picked up the receiver and was surprised to hear Steve Carstairs's voice.

'What is it, Steve?' he asked, wondering what catastrophe he was about to report.

'I've just had a call from Serena. Do you remember Serena? She was at Potwoolstan Hall when ...'

'I remember her.' Serena Jones wasn't easy to forget. 'What about her?'

'She's just rung to tell me she was round at the Hall and she saw something.'

Steve was being irritatingly cagey. 'What did she see?'

'She says Jeremy Elsham was digging up some bones in the woods.'

Wesley sighed. 'Bones?'

'Yeah.'

'Human bones?'

'That's what she said. That's why she rang me. She thought the police should know.'

'Very public-spirited of her. I suppose we'll have to check it out, but it can wait till tomorrow.'

'Don't you believe her ... sir?'

'I don't know what to believe any more,' he said softly before putting the receiver down. It could be relevant to their investigation or it could be the product of Serena Jones's fevered imagination; something quite innocent that her subconscious longing for a good story had caused her to misinterpret. Perhaps Jeremy Elsham had been hypnotising his Beings to change their wills in his favour then killing them and burying them in the woods. Or perhaps not.

When he heard a voice calling from upstairs, echoing and faint in the steamy bathroom, he bounded out into the hall and climbed the stairs, two at a time.

Arbel Harford sat in the living room of Gwen Madeley's cottage surrounded by boxes. She had been relieved when Anthony decided to return to London and leave her to it: there were some things she had to do alone.

She looked at her watch. It was almost nine o'clock and quite dark outside. At least she had managed to get most of Gwen's personal possessions sorted out. She wondered whether the police knew that, under the terms of Gwen's will, Dylan inherited everything. The person who benefited most by someone's death was always the prime suspect, so she'd heard. Perhaps she should draw DI Peterson's attention to this fact.

She went to the window and drew back the curtains. She could see the lane clearly in the moonlight.

Then, as she closed the curtains again, she heard a knock on the door. A loud, hollow sound, like a summons from the bringer of death.

Emma Oldchester switched on the television, trying to kill time before Mrs Potts called to fetch her daughter's house. It was a pretty house with frilly curtains and painted roses around the door and Emma felt rather proud of her handiwork.

When the doorbell eventually rang, she took a deep breath to calm her racing heart. She recalled Barry's instructions to check the caller's identity before answering the door. She turned off the light and flicked the curtain to one side, just as her mum, Linda, used to do when she wanted to see what the neighbours were up to. But she couldn't see the visitor clearly in the dark. At first glance it almost looked like Barry in his duffel coat.

She hesitated. Then the caller knocked again and some instinct told her to be careful. She switched on the light again, which somehow made her feel safer, and hurried into the hall.

She stood behind the front door and called out. 'Who is it?'

'Mrs Potts. I've come for the house,' was the reply. Mrs Potts had rather a deep voice.

Emma shot back the bolts she had so carefully fastened when Barry had left. The thought of the money she'd receive for the finished house spurred her on and she fumbled with the catch.

The door opened and the hooded figure pushed forward. As Emma backed towards the stairs, the front door was closed and the key turned in the deadlock with a final click.

'Please go. Please,' Emma whispered as she flattened herself against the wall.

Chapter Fourteen

Penelope is with child and although I should be joyful I am uneasy in my mind. I have discovered certain charms and powders amongst her possessions that I cannot but think she has used in spells and witchcraft. I think now upon the manner in which she bewitched me and blinded me with lust and I weep at what I have done. She has persuaded men of influence to elect me to the Council yet still she urges me to return to England and when I refuse she becomes angry and will not speak. She refuses to do aught in the house and I fear what will become of us when we have the winter to face and most likely great hardship.

I fear there may be murder in my heart. How I fight the temptation to put my hands around her pretty neck and force the life out of her. She desires to be a fine lady, to have riches and respect and so fierce is this desire I fear what she will do.

She speaks of Potwoolstan saying that it is only my brother who stands between me and the estates. I know what is in her mind but I am no Isaac Morton. I have great love for Richard, bound together as we were in tragedy and shame.

I pray for guidance and forgiveness but I fear the Lord will not listen for I am so sunk in sin.

Emma raised her arms in defence, hiding her face and sliding down until she crouched on the floor, a bundle of terror and sobbing.

'I can't tell them anything,' she sobbed. 'I don't remember.'

'Liar.'

Emma uncovered her eyes for a moment and looked up at her tormentor towering over her. 'Please. Leave me alone.'

A hand grabbed at Emma's hair and yanked her upwards. But Emma lashed out, scratching, kicking. Fighting for her life.

Something flashed in the dull light of the hallway's sixty-watt bulb. Something bright. A blade. It was there above her, hovering like an angel of death.

As the blow was struck, there was a thump on the front door. 'Emma. Are you there, love? Open the door, will you? Come on.'

As Barry Oldchester hammered at the front door the intruder dashed out through the French windows and flitted across the back garden, leaving Emma crouched in the hall, her life blood draining away, soaking into the new cream-coloured carpet.

When the telephone rang Amelia awoke and started to howl. Wesley and Pam's snatched escape into pre-baby freedom had been all too fleeting. The bottle of wine shared in a steamy bath followed by leisurely lovemaking now seemed like a distant memory. Pam struggled out of bed to attend to Amelia while Wesley answered the phone with a sleepy grunt.

But he was soon wide awake. A patrol car and ambulance had been called to the Oldchesters' house by Barry,

317

who had found his wife collapsed in the hall, semi-conscious and bleeding from a stab wound. She had been taken to Tradmouth hospital where she was undergoing surgery.

Half asleep, Wesley pulled on his clothes, muttered his apologies to Pam and left the house. A patrol car was coming to pick him up and he was to meet Gerry Heffernan at the Oldchesters'.

When he arrived at his destination he found the DCI there, annoyingly awake. The entrance hall had been taped off as a crime scene and a group of scene of crime officers in white protective suits were giving the place a once over.

'No sign of a break in,' Heffernan said. 'Looks like Emma opened the door to her attacker.'

'I thought her husband was going to stay with her.'

'He had a call from someone who said they had a burst water tank and their house was flooding but he found the address didn't exist. It was a hoax to get him out of the way.'

'Who made the call? Man or woman?'

'Barry thought it was a woman but he said the voice was quite deep. It could have been a man. And Emma was expecting a woman to pick up a doll's house she'd ordered for her daughter. A Mrs Potts.'

'And did she turn up?'

Gerry shook his head. 'That's the thing, she didn't. And according to Barry the house was ordered over the Internet. Emma never met this woman.'

'You think the attacker was a woman?'

'Or a man pretending to be a woman to put us off the scent. I think this was a setup. Someone wanted to get at Emma and planned it all.'

'Nigel Armley?'

'Or Nigel Armley and his wife. Jeremy and Pandora Elsham?'

'We've no proof it was them, Gerry.'

'We'll get it.'

318

'And if Elsham wanted to get rid of Emma why didn't he do it while she was at Potwoolstan Hall?'

'Because he would have been a prime suspect.'

'Even if she didn't remember everything when he regressed her, he knew you were trying to persuade her to see someone professional. It was only a matter of time before the truth came out.'

Heffernan put his head in his hands. 'Me and my big mouth.'

'I had a call from Steve earlier. Some garbled story about Elsham digging up some bones. I was going to send someone round first thing in the morning.'

'Well, there's no time like the present, Wes. Dragging people out of bed in the middle of the night always puts them at a disadvantage in my experience.'

'Don't I know it,' Wesley muttered under his breath. But the chief inspector was right. If they called on Elsham now before he had the chance to destroy any evidence and think up a convincing story they might just get somewhere.

Rachel Tracey appeared in the doorway. She managed a weak smile. 'Trish has just rung from the hospital. Emma Oldchester's still in the operating theatre. Touch and go.'

For the first time Wesley noticed that Rachel was dressed in a short denim skirt and chiffon top with full make-up. 'Hope this hasn't ruined your evening,' he said, subconsciously aware that he was fishing for information.

'Not really. I didn't have much on.' She blushed and Wesley felt a sudden rush of envy that he quickly suppressed. Rachel was a free woman. And he was a married man.

Gerry Heffernan never ceased to be fascinated by people's choice of night attire. The most hard-bitten matriarch of some criminal clan would, in his experience, be discovered in Mickey Mouse pyjamas when the police battered her front door down in an early morning raid. Jeremy Elsham's pyjamas, however, were plain and expensive, probably silk

– although silk pyjamas were uncharted territory to Gerry Heffernan – and he covered them with a pristine white towelling bathrobe before leading them into his office. Pandora followed in a matching bathrobe, only hers had a smudge of make-up on the collar and the nightdress underneath was cream satin.

'What's this all about?' Pandora asked. She sounded annoyed. Her husband said nothing.

There was no sign of bloodstained clothing in their room and, according to Forensic, Emma's attacker would probably be splashed with her blood. However, a couple of uniformed officers had been called to make a search of the Hall.

Heffernan sat himself down in Elsham's leather swivel chair, making himself at home. Wesley took the smaller visitor's chair and moved it beside his boss's, leaving Elsham and Pandora a couple of low seats, designed to make their occupants look up to the man behind the desk, putting them at a disadvantage.

Heffernan leaned forward and looked Elsham in the eye. 'Where were you at nine forty-five last night?'

'Here of course. Where else would I be? What's this about? What are those policemen looking for?' There was no mistaking it, he looked terrified. So did his wife.

'Emma Oldchester was attacked last night,' said Wesley. 'We think she was targeted because of what she knew about the murders here in 1985. You claim she didn't remember much about it.'

'You've heard the tape for yourself.'

'Have you ever heard the name Nigel Armley, Mr Elsham?'

Elsham and Pandora glanced at each other. 'Wasn't that the name of one of the people who died here?' He looked Wesley in the eye, the picture of innocence.

Heffernan leaned forward. 'You see, Mr Elsham, we've tried to check out your background and we've come up with a blank.'

Elsham swallowed hard. 'Really?' The word came out as a squeak. He was on the ropes.

'What did you do with the bones you dug up yesterday?'

Elsham opened and closed his mouth like a goldfish. 'Who told you . . .?'

'Where are they now?'

There was a long period of silence before Elsham spoke. 'A tree fell in the high winds the other night. I noticed the bones tangled up in the roots when I was down in the clearing meditating and I thought that if they were found it would only lead to more trouble. We've had a murder in the grounds already, police crawling all over the place. It's been a disaster for the business. We've had cancellations, haven't we, darling?' He looked to Pandora for confirmation and she nodded dutifully.

'Jeremy's right. It has hit us badly. Nobody wants to come to a place crawling with police and reporters when they're searching for tranquillity and spiritual renewal. Jeremy moved those bones to save our business.'

Wesley found himself believing every word they said. Almost. 'Show us the bones and where they were found.'

After dressing, Elsham led the two policemen to an outhouse, maybe the one where Gwen Madeley had had her amorous encounter with Nigel Armley. The skeleton had been packed into a plastic crate, once used to store plant pots. When Wesley examined it, he found that it was almost complete, give or take a few fingers and toes. Elsham then took them to a clearing in the woods where a tree hung at a dangerous angle, supported only by its fellows. The roots had been torn out of the earth and Elsham pointed to the cavity they had made.

'It was in there.'

'I'd like to get this hole examined properly. There might be some clue to his identity in there.'

'He? It's a man?' Elsham sounded surprised. 'I thought it was something to do with that old story. Wasn't the man who built the Hall supposed to have murdered a girl and

321

buried her body in the grounds? I thought . . .'

Wesley said nothing. Jeremy and Pandora Elsham were bound for the police station for more questioning while the Hall was searched.

Before they left, Wesley retrieved a paperweight from Elsham's desk, a glass sphere, undoubtedly covered in Elsham's fingerprints. It was about time they found out who Jeremy Elsham really was.

The postman reached Gwen Madeley's cottage at around eight o'clock, just as he did every morning. He had heard that the woman who lived there had been found dead in the river and curiosity made him pay particular attention to her post. The fact that a friend of the dead woman's from London had been staying there off and on had stuck in his mind, along with all the other snippets of local information he gleaned during his round.

Examining the label on the parcel, he discovered that it had been sent by a firm that sold artists' materials; hardly unexpected as Ms G. Madeley had been an artist. He knocked twice, three times, but there was no answer. There were no neighbours to leave it with in this isolated spot. But there was a porch at the back of the cottage where he'd left parcels before.

As the postman walked round the side of the building his heart beat slightly faster in anticipation. A murdered woman had lived here and he felt a thrill of excitement at this small and vicarious contact with the drama.

The porch protecting the back door was unlocked and once the parcel was safely deposited, the postman yielded to his natural curiosity and peeped through the back window; tentatively at first then, when he saw no movement within, more boldly. He pressed his face against the glass and looked into the room. And when he saw the body lying on the floor, he jumped back and caught his breath for a few seconds before dialling 999 on his mobile phone with trembling hands.

Chapter Fifteen

15 June 1606	*Mistress Selbiwood delivered of a son named Thomas.*
25 June 1606	*Mistress Radford died of the bloody flux, her body bruised and swollen.*
5 July 1606	*Thomas Selbiwood, son of Master Edmund Selbiwood, baptised.*
25 July 1606	*Master Edmund Selbiwood is exceeding sick of a mad fever. His skin doth peel.*
1 August 1606	*Master Edmund Selbiwood died today of the bloody flux.*
4 August 1606	*Captain Radford is sick of the mad fever and in a furious distracted mood did come openly to the marketplace blaspheming. He then fell sick of the flux, his body bruised and swollen.*
10 August 1606	*Captain Radford was today trans-lated from this uncertain and troublesome state.*

Because of his early return from the States, Neil Watson found himself at a loose end. He had the option of catching up on his paperwork. But paperwork had never really been his forte. He longed for action; he yearned to get his hands dirty. So when Wesley rang to ask him to use his archaeological expertise to help the scene of crime officers excavate the site of a burial, he felt pathetically grateful for the distraction.

When he arrived at Potwoolstan Hall the bones themselves had already been removed to the mortuary to await Colin Bowman's attentions. Neil was there to examine the place where they had been buried.

It was always possible that the mystery man had been buried naked, but Wesley, perhaps optimistically, was counting on finding something in the makeshift grave that would lead to an identification. That was where Neil came in.

Neil put on the white-hooded boilersuit the police forensic team habitually wore – if this was a murder scene it was important that the evidence shouldn't be contaminated – and after two hours of painstaking scraping and brushing a strange array of objects, some so tiny they would have been missed by an inexperienced eye, lay on a white sheet beside their former resting place. They had been arranged carefully and the whole procedure had been photographed and recorded. Neil looked at his haul: an assortment of buttons and metal eyelets; a rusted zip; a few coins and the corroded remnants of a belt buckle. Fragments of cloth had been collected and bagged and samples had been taken from the surrounding soil.

By the time Wesley arrived, the job was almost done, and he stood beside Neil looking down at his grim harvest. He had just come from a meeting with Colin Bowman at the mortuary. Colin had joked that they were keeping him in work. Somehow, Wesley hadn't felt like laughing.

'Colin said anything about the bones?' Neil asked after a long period of silence.

'He said there's a healed fracture on the right femur. And it wasn't a particularly old one. There's also some dental work. Rather rules out the theory that he's been there for centuries. He has someone tracking down medical records at the moment.'

'Why are you looking so pleased with yourself?' Neil asked.

'No reason.'

Neil walked away and when he came to the line of blue and white crime-scene tape he began to take off his protective suit.

Every time somebody entered the CID office, Gerry Heffernan looked up, then looked down again, disappointed. There was to be no distraction from the divisional crime figures which hung over him like a long jail term.

So at ten o'clock when Steve Carstairs burst in with the news that a postman had summoned a patrol car to Gwen Madeley's cottage because he'd looked through the window and seen a body lying on the floor, the chief inspector leapt to his feet at once, knocking the crime figures to the floor, where they landed in an untidy heap.

'A woman's body?'

'He didn't say.'

'And you didn't think to ask.' He began to pace up and down. 'Arbel Harford was at that cottage. Hell. Why didn't we offer her some protection?'

Steve shifted from foot to foot, uncertain what to do next. There were dark rings beneath his eyes and he hadn't shaved that morning. He looked exhausted. Maybe Serena Jones was a demanding woman, Heffernan thought fleetingly. She certainly looked the type.

'Inspector Peterson in yet?'

Steve scowled and shook his head. 'He's gone to Potwoolstan Hall. That skeleton. He's asked me to check Gwen Madeley's bank account and . . .'

'You done it?'

'Yes but . . .'

'You up to driving?'

There was another scowl that Heffernan took for a yes.

'We'd better get over to Gwen Madeley's cottage. And,

before we go, see if Dylan Madeley's turned up yet, will you.'

Gerry Heffernan stood for a few moments staring at the gruesome pictures on the notice board, fearing that it wouldn't be long before Arbel Jameston's image was up there and cursing himself for not watching her more closely.

Wesley often wished the mobile phone hadn't been invented. He wanted time to think. He had answered it after the seventh ring and heard Gerry Heffernan's voice telling him that a body had been discovered at Gwen Madeley's cottage: Arbel Jameston had been there alone.

It seemed that the killer wouldn't stop until all possible witnesses to what had happened at Potwoolstan Hall in 1985 had been eliminated. Emma Oldchester was still unconscious in hospital under police guard but the operation had gone well and the doctors were optimistic. Now all they had to do was guard her well and hope she would be able to tell them what they needed to know. But maybe he was expecting too much. And he had a nagging feeling that it might not be right to encourage Emma to relive the horror of what she had witnessed when she was seven years old. However, the thought that she had gone to Jeremy Elsham voluntarily because she wanted to remember helped to salve his conscience.

He was about to return his mobile phone to his pocket when it began to ring again. This time it was Colin Bowman, sounding inappropriately cheerful as usual.

'I've got some news for you, Wesley. I've had someone going through medical and dental records and I think we have a name for our skeleton.'

'It wouldn't be a Nigel Armley by any chance, would it?'

Colin sounded deflated. 'How did you know?'

'I'm clairvoyant.'

He rang off and returned to his car. And as he drove to Gwen Madeley's cottage, he hoped that he wouldn't have to be the one to break the news to Arbel's husband.

Emma Oldchester opened her eyes then she closed them again.

A shout went up from the man seated by the bed. 'Nurse. Nurse. She's moved her eyes.'

How Emma wished that Barry would leave her alone sometimes. Half aware of his presence, she tried to lift her right arm to shoo him away like an annoying insect but she found she couldn't move. Her limbs felt like lead and there were things attached to her arms. Tubes and lines. She tried to open her eyes again and succeeded for a couple of seconds. She was in a bright room with blue walls; a strange room.

She tried to speak but she only managed a squeak. There was a machine nearby that bleeped.

'You're OK, love, you're in hospital. Your dad's here.'

She heard Joe Harper's gruff, loving voice and felt him squeeze her hand gently.

She tried to speak but her throat was dry and sore. She mouthed the word 'water' but nobody seemed to hear. She closed her eyes again. Sleep was better than trying to talk about trivia.

Memories of that night all those years ago – the night her mother died – were starting to swim into focus. She wanted to see the doctor the police had talked about. She wanted him to help her remember properly. She was ready to face the past.

'The doctor's with her now but he says she's not up to making a statement yet,' said DC Paul Johnson, averting his eyes from the corpse that lay on the floor of Gwen Madeley's sitting room.

Gerry Heffernan scratched his head and stared down at the mortal remains of Dylan Madeley. The dead man's lips were curled upwards in an unpleasant snarl and it seemed he looked more vicious in death than he had done in life.

There was a crusted wound on the side of his head where he had apparently fallen against the hearth. In his hand was a knife with a narrow blade. Probably the knife that had killed Patrick Evans.

'We should have made sure Arbel Jameston wasn't alone here at night.'

'Do you think she would have taken any notice?' said Wesley.

'He obviously came here to kill her. This was self-defence. No jury would convict her of murder.'

'You think he killed the Harfords?'

Heffernan sniffed. 'No doubt about it. It had his signature all over it.'

'So why was Nigel Armley's body buried in the woods at Potwoolstan Hall?'

Heffernan turned and stared at him. 'Those bones belong to Nigel Armley?'

'Colin Bowman traced Armley's dental records and, according to his medical records, he broke his right femur in 1982. The bones are Armley's all right.'

'And why have you been keeping this little gem of information to yourself?'

'I only found out before I set off. I haven't had a chance to tell you.'

Heffernan paused for a moment while he absorbed the information. 'So Armley swapped places with Bleasdale who was killed in his place, shot twice in the face with a shotgun to destroy the teeth and make identification extremely difficult in the days before sophisticated DNA testing. And as it was an open and shut case, everyone accepted what the killer wanted them to accept. Armley changed his identity and took up that gardening job in Yorkshire. Why? What was his motive? And where did Dylan come into it?'

'Perhaps they were in it together, Armley and Dylan and Dylan killed him when they fell out.'

'Dylan I can understand. He hated the Harfords. But

328

Armley was a respectable naval officer engaged to the daughter of the house.'

'Maybe he wasn't as squeaky clean as people thought. I had another call just as I was leaving the office. It seems that there was a question mark over the deaths of Armley's parents. Their boat blew up. Nothing was proved of course and the coroner brought in a verdict of accidental death.'

'Where was Armley when it happened?'

'It seems he was due to go sailing with them but he said he felt ill.' He raised his eyebrows.

Heffernan said nothing.

Wesley stared at the body of Dylan Madeley; Dylan would have stood for everything Nigel Armley despised. But sometimes opposites attract. Perhaps Armley was having a sexual relationship with Dylan as well as his sister, Gwen. Or they were planning to steal from the Harfords. The possibilities are endless. Armley wouldn't be the first apparently upstanding member of the community to resort to murder.

'Do you want to interview Arbel Jameston when she's up to it?'

Wesley shook his head. 'I think I'll leave that to Rachel. I have to get back to the office anyway. I've some things to check out.'

Heffernan looked at him ruefully. 'Suit yourself,' he said as he stepped out of the way of the police photographers. His mobile rang and he answered it. When he'd finished his conversation he looked at Wesley.

'That was Trish at the hospital. Emma Oldchester's come round. She's saying she wants to talk to Clive Wellings and I've told Trish to call the psychiatry department and let him know.'

'He might be busy.'

'Never too busy to do a mate a favour,' he said with a grin as Wesley left the room.

Arbel Jameston had been found crouching in a torn white

329

cotton nightdress splashed with blood, on the guest bed upstairs. She was shaking, too terrified to venture downstairs in case Dylan came round. For a while she had been too upset to speak but after the doctor had checked her over, Rachel had encouraged her to wash, dress and put some make-up on. And with some coaxing, and something from the doctor to calm her down, she had eventually managed to tell them what happened, still on the verge of tears but considerably calmer.

Rachel put the bloodstained nightdress in an evidence bag discreetly, hoping Arbel wouldn't notice. Then she sat beside her on the bed as she explained how Dylan Madeley had let himself into the cottage at around six thirty in the morning. She had woken up to find him standing over her and he had attacked her, furious at her accusations of attempted rape that had been dug up again after all this time. He had threatened her, implying that this time any accusations she made wouldn't be unfounded. Her body shook as she repeated his words in a whisper.

She had managed to break away from him and get downstairs and, when she fought him off, he had fallen and hit his head on the stone fireplace. It had been an accident. When Rachel asked her why she hadn't escaped and called the police, Arbel said that she'd dashed upstairs and locked the bedroom door, not realising he was dead and had been too frightened to venture down again. Her mobile was in her coat downstairs and Dylan had pulled the telephone wires from their socket so there was no way of calling for help.

Rachel believed she was telling the truth. The woman had been paralysed with fear for what must have seemed like a lifetime. Thinking it best to get Arbel away from the scene of her ordeal, she drove her back to the Marina Hotel and stayed with her, providing tea and sympathy. In the privacy of her room Arbel showed her the fresh cuts and bruises she had sustained during Dylan's attack. She had been fighting for her very survival. She had been doing a

330

last favour for a dead childhood friend and had almost paid with her life. Rachel thought she deserved a medal for ridding the world of the likes of Dylan Madeley but she tried to preserve her professional neutrality and said nothing.

Anthony Jameston was travelling from London to be with her, bringing a high-profile solicitor with him. Rachel found herself hoping that no charges would be brought, especially in view of what Arbel had been through in 1985.

Arbel Harford was the victim here.

As far as Gerry Heffernan was concerned, the murderer of Patrick Evans, Gwen Madeley – and probably the Harford family too – was dead. He even put forward a theory that Nigel Armley had been suffering from amnesia brought on by shock when he travelled to Yorkshire. Then, as soon as he remembered, he had returned to accuse Dylan, who promptly killed him and buried him in the woods. It was possible, of course. But Wesley wasn't altogether convinced.

At three thirty Steve Carstairs deposited a computer printout on Wesley's desk: Gwen Madeley's bank account. When a report came in from Forensics, he set it aside to deal with later.

They had managed to get prints off Jeremy Elsham's glass and when they'd been put through the computer, the results made interesting reading. Wesley smiled to himself. A small triumph on a rainy afternoon. But the phone call he was waiting for still hadn't come and at five thirty he made for home, hoping he would hear from Jocasta Mylcomb the next day.

It was disappointing that the one day he arrived home at a civilised time, Pam was out. The note left on the kitchen table said that she'd taken the children to her mother's and they would be staying for tea. Wesley screwed up the note and threw it with some force towards the bin.

He was surprised to hear the doorbell ring. He hadn't

331

been expecting visitors. But when he opened the door and saw Neil grinning on the threshold, he felt relieved that he wouldn't have to eat a meal for one alone.

Food was at the forefront of Neil's mind and once a take-away pizza was ordered the pair made themselves comfortable. Neil had even brought some cans of beer with him.

'Pam said she was going to Della's,' he said. 'Thought I'd come and keep you company.'

'Glad you did,' Wesley said, wondering why Neil always seemed to know more about Pam's movements than he did.

'Hannah emailed me today.' There was a faraway look in Neil's eyes when he mentioned Hannah's name that made Wesley feel unexpectedly relieved. He hadn't been conscious of being worried about Neil's closeness to Pam. But perhaps it had always been there, tucked away at the back of his mind. Hannah Gotleib had been a godsend.

'What did she say?' Wesley asked, taking a long swig of beer. He needed something to relax him after the day he'd had.

'Professor Keller sent a sample of some of the bones from the Annetown site off for analysis. They were analysed using a plasma mass spectrometer; state of the art equipment that can detect the tiniest traces of elements. It was unlikely that anything could be detected after four hundred years but Keller knows this toxicologist who uses a very sophisticated testing technique.' He paused, as though he was about to impart some world-shattering piece of information.

'Well?'

'Did you notice anything strange in the early Annetown records I gave you?'

Wesley didn't answer. The truth was, his mind had been on work and he hadn't been paying that much attention.

'Ever arrested a poisoner?'

'Can't say it's an everyday occurrence.'

'There would have been a lot of arsenic lying around on

board the *Nicholas* and in the early Annetown settlement. Ratsbane was used to control vermin. And women used arsenic then as a beauty product. They'd have a little taste of the stuff every so often to make their skin fashionably pale. Mad, but there you are. Things people do for fashion.'

'And?' Wesley wished he'd come to the point.

'Look at the symptoms: bloody flux – diarrhoea to you and me, mad fevers, bruising and swelling, peeling of skin. I think people were being poisoned with arsenic. Two of the skeletons tested – adult males – contained traces. And it couldn't have been absorbed from the environment because all the others were clear.'

Wesley sat up straight. The inner policeman was taking over. 'So who was the poisoner?'

'Look at the records and see if you come up with the same answer as I did.'

Wesley looked at his watch and took hold of Neil's photocopied sheets, wondering why he was spending his leisure time solving a crime that was no concern of his.

First thing the next morning Wesley wandered into the office, feeling the effects of the beer he'd consumed with Neil the night before. His mouth was dry and he had a slight, nagging headache but he tried to put this temporary discomfort out of his mind when Rachel caught his eye.

'You've had a call from a lady. Name of Jocasta. I said you'd ring her back as soon as you came in.'

'Thanks.' As he took the sheet of paper from her their fingers touched and Wesley moved his away rapidly.

Somehow he hadn't expected to hear from Jocasta Mylcomb again. He picked up the phone and dialled her number and, to his relief, when she answered she sounded completely sober. She began their conversation with a litany of complaints against her neighbour and his anti-social hedge and Wesley listened patiently until eventually she came to the point. When he finally managed to put the receiver down he had the feeling that the information she'd just provided could be the last piece in the jigsaw.

He made a call to the Met and when he'd finished he sat quite still for a few moments, staring into space. A picture was emerging. And if the answer from London was the one he expected, it would all begin to make sense.

The consultant in charge of Emma Oldchester's case insisted that she wasn't well enough to be moved just yet. But he agreed that Dr Wellings, his colleague from the hospital's psychiatric department, could see the patient as long as she wasn't upset. Clive Wellings agreed readily, almost enthusiastically. From what Gerry Heffernan told him, Emma Oldchester's case was an interesting one. And the sooner he saw her, the sooner she would be out of danger.

Emma herself said that she wanted Gerry Heffernan and his colleague, DI Peterson, to be present and Clive Wellings agreed to this unconventional arrangement.

Clive Wellings was a small, quiet man with a balding head and a neatly trimmed beard. He wasn't the sort of man you'd notice in a crowd but his unassuming manner inspired confidences. He sat by Emma's bed, speaking softly, taking her back gently to that dreadful day, constantly reassuring her that she had nothing to be afraid of.

Wesley and Heffernan sat motionless in the corner of the room as they listened to the small child's voice reciting the dreadful facts, describing the scene.

'Where are you, Emma?' Clive asked.

'Going upstairs.'

'Why?'

There was an awkward silence. Then the little girl's voice answered. 'I want to see the doll's house. Mummy's in the kitchen with the radio on loud so she can't hear me.'

'Why don't you want her to hear you?'

The little girl sounded coy, as though she knew she was

334

doing something naughty. 'She thinks I'm in bed. She told me not to go up there.'

'Where?'

'The old nursery. I want to see the big doll's house. I'm not allowed to play with it. Only look.'

'So you're sneaking up to the old nursery? Aren't you afraid someone might catch you?'

'Mr and Mrs Harford are in their bedroom and the others are in the drawing room. I can hear them talking.'

Clive brought her forward in time half an hour. 'Where are you now, Emma?'

This time Emma spoke in a whisper. 'Behind the big chair in the hall. He can't see me. I've got to tell Mummy.' The small voice was desperate, terrified.

'What are you doing there?'

'I heard someone coming so I hid. He dragged Mr Bleasdale into the hall. Mr Bleasdale was asleep ... or dead. I don't know. Then there were two big bangs. Then someone shouted and there were more bangs. I'm scared.'

'Can you see what's going on?'

'No. I don't want to move in case he sees me.'

'It's all right, Emma. You're safe if you stay where you are.'

'He's on the stairs. I can hear them creaking. He's going upstairs. There's voices. Mr and Mrs Harford are shouting.'

'OK, Emma. Just keep still. You're going to be all right.'

Emma shuddered and froze.

'It's later now. He's gone. You can come out now. What can you see?'

Emma started sobbing and breathing rapidly. 'Mr Bleasdale's got no face. Blood. Lots of blood everywhere. And they're lying there with their eyes open but they're not moving. There's blood on my feet. It's on my nightie.' She became more agitated, kicking the imaginary blood off her feet with noises of disgust.

335

Clive brought her forward in time again, assuring her once more that everything was going to be all right.

'Where are you now, Emma? Are you still in the hall?'

Her breathing became shallow, terrified. 'No, I'm in the pantry. I'm hiding,' she whispered. 'Mummy's not moving.'

Then Clive asked the six-million-dollar question, gently, calmly. 'Is someone else there?'

'Yes. He's got a gun. He's switched off the radio so I can't make a sound. I've got to be quiet as a mouse.' She put her fingers to her lips.

'Who's holding the gun, Emma?'

'Catriona's boyfriend. Mr Armley. He looks funny. He's wearing the clothes Mr Bleasdale wears in the garden. I thought he was Mr Bleasdale at first.'

'Was it Mr Armley who shot the people, Emma?'

'Why isn't Mummy moving? Why won't she wake up?' Tears began to run down her cheeks.

'It's all right, Emma, you're safe. Be a brave girl now.' He waited a few moments before speaking again. 'It's light now. It's morning. What's happening? Is Mr Armley still there?'

'They're in the dining room. I can hear them talking.' Her voice was weak, barely audible.

'Are you still in the pantry?'

'Yes,' she whispered. 'I came out when he'd gone but Mummy wouldn't move. Then he came back. And she came.'

'It's all right, Emma. What did she do?'

'She had crows. Dead ones. I hate crows.'

'What did she do with the crows?'

'She put one on the back door. The feathers fell off on to the floor. There's lots of blood. Blood everywhere.' She paused. 'Then she kissed him. Proper kissing.'

'Who is she, Emma?' Clive asked gently.

Tears streamed down Emma Oldchester's face as she whispered the name.

336

Chapter Sixteen

I fear I am near death. Such pain, such weakness as the body cannot endure overwhelms me and I have barely strength to write. But I confess now that my father took the blame for my sin, saying he ended the life of that girl when it was I, yielding to base lust, who took her against her will and strangled the life from her, burying her body near the river bank. And for lust and desire for Penelope I shot Isaac Morton at her behest. The curse pronounced upon my innocent father and our house has come upon me. In my agony I pray for forgiveness.

Set down by Edmund Selbiwood, Gentleman, who awaits death and hopes for God's mercy.

Extract from Annetown Records:

12 August 1606   As President of our Council Captain Radford was honourably buried having all the ordnance of the fort shot off in many vollies.

15 August 1606   Lord Coslake is chosen President of our Council.

2 October 1606   Lord Coslake is married unto Penelope, widow of Master Edmund Selbiwood at Annetown this day.

18 July 1607   Penelope, Lady Coslake did die in

*childbed this day and is honourably
buried.*

Anthony Jameston blocked the way. 'Is it necessary to upset my wife again, Inspector? It was a clear case of self-defence.'

'I'm afraid we need to clear up one or two things.'

Jameston stood his ground defensively while Wesley waited. This would be a battle of wills. It was a full minute before Jameston stood aside and allowed him and Gerry Heffernan into the room. Arbel was seated at the dressing table, brushing her smooth brown hair and when they entered she twisted round, frowning.

'I told the police it was an accident. I didn't mean to hurt Dylan. I was scared. He's always scared me. I pushed him and . . . You're not going to charge me, are you?' she asked in a whisper, close to tears.

'We've not come about Dylan Madeley, Mrs Jameston. I've just been talking to a colleague at the Met.'

Arbel's frown deepened. 'I don't understand.'

'Patrick Evans left a list of people he wanted to interview about the murder of your family. There was one name that puzzled us– a name that hadn't cropped up in the enquiry. You say you spent the night your family were killed with a friend of Jocasta Childs's brother, Guy.'

'You make it sound so sordid. I didn't spend the night with him like you mean. We just talked. And in view of what happened, we never got round to seeing each other again. I've told you this already.'

'As luck would have it, Guy Childs has kept in touch with this man and was able to provide us with his current address.' He smiled. 'Gregory Parkes remembers that party very well. It's not every day you chat up a girl only to hear that the next day she's become embroiled in a notorious murder case. He's made a statement.'

Arbel raised her eyebrows. 'Really.'

'Patrick Evans got there before us, of course. He traced

338

Jocasta and she wrote to her brother in Australia but, unfortunately, she's only just had the reply. You see, Evans knew he was on to something. He just had to check it out. But he never got the chance.'

Arbel looked him in the eye. 'I don't see what this Greg Parkes could possibly tell you. He was just someone I met at a party. He hardly knew me.'

'On the contrary, what he told us was very interesting. He said you left the party immediately after your friend, Jocasta, saying that you intended to drive down to Devon right away. He reckons you left around eleven. He had the impression you were trying to avoid going home with Jocasta. He watched you from the window. He saw you get into your Mini and drive away. Why the crows, Arbel?'

She was staring at him, her eyes wide. Wesley found it impossible to read her expression.

Anthony Jameston stepped forward and put his face close to Gerry Heffernan's. His breath smelled of mint. 'This is outrageous, Chief Inspector. What you're implying is nonsense. My wife has just been the victim of a dreadful crime.' Jameston's voice had become louder and he was bristling with indignation. 'I've a good mind to put in a complaint to your superiors.'

'You do that, sir.' He turned to Arbel, who had just risen from her seat. 'When you stabbed Emma Oldchester you didn't finish the job, did you, Mrs Potts? Emma fought back. That's how you came by those cuts and bruises, isn't it? Dylan Madeley never tried to rape you, either yesterday or twenty years ago. It suited your purposes for him to be a likely suspect if your original plan failed, didn't it?'

'I don't know what you're talking about,' Arbel muttered.

'Dylan was weak and he was addicted to drugs but he was no rapist. And he didn't have a particular grudge against your family, only against you for making false allegations that he couldn't disprove. In fact, I've asked for his body to be tested for tranquillisers. I bet you gave him a

339

massive dose – just like you gave Gwen – the ones from her bathroom cupboard, were they? He was probably lying there all night before you decided to kill him, getting the timings right to fit in with your story. Ripping out the phone wires. Messing the place up.'

Arbel stared at him.

Wesley took over. 'You might be interested to hear that Emma Oldchester saw a psychiatrist this morning and with his help she's remembered everything about the night your family died.'

He watched her face for a reaction but saw none.

'She saw Nigel Armley drag Victor Bleasdale into the hall and shoot him in the face. Was Bleasdale drugged? Is that how Armley was able to change his clothes? Pity about the ring being on the wrong finger. When Armley killed them all he was dressed in the gardener's clothes. Whose idea was it to swap places with Victor Bleasdale to make everyone think he was dead?'

Arbel smiled. 'Nigel and Vic were quite alike: Nigel must have decided to take on his identity. But I knew nothing about it.'

'If Nigel took on Bleasdale's identity it must have taken a lot of planning: the application for the job in Yorkshire for instance. Why Gristhorpe Hall? Is there any connection? We can find out.'

Arbel said nothing. She turned back to the mirror and carried on brushing her hair while Anthony looked on in horror, as though he couldn't quite believe what he was hearing.

'A witness up in North Yorkshire saw you with Nigel Armley.'

She snorted. 'It was twenty years ago.'

Wesley didn't argue. He didn't want to mention that the witness who had seen Nigel Armley with the young, brown-haired woman who fitted Arbel's description – and that of a thousand other girls of her age – had been an old lady, lonely, anxious for company and anxious to please. It was hardly evidence. And besides which, the witness was dead and couldn't give evidence in any court. But Arbel wasn't to know that.

'Emma saw you nailing the crows to the door. Why did you do that?'

'She's imagining things. After all she's been through she must be mentally unstable,' Arbel said lazily, as though she was bored by the whole thing.

'You couldn't stick to the agreed plan, could you? You were supposed to stay the night in London but you couldn't wait to see if everything had gone to plan. And you couldn't resist the crows, could you? The old legend of the curse. A little theatrical touch. What did Nigel Armley think of that? Did you know his body has been found in the grounds of Potwoolstan Hall?'

There was no mistaking it. Arbel was genuinely surprised. 'I heard something about a skeleton. What makes you think it's Nigel?'

'Dental records, medical records. It's him all right.'

For the first time the cool mask slipped. Arbel looked stunned. If Wesley hadn't been so certain that she had used Nigel to dispose of her family so that she would inherit the wealth of the Harfords, he might have believed in her innocence.

Wesley took a deep breath. 'I think we should continue this down at the station.' He spoke the familiar words of the caution but something told him this one wouldn't be easy.

Hannah Gotleib had sent a photograph of herself by email, dressed in a check shirt tied at the waist and skimpy shorts, smiling as she stood astride a trench, brandishing a trowel. Neil handed it to Pam.

'Couldn't she find any longer shorts?' Pam said, regretting the words as soon as they were out of her mouth. She sounded like a jealous bitch.

But Neil hadn't seemed to notice. He sat on the

Petersons' sofa, sipping from a mug of tea. 'Has Wes had a chance to read those old records I lent him?'

'I don't know.' She wandered over to the sideboard and picked up some photocopied sheets. 'But I have.'

'What's your conclusion?'

'That Penelope's ambition and desire for status turned her into a ruthless, manipulative killer. She got her brother-in-law to kill her husband – paying him in kind as it were – then she persuaded Edmund to get rid of him. Edmund had already killed: he'd raped and murdered a girl in Devon and let his father take the blame. That's why he fled to Virginia. Penelope wanted him to return to Devon and dispose of his brother so he could inherit the estate but when he refused to go along with it, she poisoned him. She'd hit on a plan to marry Lord Coslake and make him president of the colony so she poisoned the old president and other members of the Council and got what she wanted.'

'But not for long because she died in childbirth.'

Pam glanced at Amelia, who was attempting to crawl towards the fireplace. 'She deserved to be hanged.'

'They do say women are particularly hard on other women,' Neil observed with a grin. 'And she was an ancestor of mine, don't forget.'

'Well, none of us can choose our families, can we?'

Pam swung round to see Wesley standing in the doorway. She felt her face going red.

'I wasn't expecting you home.' She was aware she sounded guilty.

'Obviously. Sorry to interrupt. I thought I'd grab some lunch. We've made an arrest in the Patrick Evans case.'

'Who?'

'Arbel Harford. She persuaded her sister's fiancé to kill her family so that she could inherit everything.'

Pam's mouth fell open. 'The mercenary bitch.'

'I don't think she did it just for the money. Something Jocasta Mylcomb said about her relationship with her

342

family bothered me. Apparently, her brother, Jack Harford, had taken great delight in telling her that she was adopted. She probably never felt she really belonged and when she was sent away to school she interpreted it as a rejection. It must have eaten away at her until . . .'

'Have you arrested the bloke?' Neil asked.

'I'd have a job. She killed him after he'd outlived his usefulness.'

'The female of the species is deadlier than the male,' observed Neil, giving Pam a meaningful look.

Wesley looked at his watch. 'I'll grab something to eat and I'll be going. Might be late tonight.'

'So what's new?' Pam muttered under her breath.

Wesley picked Amelia up and cuddled her, kissing the top of her head. He hesitated, as though reluctant to go. Then he placed her gently on the sofa beside her mother, who glanced up at him resentfully.

When the front door had closed Pam went upstairs with Amelia, sending the papers flying on to the floor as she left. The baby was tired and she hardly complained at being put down in her cot. Once her daughter was settled, Pam hurried downstairs. When she entered the living room Neil was squatting on the floor, picking up the photocopied sheets, trying to get them into some sort of order. Pam knelt down to help him and they reached for the same sheet of paper, their hands meeting. Neither made an effort to pull away.

'I missed you when you were in the States.'

Neil didn't answer. He leaned towards her and she stayed quite still. Then he kissed her, first tentatively on the cheek, then on the lips, gently, slowly.

'I think you'd better go,' she whispered.

Neil Watson didn't move for a moment. Then he stood up.

'I'm sorry,' he said softly before taking his leave.

'Prove it,' was Arbel Jameston's only answer to their accusations.

343

'I must say, Inspector, your evidence is purely circumstantial.' The solicitor from London spoke with a lazy drawl, as though the whole process was boring him. But Wesley suspected he was as sharp as his pinstriped suit. 'And the testimony of this ...' He consulted a sheet of paper. 'Emma Oldchester would never stand up in court. It could be pure fantasy. There have been many recorded cases of false recovered memory, particularly in abuse cases. And this case ...'

Gerry Heffernan glanced at the whirling tape machine and leaned forward. 'You might be interested to know that the postmortem on Dylan Madeley showed up something interesting. Your statement says he hit his head on the hearth but the pathologist thinks his injuries were caused by a blunt instrument of some kind. And he'd taken enough tranquillisers to floor an elephant.'

'The pathologist is wrong. I'll demand a second postmortem. And of course there were drugs in his system. He was an addict. He'd take anything he could lay his hands on.'

'You had plenty of time to arrange the scene and destroy evidence before we arrived. Was he lying there unconscious while you drove to Neston to stab Emma Oldchester? Or did he arrive at the cottage later?'

'This is outrageous,' interrupted the solicitor. Heffernan ignored him.

'I must say you put on a good act. All that hysteria. It was a bit out of character though. When you found your family slaughtered, reports say that you were remarkably calm. Did Dylan suspect you'd killed his sister? Is that why he came calling?'

'I told you. He wanted money for drugs and he attacked me.'

'I thought he tried to rape you,' Heffernan said.

'Look, I was the victim. I have the cuts and bruises to prove it.'

Heffernan shook his head. 'I'm told Emma put up quite

344

a fight. You told us some porkies, didn't you, love? You said Gwen Madeley had been the one who was having it off with Nigel Armley in the potting shed. But it was the other way round, wasn't it? She saw you. And you had to make sure she didn't tell. She knew what really happened, didn't she? She was at the crime scene before the police. Did she just wander in on it or did you and Nigel let her in? Did you know she'd painted what she saw? She knew what you were, didn't she, Arbel? She knew the truth. That's why you killed her.'

Wesley looked Arbel in the eye. A two-pronged attack. 'It must have been a terrible shock to you when you found out that Patrick Evans was writing a book about the case. Did he tell you what he'd discovered when you met him?'

She pressed her lips together then she looked at her solicitor, who shifted uncomfortably.

Wesley repeated the question. 'Did Patrick Evans tell you what he'd discovered? You did meet him, didn't you?'

She took a deep breath. 'OK, I met him. He said he knew Martha Wallace was innocent. He'd been up to Yorkshire to find Bleasdale and suspected something was wrong. He even found out I had a link with Gristhorpe Hall: I was at school with Sophie Pickrington, the Earl of Pickrington's daughter.'

'Is that how you found out they had a vacancy for a gardener?'

She smiled. 'Sophie's favourite bedtime reading was *Lady Chatterley's Lover*. She kept saying she hoped they'd get someone gorgeous. I think his Lordship's other gardeners were a bit of a disappointment.'

'So Evans was getting close?'

'He kept visiting Gwen, trying to wheedle things out of her. But she told him nothing.'

'And you had to make sure she never talked, so you killed her.'

'Nonsense.'

'Evans told you what he knew. He was very thorough.

345

He even tried to find the boy you were with on the evening of the massacre, something the police never thought of. If Gregory Parkes had been interviewed they'd have found that his story didn't match the one you told at the time. If Gwen had told Evans what she knew . . .'

'Gwen wouldn't have talked to Evans.'

'No, she probably wouldn't. She had her own agenda, didn't she? Her own interests to protect. She was black-mailing you, wasn't she?' said Wesley, watching her eyes.

'Of course not.'

'Then why did you deposit large amounts of money in her bank account? And, if you were such bosom pals, how come she never mentioned you were coming to stay to any of her colleagues at the Hall? And I've checked Gwen's will. You're not her executor at all: Dylan was, blood being thicker than water, so they say. Gwen's solicitor said Dylan had been disinherited by their parents and Gwen felt bad about it and tried to do her best for him. She kept trying to give him a new start but he kept blowing it. His addiction was stronger than he was. And I don't suppose you helped the situation by making poisonous accusations. There was no reason for you to stay in that cottage and go through her things. You were looking for anything that might incriminate you. Did she tell you she'd kept evidence of your involvement?'

There was no answer.

'If I could have a word with my client . . .' the solicitor said warily.

Wesley kept his eyes on Arbel. 'You killed Patrick Evans. You searched his hotel room and took his files and notes on the case. I presume you've destroyed them. Then you killed Gwen.' It was a simple statement rather than a question. 'You were in Devon last weekend. Your husband was at the Hall and he thought you were still in London. But you arranged to meet Evans at Gwen's cottage.'

'OK. Tony didn't know I'd come down and I admit I met Evans. I'd asked Gwen to go out so we could have some privacy. I made him one of her stupid freezer meals and when I told him I didn't know anything, he left. I got the impression he'd arranged to meet someone. I don't know what happened to him. And Dylan killed Gwen when she wouldn't give him money for drugs. Just like he tried to kill me.'

'Dylan would never have harmed Gwen and you know it. Evans told you he knew the truth, didn't he?'

Arbel didn't answer.

Gerry Heffernan spoke again. 'Nigel Armley was besotted with you, wasn't he? You dragged him in so deep that he couldn't escape. What did you promise him for murdering your family? A share of the spoils? How did you get him to do it, Arbel? Jocasta Childs told us you kept a picture of him at school. Why did you kill him?'

The solicitor leaned over and whispered something in her ear.

'No comment,' she said, staring ahead. 'Can I see my husband? I want to see Tony.'

The solicitor cleared his throat. 'I'm afraid Mr Jameston's gone back to London. The Prime Minister wanted to see him.'

Wesley saw tears well up in Arbel's eyes, the first genuine emotion he'd seen her display.

Emma lay in bed. In some ways she felt better, like a weight had been lifted from her. Barry was sitting by the bed, holding her hand. Sometimes she wondered if he needed her more than she needed him.

There was a knock and a disembodied bunch of flowers appeared round the door followed by the comfortable bulk of Joe Harper.

Emma tried to sit up as Joe lumbered in, beaming, holding the flowers in front of him. When Barry relieved him of his burden and went off in search of a vase, Joe bent and kissed Emma on the cheek. 'How are you, Em? Me and Barry have been worried sick about you.' He took her hand

and squeezed it. Have the police got who did it yet?'

Emma nodded. 'It was that Arbel. She nailed the crows to the doors at the Hall.' She hesitated and caught hold of Joe's hand. 'I've remembered other things too, Dad.'

Their eyes met and Joe understood.

'I haven't told anyone. I promise I'll never tell.'

He kissed her forehead gently. 'I didn't want you to see, Emmy. That was the last thing I wanted.'

When Barry returned with the vase full of bright pink carnations, Emma let go of her father's hand.

Half an hour later Joe Harper was on his way to Tradmouth police station.

Wesley stood beside Joe, who was staring down at the tree root.

'This is the place. I reckoned nobody would suspect me if I put him here ... where he'd killed all those people.'

'How did you know he'd killed them?'

'I didn't. Not until he came for my little Em. She was playing in the garden. We had a big garden in those days. It were a few months after it happened and Em still wasn't right. She couldn't talk for a year. Poor little maid, losing her mum like that and seeing things no kiddie should see.'

'So what happened?'

Wesley stood close to the man, more a companion than a guard. He wanted him to talk freely. He was a decent man, appalled at what he'd done, and if he escaped the retribution of the law that would have suited Wesley fine. Sometimes law isn't the same thing as justice, he thought sadly. He wished Joe Harper hadn't turned up at the station to confess. But he couldn't turn back time.

'I were on my own. Linda, the wife had gone into Neston shopping and I were looking after Em. She went into the garden to see the guinea pig we'd bought her – we spoiled her a bit because of what she'd been through – and I started to watch the racing on the telly. I thought Em was quite safe where she was.' He looked guilty. 'You can't watch them every second, can you? Mind you, I wish I had.'

'Nigel Armley tried to kill Emma?'

The big man nodded. 'She was a witness, see. It had been in the papers about her being found there by her mum. He probably hadn't realised she'd been there until he read about it and I expect he was afraid she might be able to tell the police what she'd seen. When I went into the garden he was trying to take her and she was just frozen with fear like a rabbit in the headlights. Couldn't even put up a fight. He was dragging her. He had a car waiting. I couldn't see it just then but I heard the engine start up.'

'Did you recognise him?'

'Not at first. But afterwards I realised it was the man in the papers. The man they said had been shot.'

'So, what happened?'

'I had to save Em so I picked up a spade I'd left stuck in the flower bed and I hit him. And I kept hitting him. Then I shouted at Em to get in the house and I took his pulse.'

'And he was dead?'

Joe looked at Wesley gratefully, as though he was glad that he understood.

'So you waited until it was safe and drove the body to the Hall? Why here?'

'I knew every inch of those woods. I'd played in them as a kid – trespassing, I suppose it was. I buried him with the spade I'd killed him with then took it home and scrubbed it. When Em could talk again she never said nothing about it. It was like it was our secret. Never mentioned in all these years.'

'You say you heard the car engine start up. I don't suppose you saw who was at the wheel, did you?' It was a long shot but Wesley thought it was worth asking.

'Oh aye. When I'd dragged him to the shed I could still hear the engine so I crept round the corner to look, just in case there was someone else there who was going to come after Em. I would have killed them too if I'd needed to.'

'I understand, believe me, Mr Harper. I'm a father myself. Who was driving the car?'

'A young woman. They must have been in it together.'

'You're sure about that?'

'Oh yes, I got a good look at her. I recognised her from all the photos in the paper. But if I'd told anyone it would have been me who'd be done for murder. But I kept a close eye on Em after that. I always thought she might come back and ... But she didn't. I suppose after all that time she thought she was safe. Until that Evans turned up and Em went to that place.'

'Do you think Patrick Evans guessed the truth?'

'About me killing Armley? Probably not. But I reckon he was on to that bitch Arbel. But I suppose she'll get away with it: she's married to some MP: friends in high places probably.'

'Oh she'll be charged, don't you worry about that.'

'What about me?'

'I'm sorry, Joe. I really am,' Wesley said. And he meant it.

'MP's heiress wife in murder quiz.'

'Tragic Arbel in massacre charge.'

'Jameston denies knowledge of wife's massacre involvement.'

'Jameston says marriage to killer heiress over.'

'PM backs Jameston.'

'I never thought we'd get her, Wes,' said Gerry Heffernan as he perused the headlines lined up in the newsagents.

'There were times when I thought she'd wriggle out of it myself. Why did she do it, a girl like that?'

'Jocasta Mylcomb said she bore the Harfords a grudge. They adopted her, then sent her away: it must have seemed like a rejection. And Jack Harford tormented her; broke the news to her that she wasn't his real sister and relished every

350

minute of it. But I think what pushed her over the edge was when he told her he was going to persuade their father to change his will so that she'd get nothing because she wasn't a real member of the family. Jack Harford wasn't a nice man. Arbel's virtually admitted that she was the brains behind the massacre. She had both Bleasdale and Armley wrapped round her little finger. All that about Gwen having affairs with them was nonsense. It was Arbel who was having it off with them in the potting shed. She persuaded Armley to do her dirty work for her, promising that he'd get her and her money. But if Joe Harper hadn't disposed of him, I'm sure she'd have done the job herself.'

'Why the crows?'

'She knew that old legend about the curse. She added the crows to muddy the waters. Or perhaps she was putting her own curse on the house.'

'Do you believe in evil, Wes?'

'Haven't got much choice in this job,' Wesley replied softly.

Gerry Heffernan picked up the local morning paper and paid the thin girl behind the counter.

The shop was just around the corner from Emma Oldchester's house. The two men walked silently down Emma's neat garden path and rang the doorbell.

They were rather surprised when Emma herself opened the door. Somehow they had expected to find a cowering invalid, protected by her husband. But there seemed to be a new confidence in Emma's eyes.

She led them into the living room. It was hot, too hot. A coal fire was glowing in the grate, giving the room a cosy feel. Wesley looked around and noticed a large doll's house standing on the stripped pine table in the corner. He recognised it at once. It was Potwoolstan Hall, just as it had been at the time of the massacre. Dolls lay splashed with red paint to represent blood. It was a horrible thing. It took his breath away.

'Bit grim that, love,' Heffernan said gently. 'Don't you

351

think you'd be better getting rid of it?'

'Barry thinks I should just redecorate it and sell it. But I'm going to burn it. It's an evil place. Cursed.' She picked up the two figures in black: the man with no face and a smaller figure carrying the tiny birds and stared at them for a few seconds. Then suddenly she flung the dolls towards the fire. The man went straight in and was rapidly enveloped in a flare of orange red flames. When the doll with the crows landed on the hearth, Wesley bent down, picked it up and threw it on to the coals where it too was consumed until all that was left was ashes.

'They've gone,' Emma whispered.

Gerry Heffernan, standing behind Emma, put a hand on her shoulder. 'That's right, love, they've gone. They can't hurt you any more.'

'I'm giving evidence at my dad's trial.'

'I wish it hadn't had to go to court but . . .'

'Surely nobody would ever send him to prison for killing a murderer and saving my life.' Emma spoke with a confidence that showed she wasn't altogether familiar with British justice.

Gerry Heffernan gave a sad smile. 'I hope so, love. I really do.'

'What's happened to Arbel?'

'She's awaiting trial.'

'I keep thinking she's going to be let off. She's so plausible. People would believe her . . .'

Gerry looked her in the eye. 'Look, love, even with the best lawyers money can buy she's not going to get away with it.'

Emma smiled. 'I didn't tell you I was going to have a baby, did I?'

'Good,' said Wesley with a forced smile. 'You look after yourself now.'

They wished her luck as they left the house.

Neil had rung three times, Rachel told Wesley with a slight

air of disapproval. But then she had always disapproved of Neil.

Wesley wondered what he wanted. He hadn't seen him for a week or so. He had called round most nights until he had started work up at Tradington Hall. Wesley had even begun to suspect that Neil was developing a secret longing for the joys of domesticity and dirty nappies. But now it seemed things were back to normal. Wesley punched out the number of his mobile and waited for an answer.

Neil had never been one for long phone conversations. He asked Wesley to meet him at Potwoolstan Hall. There was something he needed to do.

Wesley looked at his desk. A quick trip to Potwoolstan Hall wouldn't take long and the paperwork could wait. Besides, there was a loose end he wanted to tidy up at the Hall. He told Rachel that he wouldn't be long and slipped out of the office.

There was more traffic on the Devon roads than there had been a couple of weeks before. Better weather had arrived and with it the tourists. In spite of a chilly breeze it was a fine day and the River Trad sparkled under a clear blue sky.

When he reached the Hall he parked in the car park provided for the Beings, the one near the main gate, some distance from the house. He fancied a walk. And besides, he couldn't see Neil's car so he probably had all the time in the world.

But Neil's car was there all right, parked in front of the Hall in the forbidden spot. Wesley wondered how he had got away with it. But in his experience, Neil seemed to be able to get away with most things.

The man himself was standing on the steps leading to the main door. Wesley looked up at the house and shuddered.

Neil was holding a small video camera. 'I'm making a video for Hannah and the museum,' he said by way of explanation.

'You're still in touch with her, then?'

353

'I rang her yesterday. I woke her up at five in the morning. I can never get the hang of the time difference. She's saying she might come over in the summer.'

'That's good. I'd like to meet her.'

Wesley was unable to read Neil's expression. He couldn't tell whether he was pleased or not about Hannah's impending visit. It was almost as if he had something on his mind. 'Wes, I . . .'

'What?'

Neil turned away. 'Nothing,' he said lightly. 'Let's go in, shall we? I asked that bloke who runs it if I can have a look around and he says it's OK. If you ask me, I reckon he's past caring.'

'What do you mean?'

Neil shrugged. Wesley could find out for himself.

He marched ahead of Neil into the Hall and knocked at Jeremy Elsham's door. His knock was answered by a weary 'Come in,' in a tone that lacked authority; a feeble echo of former times.

Wesley signalled Neil to stay where he was and opened the door. Elsham was sitting at his desk, surrounded by what looked like bills and invoices, probably large ones. Wesley closed the door quietly behind him. This was none of Neil's concern.

'I thought we'd seen the last of you.' Elsham sounded resentful, and well he might. If it wasn't for the police investigation and the attendant publicity, Potwoolstan Hall would probably have still been doing very nicely thank you. 'All this business has ruined this place, you know that.'

'People forget.'

'I hadn't noticed.'

'As long as you're not thinking of falling back on your insurance.'

Elsham looked up sharply. 'What do you mean by that?'

'I know about the place up in Scotland you ran. And your conviction.'

A slow, bitter smile appeared on Elsham's thin lips. 'I've

354

put all that behind me. This place is kosher.'

'So why keep those tapes of your clients' confessions under hypnosis? Let's face it, John – it is John, isn't it? John Grey? – you were hoping for something to turn up. Something you could blackmail your clients over. In the place near Stirling – what was it called? Hartsmoor Glen? – a wealthy woman confessed under hypnosis that she'd slept with her stepson. You got six thousand pounds out of her before she broke up with her husband and decided to confide in the local police. What did you get? Two years? And I'm sure that wasn't the only time you were tempted to turn people's secrets into hard cash.'

'You can't prove anything.'

'No, you're right. We can't take action unless anybody complains. And they probably won't. But now you know that we know ...' Wesley smiled. 'Do we understand each other?'

Elsham didn't reply.

'I believe you've given permission for a friend of mine to look round the Hall.'

Elsham nodded. 'The archaeologist, yes.'

Wesley pointed to the portrait of the two men that hung behind Elsham's desk. 'I think that might interest him. Do you mind if he comes in here now to have a look?'

'Help yourself.' Elsham sounded as if he no longer cared who entered his private domain.

Wesley turned to go. 'Thank you. I, er ... I hope things work out. People do forget, you know.'

Elsham shook his head. 'I'm selling up. Cutting my losses. They say there's a curse on this place. I think they're right.'

Wesley joined Neil in the hall, where he had made himself comfortable on a chair, reading a glossy magazine extolling the virtues of a healthy lifestyle and a vegetarian diet. The magazine was discarded as soon as Wesley appeared.

'Do you remember I mentioned that there was a portrait

here that might interest you? It's in there.' He pointed to the door.

As Neil stood up Elsham emerged from his office and made for the stairs, ignoring the two men. Neil followed Wesley into the office, complaining that it was a pity the place had been modernised. Wesley said nothing.

When Neil saw the painting he stopped dead and stared at the two men, posed stiffly side by side, one with his right hand on his hips, the other with his left hand resting on a globe. They were young men. In their early twenties probably but with the solemn expressions of people considerably older. Neil lifted it off the wall and carried it over to the window.

He screwed up his face with concentration and began to translate the painted Latin, barely visible against the dark background. 'Ricardus Selbiwood. That's the one on the left. And the one with his hand on the globe, that's Edmund.' He looked round at Wesley, his eyes wide with excitement. 'Dated 1604 – the year before the *Nicholas* sailed for Annetown. It's our man. This is Edmund.'

Wesley stared at the young man with the sharp-featured face and the restless eyes. The young man with his hand on the globe, anxious to explore new worlds. Edmund Selbiwood, who had killed a young woman in Devon then escaped to the New World only to die in agony far from home at the hands of his murdering wife.

'The museum at Annetown would love to have this.'

'You'd better have a word with Elsham then. He could do with the money right now.'

They left that day with the picture propped up on the back seat of Neil's Mini, Elsham's desperate pleas to get the best price for it ringing in their ears.

Earlier that day Wesley had watched his wife sitting on the shingle beach at Bereton, perched on a towel folded twice so that the sharp stones wouldn't dig into her bare legs as Michael filled his plastic bucket with pebbles, totally absorbed in his task. Amelia had slept in her pushchair. It had been good to have a Sunday afternoon together. Good not to worry about the phone ringing. The Evans case had been cleared up and Arbel Jameston was still awaiting trial even though it was now June: the due process of law ground slowly but relentlessly.

He had been angry and upset when he'd heard that Joe Harper had been sentenced to five years for manslaughter. He felt for Emma: first she had lost her birth mother by violence then her foster mother, Linda, had died. And now her beloved, gentle foster father was in prison, trapped in an alien world amongst violent people quite unlike himself. Wesley just prayed that he'd survive. He had called to see Emma, now in her fourth month of pregnancy, but she had said little and Barry had hovered over her like a clumsy mother hen. After that visit he hadn't called again.

Now that the children were in bed, Pam was at the dining table, leaning over books and reports. Being back at work was tiring her, Wesley could tell. And there was something else. She had been quiet ever since Neil had announced that he had invited Hannah Gotleib over from the States to pick up the painting of the Selbiwood brothers that the Annetown Archaeological Trust had bought from Jeremy Elsham. Elsham and Pandora had put the Hall up for sale and left, destination unknown, and Wesley wondered if they'd ever cross his path again.

As he watched Pam at work, he felt suddenly uncomfortable. Then he told himself that it was just her return to work after her maternity leave that had brought about the change. There was nothing wrong that a few more family days out and the long summer vacation couldn't cure. And there was his sister's wedding in August to look forward to.

He picked up the TV remote control and pressed the button. He didn't want to miss the local news with all its possibilities of burgeoning crime and violence. He liked to know what the coming week had in store at work.

But the image on the screen made him increase the TV's

357

volume and sit forward. A building was ablaze and fire crews were desperately trying to douse the flames with their hoses; a seemingly impossible task as the fire had caught hold and was destroying the edifice like a devouring monster.

'Fire crews from all over the area are attempting to save historic Potwoolstan Hall,' the reporter announced with what sounded like relish. 'The Hall, a former healing centre, is currently empty and it is not thought that there were any casualties.'

Wesley glanced at Pam. She had heard nothing, understood nothing. He stood up, grabbed the phone and dialled Gerry Heffernan's number.

Emma Oldchester had watched for a while from the safety of the trees before summoning the courage to approach the Hall. When Barry had asked where she was going she'd told him she was fetching something from Joe's; something he'd asked her to bring when she next visited. The way he always believed her made her feel guilty, as if she was lying to a trusting child. But this was something she had to do. And Barry wouldn't stand in her way.

As she broke the glass in the back door and poured the petrol and flaming rags through the jagged holes, the crows in the trees had risen cackling and shrieking, as though their feathers were burning like the fabric of Potwoolstan Hall.

When the place was gone it would all be over. And the curse would be lifted at last.

Historical Note

When I began my research for this book I came across accounts written by some of the first Englishmen to settle at a place called Jamestown on the James River in Virginia, USA. And when I started to dig deeper in search of facts on which to base my fictitious 'Annetown', I made some surprising discoveries.

Commonly it is assumed that the arrival in 1620 at Plymouth, Massachusetts of 102 pious English men and women seeking religious freedom, heralded the birth of modern America. The truth, however, is rather less romantic. Sir Walter Raleigh made an ill-fated attempt to establish a colony at Roanoke Island, off the coast of North Carolina in 1585 and the first American child of English parents was born there in August 1587 and named Virginia Dare. Three years later, however, all these settlers had vanished, their fate a mystery to this day.

In 1606, King James I granted the Virginia Company of London permission to colonise Virginia, exhorting them to 'dig, delve and hew for all manner of deposits and residues of gold, silver and copper'. James also needed to establish a foothold in North America to halt the spread of Spanish power in the area.

In 1607 – thirteen years before the Pilgrim Fathers set sail from England – 105 men and boys from all social classes, aristocrats to artisans, arrived at Jamestown after a daunting five-month voyage. However, within months of their arrival, sixty-seven of their number had died and contemporary accounts suggest that they met their end in terrible pain. Master George Percy – brother of the Earl of Northumberland and a Councillor of that first colony – wrote 'There was never Englishmen left in a foreign country in such misery as we were in this newly discovered Virginia.' The dream of riches in the New World had become a nightmare.

Many theories about what really happened at Jamestown have been put forward over the years, the most common being that the settlers starved to death for want of adequate food supplies (even though food was abundant in nearby settlements). Accounts written by survivors tell of famine and illness. However, recent studies suggest that there might be a more sinister explanation. The skeleton of a young man was found – a gentleman buried in a coffin rather than the shroud reserved for the lower social classes – and he had obviously died from a massive gunshot wound, suggesting murder or civil unrest. Some experts who have studied the survivors' accounts have noticed that the symptoms of the settlers' mysterious illness – bloody diarrhoea, skin peeling, fever, psychotic behaviour, delusions, weakness, a famished appearance and swelling – appear to match the symptoms of arsenic poisoning (arsenic being readily available as ratsbane was used to control vermin). This might explain why the settlers were too weakened to search for food. And why the debilitating symptoms only began when the ships returned to England, and with them any hope of help.

Captain John Smith (famously rescued by Pocahontas, daughter of Chief Powhatan) wrote that within ten days of the ships' departure, hardly anyone could stand or walk – a suspiciously sudden deterioration. Was a poisoner at work in early Jamestown? And, if so, was it an attempt to sabotage the enterprise by England's principal enemy at the time, Spain?

This idea may seem far-fetched, but even in our own day the CIA and MI5 have been known to do some strange things. And the use of poison was fairly common at the time: in 1622, following a massacre of settlers by the Chesapeake tribe, the physician for Jamestown, Dr Potter, brewed up poisoned ale for a peace conference, and 200 Indians died as a result. In perilous times – and this was the era of the Gunpowder Plot – anything is possible.

So could one or more of those first settlers have been agents of an enemy power? Archaeological evidence suggests that some of the Jamestown settlers harboured secret Catholic sympathies: rosaries and medallions were found during the excavation, hardly the sort of thing one would expect in a fiercely Protestant settlement. Or was the motive personal rather than political? Some kind of power struggle, perhaps? Maybe one day evidence will emerge that will throw more light on the mystery.

Those settlers who survived abandoned the Jamestown settlement and set sail in search of a more congenial place. But they met with a supply ship from England and were persuaded to turn back. This time they made a fresh start and the settlement thrived.

The colony fell into decay after the Virginian seat of government was moved in 1699 to the Middle Plantation (later called Williamsburg) and the site of the original settlement was, for many years, thought to be lost. But now the Jamestown site has been excavated and boasts a recon-struction of the settlement complete with replicas of the ships that brought the first settlers to Virginia in 1607. After an unfortunate beginning, Jamestown lives again.